COMING HOME

BOOK TWO

THE HOME SERIES

MELISSA WHITNEY

Coming Home
Copyright © 2024 by Melissa Whitney
All rights reserved.

This is a work of fiction. The characters are products of the author's imagination, and any resemblance to actual events or actual persons, living or dead, is entirely coincidental. Although it's fair to say that anyone enjoying a life so full of love is lucky indeed.

No part of this book may be reproduced in any form or by any electronic or mechanical means, including information storage and retrieval systems, without written permission from the author, except for the use of brief quotations in a book review.

E-book ISBN INFO: ISBN: 979-8-9904334-4-1
PAPERBACK ISBN INFO: ISBN: 979-8-9904334-5-8

AI RESTRICTIONS

ABOUT THE BOOK

Coming Home
(The Home Series, Book Two)
By: Melissa Whitney
Blurb

One night. One kiss. That's all it took for everything to change between them.

Dr. Nat Owens has come home to join her family's medical practice. In the sleepy village, she struggles to be seen as a medical professional. Patients want her father. Staff go to her mother. Village residents respect her older brother. To everyone, she's just the youngest Owens sibling. Even to the one man who she's always dreamed of. Or so she thinks.

With the sexiest dimpled smile, Marine veteran Noah Wilson appears to be just the village's handsome brewery owner. He protects and supports the community and people he loves, including his best friend's younger sister. To the village, she's just Dr. Owens' daughter, but to him, she's his everything. A fact he won't acknowledge until he decides to ignore all the reasons why she and him are a bad idea.

But is the village ready for this? Are their families? Are they?

A brilliant doctor returns to her hometown to prove that she's more than just the younger sister in this *Little Women* inspired small town romance.

E-book ISBN INFO: ISBN: 979-8-9904334-4-1
PAPERBACK ISBN INFO: ISBN: 979-8-9904334-5-8

A NOTE FROM THE AUTHOR

Note from the Author/Content Warning

Dear Reader,

Whether this is your first or fourth Melissa Whitney book, thank you for reading. There are so many books out there and I'm deeply honored you chose mine. I loved going back to my hometown of Perry, N.Y. to write this book.

While I promise you a swoony book boyfriend that you will daydream about, this is Nat's story. One of my favorite parts about the Home Series is it's told through the perspective of the FMC. I adored telling the story of the little sister and young female doctor coming home. Being a young female anything (hell, a female anything) offers an array of challenges. Nat allows me to depict that, and I am so humbled she allowed me to tell her story. A story I believe will resonate with many women facing the conflict of how the world sees you versus how you see yourself.

Coming Home is a sexy, sweet, and heartfelt romance with a guaranteed happy-for-now ending; however, it does explore things that may be difficult for some readers. This may include consensual sex on the page (sorry Uncle Mike), depicted symptoms of PTSD, discussion of the death of a sibling, discussion of military combat, depiction of grooming and an abusive relationship (not between the FMC and MMC), depiction of a motor vehicle accident, depiction of casual alcohol consumption, blood (brief), and use of foul language. As well, Nat and Noah's relationship does have a ten year age gap. He is thirty-eight and she is twenty-eight. For some readers this may be uncomfortable, especially with the discussion of their history together. While nothing inappropriate or inappropriately adjacent occurs between Noah and Nat prior to the current timeline of the book, as a survivor of childhood sexual abuse I know this may trigger some people.

Content warnings allow you as a reader to make informed decisions and I want to support you with that. Please take care of yourself while you are reading.

Thank you for choosing to read Coming Home. I hope you fall in love with this Little Women inspired small town romance as much as I did writing it.

Cheers,

Melissa

CHAPTER ONE

"I want to do something splendid...something heroic and wonderful that won't be forgotten after I'm dead." ~Louisa May Alcott, *Little Women*

N at Owen's jaw clenched as she worked to ignore the sour expression on Mrs. Lewis' face. *Don't give the octogenarian the stink eye.* "Your symptoms are consistent with a sinus infection, but—"

"Is Dr. Owens coming in, dear?" Mrs. Lewis interrupted, her mouth pursed.

The corners of Nat's lips flattened into a firm line. "I am Dr. Owens."

"Yes, dear, but the *real* one. Your father," she said with a saccharine smile and dismissive flick of her wrist.

Do no harm, even to sexist old ladies. Well, especially to them. Tapping on her tablet to give herself time to drop into the Zen zone, Nat continued, "We'll have the nurse take a throat culture to rule out strep throat, and I'll prescribe some antibiotics."

"I'd like to have Dr. Owens see me, dear."

Never had Nat experienced such a blood-boiling urge to say, "Bitch, please!" and flash her medical license proclaiming *Natalie J. Owens, Medical Doctor*. Eyes darting to the exam room door in surrender, she broadened her smile, even though it felt as if she were tightening an already too-tight sneaker. "Certainly. I'll see if he can step in."

Stepping out of the room, she controlled the force in her arm dying to slam the door, quietly eased it shut, then leaned against it, closing her eyes. The door's reassuring stiffness soaked into her spine. "I am Dr. Owens. I am Dr. Owens," she murmured to herself.

It wasn't like this in Boston during her residency. Not entirely. At first, there were a few people who saw her petite stature as *less than*. Distracted by her assortment of bedazzled, patterned, and bright-colored shoes, they soon learned underestimating Nat Owens was a big mistake. *Huge! Godzilla-sized!* It was as huge of a mistake as that summer she'd cut her own bangs. Yet, a few weeks into her residency, she became the go-to family medicine resident.

In Boston, she only needed to overcome a first impression. In the village of Perry, N.Y., there was a lifetime of impressions, a lifetime of being the youngest daughter of the beloved Dr. Chris Owens.

For nearly one hundred years, there had been a Dr. Owens caring for the residents of the sleepy village, tucked between corn fields and cow pastures. A common trait shared by each former Dr. Owens was that they had all been the eldest son. Not the youngest daughter. That's how it had been since Nat's great-grandfather, Jacob Owens, had first established the clinic in 1925. His eldest son, her grandpa, took over, and then her dad. With two older brothers, Clayton and Evan, it was never meant to be her.

I'm not who these patients think should be here. Still fuming, she found her dad and asked him to stop in to see Mrs. Lewis. Then, she sought sanctuary in her office.

More of an alcove than an office, though. The space opposite the exam rooms was generally reserved for interns or residents from the medical school in Buffalo. She plopped into the swivel chair. It wasn't a fancy office like her dad's with its wall of windows and leather chairs. With its glittery framed photos, knickknacks, and an assortment of squishy stress balls shaped like animals, it was her refuge from the Mrs. Lewis types of the world.

"Thank you, Dr. Owens. I'll stop by the pharmacy on my way home to pick up the antibiotics. When will the results of the throat culture come in?" Mrs. Lewis' voice drifted into Nat's open office door.

Seriously? Frustration sighed through Nat. She swiveled in her chair, listening to Mrs. Lewis and her father's softening voices as they shuffled down the hall to the clinic's reception area. Picking up a squishy hot pink pig-shaped stress ball, she clenched it. *I am Dr. Owens. I am Dr. Owens.*

A few minutes later, a throat cleared, pulling her attention to the open doorway where her dad stood. "Dr. Owens." Happy crinkles kissed the edges of his blue eyes.

"Dr. Owens," she said, lips lifted in a small smile.

Dad never ceased to be amused with having two Dr. Owens in the clinic. Even if some days he seemed to be the only person who remembered that she was a Summa Cum Laude graduate from medical school. He'd chuckle, saying "Dr. Owens." as he greeted her in the morning or asked, "Which one?" when staff said, "Dr. Owens."

Nat wondered if the amusement was pride in working alongside one of his children or astonishment at it being her. The memory of his blank expression when she announced she was declaring pre-med at Boston College often made her wonder. There were so many "Are you sures?" uttered, that just for a moment, she questioned it herself. She had been sure and for the last ten years, she navigated her charted path to arrive here. She just never counted on feeling like the unwelcomed third cousin at the party.

A smile kicked across his face. "You were spot on with Mrs. Lewis' assessment."

"Thanks," she muttered.

He always gave these verbal pats on the back. It was reminiscent of being a little girl with a not-yet-dry fingerpainting that he placed on the fridge, proudly proclaiming that she was the next Picasso.

"Dad—"

He raised his hand, halting her words. "Honey, it will take time. The patients are just used to me. Soon, they'll tire of the rusty Dr. Owens and want the shiny new one," he assured in a soft and encouraging tone.

"Both my Dr. Owens." Mom's gray eyes twinkled as she stepped beside Dad and pressed a peck on his cheek. "Hello, handsome."

Pink bloomed on his cheek.

The exchange both swelled Nat's heart at the effortless affection between them and churned her stomach. They were her parents, after all. The idea of them still gettin' busy after forty years of marriage horrified her. Even if it was something she secretly hoped for herself.

"Boss." He quirked a flirtatious brow at his wife.

"Don't you forget it." Mom wiggled her hips and adjusted his bow tie dotted with tiny yellow teacups.

"Gross! I'd go to HR about the two of you, but since Mom is HR, there's no point," Nat groaned, watching the pink escalate to crimson across his face.

Who knew bow ties were a turn-on? Mom seemed to enjoy them. Ugh.

No wonder her dad had an army of fun bow ties. The

teacup bow tie had been a gift from Elle Davidson, Clayton's fiancé.

"Oh, hush Natalie Joan," Mom chided with a grin. She turned to her husband. "Are you going to wear this bow tie to Clayton and Elle's engagement party tonight?"

"It might be a little fancy for a brewery," Nat offered.

The Farmer's Ale, a local brewery owned by Todd Krueger and her brother's best friend, Noah Wilson, would host the happy couple's engagement party. Since opening in May, it had become one of the hot spots in the village. Granted, there were only four other "hot spots" opened past eight, including the VFW, the Sea Serpent Restaurant and Lounge, and the Wine Down, but she'd argue the new pub rivaled any hip brewery in Boston. Even if she was a little biased.

"Oh, I have a *special* bow tie for tonight." Dad's eyes filled with mirth.

"Oh?" Mom purred, waggling her eyebrows.

"Seriously. I'm going to need a therapist to wipe away *this* image of the two of you from my psyche." Her face scrunched up as she gestured to her parents.

"Don't be dramatic." Mom waved her hands. "Anywho, Mrs. Jarvis is here. LeAnne is weighing her and will put her in exam room two."

"Thanks." Nat picked up her tablet and stood. A pregnant mother of three was her next patient.

With a sorrowful wince, her mom held her hands up. "Sorry, sweetie. She'd prefer to see your dad. He was her doctor with her other pregnancies and she's…just more comfortable with him."

Nat forced her lips upwards as she sank back into her seat. "Totally get it."

"It will take time, honey. Change is difficult. It's slow, but it always happens," he said, placing his hand on her shoulder before turning to leave.

I am Dr. Owens. I am Dr. Owens.

If she repeated that mantra, maybe it would come true, vanquishing the fear that in Perry, she may always be Dr. Owens's daughter and not *the* actual Dr. Owens.

CHAPTER TWO

"Some people seem to get all sunshine, and some all shadow…"
Louisa May Alcott, *Little Women*

The sun's rays caressed Nat's bare shoulders as she stepped out of her sunshine yellow Jeep. Moving toward the brewery's backdoor, the heels of her strappy tan sandals clacked against the blacktop parking lot. Most customers entered through the main entrance at the front of the red brick building. She wasn't *most* customers, though. She was family.

She had no memory of a life without Noah Wilson. His dimpled grin meeting hers across the room during her parents' annual Christmas party. Those ocean-blue eyes sparking with mischief when they teamed up against Mom and Clayton in a game of cornhole at the Wilson's Memorial Day BBQ. The song of his laughter filling the dining room after teasing her at a joint Wilson/Owens family dinner. The two families were always intertwined.

"Nat!" Elle looped her arms around Nat when she walked into the bar area.

Over the last year, she'd grown close with Elle. The

auburn-haired beauty was once her favorite day camp arts and crafts instructor when she was a little girl. Now, one of her long-time favorite people was marrying one of her other favorite people.

"Look at you!" Nat took Elle's right hand, twirling the soon-to-be bride. The skirt of her purple halter maxi dress glided with the movement.

"Well, I must keep up with my dazzling soon-to-be sister."

The use of "sister" rather than "sister-in-law" fizzed like happy bubbles through Nat's bloodstream. She'd been a sister but had never had one. She'd be willing to wear any brides-maid fashion monstrosity for the privilege of calling Elle her sister. The pledge was true, but no real fear in ugly dresses. The fashionista bride would ensure all outfits were on point.

"Look at you in that dress!" Elle cooed. "Best stay clear of Aunt Janet. She may pull out a ruler to nag you about its questionable length." She pointed a manicured purple fingertip at the hem of Nat's pale green dress which stopped mid-thigh.

Outside of the clinic, where she wore her "take me seriously" knee-length pencil skirts paired with a not-so-serious pair of fun ballet flats, Nat liked to accentuate her petite legs with short skirts. The shorter the better. She had no insecurity about her body. She embraced it for what it was and wasn't, but she still enjoyed the illusion of having long legs like Elle.

"It is a little too short. Maybe wear a jacket." Clayton strode up, forehead creased and finger wagging.

Pressing a peck to his cheek, Elle teased, "Don't be a hypocrite about your sister's short dress when you're flashing those *sexy* forearms with your rolled up sleeves."

"*These?*" His lips tugged up with devilish delight as he flexed his forearms before capturing Elle's mouth in a slow kiss.

"Sister present!" Nat groaned, covering her face with her hands. "Goddess, between our parents' eye-banging at the clinic and *you* two, I'm going to need a whole lot of therapy and alcohol to get through tonight."

"Mom and Dad eye-banging? Well, that killed the mood." He winced, looping an arm around his fiancée's waist.

"How do you think I feel? They're in their sixties and are gettin' busy more than me."

"There should be *no* gettin' busy, young lady, especially while you're staying at the Little Red Barn." Clayton's mouth formed a wry grin.

At the end of May, Nat moved into Clayton's renovated barn turned Airbnb living space. The former occupant had been Elle, who'd rented it for a month last summer. Of course, her residency in the actual barn lasted barely two weeks. Upon her return to Perry, she and Clayton quickly dove into their love cocoon. In December, she moved back to Perry and officially into his farmhouse. After that, Clayton no longer listed the red barn, despite the demand for chic country spots. With Elle living with him, the overprotective Clayton didn't want "strangers" staying on the property.

Thank the goddess, because the Little Red Barn was a far better alternative for Nat than moving back into her childhood bedroom. It allowed her to settle into life in Perry while deciding whether she wanted to buy a house or continue to rent. She insisted on paying rent, even if Clayton had yet to cash her monthly checks.

"Can I remind you of the things we've done on the counter of the Little Red..." Elle's words were stopped by a red-faced Clayton placing a hand over her mouth.

"Gross! This is why I insisted on having that place professionally cleaned before I moved in," Nat grumbled.

They tried to cover their blushes with apologetic smiles. *Tried* but didn't necessarily succeed.

She motioned for them to scoot. "Go mingle."

She was always going to indulge in little sister teasing and groaning at Clayton and Elle's inability to keep their hands off each other, but happiness spread in her chest as she watched them melt in each other's embrace as they accepted congratulations from their guests.

"They're so happy." A deep baritone murmured into her ear, and the scent of fresh pine, reminiscent of a Christmas tree farm, swirled around Nat.

"Yeah." She turned, facing the calm waters of Noah's eyes.

With an unabashed grin, he claimed the stool beside her at the farm barrel-turned-high-top table. Embers sparked in the mere inches between them. Like the flick of a match, that heat tiptoed up her body and ignited tiny crackling fires at every nerve-ending.

"It's weird. This will be my second best man speech for Clayton, but I'm more nervous about this one."

"Why?" Head tilted, she gripped the pint glass, thankful the condensation on the surface cooled the heated charge zipping through her with his proximity.

How did Noah still have this power over her? The school-girl crush she'd had on her big brother's best friend should have faded with adulthood. With every boyfriend. With every bad Tinder date. With every one-night stand after too many tequila shots.

"This one counts. *Really* counts. This one will be forever. I think I knew, even before standing next to him at the church when he married Marianne, that she wasn't his soulmate. Who knew his soulmate was the girl he'd had a crush on since he was fourteen?"

Her smile bloomed large. "You knew. You always knew."

Most people only saw the amiable businessman, good-looking former high school football player, or modest veteran. Just like Nat, he fit in a single box in Perry, but she knew there was far more to him.

Most people never realized that Noah saw much more than what was visible. He was the first one to see the love Clayton had for Elle when it was merely a crush stoked in the flames of secrecy within his teenage heart. He was the first one to see the seeds of love growing inside Elle when she'd reconnected with Clayton last summer. Behind the scenes, he'd gardened that budding romance, helping them bloom with each other.

"Don't tell anyone. I have a reputation to protect." A self-deprecating lilt filled his voice.

"And what's this reputation we're protecting?"

He cocked his head to the right, his lips curved up in a playful smirk. "Well, Clayton is the perceptive one who sees everything. I'm the smiling best friend who's good with fluffy social interactions. The good-time-guy."

"You're not a 'good-time-guy'," she scoffed, making air quotes with her hands.

"Are you saying I'm *not* a good time?" he said with mock dismay. "Here I thought you enjoyed being around me."

Goddess, did she ever, but he was more than *just* that. The idea of him not seeing that, even in jest, caused a fury in her belly. "You're more than just a welcoming smile with funny anecdotes at parties."

He nodded, a small smile on his face.

"But I'll keep that to myself. Your secret's safe with me." She winked.

"I can always count on you." He placed his large hand atop hers.

An electric tingle pulsed from his palm into her body, fanning those bonfires into a raging forest fire within her. Warmth crept up her neck and heated her cheeks.

"Are you okay? You look flushed."

"Yes. Just warm in here." A small catch stole her breath.

Their gazes tethered. Maybe it was just her moth-like gaze refusing to look away from the flame of his eyes, but for a moment, it seemed as if he was as drawn to her as she was to him.

His fingers skated across the heated skin of her hand in soothing strokes. "Do you want to go—"

His words were snatched from a loud voice bellowing from the bar. "Hey, Prince Charming!" Todd, Noah's business partner, peeked over the heads of partygoers crowded at the barndoor paneled bar.

"Todd?" Noah blew out a long breath, twisting toward the bar.

"Stop flirting with Clayton's sister and come help me!" Todd's face pinched with annoyance.

"I'm not flirting with Clayton's sister."

Gut punch. Nat's smile didn't reach her eyes.

"Duty… well, Todd calls." Noah jumped up and strode to the bar.

Just the sister. Nat frowned and gulped her ale. While Noah's eyes saw so much, she feared that in his eyes she'd always be Clayton's little sister.

Nat meandered through the party chatting with the guests. It was a mixture of family and friends. Elle's two besties, Viet and Willa, held court in the corner of the room surrounded by Elle's Uncle Pete and cousin Tobey.

It felt a little too unrequited for Nat to stand, with a longing gaze, in the opposite corner of the bar watching Noah. A carefree expression on his face as he whispered something in Willa's ear. Head bobbing in laughter, her long caramel locks tumbled over her pretty face.

Nat's fingers curled tightly around her drink as she took in the sight. It wasn't the first time she'd witnessed the flirtation that flew between Noah and Willa, which had been a topic of conversation with Elle and Clayton. Nat observed it first-hand in May after Willa had flown in for the Farmer's

Ale Grand Opening. Both Noah and Willa insisted they were *just* friends, but who flies cross-country to come to a brewery opening in Perry, New York for a "friend" you'd barely known for a year?

Not buying it.

A frown formed on Nat's lips with each caress of Willa's fingers down Noah's muscular arm. The sultriness in her eyes as she looked at Noah like he was the last Oreo in the package even caused Nat's temperature to tick up.

Of course he was drawn to Willa. The sexy curves and flirtatious personality aside, she was brilliant, warm, and *not* his best friend's little sister.

I could never be Willa.

"What are we frowning at?" Summer Michaels' soft voice broke into Nat's self-loathing.

She sighed, "Nothing."

"Looks like that *nothing* is flirting with Willa."

Ugh. Can't get anything past her. She nodded.

Since coming back to Perry, Summer and Nat had formed an unexpected friendship. The single mom, nine years older than Nat, had gone to high school with Elle, Clayton, and Noah. To say Elle and Summer were high school besties was like saying great whites and seals were snuggle buddies. Summer wasn't just the former great white, but the Regina George of Perry. That was high school, though, and neither she nor Elle were the girls they'd been. After reconnecting last summer, the two became close friends.

Nat soon followed. After meeting at the Owens' annual Christmas party, they formed a fast friendship. What started as superficial bonds over a shared love of Disney movies, their favorite book *Little Women*, and being terrible cooks soon deepened.

Besides Elle, Summer was the closest friend Nat had in Perry. She was the only person who knew about Nat's long-standing crush on Noah. Elle knew that she had a crush as a little girl but had no idea that the fascination lingered like a mosquito that just wouldn't fucking leave no matter how often she'd swatted at it.

"I'm pathetic," Nat muttered, pressing her hands against her face.

Summer squeezed Nat's bare arm. "You're not pathetic. You're scared."

"I'm scared?" she scoffed.

Summer's brows lifted. "You're scared to tell him how you feel."

"It's just a crush. It will go away."

"A crush that you've had since you were ten. Eighteen years and that crush hasn't died yet."

"Can we talk about something else?" Nat rolled her eyes. "Can we discuss how fabulous this place looks?" She gestured to the twinkling purple lights crisscrossing the ceiling beams and tables bedecked with mason jars full of purple daisies and tiny barrel-shaped candles.

"Thanks." Bashful pride sparkled in Summer's dark brown eyes.

Before Summer moved back to Perry eight years ago, pregnant with her son, Liam, she worked in New York City as an event planner. Over the last few months, Carmen Herrera, the Village Mayor, convinced her to revive her skills. She'd managed several village events, including the upcoming fall fest. Several local businesses and individuals had also hired her to plan parties and events. She'd organized the Farmer's Ale Grand Opening. Now, she was helping Elle and Clayton plan their wedding and pre-wedding events.

"I see you both are *sans* drinks. I come bearing liquid courage." Todd sauntered up, carrying a tray with a stemless glass of rosé and a pint of ale.

"Liquid courage? For what?" Summer's expression twisted with confusion.

"We're some of the only single people at an engagement

party." Todd handed both ladies fresh drinks, then slid the tray under his muscular right arm.

"No courage needed. I prefer being single." Summer tossed her long chestnut hair behind her shoulder and sipped her wine.

The green in Todd's eyes sparked as he studied Summer's pink tongue darting out to lick excess wine off her red lips. Her gaze remained on Nat, oblivious to his attention.

Amusement curled Nat's lips while she watched the game of crushing cat and ignoring mouse.

"Plus, Noah and Willa are also single. Also..." Forehead puckered, Summer peered around the room full of couples.

"See!" Todd smirked with triumph. "In the sea of two-scoops, we're the single ones."

"Well, if I'm a single scoop, I'd come with rainbow sprinkles," Nat declared, raising her pint.

"I like that." Summer clanked her glass against Nat's.

"Summer would be cookies 'n cream." Todd winked.

"Oh, sweet creamy vanilla with a fun cookie surprise." Nat cheered.

"What would I be?" Todd lifted his chin.

"Rocky Road!" Summer and Nat laughed in unison.

Todd shrugged in acceptance. "A little nutty. A little marshmallowy. Lots of *smooth* chocolate."

"Not to mention too much will give you a stomachache," Summer snarked.

Todd placed his hand on his heart. "A nearly fatal blow. Here I was thinking I was growing on you."

"Like fungus."

"Don't underestimate the power of fungus. It gave us penicillin."

"Well, I'll ring you when I need a shot," Summer sassed but winced at the suggestive nature of her quip.

"Noted." The low timbre of his voice was almost purring. His gaze dragged down her curvy figure again, and then, as if chiding himself, snapped his eyes back up to Summer's face.

With an eyeroll that did nothing to cover up the crimson coloring her cheek, she shifted her gaze to the other side of the room.

Nat smiled. This game played on repeat each time Todd found himself in Summer's vicinity. In many ways, Todd was the male version of Nat, but *way* more obvious. She tipped her glass to him in salute.

"I should get back to work." He turned and walked away.

"Summer Michaels." Nat shimmied her shoulders at her friend. "I do believe I just witnessed Todd Krueger flirt with you, and *you* flirted right back."

"Stop!" Summer waved her off with a breathy laugh.

"Attention!" Mom clapped her hands, calling everyone's focus to the center of the bar.

Dad stood beside her. Tiny purple flowers peppered his white bow tie in honor of Elle's favorite color. "As parents of the groom and soon-to-be parents of the bride, we'd like to make a toast."

"Hopefully, you won't blubber like Pete did earlier." Elle's Aunt Janet nudged her husband's ribs.

"Hey, real men cry." His head tipped up and his chest puffed out in a prideful stance.

"Just wait 'til the wedding day. Clayton will be a puddle," Noah teased, putting Clayton in a headlock and giving him a noogie like they were ten again.

Nat sipped her drink, taking in the scene. Gentle waves of love washed over her. Yes, she was that rainbow-sprinkle-covered single scoop, but she was in an entire parlor of scoops that went together. Couples held hands. Fathers and sons teased. Mothers dabbed their eyes. Aunts blew kisses. Friends poked at each other. As Dad toasted the happy couple, the different types of pairings blanketed her in warmth.

I am single, but I'm not alone. She hoisted her glass into the air. "To Elle and Clayton!"

After a string of toasts, Nat stood with Dad and Clayton while Mom stood at the bar with her best friend, and Noah's mom, Maura. The two women laughed while their gazes danced around the room. Where one was, the other was never far.

Nat smiled, raising her pint glass in their direction. Both sent wry grins Nat's way, causing her to arch a quizzical brow. *What are they discussing?*

After both women pivoted away from Nat's stare to talk to Todd, Nat shrugged and settled back into her position between Dad and Clayton and once again contemplated how similar they were. Men of few words, but when they spoke, their words commanded, guided, accepted, and comforted. Each was the heart of this village. Dad had captained the Owens Family Clinic for the last forty years, while Clayton led the Village Veterinarian Clinic for the last four.

Like sturdy oaks, both men towered in the forest, withstanding any harsh winds that whipped across life. Between the two, Nat felt akin to a tiny windblown fern desperate to grow tall, but the shadows cast by her two mighty oaks blocked out the needed sun. Oaks can't help being oaks, and ferns can't help being ferns. No matter how much a fern wants to be an oak.

I'll always be a fern. She tightened her grip around her glass.

"When is the big day?" Virginia, one of the ladies who worked with Elle's aunt at the Village Rose Florist Shop, asked.

"December tenth," Clayton replied.

"Oh, an almost-Christmas wedding. I can picture the flower arrangements already. Although, with Elle, we'll need to incorporate some purple."

Dad beamed. "Our Elle loves purple."

"*Our* Elle," Virginia sighed.

Nat joined in on the sentiment of claiming Elle. Since she'd walked back into Clayton's life, the entire family embraced her with open arms. When Clayton brought Elle to a family dinner almost a year ago, she and everyone else there knew that this was his person…his forever. The moment they walked out the door, Mom proclaimed, "They'll be married within two years."

"So, why that date?" Virginia inquired.

"Because he's impatient." Nat poked Clayton's side.

He swatted her off with a laughing grumble. "Elle wants time to plan, but I don't want to turn a year older without her being my wife."

"Clayton's birthday is December twelfth. They also moved in together on the tenth, so it's *uber* romantic." Nat looked up at her brother, whose gaze drifted across the room to his fiancée.

Surrounded by Carmen and Summer, Elle's face was bright with laughter. Clayton's gray eyes sparked with contented longing. She'd never seen her brother both so happy and impatient. With one word from his fiancée, he'd not pass go, not collect two hundred dollars, and proceed to city hall to marry Elle this very instant.

Warmth spread within Nat as Elle's hazel eyes sought out Clayton. Their stares tangled in wordless conversation from across the room.

"So, he's getting Elle as his wife for his birthday. I'm trying to talk her into wearing a big purple bow on her dress, but she's not biting."

"Ha!" Virginia clucked. "Natalie, you are a card. The

patients at the clinic must leave in stitches after seeing you. Pun intended."

"Well, we charge by the stitch, so it's good for business."

Clayton rolled his eyes at his sister's very bad dad joke while Dad's lips lifted with what looked like pride.

"I bet!" Laughter bubbled in Virginia's throat. "How is it working for your dad?"

For? A crowbar may be needed to remove the tight smile she'd worn all evening.

"We're so lucky to have her. She's a huge help at the clinic." Dad grinned, placing a hand on her shoulder.

A huge help? It was like this was an after-school job or something she did on break, not a career she'd studied for and trained to do for the last decade of her life. "Yup." The battle to keep her tone light raged fiercely through her.

At nine p.m., The Farmer's Ale opened to the public. Most of the partygoers had left, but the happy couple and members of their wedding party remained. All twelve of them clustered around several high-top tables at the perimeter of the bar. Patrons filled the low farm tables in the center of the room, clanking glasses and chatting. Nat sat at a four-person table with Clayton, Elle, and Willa, discussing tomorrow's wedding party event.

"It's a twist on an English high tea," Willa explained.

The wedding party was small. Viet, Willa, and Carmen made up Elle's bridal party. Noah, Nat, and Jerome, Clayton's partner at the vet clinic and Tobey's husband, were standing up with the groom. Elle's cousin Tobey, now an ordained Internet minister, would officiate. Willa and Viet lived in Long Beach, where Elle used to reside. They'd be flying back for much of the pre-wedding shenanigans.

"Just tea, right?" Elle pointed at Willa.

Willa's lips lifted into a mischievous smile. *"Of course."*

"Wills."

"It will be a tasteful tea," she said with a demure bat of her long eyelashes.

"Your definition of tasteful worries me."

"Says the woman who has been caught dry-humping her fiancé in public by at least four people in this bar. Not to mention that poor Noah walked in on the two of you—"

Elle's face went fire-engine red, and she clamped her hands over Willa's mouth, cutting off her words.

Nat giggled, thinking about how just a few hours ago Clayton had done the same exact thing to his bride.

The covering of Willa's mouth was pointless. Everyone in the wedding party knew the story. Not because of Noah, but due to a tipsy Elle telling the story after one or six too many mimosas at her wedding dress shopping trip last week. Poor Noah walked in on a very naked Clayton and Elle "making breakfast" in the kitchen. Nat was horrified. Carmen blushed. Willa offered pointers on kitchen counter sex positions. Viet simply poured Elle another mimosa.

"This is why I always text before going to the farmhouse. Not to mention knock loudly and cover my eyes before entering." Nat waggled her brows at the blushing couple. "Mom and Dad were bad enough."

"You walked in on your parents?" Willa pushed Elle's hands away and gaped.

"Horrifying, isn't it?"

"No, impressive. Who knew a man who wears bow ties was a senior citizen sex god? Elle, if Clayton takes after his dad, we'll have *many* years of the two of you getting caught sexing each other up."

"Sex god?" Nat and Clayton guffawed.

"Who's a sex god?" Noah asked, walking up to their table.

Running a manicured finger up Noah's chest to his chin, Willa purred, "Besides you, gorgeous...Clayton's dad."

He blanched. "I did not need that mental image."

As the members of the party laughed and groaned, Nat tried to avert her focus, but it repeatedly dropped onto Willa and Noah. Willa's seductive winks. Noah's bemused expression.

Too much! She jumped off the stool. "I'm going to grab another drink. Anyone need anything?" Nat blurted, steamrolling over Willa mid-sentence.

Who knew what Willa was saying? Nat had only half listened. *Ok, not listening at all.* Guilt churned in her tummy. It wasn't Willa; she'd been nothing but kind to Nat. Any woman that Noah looked at would generate envy inside her. Any woman he looked at not as a little sister, the way he looked at her.

"I'll take another Doc Owens." Elle raised her empty glass.

The ale, named after Clayton, was the only beer the rosé-all-day Elle stooped to drink. All the brews at the Farmer's Ale were named after someone or something notable in the village. With the lifelong bromance between Clayton and Noah, it was unsurprising that he'd name a beer after his best friend.

"What's wrong with the one you've got?" Clayton teased, taking her lips in a nipping kiss.

"Ugh...get a room," Nat groaned at the now moderately PDAing couple.

"Agreed," Noah added.

"One with a door that locks," Willa laughingly joined in.

"Agreed." Laughter rumbled in Noah's chest.

Elle flipped them off while she remained lip-locked with Clayton.

There was no shame in their PDA game. As a woman who had been in a self-induced sexual drought, Nat was impressed and, perhaps, a little jealous. As a little sister, she was horrified.

"Willa, how much do you charge for therapy? I may need you." Nat winked at Willa, hoping it would make up for her earlier abruptness.

"Queen, I've got you." She placed a hand on her shoulder and squeezed. "We single gals gotta stick together. Especially since the entire male population of the wedding party is married or Noah. Hopefully, there will be some cute, single, and lady-part-loving lads invited to this shindig. We need to get our swirl on." She used her fingers to mimic a sexual act.

Married... and Noah? Nat nodded, not knowing how else to respond. Was something *not* going on between them? The words conflicted with the behavior between the two.

"There will be *no* swirling for Nat," Clayton warned, pointing his finger at Willa.

"Looks like you activated overprotective big brother mode." Nat rolled her eyes. "On that note, I'll grab Elle and my drinks."

Nat threaded through the crowded room and found an open spot at the end of the bar near the front entrance.

Todd waved from the other side of the bar, mouthing, *Be with you shortly.*

With a smile, she pivoted and leaned against the bar, marveling at all Noah and Todd had achieved. Five years ago, Noah moved back to Perry from San Diego, where he'd lived after being discharged from the Marines. After buying the Farmer's Wife, the local bakery, and opening the Wine Down, Main Street's only wine bar, he'd partnered with Todd to open the brewery.

"Natalie Owens." A familiar low voice jolted her.

She twisted around, and her heart thumped like a kangaroo on a trampoline. "Duncan Ellis?"

CHAPTER THREE

---

*"You don't need scores of suitors. You only need one…if he is the right one." ~*Louisa May Alcott, *Little Women*

Duncan Ellis. Butterflies twerked in Nat's stomach as she stared into a pair of familiar bourbon-colored eyes. It had been ten years since she'd stood in front of her high school boyfriend.

That early May rain had drizzled as they stood on his front porch. A shopping bag full of things he'd given her dangled from her hand. His letterman jacket she'd worn cheering from the stands at his baseball games. His royal blue homecoming hoodie she'd pulled on to keep warm at parties hidden within the cornstalk confines of his parent's farm. His DVD of Pirates of the Caribbean she'd never watched. You didn't break up and get to keep things.

"How are you?" Duncan wrapped his muscular arms around her.

"Good." Nat pulled back, brushing a wayward tendril of sandy hair behind her ear.

"I heard you were back in town working with your dad."

"Yeah." She smiled. It was nice to have someone say *with* and not *for.*

"You did it. You became a doctor."

"Yup." Shifting foot-to-foot, her gaze flicked to her table and back to Duncan.

He looked the same and, somehow, entirely different. Those same slightly ruffled floppy blond waves. The once-rounded features had been replaced by sharp angles and a strong jawline. But a familiar bashful smile rested on a now chiseled face.

"What are you up to? Are you back in Perry or just visiting?" she asked.

"I moved back six months ago. I'm working as an Assistant District Attorney at the County Courthouse in Warsaw." That self-conscious smile dissolved into a prideful grin.

"Amazing!" Her face lit up. "I remember when we'd watch those *Law & Order: SVU* marathons in high school. You talked about wanting to be a prosecutor."

He combed his fingers into his hair. "And you'd talk about taking over the clinic someday." The gaze he skimmed down her body was heated, as if filled with memories. "Although, I see you have opted to *not* go with his signature bow tie."

"Yeah," she said, trying to stamp out the breathiness in her voice.

A tingle pulsed along her skin at his proximity. Duncan, the first boy she'd really kissed. The teen she'd called boyfriend for almost two years. The person she'd lost her virginity to.

He's no boy, though. That muscular frame, full lips, spicy male scent, and corded forearms were so unlike the unsure lanky teen she'd dated. Had he somehow gotten taller?

"I heard you're living with your brother," he said.

"Not with him. I'm staying at his former Airbnb. It's on his property but my own place. It's a converted barn space. *Tres* cute and trendy. I'm lucky he's letting me stay there."

"Nice. I'd love to see it sometime." His deep timbre almost rumbled.

Heat snaked up her spine. "Umm…there are pictures online if you look up the Little Red Barn in Perry." She tugged at the hem of her too-short dress. *Why are you being awkward? He's seen you naked before.* She pulled on the fabric harder, wishing she'd worn something longer.

Nodding, he slipped his hands into the pockets of his dark denim jeans and rocked on his feet. "Not surprised he's letting you stay there. Your brother was always overprotective. He probably likes that he can keep an eye on you. I bet he's staring at us right now." With a playful arch of his right brow, he leaned around her toward the other side of the room where the wedding party sat.

She twisted her head, following his gaze. Sure enough, there was Clayton'; his brow puckered and gray eyes fixed on them.

"He is, isn't he?"

Nat nodded. "Yup."

"He never liked me." Light laughter rolled through him. With a cheeky grin, he raised his hand and waved. "Hi, Clayton!"

Wide-mouthed, she grabbed his hand and yanked it back down. "Don't poke the bear."

"Should I poke you instead?" He gently tapped her upper arm.

Something buzzed across her skin and for the first time all night, and she beamed an honest-to-goddess actual smile. No tightness. No guarded firm lines. No almost reaching her eyes. It was unbridled and so delicious.

"Do you have the same number?" he asked.

"I do."

"Me too."

"Nat." Noah appeared, placing his hand on the small of her back.

What is he... The touch melted her ability to think and caused her already-heated skin to become molten.

"It looks like it's a madhouse. I came to get Elle and your drinks since it's taking so long." Noah motioned to Todd. "Two Doc Owens, please."

"Yeah, yeah. Keep your crown on, Prince Charming," Todd snarked, pulling a couple pint glasses down from the iron wagon wheel shelf hung above the bar.

He just shrugged at Todd before facing Duncan.

"Noah." Duncan greeted, amusement sparking in his eyes.

"Duncan," Noah returned the greeting while something besides amusement darkened his eyes.

Nat cocked a brow at the standoff between the two men, like gladiators meeting center ring. No doubt Noah came over on Clayton's behalf. He always did this. People assumed Clayton followed Noah around, but it was quite the opposite. Noah often played guard dog to, or for, Clayton. As the younger sister, she'd borne the brunt of this her entire life. If it wasn't one of them, it was the other.

"Well, I should get going. Natalie, it was wonderful seeing you." Duncan leaned in, giving her another hug. "Call me. I'd love to get together and catch up."

"Sure," she said as he ended their hug and turned for the door.

"I bet he'd like to *catch up*," Noah added an almost sneered emphasis as Duncan walked out the front door.

Nat spun to face him. "What the hell was that?"

"What?"

She stabbed her index finger into his chest, trying to retain her annoyance and not swoon at the firmness under his shirt. "I already have one overprotective big brother. I don't need another."

Noah flinched.

Why is he flinching? No way had her poke done any damage.

"Here you go, your highness." Todd plopped down two pint glasses with the right amount of head on them on the bar.

"Thanks," Noah grumbled, his eyes fixed on her.

Todd's gaze bounced between them. With a wry smile, he shook his head and walked away.

Pivoting to grab the drinks, she blew out a heavy breath. *Ugh! This man!* Plopping the drinks back on the bar, she whirled. "I don't need Clayton nor you butting into my life. I'm twenty-eight. I've had boyfriends. I've had sex. Lots of sex."

"I know." He swallowed thickly. "I just want to look out for you."

She threw her hands up. "I'm *not* a little girl anymore!" Granted, her rebuttal was little girl tantrum-like, but utterly justified. Even if only to herself.

Who was *he* to butt in? Her brother's obnoxiously intrusive overprotectiveness, while just as annoying, was one thing. But Noah indulging in that behavior by intervening was quite another. With Clayton, she was the little sister. She knew that. Noah's action was akin to rubbing salt in the "you'll only ever be my BFF's little sister" wound.

"I know you're not a little girl." His blue eyes heated as their gazes twined together.

Something sparked in the bonding nature of their interlocked stares. The intensity forced her to step back, bumping against one of the stools at the bar. Stumbling, she started to fall backward until Noah's strong hands clamped on her shoulders and steadied her.

A charged electrical current coursed from his palm. The air between them snapped, crackled, and popped like Rice Krispies with the first splash of cold milk. His thumbs stroked circles on her bare upper arms. Each caress calmed and inflamed her scorched skin.

What the fuck is happening? Her breath shallowed.

"Sorry." He released her, his hands threaded into his short dark hair. "You're right. I'm just used to looking after you. Clayton is like a brother, so you're…"

"Like a little sister." The sting was not dulled by the words coming from her own mouth.

With a firm line sketched on his face, Noah grabbed the drinks. "I'll carry these." He turned, looked at the table, and then back to her. "Sorry. I just remember when you dated Duncan. You two broke up so soon after Evan that… It just didn't sit right with me that he'd break up with you right after your brother died. It speaks to his character."

Evan? The mention of her long-dead brother slammed into her like a freight train. Instead of the sensation of being crushed, red-hot anger surged in her.

Nat clenched her jaw, yanking the drinks from him, some of the creamy red ale sloshed onto both their hands. "I can carry my own damn drinks and decide who I spend time with." She stomped toward the table and then whirled on him with narrowed eyes. "For the record, I broke up with him. I'm not some damsel who got her heart broken that you need to protect from the big bad ex-boyfriend. Why don't you focus on your…*whatever* you have going on with Willa and let me make my own decisions."

"Nat—"

She ignored him and walked away.

CHAPTER FOUR

*"I don't pretend to be wise, but I am observing, and I see a great deal more than you'd imagine." ~*Louisa May Alcott, *Little Women*

S *tupid Noah Wilson!* Teeth gritted, Nat brushed her shoulder-length hair up into a ponytail in preparation for high tea at the farmhouse. It would only be the wedding party. Plus, Jerome's husband Tobey, Mathew, Carmen's husband, and Ryan, Viet's husband. Including Noah and Willa with *whatever* they had going on, she'd be the rainbow sprinkled single scoop... *Again.*

"Fuck it!" she said aloud, putting on the glittery rose teardrop earrings Elle had given her last year. If she was going to be the single scoop, then she'd put on all her rainbow sprinkles.

After shimmying into her hot pink dress with a tulle skirt that stopped just above the knees, she twirled in front of the sleeping loft's gold-framed mirror. Yes, she actually fucking twirled. If everyone was going to treat her like the little sister, she'd do what she'd done throughout her residency program when others discredited her for her being younger than everyone else, her petite size, or her gender; she'd put on something that surged her confidence and shake it off before facing them. Even if she chose her battles, she could always be prepared with a cute outfit and an assured smile.

With her newfound confidence, she descended the stairs to the living area. Stretching her arms, she let out a small yawn. All night, she'd tossed and turned. She'd flipped between stewing about Noah's unwanted intervention with Duncan and fixating on that electric heat that came with proximity to both men. Two men. The same reaction.

Plopping onto the green couch, she leaned her chin on her hands. Noah had been the real-life Prince Charming who'd starred in her daydreams from the age of ten. Eighteen years ago, he'd gone from Clayton's best friend to the star of all her schoolgirl fantasies when he'd come down the escalator at the Buffalo-Niagara Airport in his Marine uniform. Both families greeted him with signs welcoming him back after his first deployment. Excitement rioted through her as she held her handmade *Did you bring me a present?* rainbow-glitter-covered sign.

Noah's stoic face erupted in a million-watt smile, and laughter rumbled as he pointed to the sign proclaiming, "That's my girl!"

He'd never called her "his girl" before. It was always "Nat" or "Little Sis." It would be eight years before he called her "his girl" again. It would also be the last time. The memory of *that* moment ten years ago both soothed and tormented.

Nat's cell pinged, pulling her from the walk down crush-memory lane.

Duncan: Call me impatient. Dinner this Wednesday?

A hesitant giddiness accompanied the message. Duncan Ellis was asking her out. Dinner would not be a platonic catch-up session. It was the first flick of a lighter to rekindle what had once been.

She worried her bottom lip with her teeth. Did she want that old flame to reignite?

Nat lifted her head at the sound of a soft rap on the front door. Placing her phone on the coffee table, she stood and walked to the door.

Her breath caught. "Noah."

Of course, he stole her breath. He stood there in all his sexy small-town-hero glory, holding a bouquet wrapped in the signature rose-patterned paper of the Village Rose Florist. Dark stubble outlined the contours of his strong jawline. A button-up shirt that matched his blue eyes molded to his muscular frame. His throat was exposed by the unbuttoned collar, and the rolled sleeves of his shirt revealed corded forearms.

He was the living, breathing embodiment of her fantasies. How often had she daydreamed of him standing at her door, dressed like the handsome lead of a rom-com, and holding flowers? How often had she fantasized about him saying, "It's you," and taking her lips in a long kiss?

Only he wasn't dressed up for her. He was here for the tea.

He will never be for me. Nat stiffened. To him, she was only Clayton's little sister. Someone to protect. Someone to not take seriously.

"You look pretty," he said, his gaze sweeping over her. "May I come in?"

Disarmed by his compliment, she stepped to the side to let him in. "Are those for the tea? Did Willa wrangle you into helping with decorations?" A soft sigh captured her tone.

Ugh! Don't be that girl. Willa's nice. Noah's nice. They deserve each other. She glanced downward, focusing on her hot pink ballet flats.

He handed her the arrangement. "They are for you. An apology for last night. I'm really sorry."

She took them. "Noah—"

"I know what you're going to say."

"Well, if you know what I'm going to say, then you don't need me here for this conversation," she sniped.

"Damn it, Nat." He took the flowers back and stomped to the small island that separated the kitchen from the rest of the open space and set them down. Sucking in a deep breath, he placed his hands flat on the counter as if anchoring himself. "Why are you so pissed at me? It's not like you to get so angry. Are you okay?"

The earnestness in his words softened the tension in her muscles. "You're right. I'm sorry. It's fine. I'm fine," she said, deflated.

Twisting to face her, he leaned on the counter. Forehead creased, he studied her. "No, you're not, and it's not. Talk to me."

His gaze was like a thief stealthily breaking into a safe, eager to coax all her secrets out.

He took two steps forward and then stopped. "We've always been able to talk to each other. You're one of my favorite people."

"You're one of my favorite people." A tiny quake trembled in her voice.

"Nat, what's going on? I know I stepped over the line about Duncan last night, but you were tense before then. You weren't smiling last night. Not the real Nat smile."

The real Nat smile? She moved her fingers to her lips, tracing their outline. "You really do see so much, don't you?"

"I see you," he said, his stare tight on her, almost possessive.

What? Her heart thundered. Surely Clayton and Elle could hear the erratic thump in the farmhouse. Hell, her parents may hear it from their house two miles away.

The reaction her body had to him wasn't new, but the way he looked at her was. What did his attention mean? Was it just more of someone with the protective gene looking out for someone as, say, a little sister? *Probably.* Everyone saw her as the youngest Owens, a little girl. Why would he be any different?

He cleared his throat. "You're not happy."

"It's been hard since I've come home." She exhaled, walked to the couch, and sat.

"Why?"

"Because I'm Natalie Owens here."

His head jerked. "What's wrong with being Natalie Owens?"

"You wouldn't understand. You're Noah Wilson. The former high school quarterback. The decorated veteran. The one who came back to revive the village with not one but three businesses. People respect you."

"Who doesn't respect you?" The calm seas of his blue eyes almost stormed.

She tossed her hands in the air. "Everyone!"

"I respect you."

"You protect me. Big difference." She crossed her arms.

"Do you think I respect Clayton?"

"Yes."

"Do you think I protect Clayton?"

She didn't say anything. Just nodded. *Damn him and his logic!*

"So, we've established that I respect you. Anyone else that doesn't respect you…fuck them."

Her eyes widened. "Did Noah Wilson, the man that is nice to *everyone*, just say, 'fuck them?'"

Noah smirked. "Yup. Fuck them."

She couldn't fight her grin. It spread like peanut butter on hot toast. This is why Noah remained one of her favorite people. It was why this goddessdamn crush wouldn't go away anytime soon.

"Thank you."

"I'm here anytime you want to talk. I know I'm Clayton's best friend, but I'm also your…"

Nat prayed he wouldn't say big brother.

"...friend."

Not sister, but friend. A quiet happiness bloomed in her chest. She may never be the woman he looked at with heated eyes or pulled into his arms to kiss, but as a friend, hope lived that she was no longer relegated to the little sister image in his vision. Most people loathed the idea of being friend-zoned. At that moment, she was living for it.

She jumped up from the couch and walked to the counter. "Let's see these flowers. Isn't the Village Rose closed on Sundays?"

"I called in a favor with Janet."

"Nice." She ripped open the paper.

"*Typical...* You open everything like it's Christmas morning." The corners of his mouth turned up in amusement.

Delicate yellow gardenias sat in a clear glass vase tied with a rainbow ribbon. Breathing in their scent, Nat closed her eyes. "Beautiful."

"Yeah," he murmured.

She turned her gaze, finding his stare fixed on her.

Like a killer from a slasher movie who refused to die, the electric heat of her long-standing attraction to this man returned. Each nerve ending exploded into awareness as the tropic-level heat radiated in the inches between them.

The muscles of his throat worked. Each flex and swallow telegraphed the careful consideration of what to say. He cleared his throat. "Janet has an eye for flowers."

"She does... Thank you for these."

The elixir of his pine and mint scent coiled around her. It both tensed and relaxed her muscles. It had never been like this. Awkward and comfortable at the same time. Even with her long-lasting crush, the space between them had never been clumsy. They'd never sniped at one another. There'd never been a reason for either to apologize. She didn't like it.

She'd never have him the way she wanted, but she could have his friendship.

"Noah, I'm sorry about snapping at you last night and my snide comment about Willa. I like Willa a lot, and I'm happy for the two of you."

"There's nothing going on between Willa and me. We're just friends."

Friends? Like us? Only you don't let me touch you the way you let Willa. Of course, I'd never dare.

Shaking away the errant thought, she said, "Okay."

"Let's head over to the farmhouse." Noah tipped his head toward the door.

"Okay, let's go…friend."

CHAPTER FIVE

"Let us be elegant or die!" ~Louisa May Alcott, *Little Women*

Nat was in awe. The farmhouse kitchen and dining area had transformed from modern country chic to sophisticated English teahouse. Tiered silver trays of scones, tiny sandwiches, and cookies sat atop violet-hued linen tablecloths. Elegant string quartet music hummed in the background. The aroma of white roses and lavender mingled with the scent of fresh scones.

Guests sipped tea from petite purple teacups rimmed in gold and munched dainty snacks. Laughter filled the room from Mathew's ill-begotten demonstration of how to drink pinkies up, resulting in tea sloshed onto his white shirt.

In the middle of everything were Clayton and Elle. In the constellations of love filling the home, they were the North Star. Love filled every corner of the farmhouse. Couples held hands, kissed, or enveloped one another.

Longing ached in Nat's chest. She wanted that kind of love. Not just the sweetness but the kind of love where you're seen for all that you are and aren't. Truly seen.

I see you. Noah's words lingered in her ears as she stood

with Carmen and Willa. Her gaze drifted across the room to where he stood talking to Mathew. For a moment, their eyes met. What did he *see* when he looked at her?

"Willa, this high tea is adorable," Carmen gushed, pouring peppermint tea from a purple porcelain teapot.

Nat shifted her focus back to the little group. "Agreed." She raised her cup in salute. "You're a goddess among queens."

"Thanks." Willa curtsied. The long strapless blue dress and peacock feather fascinator she wore added to the whimsy of the day.

Viet sauntered up, a teacup and saucer in hand. "This is classy, Wills. When you said you were planning high tea, I expected Long Island Iced Teas and strippers."

"Well, the tea party is still in diapers." She winked before stepping into the center of the room. "Everyone, may I have your attention!"

"Oh no, if a stripper jumps out of a scone, I'm out of here," Viet quipped.

"That'd be *one* tiny stripper," Nat joked, lifting a white-chocolate raspberry scone and breaking it in half. "Boo, mine has no stripper."

"You've been working with Dad too long," Clayton groaned, pinching his nose.

"No strippers, but we do have a special activity. Let us proceed to Clayton's mancave. Leave your tea. I have proper drinks down there." Willa regally waved her hand, directing the party to the basement door.

"It's not a man cave," Clayton protested.

"Knowing those two, it might be a sex dungeon," Viet deadpanned.

Blushing like a cinnamon red-hot, Elle narrowed her eyes at her old friend.

"Come on, *Fifty Shades,* let's go." He looped his arm in hers and headed to the door.

"They joke about the basement being their sex dungeon after we spent an hour eating scones from the counter where I caught them having sex on," Noah whispered in Nat's ear.

Goosebumps bloomed across her skin. When did he move close to her? Just a few minutes ago, he'd leaned against the kitchen counter on the other side of the room, sipping tea and smirking at Mathew.

"You poor thing," she teased.

"No coming back from seeing that." His face creased with a mixture of horror and humor.

Elle had shared it in tipsy detail. Her body bent over the counter, and Noah walking in. Nat couldn't imagine the embarrassment for all involved. She'd be horrified if she was Elle and someone walked in on her and…

Great! Now she was thinking of Noah bending her over the kitchen island.

"I don't want to think about it." A breathiness took control of her voice.

He gestured to the door. "After you."

They headed down the stairs. He was just a heartbeat behind her. With each step she took, his fresh pine scent enveloped her. A familiar charge zipped along her veins with his closeness. *Just friends,* she reminded herself.

Reaching the bottom step, she stopped to scan the room. Noah's firm chest collided with her back. The contact dissolved the goosebumps into lava swirling across every inch of her skin.

"Sorry." She swallowed thickly.

His hand grazed her bare upper arm in a soothing stroke. "It's okay."

With a deep inhale, she stepped into the room. Willa had worked her decorative magic, transforming Clayton's soft cream, beige, and hunter-green basement into an explosion of the wedding colors of purple and silver. The sectional couch and chairs were draped in deep violet fabric with silver heart-shaped pillows. Twinkling white and purple lights criss-crossed the ceiling. Purple roses in silver vases sat on each end of the bar. Tealights flickered in silver and purple stained-glass candleholders on the end tables.

"It's *so* cute in here!" Nat gave a thumbs up to a preening Willa.

"Thanks, queen." She pointed to the couch. "There are seats there for you two."

"Uh… Okay." Nat nodded.

The only seats available for her and Noah were beside each other on the sectional couch between Elle and Clayton, and Viet and his husband, Ryan. Both couples' laps were occupied by Clayton and Elle's dogs: Fitz and Lizzie. The addition of the dogs squeezed them tight against each other on the couch.

She took her seat, and so did he.

She yanked at the hem of her dress. The fabric had ridden up to the middle of her thigh, exposing more bare leg than she felt comfortable with, especially sitting so close to Noah. A dip in a bath of ice water was needed. The molten tempera-ture of her body pooled sweat in unladylike spots. Places that clenched with a wanton ache.

"Here you go." Willa handed them each a champagne flute filled with mimosa.

"Wait, is Nat old enough to drink?" Mathew mocked.

"I'm twenty-eight!" she scolded, taking a swig of her drink while side-eyeing Mathew, who sat diagonal from them on the floor in front of Carmen.

"Hush, or she won't write you a prescription for that rash you have." Noah narrowed his eyes and tossed a heart-shaped pillow at Mathew.

"Dude, I told you that in confidence!"

"Thanks," she whispered to Noah.

He nudged her side. "I got you."

Oh, goddess! More sweating.

Willa finished dispensing the mimosas. "As you know, this is a Willa twist on a tea party. Elle got her fancy Austen-inspired tea party, but what Willa-inspired version of anything wouldn't come with a *sexy* surprise?" She wiggled her curvy hips.

"Willa, what did you do?" Elle arched a brow.

"Honey, I told you we should have got cash out. She totally got a stripper." Ryan elbowed his bemused husband.

"Even better. May I introduce Ms. Coco ChaNUT!" Willa cheered.

A drag queen with a short black bob and ruby-red lips sashayed into the room. A black cocktail dress hugged her statuesque figure. "*Bonjour, mon petites,*" Ms. ChaNut purred in a thick French accent.

"Oh my god!" Viet and Elle squealed happily.

"By the end of my seminar, your lovers will be saying that," she sassed.

"Who's Ms. ChaNut?" Nat's head tilted, looking between Willa and Elle.

"Ms. ChaNUT is a fabulous drag performer and sex therapist who runs workshops on how to give..." She motioned with her hands.

She didn't have to finish the statement. Nat knew exactly what she was saying. Mortification engulfed her. What could be worse than sitting in her brother's mancave learning how to...

"*Mademoiselle,* when we last met at that handsome man's bachelor party..." Ms. ChaNut pointed a red manicured finger at Viet, "...that was for a room full of the penis lovers. Today we are in mixed company. We will tap into your oral fixation for both. Whether you prefer a baguette, a quiche, or both. I don't judge."

Ok, that's worse. Nat's eyes widened in horror. *This is not happening.*

"Aw, Nat, your face is beet-red," Mathew taunted.

"Hey, Mathew, why don't you pay attention? You may learn something," Noah said. Lines of frustration creased his face.

"Well, I could probably teach the quiche section."

"Here," Carmen said, handing her husband a notebook and pen. "Take notes."

Mathew blanched as laughter filled the room.

Noah bent close to her ear and murmured, "Ignore Mathew. I think we're all equally uncomfortable."

"Willa's not." Her eyes drifted to Willa, an amused smile hidden behind her Champagne flute.

"Confidence and insecurity sometimes look the same."

She tilted her head to him. "What does that mean?"

"Some people overcompensate for insecurities with false bravado, while some deliberately hide their confidence to appease the insecurities of others."

Which am I? Which are you? She blinked, breaking their woven gazes.

"Pay attention, Wilson, you may learn something," Mathew chastised with a twinge of mockery.

"Hey, if he's distracting Nat from paying attention, that's okay with me. In fact, Nat, do you want to take Fitz and Lizzie for a walk?" Clayton's tone was half-joking, but his tense expression displayed his overprotective big brother side.

"Nope," she said, lips pursed.

This was uncomfortable for both of them but for different reasons. Her discomfort was at the fact that she was learning sexy time activities at a pre-wedding activity for her brother in his house. Clayton's blush and stuttered, "ex...ex...excuse me?" when she'd first brought up sex in his presence flashed in her mind. Despite her twenty-eight years, her brother still treated her like a little girl. He'd have a coronary if he knew about the vibrator in the nightstand in the Little Red Barn.

"Carmen, can I borrow a piece of paper and pen?" Smirking, her audacious gaze remained fixed on her brother.

Clayton grunted.

Elle patted his cheek. "She's an adult."

"But she's still my little sister." The protest was dipped in regret. As if he'd failed somehow.

Nat wanted to quell his feelings. So much of his life was spent as a big brother and her a little sister. It had to be hard to realize she wasn't that pigtailed little girl anymore. Part of her wanted to put the notebook down, make a joke, and take the dogs for a walk, allowing his discomfort to dissolve.

Not discomfort, but his insecurity. She gnawed on her lip, thinking of Noah's take on Willa's over-the-top confidence versus the limitations some put on themselves to make others feel better. Was Nat the latter and not the former?

This was far too much introspection in the middle of a sex workshop. Pushing those thoughts away, she settled the small notebook Carmen gave her on her lap.

She scribbled notes in her sloppy doctor's handwriting. It was like being in medical school again. Only instead of the technical terms, Ms. ChaNUT used a fun mix of half-French/half-English and totally dirty versions to describe human anatomy and sexual positions. She'd never look at hollandaise sauce in the same way.

Shifting on the couch beside her, Noah cleared his throat.

Face tipped toward Noah, her eyes snagged on his gaze, which was locked on her paper. Fat cursive outlined Ms. ChaNUT's suggested tongue techniques. The cool calm blue of his eyes darkened like a stormy sea.

Nat's breath hitched. Had his eyes flicked between the words scrawled on her paper to her lips? Did he imagine the slickness of her tongue trailing down the contours of his body? The heat of her mouth moving lower and lower until…

Like the turn of a crank, tension built between her legs. Breath ragged, she looked back to her paper.

"Now, when you want to pleasure a lady…" Ms. ChaNUT went on.

Don't look at Noah. Don't look at Noah.

She looked at him.

It had to be a trick of her crush-logged and sex-deprived brain. Had she imagined the smolder in his eyes? His uneven breaths? The lick of his lips like a wolf ready to devour its first real meal in days? The grip of his hands around his knees as if battling for control? None of that was real. It couldn't have been.

I'm just Clayton's sister to him.

As Ms. ChaNUT described dual stimulation of a woman during oral sex, Nat pulled harder at the hem of her skirt. With each detail, Nat could imagine being alone in this room, on this couch with just Noah. His head between her legs, mouth drinking her up, and fingers pushing inside her. A hot flush invaded every inch of her.

"Are you okay?" Noah whispered.

Stupid body! Ice baths all week! Nat pressed her legs tight, trying to fight that throbbing ache. This was ridiculous. Her own form of torture.

"Warm…in…here," she said, her words came out like a tripping response. It was the same excuse she'd given last night. She hoped he bought it.

"I feel it too." He shifted. "The heat…it's sweltering in here," he sputtered, standing up. "I'm going to turn the air conditioning down a bit. It's a little warm in here."

After the sexually titillating workshop ended, the guests lingered, sipping mimosas and mingling. Nat slipped upstairs to take Fitz and Lizzie outside. Frankly, she needed a break. Sitting a breath away from Noah for an hour-long seminar about oral sex had taken a toll on her body. Every muscle was coiled tight. and her core pulsed with an unrequited ache. The fresh Noah-free air soothed the tension rioting within her.

After the quick walk, the dogs padded behind her toward

the kitchen cabinet where their treats were kept. Sound filtered up from the basement. In the cacophony of voices, she could make out Noah or, perhaps, it was just the echo of him murmuring in her ear.

Today, he saw her. He supported her. He set her on fire. The way Noah's gaze flitted between her notes and her body. The pink that kissed his cheeks after he looked away from her. How his hand, which sat inches from her leg, had grazed her bare skin. Likely accidental, but she could always dream the touch had been intentional.

"Only you would plan something like this." Noah chuckled, emerging from the basement. He glanced over his shoulder as he spoke.

"You *loved* every minute of it," Willa teased, following him. "I bet you learned a few things. Care to try them out?"

Noah's laugh echoed mockingly as they strode into the living room.

It was like a bucket of cold water tossed into the warm bubble bath she'd been mentally luxuriating in since he'd shown up at the Little Red Barn earlier. Nat's heart sank with each muffled laugh, giggle, and word wafting from the living room with the unwanted stench of truth.

No more. Nat retrieved her rainbow patchwork purse from where she'd left it on one of the kitchen island barstools and pulled out her phone. It was time to give up childish things, including crushes.

Especially crushes. She pulled up Duncan's message and responded.

Me: Absolutely.

CHAPTER SIX

"Watch and pray, dear, never get tired of trying, and never think it is impossible to conquer your faults." ~Louisa May Alcott, *Little Women*

The rain tapped against the windowpane in cadence with Nat's fingers on the laptop keyboard. Rather than heading out for lunch, she took advantage of the quiet of the closed clinic to update patients' charts. Tuesday was one of the days they closed from noon to three for an extended mid-day break before staying open until seven to see patients. Dad started this when he took over the clinic from Grandpa. Thanks to Dad, the Owens Family Clinic offered evening and Saturday appointments.

The increased availability offered access to care for those who may not have the luxury of taking off work to see a doctor. During Nat's Emergency Medicine rotation, while completing her residency, she found many people visiting the ER with exacerbated conditions that could have been prevented by regular health checkups. A lack of health insurance and limited healthcare services detoured many from getting needed care. Nat knew that preventive health services not only promoted good health but, in some instances, saved someone's life.

This was just one of the many reasons Nat wanted to be a doctor. To help. To be of service. To change things for the better. Just like her dad.

Just like Evan would have done. Her gaze dropped to the rainbow-glitter framed photo sitting on the corner of her desk. In it, she wore a birthday girl sash and crown and was surrounded by Evan, Clayton, and her parents during her eighteenth birthday party. It was the last complete Owens family photograph taken. A month later, Evan died. Beside that picture was a simple wood-framed photo of Nat and Clayton flanked by Mom and Dad at her medical school graduation.

The incomplete Owens Family. She frowned, swiveling back and forth in the chair.

Like an unyielding current, time had differed since Evan died. The memory of that night still echoed inside her. The somber Perry Police Officers on their front porch. Mom's howl. Dad's blank stare. Nat, alone, on the bottom step in the foyer watching the strongest people she knew crumble.

The pain had dulled over the years, but the nagging ache never went away. Evan's presence haunted each of them in different ways.

Nat returned her gaze to the two photos and studied the variations in her parents' smiles. In the complete Owens family photo, each unabashed grin reached their eyes. In the incomplete Owens family photo, those smiles were large, but grief and wistfulness shaded their eyes.

She worried that it wasn't just because they missed Evan in the big moments, but also because they wished they were celebrating his medical school graduation. Wished that Evan was the new Dr. Owens sitting in this chair.

Don't let yourself go there. Nat pushed up from her desk to head to the front to prepare for the clinic's reopening.

"Dr. Owens isn't back from lunch yet," LeAnne's muffled voice filtered through the red door between the clinic's lobby, where patients checked in, and the back area where the exam rooms and offices were.

Nat stopped, hand on the doorknob, and inhaled deeply, fighting her irritation with the medical assistant. *I'm Dr. Owens.*

"Is the boss around?" a deep voice asked, a soft chuckle punctuating the question.

"Mrs. Owens is at lunch with Dr. Owens. You can—"

"I'm Dr. Owens." Nat stepped into the patient check-in area.

"Well, you don't look like Dr. Owens." The gray-haired man cocked a teasing brow.

"I'm Dr. Nat Owens. I joined the practice in May." She extended her arm.

The man took her hand in his leathery grip. "Little Natalie Owens. All grown up and working for your dad."

Her smile smoothed to a firm line. "I'm sorry. Do I know you?"

"You probably don't remember me. I'm Jack Simmons, the rep from J&C Medical Supplies. Your dad's clinic has been in my territory for thirty years."

"Oh, Mr. Simmons. You're right...I didn't recognize you."

Jack stroked his chin. "It's the beard. Can't grow hair on my head anymore, but it seems to come in like I'm Father Christmas on my face."

She nodded and forced a laugh.

"Your dad mentioned you'd be coming to work for him."

With him, not for him. She pushed her clenched fists into the pockets of her white lab coat.

"I remember you running around here as a little girl with your Fisher-Price doctor's bag."

"That was a long time ago." She blew out an annoyed breath and tried not to say that she remembered him with hair. "So, you wanted to speak to Dr. Owens. Well, I'm Dr. Owens. How can I help you?"

"Of course. I've got some new blood pressure cuffs and—"

"Jack!" Mom strolled into the clinic, causing Jack to turn toward the front door.

"Well, there's the boss." He opened his arms wide.

"Simmons," Dad grinned, following close behind Mom.

"Dr. Owens, I was just chatting with Natalie."

She dug her fingernails into her palms which were still hidden in her pockets.

Jack pointed to a large black roller bag near the check-in desk. "I've got new doctor gadgets to show you. Got time?"

"I do love doctor gadgets," Dad chuckled and looked to Mom, who nodded. "The boss says I have time." Placing a hand on Jack's shoulder, he guided him toward the red door. "Let's go to my office."

"Wonderful." Jack grabbed his bag, pivoting to Nat. "Natalie, great to see you again."

DR. OWENS, NOT NATALIE!

With a tip of his head, Jack disappeared behind the red door with Dad.

"Did you take a lunch break, sweetie?" Mom looped her arm around Nat's shoulder.

"I ate a yogurt while I was charting."

"That's not a proper lunch break. You know you get… what do you call it… hangry?" Mom made air quotes with her fingers. "You have a good thirty minutes before your next patient, why don't you go grab something."

Did Mom ever worry about Dad getting hangry? It was like being five again, with snack time and nap breaks. Any minute, Mom may pull out Wrinkles, the stuffed bulldog Nat had as a kid, and tell her to take a nap. Was Nat Dr. Owens, or was she still that little girl with her Fisher-Price medical bag?

CHAPTER SEVEN

"You have found your style at last." ~Louisa May Alcott, *Little Women*

Nat stood, hands on hips, in front of the wardrobe. How was it possible to own so many clothes and still have nothing to wear on a date? Yes, Duncan had seen her naked. No doubt, he maintained an entire mental catalog of her questionable high school fashion. The thought did nothing to quell the nervous flutter in her stomach.

The dark-oak wardrobe shined with a rainbow of bright-colored clothes. Not a single little black dress to be had. At that moment, all she wanted was a sexy little black dress like Audrey Hepburn or a sophisticated red dress like she was... well, anyone but her.

"Ugh!" She fell onto the bed. Why didn't she own a fucking little black dress? Who bought her clothes? Sailor Moon? "Double ugh!" she groaned.

Twisting on the bed, she grabbed her phone and texted Elle for backup. While Summer was her go-to for most things these days, the former high school fashionista lived in jeans, cut-off shorts, and T-shirts. Thank the goddess for her fashion-forward, soon-to-be sister who always had the perfect outfit for any occasion.

Ten minutes later, Elle stood in front of the wardrobe. Nat's clothes and a few pieces that she'd brought were strewn across the bed. Elle was a good five inches taller. In no *Sisterhood of the Traveling Pants* alternative universe would the clothes that hugged her trim, athletic curves and accentuated her long legs look good on Nat. Thanks to Nat's petite figure and short legs, she'd appear like a little girl playing dress up in her big sister's clothes.

If things progressed with Duncan, there'd need to be some future shopping trips with Elle to level up her clothing. The vision of a makeover montage to some sugary pop song danced in her head.

"I don't know why you think you have nothing to wear. This is darling." Elle pulled out a silky knee-length peach dress.

"Darling is for little girls," she grumbled like the little girl she was complaining about. "I don't want to be darling. I want to be sexy and sophisticated."

"Don't we all."

"You are. As vomit-inducing as this is to say, Clayton looks at you with a mixture of respect and pervy intentions. I want Duncan to look at me like that."

Elle sat down beside her on the bed. "I snuck a peek while you were at the bar talking with Duncan, and he already looks at you with very *pervy* intentions. I think that's why Noah went over there to play guard dog."

Nat's eye roll could likely be heard at the farmhouse where Clayton was making dinner. "I'm sure Clayton didn't like it and ordered Noah to come over."

"Noah went over there on his own accord. After Duncan waved, I was distracting Clayton with..." she trailed off with a devilish lift of her lips.

"No, no, no! I don't want to know," Nat groaned, standing

up and grabbing the red dress that Elle brought. Her nose scrunched as she held the dress to her body in front of the gold-framed mirror. *This won't do.* The soft cotton fabric of the dress would swim on her smaller hips and breasts.

Damn clothes punctuated the cruel reminder that in Perry, she was still seen as girlish rather than womanly. Little girls wore peach-colored dresses. Women wore sexy little black dresses. She was no Audrey Hepburn. No Elle Davidson. She was just Nat.

"I've never seen you get nervous like this before. Of course, this is my first experience with you dating someone."

Nat placed the red dress on the bed. "It's been a while since I've been on a date. For the last year, I've been so focused on finishing my residency and establishing myself in practice, I kind of forgot to date *or* have a life."

"When was the last time you dated someone?"

She tapped her right foot. "The last date was two years ago, the last boyfriend was four years ago, and my last one-night stand was a year ago. So, it's been a while."

"Are the nerves because it's been a while or because it's Duncan?" Elle asked, walking to the wardrobe.

She shrugged. This wasn't like her to get anxious about a date. It wasn't like her to fret over what to wear or to look at her clothes and think none of them would do. That *she* wouldn't do. Self-doubt and second-guessing were a new bag of chips for her. The taste was sharp, like salt and vinegar in her mouth, but had, nonetheless, taken root since coming home.

She studied her reflection in the mirror. Where once she reveled in her wavy sandy hair, eyes the color of a stormy sky, and soft yet strong, petite frame, she cringed at what she saw now. The image seemed distorted, like a cruel funhouse mirror pointing out every flaw. Both seen and unseen.

Elle went on. "I was so nervous with your brother, but it was that excited nervousness. Although, I never worried about what I was wearing because he loved me in anything." Her hazel eyes sparkled.

"I think he loves you best in nothing at all."

Pink rouged Elle's cheeks. "My point is...dress for yourself. The right person will see you because you're showing yourself. For the record, I think who you are is amazing." Elle held up a spaghetti-strap fuchsia, fit-and-flare dress.

"Easy for you to say. You're you." She flinched as insecurity slipped out.

"For a long time, I thought I wasn't enough. Your brother once said to me he wished I could see myself through his eyes. It took time, and it's still a battle, but I see myself...not through his eyes but with my own. I see what he sees in me... and I like me. I can only hope you'll see yourself the way the people that love you do. You're a perfect summer day... warm, full of sunshine, and missed when away."

With a small grin, Nat took the dress.

Thirty minutes later, Nat arrived at the Sea Serpent restaurant, parked her sunny yellow Jeep, and jumped out. The kitten heels of her white shoes kicked up loose gravel with each step toward the entrance.

Duncan waited just inside the door. In a fitted navy suit that molded over his muscular physique and those reckless blond waves smoothed with product, he appeared the dashing do-gooder attorney from a TV courtroom drama.

"Natalie," he greeted her with a smile.

A flutter bloomed in her abdomen and wiggled across her entire body. "You look very fancy."

He leaned in, placing a chaste kiss on her cheek. "I came from the courthouse. My last case ran late, so I didn't have time to change."

"No problem for me. You look handsome."

His bourbon-colored gaze dragged over her figure. "You look…cute."

Cute? Her stare flicked down to the simple fuchsia cotton dress. *Maybe I should have borrowed Elle's red dress…and a belt.* What twenty-eight-year-old doctor wanted to be cute? Hell, what twenty-eight-year-old *period* wanted to be cute?

Sigh. Ask Elle to go shopping for some pervy-intention-inducing clothes.

"Welcome." The hostess appeared. "Let me take you to your table." She pulled two leather-bound menus from below the hostess stand and motioned for them to follow.

Their corner table overlooked the serene waters of Silver Lake. A blood-orange glow permeated the room from the setting sun streaming in through the floor-to-ceiling windows. On the table, light flickered from the jade-green sea glass candleholder like a witness to this second first date.

That knowledge released a strange swirl through her. This wasn't the first time she bit her lip and fidgeted with the hem of her skirt, wondering what to say to Duncan on a first date. For a moment, she was sixteen again, smoothing down the satin fabric of her tea-length dress as they sat side-by-side on gymnasium bleachers at the homecoming dance.

He leaned across the table. "Nervous?"

The question was a balm for her nerves. It was like a diagnosis. Once you identified the problem, you can treat it.

She blew out a breath. "I know I shouldn't be. We've done this before."

"I don't think we've done *this* before."

"What?" she guffawed. "We dated for almost two years."

"That was high school. We were kids. We barely knew what dating was."

Her brows knitted together. "I think I barely know what dating is now."

"Sounds like you've dated the wrong men. Good thing I

came along to help refine your understanding of dating." His low voice almost dripped with smooth caramel.

She arched an eyebrow. "Dating the *wrong* men? You remember I dated you, right?"

"I said men. I was a boy then. I'm not a boy anymore."

Her lips curved up. "So, this is a date and not just old friends catching up?"

"Correct." He closed his menu. "I'm not going to be coy with you. I'd like to date you. I won't pretend that I haven't checked up on you via social media a few times over the years and thought about reaching out. When I saw you Saturday, I knew it was my chance to do what I should have done a long time ago."

"Ask me to dinner?" An uncomfortable laugh whooshed out.

"Win you back."

Her forehead creased. *Win me back?* What did that mean? "I'm not a prize or a trophy," she said in a clipped voice.

"I know." He reached across the table, brushing his fingers over her hand. "Although, being with you did make me feel like I'd won every trophy."

Gooseflesh bloomed with each soft stroke across her skin.

"I was a dumb kid when we dated. You were right to break up with me."

Nat's face pinched with remorse. Awkward regret twinged with the memory of his stricken face and croaked, "Okay," when she'd whispered, "I think we should break up." Not because she broke up with him but for the impact on him. Despite her reasons, she always regretted hurting him.

"It was just all too much then. Evan had just died. My family was…" A dull ache choked off her words.

Moving her hand away from his, she unwrapped the silverware and unrolled the cloth napkin. The action anchored her in the here and now. Reminding her that she was ten years away from that night, even if the pain sometimes felt like it was right now. Like a thief, *that* night crawled into the room and replaced the muffled chatter of other patrons, the clank of dishes, and the soft instrumental music. The voices from that night echoed in her heart.

You're making a mistake.

We're sorry, Dr. and Mrs. Owens.

Not my son!

I've got you, Nat, I'm coming.

She pushed the echoing voices of that night down...deep down.

"Hey." Duncan uncoiled her fingers from the napkin, wrapping his warm hand around hers. "It was a tough time for you. I didn't understand then. I was a selfish asshole only thinking about why my girlfriend didn't want to spend time with me. I didn't consider what you were going through. I can't change the past, but I am sorry I wasn't who I should have been. Who you needed then."

"Thank you." Her voice wobbled.

It wasn't just him. She'd pulled away from him then, and she knew that. Everything had changed when Evan died. She'd changed. She wasn't the girl he first asked out. He deserved that girl and she couldn't...or wouldn't be her ever again.

"We were both kids, and neither of us knew how to navigate what was happening," she offered.

"We're not kids anymore." He squeezed her hand, his lips flexed into a soft grin.

Her eyes met his. The searching gaze of a slightly clumsy boy had been replaced by the confident certainty of a man.

"Hello, folks. Do you know what you'd like?" the server asked, interrupting them.

"I do." Duncan's eyes almost smoldered as he gazed at her.

Am I on the menu? Her mouth went dryer than the Sahara.

Crisp pear cider bathed her bloodstream in a fizzy happiness while Duncan filled in the blanks of the last ten years between sips of scotch. After they broke up, she did the very mature thing of unfriending and unfollowing him on social media. So much of the last decade of his life was an untouched piece of plain paper.

He had fewer questions and more knowing statements about her life. Unlike her, he followed her on Instagram. Followers were something she never paid attention to, so she had no idea he knew about her many, *many* posts about crafty activities, dishes eaten at restaurants, and endless snapshots of Fitz and Lizzie.

"I see from Instagram that you do a lot of crafting projects," Duncan said, wiping his mouth.

"Wow, you really did your homework," she teased, spearing a green bean.

"Ninety percent of being a good attorney is research."

"What's the other ten percent?"

"A pact with the devil," he said with a wry grin.

"Funny, and they say most doctors have God complexes."

"Guess we're two sides of the same coin." His voice was seductive and buttery.

Nat cleared her throat. "Back to your original question. Yes, I'm still a crafter. It helps me relax and destress. I'd be lost without my hot glue gun."

"Boxing is my stress reliever. I started boxing my freshman year. It helped channel my anxiety in a constructive way."

Laughter rumbled through her. "By punching someone's face?"

"Ha!" he barked. "Most of it is with a punching bag. There's a small boxing gym in Geneseo that I go to a few times a week. You should come. Great stress reliever and a workout."

"That explains the muscles." Her mouth dropped open. "Did I say that out loud?"

Pleased smugness lit his expression. "Yes."

Her face scrunched. "Sorry."

"I'm not. I like that you noticed my muscles. I've noticed a few things on you, as well."

"Oh…care to share?" Her voice came out a high-pitched squeak.

"In time."

"Tease." She offered a sassy waggle of her eyebrows.

"I'm only a tease if I don't follow through." His fingers skimmed the rim of his glass in slow sensual strokes. "And I always follow through."

Oh my!

After dinner, he escorted Nat to her Jeep. The mid-August night air was still warm, but goosebumps pricked her skin when his hand came to rest on her lower back. Her body reacted to him in a way it never had when they dated. Even when they had sex. It had been the first time for both of them. Just like her decision to have sex with him, it was clumsy and quick.

"I had a wonderful time, Natalie."

Propped against the driver's side door, her eyebrow ticked up. "You keep calling me Natalie. You used to call me Nat in high school."

"We're not in high school anymore." He stepped close and the low timbre of his voice caressed the space between them.

"No, we're not," she whispered.

He raised his index finger to her face, outlining her lips. "I remember how nervous I was to kiss you for the first time after that homecoming dance."

"You don't seem nervous now." She almost gulped.

"That's because I'm not going to kiss you now." He released her and stepped back.

"What?" Her face tipped up, eyes blinking.

"I have to give you something to look forward to on our second date." Mischief glinted in his gaze.

"What makes you think there'll be a second date?"

Those full lips of his lifted in a cocky grin. "Oh, there will be a second date."

"Aren't we confident?" Smirking, she pulled out her keys from her purse and unlocked the door.

He stepped closer, holding the Jeep door open for her. Bending, he pressed a kiss to her cheek and murmured, "Not only will there be a second date, but I'll kiss you in a way that will obliterate anyone's kiss that came before… even mine."

The air caught in her lungs, stifling her ability to say anything. *Oh, my goddess.*

"Good night, Natalie," he said, shutting her door and walking away.

Her gaze followed him into the shadows of the parking lot. Not once did he turn back to look at her, but her eyes remained transfixed.

Had that just happened? Shaking her head, she started the Jeep and headed home.

Frustration and giddy expectation battled for control as she drove up the driveway to the Little Red Barn. Duncan had left her topsy-turvy. She was both wanting and angry. How could he declare he wanted her with one breath and walk away when he had her with the next?

Sliding out of her Jeep, she shut the door and leaned against it. Her stare was drawn to the glow of white light from the farmhouse porch. The turquoise door opened, and Noah emerged.

"What is he doing here?" she asked aloud to the inky sky, which remained tight-lipped.

No doubt, he was heading home after an evening with Clayton. Through the darkness between the farmhouse and the Little Red Barn, Noah's trademark dimple-punctuated smile popped. Hands in his pockets, he descended the stairs. Bypassing his parked SUV, he strode down the stone path to her.

The rapid *thump, thump* of her heart rattled in her chest. *Why is he coming this way?*

"Nat." He grinned, reaching the border of the stone path and gravel driveway.

He calls me Nat. Her fingernails dug into her palm. Was she Nat or was she Natalie? More importantly, which did she want to be? Nat was the girl-woman in a flirty fuchsia dress. Natalie would be the sophisticated sexy woman in a slinky black dress. Nat was the girl who pined, while Natalie would be the woman who devoured lovesick men.

With each jackhammered beat of her heart in his presence, she knew she was still Nat. All pining. No being pined for.

He cleared his throat. "How was your date?"

"Did Elle tell you?"

Elle had likely told Clayton, who told Noah. The two men may be plotting Duncan's demise. No wonder she'd not dated since returning home. One hard-to-impress giant big brother was bad enough. Let alone his Marine Corps veteran best friend. Together, they'd intimidate any man who dared to date her.

"Yeah." He nodded. "Did you have fun?"

"Yeah."

"Good." His tone was quiet.

Strangled stillness enveloped them. The silence between them was pierced only by the shuffling of his sneakers at the edge of the stone pathway. Each movement seemed to communicate indecision; whether to step over to her side or not.

"You look beautiful." His earnest blue eyes shimmered with regret.

Why is he looking at me like that? Fidgeting with the skirt of her dress, she looked down. A languid want in her belly pushed her eyes back to his as if starved for his gaze.

"Thank you." She tucked her hair behind her ears, hoping the motion would calm the anxious whirlwind inside her. *What the actual fuck was happening?*

"I..." He stopped and swallowed thickly. "I should go. Goodnight." His soft footsteps tapped on the stone as he walked away.

"Goodnight, Noah."

It was barely a whisper, but he stopped and turned back to face her. His mouth opened and then closed. With a nod, he pivoted and left.

For the second time tonight, she was left confused by a man.

CHAPTER EIGHT

"Love, Jo, all your days, if you choose, but don't let it spoil you, for it is wicked to throw away so many good gifts because you can't have the one you want." ~Louisa May Alcott, *Little Women*

With each flip in the bed and punch of the pillow, Nat tossed and turned between her attraction to Noah and the allure of reuniting with Duncan. Even though she was the only one in the bed, it was filled with reminders of both men. Noah's forlorn blue eyes staring at her from the stone path. The softness of his words as he told her she was beautiful. The way Duncan's scent of spicy enticement had wrapped around her. The primal possessiveness in his voice as he bent close, promising to obliterate all past kisses with his future one. The seductive glint that swam in his eyes should erase any thought of Noah, but it didn't.

Kicking her blankets off, she shot up. "Fuck it!"

No use trying to sleep in a bed full of phantom men. One a promise of the future and the other a specter of what would never be. The dull ache in her chest sparked from the pain of unrequited affection. It was called a crush because to care and not be cared for had the power to destroy.

"I'll only ever be Clayton's little sister to him."

Then, why did he say you were beautiful?

"To be nice!" she gritted, answering herself.

Plucking her phone from the bedstand to check the time, she decided to exercise this angst away with a jog. It was almost six a.m. The gray light of breaking day slinked into the sleeping loft through the partially opened blinds. Tugging on hot pink running shorts and a black sports bra and tank, she plopped onto the bed to put on her socks and sneakers.

Walking to her car, her gaze drifted to the farmhouse. Clayton's red pickup was gone. Most mornings, he and Elle jogged at the Greenway before work. Since they'd be at the Greenway, she decided to go to the village park to get a run in before coming back to get ready to head to the clinic for the day. Neither of the Owens siblings jogged the country roads of Perry.

Not anymore.

This early in the morning, the village was quiet. The row of gravel parking spaces along the front of the park was empty. She parked her Jeep and hopped out. Inhaling the coolness of dying night and the warmth of waking day, she cut through the playground toward the paved road that encircled the park's baseball fields.

Down the street and around the corner stood the yellow Victorian she'd called home for the first eighteen years of her life. Growing up near the park, she spent plenty of time here and scenes of her childhood were fond memories. The safety of Dad's arms catching her as she shot down the slide, arms up and squealing. Her mom's musical laughter as she pushed Nat on the swings. Clayton and Evan playing basketball on the court while she cheered in between whines for them to let her play. Clayton, the eldest, always succumbed to her tantrums. Evan, the middle child, shook his head before he relented and handed her the ball.

"Evan," she croaked at the remembrance. Increasing her speed, she ran as if trying to outrun the memories.

Despite being seven years older, Evan was more best friend than big brother. While Clayton was the quintessential big brother, doting and overprotective, Evan straddled the line between protective and "I got your back." He'd tease her but also listen. From the time she was thirteen, they'd go on long runs together and talk the entire time about anything and everything. There had been few secrets between them.

Evan was the favorite of all her favorite people. He'd been a bright light that flickered for just a moment, leaving her cold in the darkness of facing a life without him.

"Oh, Evan. I miss you," she whimpered.

Hot tears rolled down her face, accompanying the painful widening pit in her stomach. The rapid pace of her run slowed with each teardrop. Salty tears and sweat blurred her vision. She stopped, pitching over with her hands on her knees, and gulped for air.

"I got you," a soft baritone soothed, and a palm rubbed calming strokes down her back.

Lifting her head, she murmured, "Noah."

"I've got you," he repeated, placing his strong hands on her arms. With firm gentleness, he raised her to a standing position.

"Noah." His name said everything and nothing all at the same time. She pressed her face into his chest, allowing his arms to tuck her in close and his embrace to ease her sadness.

They stood there for what may have been hours or only minutes.

Noah's arms clenched around her. "I've got you. Let it out."

Not once did he say, "It's alright," or "Don't cry." In that moment, he just let her be sad.

"I'm sorry," she said. Her voice was muffled by his chest.

"Nothing to be sorry about."

"But I'm using your T-shirt as a tissue," she sniffled.

"What else are T-shirts good for?"

She tipped her head up. "How are you here? The park was empty when I got here."

He grinned. "I live three doors down from the park. I got up early for a run and I saw your Jeep."

Nat's gaze fell to the yellow Jeep parked on the other side of the playground. "I guess it's a conspicuous vehicle."

"It stands out, but so does the driver."

"Especially when she's having a crying fit in the middle of the park," she muttered, wiping away excess tears from her face.

"Hey, I bawled like a baby while having lunch at Cassie's Corner Café the other day when Todd showed me a video of a soldier reunited with their dog. So, no judgment about public crying."

"You are such a sucker for those videos." Her laugh was watery.

"Yep." His hands skimmed down to her waist.

Her body hummed from his touch. Every nerve screamed, *melt into him.*

"They get me every time."

"I'm surprised you don't have a gaggle of dogs, considering how much you love them. It blows my mind that you don't even have one." Her breath hitched at the warmth that pulsated across her body from his palms resting on her hips.

As if where his hands were had just dawned on him, he dropped them. Raising his right hand, he tugged his short dark hair.

"I'd be a wreck if I had a dog. I'd be a puddle each time they waited for me at my door. I almost cry when Fitz and

Lizzie greet me at your brother and Elle's place." A self-deprecating smirk washed over his features.

"Why do you get so emotional about dogs greeting people?"

"I think it's both the reunion of loved ones and the thought of what that image would look like if they hadn't come back."

A single tear, late for the party, tumbled from her left eye.

"Hey," he whispered as he swiped away her errant tear. "Evan?"

"How did you know?"

"I've only seen you cry like this one other time."

Nat clamped her eyes shut. The memory drowned her. When Evan died, she'd not cried—not right away. While everyone else fell apart in their own ways, she'd smiled. Not the "Nat smile" that Noah mentioned the other night, but a helpful soother of the storm of tears that had gripped Mom, somber stoicism that had engulfed Dad, and grieving loud-quiet that had held Clayton captive.

It wasn't until Noah arrived that she'd cried. *He found her alone in the gazebo in the backyard. With his arms around her, he pulled her into his embrace and murmured, "That's my girl. Let it out."*

"Sorry." She took a step back from Noah and the memory of that day. "I don't know why I'm so emotional. I was jogging and started thinking about Evan and just... ugh... now I'm a baby." She covered her face.

"Hey." He raised his hands to hers, shepherding them down from her face. "It's not baby-like to miss someone...to grieve them."

Nat coughed, pushing down the lump in her throat. "I miss him and..."

The words clustered in her throat, so many of her emotions over losing Evan locked inside. Grief. Anger. Guilt.

Resentment. They all colluded in a sad bitter stew within her belly.

"It makes sense that you'd feel raw coming home. This is the longest you've been home since he died. You left for that Boston College summer program three months after he'd passed. Besides a few weeks over breaks, you've been in Boston since you were eighteen."

"I can't believe you remember that. You were in San Diego for most of that."

Noah turned, placed his hand on her shoulder, and led her in a slow walk toward the playground. "Well, I noticed when one of my favorite people wasn't here when I visited."

"Also, your mom."

"Also, my mom."

They looked at each other with knowing grins. Mom and Maura, Noah's mom, were the definition of BFFs. Since they were fifteen, they'd been inseparable. What one knew, the other soon would know.

A warm chuckle rolled through him. "I didn't even need to talk to Clayton or read the letters you sent when I was in the service to know what was happening."

"Oh, my goddess, those letters and care packages I'd send. I was such a dork," she cringed.

Twice a month from the age of ten until she was seventeen, she used different colored gel pens on rainbow-themed paper to write letters to Noah wherever he was stationed. Once a month, she filled a shoebox full of Twix, his favorite candy, Austen Cheddar and Peanut Butter crackers, and a homemade crafting project.

"If you were a dork for sending, then what does that make me? I lived for those letters and care packages. Well, 'til I got in trouble with my commanding officer when some of the loose glitter from an Origami star you'd put in a package got all over my uniform." He nudged her shoulder with his as they walked across the dew dampened grass toward the teeter-totters.

"I was doing my patriotic duty with that excess glitter. Military uniforms are far too drab."

"I should have given my CO that defense before he made me do all those pushups for penance." He stopped at the long plank supported in the middle by a metal fulcrum. Mischief lifted the corners of his lips. "Care to have a go?"

When was the last time she'd teeter-tottered? Besides the metaphorical one that she was on now, between her crush on Noah and rekindling a relationship with Duncan. The one between being Dr. Owens or Dr. Owens' daughter.

Part of her knew she shouldn't. She should tell him goodbye and head to her Jeep. That would be the adult thing to do.

"Sure." Even as she agreed as apprehension reared up in her torso.

He lowered the teeter-totter closest to them and held it waist-level. Tentatively, she grabbed the handle, wrapping her hands around the cool metal. Their gazes twined together as she straddled the seat.

The planes of his chest constricted and expanded with quickened breath. "You secure?" His eyes raked down her.

His sweeping gaze tiptoed down her body, from chest to hips, to her bare legs, and back up. Heat sparked on each part of her where his eyes lingered.

"Yup." She bit her lip, stifling the sex phone operator quality of her voice.

"Okay." Letting go, he pivoted and jogged to the other side and settled onto his seat. "Ready?"

"Yep!" she squealed as the teeter-totter blasted into the air.

"Still got it," he said with laughing smugness.

"Got what?"

"The ability to make you smile."

And he did. The smile spread on her face like hot syrup on

pancakes. No corner of her face was untouched by its sweetness.

"Aren't we Count Confident?" she teased.

"Yup." He smirked, pushing off the ground and flying his side into the air.

"Noah!" She closed her eyes, bracing for the thudding impact. Just as the bottoms of her sneakers grazed the grass, she flew back into the air. "Noah!" she squeaked with glee.

"Still got it," he rumbled with self-satisfaction.

Teetering between the exhilarating sensation of weightlessness and protected falling, happiness fizzed inside her. Each time her wooden seat hurtled toward the ground, she'd gasp but knew he'd never let her hit the bottom.

CHAPTER NINE

"Women, they have minds, and they have souls, as well they have just hearts." ~Louisa May Alcott, *Little Women*

"**Y**our life is like a *bad* romance novel." Summer arched a taunting eyebrow.

"I know." Nat lowered her head to the table cluttered with homemade invitations.

For this week's takeout and movie date at the Little Red Barn, they skipped the movie to discuss her disastrous romantic entanglements while handcrafting invitations for Elle's bridal shower.

Summer had settled into her new-found role as party planner to the Perry elite, AKA anyone in the village that would hire her. Between shifts at Cassie's Corner Café and mommy duty with her son, Liam, her business had exploded. In addition to wedding-related festivities, she agreed to plan the village's Fall Fest scheduled for the end of September. With no excuse needed to pull out her trusty hot glue gun, Nat volunteered to assist with all crafty needs.

"You could at least get kissed by one of them," Summer teased, stamping a purple teacup seal on the envelope.

Nat lifted her head. "I know."

Unbridled laughter *swooshed* out of Summer. "Girl, you're a mess. You have glitter all over your face."

"Oh, goddessdamn," she grumbled, swiping at the glittery grains.

"Why do you always say goddessdamn instead of goddamn?"

"Because God is a woman."

Summer's brow creased. "What makes you say that?"

"Because women can have multiple orgasms. No *way* a man thought of that."

"Sound argument," Summer paused, her face scrunched in thought. "Have *you* had multiple orgasms before?"

She sighed. "Only with Henry."

"Who's Henry?"

"My vibrator."

"Why Henry?" Summer's head tilted to the right.

"For Henry Cavill." She fanned herself with an invitation, scattering even more glitter on her face.

She'd had good sex. There had been lots of *okay* sex. However, there'd never been the leg-trembling great sex that Nat read about in novels or had seen when bingeing old episodes of *Sex in the City*. Not a single boyfriend or hookup made her scream their name and dig her nails into their shoulders, only to leave her in a puddle of jellied muscles after a mind-blowing orgasm. Let alone given her a second one.

Thank the goddess for Henry getting her through this very long dry spell. Although it was less a dry spell and more a self-inflicted convent living at this point.

"I think that is the one thing I miss about Max." Summer frowned, referring to Liam's dad.

Summer had been tight-lipped about all things Max. The only item she'd offered about her New York City live-in boyfriend of four years was that he wasn't nice to her. When she discovered she was pregnant, she left.

Nat nodded, continuing to brush her face with her now-glittered hands. *Goddess, I'm a mess.*

"You're making it worse." Summer shook her head. "Stop what you're doing." She got up and walked to the sink. Wetting a tea towel, she moved back to Nat.

"You're such a mom sometimes." She giggled as Summer swiped the lukewarm towel along her face.

"I know. Maternal aptitude oozes out of me." Summer's grin was self-deprecating.

"You're a good mom…one of the best. And I know good moms. You've met mine, right?"

Summer nodded, placing the towel on the table. "Thank you…I needed to hear that."

"Why? What's going on?"

It wasn't like Summer to question her mothering skills. There were so many things she excelled at. The way she never forgot customers' names and orders despite the chaos of the cafe. How calmness vibrated off her while coordinating an event. The steadiness of her shoulders as she supported her friends. Above all, she shined brightest with the supportive, loving, and patient nurturing of Liam.

"Liam's struggled a lot this year. Academically he's killing it, we're dealing with some behavioral and social challenges. The school psychologist recommended an autism behavioral specialist in Buffalo."

Two years ago, Liam was diagnosed with autism spectrum disorder low needs. Since then, Summer devoured literature, joined mailing lists, and visited message boards to identify various resources and strategies to support his success. In a small rural community like Perry, the services were limited for children on the spectrum. That didn't deter Summer from being focused, resourceful, and a tenacious mama bear.

"Are they taking new patients?" she asked.

"Yes, in the fall, but it's mid-day Thursdays. So, I'll need to take off work, pull Liam out of school, and drive up there. Round trip it will be three hours, including his appointment, which I'm fine with. I just hate taking him away from school so much. Routine is important with Liam, and this will jack his routine up."

"There's nobody closer that offers the same services?"

She knew the answer before the question left her lips. There were limited healthcare services in the county, let alone behavioral health ones. The Owens Family Clinic had been the village's only primary care service for nearly one hundred years. Outside of the optometrist clinic across the street from Clayton's vet clinic and two dentists, there weren't any other healthcare providers in Perry.

"I wish there were more services in the county for kids. When Liam was first assessed, I had to take him up to Buffalo. There are a few other parents at the school who also take their kids to specialists in Buffalo or Rochester."

Nat nodded.

Summer sighed, sweeping her long chestnut hair up into a messy bun. "I just want to do what's best for him. Sometimes I think about us moving to a city, but here we have my mom and dad. I...we have support. Over the last year, I feel like our circle has gotten so big." Her chocolate eyes glimmered with threatening tears.

"The Liam and Summer Team has a deep bench."

Since Summer reconnected with Elle last year, a whole new social network opened up to them. During school breaks or on the weekends, Liam, a budding future vet, visited Clayton's clinic. Carmen and Mathew adjusted the weekly story time at Cow Tales, the village's bookstore/coffee shop, to be accessible to individuals with sensory disabilities and challenges. Noah, and sometimes Todd, met them at the park to run around with Liam.

The nine-year-old was one of Nat's favorite board game buddies. Although she could do without him destroying her at Connect 4 time after time. He was merciless.

Despite the many things Perry didn't have, it offered so much love and support for Summer and her little boy. It was one of the reasons Nat came home... because Perry always made up for things it didn't have with an abundance of what it did have: love.

Summer leaned back in the kitchen chair. "When I first came back, I was still Summer Michaels, the bitchy popular girl from high school. To so many in the village, I'm still that mean girl. At least, that's how they see me. Over the last few months, I've started to feel like I'm more than that. More than just the girl people were happy to see leave and even happier to see come back knocked up with her tail between her legs."

Nat placed a hand on Summer's cheek, repeating Noah's words. "Fuck them."

"Asshole!" Summer laughed, swatting her hand away. "You glittered me."

"Just so you remember that you sparkle." She winked.

"How are we friends?"

"Because you *love* me." Nat rubbed her glittered hands all over Summer's face, who protested despite her deep-belly laughs.

"Speaking of *love*." Summer waggled her now glitter-speckled eyebrows. "Can we go back to your little *love* triangle?"

Nat's gaze drifted to the yellow gardenias from Noah taunting her from the kitchen counter. "First, I don't think I appreciate the salacious way you say *love*. Second, there's not much to talk about."

"Well, I know you've been gaga for Noah since before it was age-appropriate for you to have those feelings, but what about Duncan? Were you in love with him?" Summer walked to the sink and cleaned the glitter from her face.

"I don't..." Nat bit her lip.

"So, that's a no."

"It was high school. I mean, who falls in love when they are in high school?"

"You mean besides your parents, my parents, your brother, and half the village?"

Her lips puckered. "Clayton doesn't count. His love was one-sided 'til Elle came back last year."

"You know, the irony that your soon-to-be sister-in-law and you both crushed on Noah is not lost on me. Although, her crush is past tense." Summer patted her face dry with a paper towel.

"Back to Duncan." She puffed out a long breath.

Noah infiltrated far too much. Tamping down his presence in her life was reminiscent of trying to keep the sunshine out of a glass house.

"You lost your virginity to Duncan, right?"

"I didn't lose it. I gave it to him."

The eye roll at the idea of losing one's virginity couldn't be avoided. As if it was half of a pair of socks that went missing in the dryer. It's not like she woke up and misplaced her hymen. It was a decision. Perhaps not a thought-out one, but a decision she made, nonetheless.

Summer sat in the chair, crossing her legs. "I take it there were no multiple orgasms."

Nat grimaced.

"So, there were *no* orgasms."

"We were eighteen. Neither of us knew what we were doing. Plus, we only had sex once."

"Why only once? Was it *that* bad?" Summer's face contorted in apologetic lamentation.

Nat blew out a heavy breath. "No. It was fine. It's just...it was a mistake."

Summer's head jerked. "Mistake? What happened?"

"No. Not like that. It was consensual. I just wasn't in a

good headspace. We dated for almost two years. There was lots of kissing and a few make-out sessions worthy of a CW show, but I wasn't in a rush to have sex."

"Was he?"

"No… I mean, he was a teenage boy, so he was down. He never pushed me, though. Not for sex."

"Why'd you have sex then?" Summer's tone was soft and coaxing.

"Evan." She closed her eyes. "He'd died. Everything was a mess. I just wanted to feel anything but what I was feeling. It wasn't fair to Duncan. It wasn't fair to me. We had sex, and two weeks later I broke up with him."

"Because of the sex?"

"No. I mean, I don't know. He just wanted more of me than what I was able to give. The sex took the relationship to the next level. Only while Duncan and the relationship were at that level, I was still a step below."

That day flooded her senses. *Duncan's red-rimmed eyes imploring her to stay. The things she returned clenched in his hands. The tapping of the rain on the porch roof. The squish of her sneakers in the wet grass as she left him on the porch and crossed to her car.*

"He deserved better. He still does. I can't keep letting myself get caught up with what will never be."

Summer placed a hand atop Nat's. "It will never be if you never tell Noah how you feel."

"Despite what you say, my life isn't like a bad romance novel. Noah's not going to fall head over feet for his best friend's little sister."

"Who says he hasn't already?" Summer asked smugly.

"If the people who think you're still Regina George only knew you're actually a cross between Marmee and Beth from *Little Women*."

A bashful smile tugged at her lips. "Thanks."

"Of course, we know I'm Amy March." Naturally, she'd

be the youngest March sister whose artistic skills matched her own craftiness.

"And Noah's your Laurie."

Forehead wrinkled, Nat slipped her hand from beneath Summer's and glittered her face. It was a very Amy March thing to do, after all.

CHAPTER TEN

"Be comforted, dear soul! There is always light behind the cloud."
~Louisa May Alcott, *Little Women*

"Are you a doctor?" Sally asked, swinging her tiny legs over the edge of the exam table.

"I am." Nat smiled, placing her tablet on the small desk anchored to the wall.

"But you don't have a bow tie."

"Sally," Emma, her mom, chided, twisting to Nat with an apologetic expression.

"It's alright." A wry grin spread on Nat's face. "Nope. I don't have a bow tie."

"Why don't you have a bow tie?" Sally looked at Nat and then at her mom, who sat in an uncomfortable plastic chair in the corner.

"Don't need one since I wear fun shoes." She lifted her left foot and pointed to the fluorescent orange ballet flat.

Dad had his bow ties. She had a rainbow assortment of shoes. Fashion choices aside, they were both doctors. Whether it was her lack of bow tie, her gender, her age, or whatever else individuals used to assess her as "not a doctor," this conversation repeated far too often. And not just with the little Sallys of the world but with people like Jack Simmons and Mrs. Lewis.

"*Oh*, pretty," Sally breathed. Her tiny face scrunched in thought. "Also, you have a white coat like a doctor, so you must be a doctor." With a first place in the spelling bee smile, she beamed.

"You're very smart." Lips curled in a grin, she lifted Sally's shirt and blew gently on the stethoscope before positioning the flat disc on the child's back. "This may be cold."

It was so simple that a five-year-old could see it. She was a doctor. She wore the white coat, damn it! Now, she just needed to figure out how to transplant Sally's vision to the rest of the village.

"Natalie Joan Owens," Mom tutted.

Nat's head jerked up from the other side of the reception-ist's desk, where she tapped orders into her tablet after Sally and Emma left. *Oh, shit.* She was reduced to a recalcitrant child the second her mom two-named her. "Yes?"

Her mother's use of her full name, in conjunction with that accusatory tone, conjured memories of getting caught eating peanut butter out of the jar with her fingers. In her defense, she was seven and all the spoons were in the dishwasher.

Mom stood, hands on hips, and one brow ticked up. "Someone got a delivery." Mischief flooded her gray eyes as she gestured to a bouquet wrapped in rose-patterned paper.

For a moment, Nat's breath faltered. *Noah?* Had he sent flowers because of her micro-meltdown at the park?

"Are you going to open them? I'm *dying* to see. Janet was tight-lipped when she delivered them from the Village Rose."

You'd think with us being almost family, she would loosen the vow of silence the ladies of the florist shop have taken. They never spill the tea." A slight pout dragged Mom's lips downward. Far too undignified for a woman in her sixties.

"Do you even know what spill the tea means?" Nat teased, pushing open the small half-door between the reception and patient check-in areas.

"Of course. I watch the *Real Housewives.*"

Rolling her eyes, Nat ripped the paper off the bouquet. Sweet perfume wafted off long stem red roses. While lovely, something told her Noah wouldn't send roses. They somehow felt impersonal and sterile. The blood-red petals lacked the brightness of the yellow gardenias.

Tiny crinkles kissed the edges of Mom's eyes. "Gorgeous."

Plucking the card from the tiny plastic holder in the arrangement, Nat unsealed it and read.

Meet me at Tucker's Boat Launch at seven. Dress for boating.
~Duncan

"Duncan?" Mom asked, reading over her shoulder. "As in Duncan Ellis?"

Nat folded the card in half and shoved it into her pocket. "You're so nosey," she grumbled.

"I'm a mom. It's in the job description." She twinkled. "So, you two are seeing each other again?"

Nat shrugged. Were they? They'd been on one date. There'd been only a promise of a kiss. Duncan's intentions were as crystal clear as the vase the roses sat in. The only question that remained… What were Nat's intentions with Duncan?

"We're spending time together. Seeing what happens."

That was a good enough answer for Mom and for herself. At least for now.

CHAPTER ELEVEN

"Be worthy of love and love will come." ~Louisa May Alcott,
Little Women

The gravel in the parking lot for Tucker's Boat Launch crunched beneath Nat's white Converse sneakers. She strode toward the low, gray-roofed building tucked up against the Silver Lake shoreline. As she strolled down the sloped sidewalk toward the U-shaped dock, she tugged at her caramel-colored shorts, regretting their length. The air was warm but would be cool enough on the lake to need the pale pink Boston College hoodie she wore.

Apprehension snaked through her veins. The invitation from Duncan was more direct than he'd ever been. Well, besides his promise…or threat…of an earth-shattering kiss. Gone was the seventeen-year-old whose eyes remained cast down when he'd asked her to the Homecoming dance. Was she unnerved because of the starkness between that shy teenage boy and the directness of the confident man? Or was it the idea of Noah that slowed her steps? No clear answer occurred by the time she reached the junction where the sidewalk ended, and the dock began.

At the end of the floating metal dock, Duncan leaned against a pylon, an enormous smile sketched on his face. His hands were balled into the pockets of faded dark blue jeans, that hung low on his hips. A gray NYU T-shirt stretched over his sculpted chest and shoulders. Loose wavy blond strands that reminded her of the boy he'd been replaced the sleek, styled hair from the other night. With each step closer to this version of him, her tight muscles eased.

"Fancy meeting you here," he drawled.

"Well, I was summoned," she teased, dropping into a princess-worthy curtsy.

Duncan winced. "Ouch. I thought that my note was going to read smooth, not Joffrey Lannister-like."

"I've never had someone ask me out with a card for the same night."

"I do enjoy being your first." He winked with playful wickedness.

Duncan assisted her into a small white speed boat trimmed in blue and settled her on the white bench at the back of the boat. Then, he sat in a small blue captain's chair, turned over the engine, and launched them into the serene lake waters.

"Is this your boat or did you rent it?" she asked, raising her voice over the loud engine, whipping wind, and lapping water.

"It's my dad's. He got it when he retired last year."

"Who's running the farm?"

"My older brother Jacob. He and his wife live in my parents' house. Mom and Dad have a cottage on the other side of the lake. They stay there in the summer and are in Florida with my uncle during the winter," he explained, slowing the boat. "This will be perfect."

"For what?" Her head twisted, surveying their surroundings.

The boat bobbed in the middle of the mostly empty lake.

Streaks of pumpkin, crimson, and amethyst splashed across the sky in a brilliant sunset.

Duncan dropped the anchor. Reaching under the steering wheel, he pulled out a small blue cooler. "For this," he said.

Placing the cooler in front of her, he lifted the lid and plucked out a chilled bottle of champagne, plastic wrapped cheeseboard, and two glasses.

"I thought we'd have a picnic at sunset."

"This is pretty romantic." She bit her lip.

A self-assured grin lit his features. "Exactly what I was going for."

After arranging their little picnic on the top of the closed cooler, he popped the cork on the bubbly and poured two glasses. "Here's to second chances."

After a moment of hesitation, she lifted her glass to tap the rim against his. "Second chances," she murmured. "How do your parents like retirement?"

"They love it. Between here and Florida, Dad fishes year-round and Mom loves not dealing with snow." He grabbed a slice of salami from the cheeseboard. "How about your parents? With you being back, they must be thinking of retiring. They've run the clinic for forty years."

Nat frowned, grabbing a piece of gouda and a cracker. "I don't know. It doesn't seem like they're in any hurry to retire."

"How is it working with them?"

"Fine." The firm line that all too often rested on her face these days settled into its usual spot.

"Natalie, I don't need to use my lawyer intuition to tell that you've just perjured yourself."

"Don't use your attorney voodoo on me," she warned, pointing her cheese and cracker at him.

His eyes narrowed. "I'm serious, Natalie." Clearing his throat, his tone softened. "How is it?"

She blew out a long breath. "In Boston, the attending physician accepted me as a colleague. Here…it's hard."

Since she was a little girl, she'd wanted to work with her dad, to be her dad. To be Dr. Owens, not just Dr. Owens' daughter. The unspoken truth twisted in her abdomen.

Duncan's lips pursed. "Sometimes, Natalie, we make it hard on ourselves and blame others."

"What does *that* mean?"

"You have to demand respect, not ask politely or remain quiet and hope people figure it out." He gestured to himself. "Look at me. When I clerked at the DA's office in New York City, I was the kid. When I graduated, passed the bar, and went to work at that same DA's office, they still called me 'kid.' They'd undermine me with comments. I had a mentor who told me what you permit, you promote. I realized I'd given them permission to treat me like a kid. So, I stopped acting like a kid. Spoke up. Dressed more professionally with tailored suits instead of mismatched sports jackets and slacks."

Nat studied the plastic cup.

"As much as I loved that dress you wore the other night or these"—he pointed to her shorts—"it screams co-ed fashion rather than young professional."

Gaze turned away, she focused on the rows of cottages that poked out from thickets of trees along the lakeshore rather than the swirl of emotions that pricked inside. Was Duncan right? Had she shaped how people saw her by playing the part of the daughter instead of the doctor? The image of her in a lab coat and bright-colored ballet flats flashed in her vision. She'd always thought the colorful shoes made kid patients more comfortable with her as a doctor. She'd appear more approachable and fun. Not to mention, she just liked cute, comfortable shoes. But now she feared she was seen as a little girl playing doctor instead of an actual doctor.

"Natalie, you're very special, but people will miss it if you don't show them you're someone to be respected," Duncan said, placing his hand on her thigh and pulling her attention back to him.

"You've given me some things to consider."

He placed his large palm over hers. "I mean it. You're special. You've always been."

They sat, quiet, allowing time to drift. Darkness blanketed the sky. The gentle current of the lake swayed the boat back and forth.

Her thoughts bobbed with their boat. Was she the key to changing the village's and her parents' perceptions? If she wanted to be taken seriously, did she need to be more serious? Did she need to change who she was?

"I made you a promise," Duncan murmured. The low timbre of his voice pierced her roaming thoughts.

Nat shifted on the bench, facing him. "You did."

He took the cup from her hand and placed it on the cooler beside his. Licking his lips, he raised his hand to her face. The smooth pads of his fingers skated across her cheek to her lips. With aching slowness, he traced her mouth with the tips of his fingers.

Her body convulsed in confusion. Some muscles tightened in anticipation. Others jerked as if trying to get away. Closing her eyes, she tried to relax both. To just be in the moment. To be open to this second chance.

Duncan is real. Duncan is here.

"Open your eyes, Natalie," he commanded.

Her gray eyes opened at the gruff nature of his voice. "I'm sorry. Is there something wrong?"

"I want you to experience this with all your senses. To see." He leaned in. The heat of his breath was a prelude to what was coming. "To feel." His full lips pressed, imprisoning her lips in a slow, demanding kiss. "To taste." The wetness of his tongue licked the seam of her mouth, prying it open. Like a predator, his tongue stalked hers until it found its prey and devoured it.

Duncan's hands strolled down her torso to her waist. His grip tightened on her middle.

A tornado roared through her. Every muscle grew stiff as if grinning and bearing the whole experience.

Duncan's kiss slowed and then ceased. "I keep my promises."

She bit her lower lip.

It was a promise half-kept.

CHAPTER TWELVE

"Jo had learned that hearts, like flowers, cannot be rudely handled, but must open naturally..." ~Louisa May Alcott, *Little Women*

The slick condensation coated Nat's hands in wet coolness as she clutched the iced hazelnut latte. Every other Saturday, she and Dad swapped who managed the half-day clinic. This was a rare Saturday where both she and Summer were free to wander the farmer's market.

"So, we have fifteen minutes before Carmen brings Liam back from story hour at Cow Tales." Summer tipped her head toward the coffee shop/bookstore down the street from the city hall parking lot turned open-air market.

The colorful stalls were filled with fresh produce, baked goods, homemade jam, and honey. An abundance of craft stands pulled Nat's attention with an array of jewelry, knick-knacks, and clothing.

"How was the date? Did he kiss you?" Summer waggled her brows.

"Yes."

"How was it?"

"It was good." Nat shifted her eyes to a pair of ruby-red

slipper ballet flats displayed on a folding table at one of the artisans' stands.

Sometimes you must play the part. Duncan's words echoed in her ears, forcing her gaze away from the tempting shoes.

"Did it erase *all* past kisses?" Summer asked with a cheeky grin.

Nat took a long drink of her latte.

"So, that's a no."

She sighed. "It was a good kiss. It just… It just didn't erase an almost kiss."

Summer's forehead wrinkled. "With whom?"

She looked around. There were too many people. Grabbing Summer's arm, she dragged her to a green iron bench on the sidewalk outside the farmer's market. It was far enough away from the clusters of perusing patrons to not be overheard but within sight for Carmen and Liam to find them.

"Noah and I almost kissed," she whispered.

"What!"

Nat's eyes narrowed, and she motioned around them. "Inside voice, please."

"Sorry." Her tone was soft, but her eyes were loud with giddy excitement. "When did this happen?"

"Ten years ago."

"Ten. Years. Ago." Summer repeated with deliberate slowness.

"It was after Evan died. It was the night of the funeral. It was…" A tremor broke loose in her voice. "…It was a lot. Mom was a mess. Dad was trying to take care of her. Clayton was distant. I felt so alone."

Summer threaded their fingers. "And Noah was there for you?"

"Yeah." She smiled through a long sigh. "He'd found me crying in the gazebo in the backyard. I was alone. He held me for the longest time. Just telling me to let it out. That he was there. That he had me. After there were no more tears, he kissed my temple. My head tilted up, and there was this moment. Like when you hold two magnets close enough to pull to one another but not connect. Then Clayton came outside, and Noah backed away."

"Did you two ever discuss this?"

Nat shook her head.

"Nat." She pushed out a disappointed but understanding breath.

"Mom!" Liam bounded down the street.

Nat and Summer's heads jerked toward his happy squeal. Liam skipped alongside Noah, who wore an amused grin. Noah and Clayton had befriended the little boy over the last year, taking him fishing, to the library, or for play dates with Fitz and Lizzie.

"What? Is he like Beetlejuice?" Nat muttered under her breath.

"You didn't even have to say his name three times," Summer said through a fixed smile. "You, okay?"

"Yup."

"Hey, baby. How was story hour?" Summer knelt, opening her arms in greeting.

"Mathew dressed up like a bear," he chirped.

Summer cocked her face to Noah.

"The story was about a bear. You know Mathew, he loves a costume." Noah grinned, pushing his hands into the pockets of his dark blue jeans.

Oh, goddess! Stop looking at how those jeans caress his muscular legs. Nat averted her gaze.

"Speaking of costume. Little Francisco needed an outfit change, so I volunteered to walk my man here to meet you ladies," he said, referring to Carmen and Mathew's nine-month-old son.

"He pooped his pants," Liam whispered.

"Yeah." Noah chuckled, shaking his head. "It was a scene. Mathew forgot the change of clothes in the diaper bag."

"But he remembered his bear costume," Nat chimed in with a small smile.

"Yep." Noah gazed at her, a strange intensity in his blue eyes.

"Well, at least Francisco will grow out of it, but Mathew…" Summer trailed off as all of them laughed.

"If you ladies don't have plans, I was headed to the bakery to do some taste testing of a few of the autumn treats we'll launch at Fall Fest. We could use some free focus group people. Otherwise, it will just be Todd and me."

Summer and Nat's gazes darted back and forth in their own visual morse code. In the quick exchange, Summer's chocolate eyes seemed to ask if Nat was okay or if an excuse was needed.

She could do this. "Yeah. That'd be great," Nat verbalized what her eyes had communicated to Summer.

The foursome walked down the street to the Farmer's Wife. The Main Street bakery had been in the village for forty years. Five years ago, Noah bought it from the previous owner who wanted to retire. It was his first venture into the business world, and soon the budding mogul expanded with the wine bar and brewery.

The bell above the door chimed as Noah opened and held the door. Liam scampered into the half-filled bakery, claiming a large round table near the front windows.

"Nat!" Liam shouted.

"Inside voice, baby," Summer corrected with a warm smile before looking at Nat.

"Like mother, like son." Nat elbowed her friend.

Summer poked Nat's ribs.

"Nat," Liam said with his indoor voice. "They're the color of your Jeep." He pointed to the sunshine-yellow painted walls, dotted with framed pictures of old-timey country kitchens.

They are. Nat's mouth dropped open. She'd never noticed

that before. Until Noah bought and renovated the bakery, the walls had been off-white. In fact, Noah teased her when she'd posted a picture of her obnoxious bright-yellow Jeep on Instagram after she'd bought it five years ago.

Summer placed her right hand beneath Nat's chin and pushed up. "You'll catch flies."

"Well, well, look at what the tomcat dragged in." Todd sauntered through the swinging white kitchen door. His muscular arms and cut torso on full display in a form-hugging sky-blue T-shirt.

Summer's mouth dropped open. Nat placed her hand below Summer's chin and repeated the same action. Both women giggled as Summer batted her hand away.

"Mom, what are you and Nat doing?" Liam asked, face pinched.

"Nothing," they replied in unison.

"Girls are weird," he groaned, turning to Noah.

"One day you'll like weird," Noah said, his eyes anchored on Nat.

Is he… No. Her throat grew dry.

"I love weird." Todd's focus settled on Summer like she was a tray of pastries and he was starving.

Nat squeezed Summer's upper thigh from below the table. Summer kicked her with her flip-flopped foot. They were both acting like twelve-year-olds. One with a self-admitted crush and one refusing to own up to hers.

"We created a few new treats for the fall," Todd explained, pointing to the different goodies. "This is a cinnamon vanilla chai-inspired scone." He picked up a knife from the tray, cutting the pastry into four pieces.

"You're doing it wrong." Liam frowned.

Todd winked, silencing Summer's readied correction. "I'm always open to feedback. How should I do it?"

"Five pieces. There are five of us. You need a piece too."

Todd's lips lifted in an appreciative smile. "You got it, little dude."

The five of them laughed, trying the different pastries. Liam copied Todd taking thoughtful bites, followed by a nod of his head, and a thorough assessment of the consumed baked good while tapping on his chin.

The smile Summer beamed was unguarded. It wasn't like she never smiled, but they were tight or cautious, as if she didn't deserve to smile or was scared each smile would be her last.

"Have you noticed Todd doesn't give me shit when Summer and Liam are around?" Noah bent, whispering in Nat's ear.

The low vibration of his voice ignited a crackling heat inside her. "He's on his best behavior," she whispered back.

Their joint gazes dropped on Todd, who had a light blush on his cheeks as Summer giggled about something he'd said.

Nat looked back to Noah. "He's a good guy." It was a quiet statement laced with inquiry.

"He's the best," Noah reassured her with a pat on her upper thigh.

The former chemist had a good reputation in town. Nat knew that, but she needed the confirmation. Todd and Noah had become closer after they both moved back to Perry around the same time. A few years ago, Todd had left his job at a lab in Rochester to work with Noah.

Like most people in the village, there were six degrees of separation from either one of the Owens siblings or their parents. Todd had been in Evan's class, but they weren't close. Evan was the Noah Wilson of his class. The good-looking, popular jock who was nice to everyone. Even the scrawny band geek that Todd had been in school.

Just like Summer, Todd wasn't the same person he'd been in high school.

"We're going to need all the broccoli tonight. Too many sweets," Summer laughed, leaning back in her chair.

"I make a mean broccoli casserole," Todd offered with a waggle of his eyebrows.

"I'm not a fan of casseroles." Summer flipped her chestnut hair as if flicking the veiled date request away.

Noah and Nat's eyes met. Both smirked as Noah squeezed her shoulder.

This is why she couldn't stay away from him. Despite the crush that left her feeling—well, crushed—an easiness always remained between them. An ability to fall into step with one another. To know what the other was thinking just by reading each other's glances. That's how she knew that day he held her after Evan's funeral, his blue eyes burdened with regret… that he didn't want her. It was a moment clouded with mutual grief and sadness.

Nat understood regret. It flooded her after having sex with Duncan. The same regret that had dulled Noah's eyes glistened in the remorse filling her eyes with tears as she'd looked in the mirror two days after having sex with Duncan, knowing she'd made a huge mistake.

"Natalie." Duncan's voice pierced their little group and her thoughts.

Nat raised her head. Had she conjured another man? Maybe she should start thinking about Henry Cavill to see if the man of steel would walk through the bakery door. Her gaze darted to the door, but a stocky man in his sixties shuffled in. *No Henry Cavill.*

She stood up. "Duncan."

Duncan dipped his head, giving her a kiss. "I thought I saw you when I walked by." His palm settled on her lower back as he turned with a charming smile. "I'm Natalie's boyfriend, Duncan."

Boyfriend? Nat gaped.

Todd stood, a tight smile on his face, and held his hand out. "Todd Krueger."

"Sheriff Krueger's son." Duncan's eyes widened, shaking Todd's hand.

"Yep," Todd grunted.

Nat's eyebrow ticked up at the chilliness from Todd. None of his trademark playful sass had filtered into the greeting.

"Hello, Duncan. I am Liam. Nice to meet you." Liam looked to his mom as he held out his hand toward Duncan.

"Nice to meet you." Duncan formed a fist with his left hand, reaching across the table to fist-bump Liam.

A scrunched-faced Liam stared at the fist. The wrongness of the gesture danced in his frustrated eyes. Liam had a particular way of doing things. A script to follow.

Duncan didn't know the script. Didn't know Liam. But when someone reaches their hand out, the polite thing to do is to take it. Nat bristled at the portrait of a boy offering his hand and a man's outstretched fist, almost saying, "No...No that's not good enough."

Summer swiveled in her seat, facing Duncan with a firm line and narrowed eyes. "He was trying to shake your hand, not fist bump it." Her tone was clipped.

"Sorry." He shrugged. "Anyway, I don't want to disturb you all, but Natalie, can I borrow you for a minute?"

"Sure," Nat said, ignoring Summer's chilly expression. "Be right back."

She needed to talk to him about the boyfriend label. Kiss aside, the last time she checked, she'd not signed up to play the role of girlfriend.

They headed outside and his hand found the small of her back. Its heat almost burned, guiding her down the street. Rather than stopping at the empty sidewalk, he ushered them around the corner.

"Umm...what is going—"

Duncan's lips crashed against hers. The kiss not only

stopped but stole her words. The force of his body propelled her against the firm brick wall of the building.

Finding purchase against his chest, she shoved him off. "What the hell, Duncan?"

"I'm sorry." His fingers raked into his hair. "I saw you with Noah, and I got jealous."

"We were sitting at a bakery with friends. It wasn't like he had me bent over the table."

"I know. It was just the way he was looking at you and kept touching you." Worried lines creased his face. "How can I compete with him?"

"This isn't a competition," she said through gritted teeth.

The truth in that statement sunk in. Even if she were a prize to win, Noah would never compete for her.

"I'm trying to play this whole thing cool, but I'm failing." Those bourbon eyes beseeched hers. "I never stopped loving you."

"What?"

CHAPTER THIRTEEN

"I wish I had no heart, it aches so…" ~Louisa May Alcott, *Little Women*

Had Duncan just said he was in love with her on a street corner? With frantic blinks, Nat tried to will this away. This was all wrong.

So. Very. Wrong.

"I'm in love with you. I've been in love with you since we were seventeen." He grimaced as if the admission pained him.

Did loving her hurt him? The expression was akin to that of someone accidentally slamming their thumb with a hammer while hanging a photo. He didn't look any more pleased to be saying it as she felt hearing it.

Leaning against the cool brick wall, eyes closed, she proceeded with trepidation. "I didn't know."

It was such a poor response to such a big declaration, but the truth often was. The scrapbook of their eighteen months together held no page dedicated to their first *I love yous*. No picture existed of them staring with adoring eyes as little red hearts fluttered between them. No memory of her belly twisted in girlish delight when he tugged at his blond hair with a bashful confession of love. No image of her raised to her tiptoes, smile broad, with an *I love you* in return.

"I never said anything." His gaze fixed on hers.

Clumsy silence stretched between them. She fiddled with the frayed hem of her denim cutoffs. The blizzard of her thoughts was drowned out by the rapid thump of her heart. Her eyes flicked to Main Street, where people meandered down the street with reusable shopping bags filled with produce from the farmer's market.

It was a typical mid-August Saturday morning in Perry—except it wasn't. Duncan said he loved her, and her response was to blink it away like it was a bad dream.

"Duncan—"

"Natalie." He twisted to face her, his eyes pleading. "Please, don't say it. Give us a chance. A *real* chance. This time at least."

"This time?" Her head tipped up to him.

Duncan stepped close. "You never gave us a chance back then. You always held me at a distance."

"That's not true."

"It was." A harsh laugh burst from his lips. "But I was so fucking in love with you that I didn't care. Any bit of you was better than nothing at all."

She raised her hand to comfort him but crossed her arms over her chest instead. The desire to soothe was shadowed by the anger flashing in his eyes.

"Natalie, I love you. And, I think if you gave us a chance, you'd love me, too," he said, turning his stare back to her.

The glimpse of possessive impatience flaring in his gaze sent a chill up her spine.

"I...I don't love you, and I don't think I ever will. I'm sorry, Duncan. It's not fair to either of us to drag this out. I am so sorry. I had no idea you felt like this, and if I had, I would have never—"

"Sure," he hissed. "I was never good enough for you, was I? Just a farm kid who thought he was lucky enough to date the princess."

She flinched. "I'm not a princess. It's not like that. You were…are good enough. I just—"

"Damn right, I'm good enough," he sneered through clenched teeth.

"Stop fucking interrupting me," she snapped, pushing away from the wall to walk away. "I'm not doing this with you. I'm sorry I hurt you, but—"

"But what?" He grabbed her upper arm, fingers biting into her bare skin, and dragged her back to him.

"You're hurting me!" She yanked, but his hand tightened in a bruising grip.

"Is the little Owens princess done with me? Well, I'm not done with you. I won't be dismissed. I'm not that lovesick boy I was in high school. I'm a man. Maybe that's the problem. You're still a little girl," he snarled. "No wonder people don't take you seriously."

Like a gut punch, his words slammed into her, almost knocking the wind out of her.

She jerked her arm away. "Fuck you, Duncan."

His serpentine smirk went slack as a force hurled him into the brick wall. Jolted backward, she gasped. Her chest puffed in and out with rapid gulps. Her eyes were wide.

"You don't fucking talk to her like that," Noah growled, gripping the fabric of Duncan's collared shirt as he held him firm against the wall.

Duncan twisted his head to Nat. "Looks like your knight in faded blue jeans is here, princess."

Jerking Duncan forward, Noah then slammed him back against the wall. "You don't look at her. You don't speak to her. You don't fucking think about her."

A shuddering wince darkened Duncan's features. "Let me go," he ordered, squirming to extricate himself.

The normally calm ocean of Noah's eyes raged like a hurricane. Muscles in his corded arms flexed. The grip was so tight that the knuckles of his tanned hands paled. The charming, dimpled smile morphed into a clenched, bared-teeth snarl. It was like a wolf ready to rip out the throat of his prey.

It had always been hard for her to picture the carefree Noah of her childhood as a Marine. To envision him in the heat of battle, aiming a gun, intent on taking a life. Even when defending his fellow Marines. The furious, glazed look in his eyes confirmed that Noah could, if pushed, do harm.

"Noah." She placed a calming hand on his arm. "I'm okay. Let him go."

The rigidity of his muscles relaxed beneath her touch. The breakneck speed of his breath slowed. His grip loosened. Noah released Duncan and stepped back but positioned himself in front of Nat like a loyal soldier.

"I could press charges," Duncan said, smoothing down his rumpled shirt.

"So could I." She narrowed her eyes, shaded in steely fierceness.

"He shoved me into a wall," he scoffed, gesturing to Noah.

"You grabbed me." She pointed to her bicep, red splotches left behind from his hand. "I wonder how your DA boss would like to hear that one of his Assistant DAs was charged with assault, *especially* on a princess." Venom dripped from her words.

"I didn't..." He blanched, his eyes dropping to her arm. The realization of what he'd done splashed over his features. "I didn't mean to... I'm sorry. Natalie..."

Noah growled, silencing him.

Nat placed a hand on Noah's arm. The snarl in his throat quieted under her touch, but his stare remained focused on Duncan.

"I'm sorry I wasted my time thinking you were something

you're not... a nice guy. Lose my number and never speak to me again. If you don't, Noah will be the least of your worries."

Duncan opened and then closed his mouth. Shaking his head, he turned and walked by them. Noah's gaze followed each step until he disappeared down the street.

He turned, his forehead creased with worry. "Are you okay?"

"Yes."

His gaze zeroed in on her bicep, where Duncan's handprint was already fading. "Are you sure?"

Was she? Had this all just happened? One minute, she was enjoying pastries in a bakery and the next moment, Duncan grabbed her. Then Noah charged in just like that knight that Duncan sneered he was. The reverberations of what just happened quelled the anger boiling in her.

She swallowed that anger down. "I'm fine. Are you?"

He sloshed a long breath, and the tension in his shoulders seemed to dissolve. "Yes."

"Okay. I'm leaving. Bye." She pivoted and strode down the street toward the alley that led to the small parking lot behind the Wine Down, where she'd parked her Jeep.

With each step, the swallowed anger built like a volcano ready to explode. *What the actual fuck!?* She balled her fists, stomping into the parking lot.

"Nat!" he called, running after her. "Where are you going?"

"Home." Her tone was curt.

"Wait." He caught up, stepping between her and the Jeep. With a gentleness so starkly different from what she'd just witnessed, he placed his hands on her shoulders. "You're not okay. Let's talk, please."

"I didn't need you to rescue me!"

"He touched you. He—"

She threw up her arms, pushing away his hands. "You

don't think I've dealt with grabby assholes before? You weren't there when some frat guy grabbed my ass in college. I handled that all by myself." She motioned to herself. "I was the one who slapped him and dumped a beer over his head. You weren't there when I dealt with jerks in my residency program who thought they could intimidate me but soon found themselves eating my badass dust as I surpassed them in our program. I can take care of myself."

Eyes raised to the sky; he sucked in a steadying breath before looking back at her. "I know, but he *touched* you."

"Damn it, Noah!" she exclaimed, kicking a crushed soda can on the ground. "I'm tired of being the little sister everyone feels they need to protect."

"I don't see you as *my* little sister."

"Bullshit," she huffed and pulled her keys out of her pocket.

"I don't."

"Sure." Her tone mocked.

"I don't see you like that."

"Prove it," she said, her steel-gray gaze slammed into his.

"Okay." It was uttered like a dare. Charged determination shaded his eyes.

Graceful as a jungle cat, powerful and primal, he moved closer. She stepped back. He followed. With each tandem step, electricity buzzed between them.

Disbelief flooded her veins, quickening her pulse. *Is this happening?*

Her back hit the building's cement wall. "What are you doing?" she asked, a slight breathy tremble in her voice.

"Proving it." His hand raised to her hairline, tracing down to her cheek. "Is this okay?"

"Yes." It was barely audible over the drumbeat of her heart.

"Good." He dipped his head, meeting her lips.

Each muscle of her body rang out as if it was an instrument being played. *Good goddess, is this really happening? Don't pinch me.*

On raised tiptoes, her hands lifted to his shoulders, finding purchase. A tiny whimper escaped with the strong angles of his chest pressed against her, pinning her between his body and the wall.

This is where I live now! Have her mail forwarded. A crowbar would be needed to pry her from this Noah and wall sandwich.

"Mmhmm," he moaned. He nibbled open her mouth with soft bites.

The slick heat of his tongue explored her mouth until it found its desired playmate. In a languid game of tongue twister, they luxuriated in each other's tastes. The sweetness of the pastries still lingered, coating their kisses in vanilla and cinnamon.

His muscular arms slid between her and the wall, cushioning her and enfolding her deeper into him. Their small gasps and relieved moans masked the sounds of people talking, children squealing, dogs barking, and doors screeching open.

Wait. Door opening?

Breathless, he pulled away as if he heard her thoughts. Both their gazes dropped to the open backdoor of the Wine Down, where Todd stood, right eyebrow cocked, a shit-eating grin on his face.

"Looks like you finally stopped kissing the frogs and landed yourself a prince," Todd snarked.

"Oh my goddess." Mortified horror rippled through her.

"Don't worry, this stays with me." Hands raised, Todd paused with an amused expression. "Nicely done, Prince Charming. Oh, Nat… Summer had to take Liam home. She knew Noah was checking on you and the dillweed attorney-at-law, but text her. She was worried."

Nat nodded.

Smirking, Todd went back into the wine bar to prep to open for the day.

Their eyes fell back to one another. A quiet beat allowed what just happened to settle.

She just kissed Noah Wilson. Correction, Noah Wilson just kissed her. Scratch that, they'd just made out behind his downtown wine bar and got caught. By Todd.

He stepped back, putting distance between them. "I'm sorry."

The empty space between them was now filled with his regret. The same remorse that swam in his eyes *that* night was back.

Her heart dropped to the soles of her pink Converse sneakers. "Don't give me the best kiss of my life and say you're sorry." She pushed off the wall and strode to her Jeep.

"Nat," he beseeched, touching her arm and halting her steps.

She turned to face him.

His gaze met hers and his mouth opened, but no words came. All that spoke between them was the regret twisting his features.

"I can't have you look at me like that," she said, her voice sad but resolute.

"How am I looking at you?"

"Like you regret kissing me. Just like how you looked at me that night you almost kissed me. I won't be your regret."

She opened her door, got in, and drove away, leaving Noah, and her crush, in her taillights.

CHAPTER FOURTEEN

"I have nothing to give but this heart so full and these empty hands. They're not empty now." ~Louisa May Alcott, *Little Women*

Gravel popped, like her dreams, as she drove onto the driveway of the Little Red Barn. Putting the vehicle into park, she yanked out the keys and leaned back against the headrest. Hot tears trickled from her eyes, and she let the last twenty minutes crash over her. Duncan was an asshole. Noah kissed her. Then looked at her with regret.

"Nope. You're not going to cry over Noah Wilson. Not anymore." She dashed away the tears.

Her gaze flicked out the window. Across the property, Elle and Clayton were loading suitcases into the bed of his truck.

She looked in the mirror and wiped her face. Thank the goddess she didn't wear mascara. There'd be no raccoon eyes to take care of. No evidence of her sadness.

"Natster!" Clayton shouted from across the property, waving his hand at her when she hopped out of her vehicle.

"Clay Pot!" she called, walking toward him.

His expression scrunched up from her use of the nickname. As a child, she'd bestowed many, many nicknames on him.

To him, though, she'd always be Natster. The endearment both warmed and chilled her heart with lukewarm understanding. How could Noah look at her with anything but regret? She was the little sister of his best friend. Nothing more. Even if, for just a few moments today, she'd hoped that was no longer true.

"Clay Pot?" Elle gaped, her hands on her hips.

A smile curled on Nat's lips. "I also called him Clay Pigeon, and then there was the unfortunate Clay Aikens period. He did not appreciate that one."

"He was so overrated. Not to mention that 'Invisible Man' song was the national anthem for stalkers," he chuckled, hoisting a suitcase into the trunk.

Lizzie and Fitz barked and danced at their feet. Lowered to her haunches, Nat gave both pups ear scratches. The plump pug snorted while the brown and white pit bull licked her face. No matter what ailed the heart, puppy love was almost always the best cure.

With one last belly scratch for Lizzie, she straightened. "You two are off for your romantic weekend?"

"Yup." The giant grins perched on their faces were blinding.

To celebrate their one-year anniversary, they rented a cabin on Lake George. For the next week, they and the puppies would enjoy lakeside strolls, campfires, and a lot of something that Nat didn't want to think about her brother doing.

"We'll have cell service if you need anything. I've asked Noah to stop by to check in on you, and, of course, there's Mom and Dad," Clayton said.

Hard pass! The last thing she wanted was Noah stopping by.

She rolled her eyes. "You realize I am almost thirty, and I used to live in Boston. Perry isn't exactly Dorchester."

"If it makes you feel better, Noah pops by to say hello"—Elle made air quotes—"when your brother is at the clinic, and we have bad weather. It's *so* obvious Clayton sent him to check in on me." She nudged his ribs.

"I worry about my girls." He flung both arms around his fiancée and sister, tucking both close to his chest.

"You're such an overprotective softy," Elle cooed.

Alone in the sanctuary of the Little Red Barn, Nat sat on the kitchen floor, its linoleum cool against her legs. The temperature and today's events coated her body in a salty gloss of perspiration. The day had been so, so much. Almost too much, and she just wanted to put it behind her. The confrontation with Duncan, that scorching hot kiss with Noah...the agonizing rejection at the end of that encounter.

She needed her glue gun and a craft project...stat! But first, she texted Summer. No doubt, she worried about Nat after all that happened.

Me: Sorry about earlier. I'm okay, but I need time to craft this out. Can we do dinner Monday night?

Summer: Of course. One question, though. Is Duncan in the picture still?

Me: GODDESS NO!

There may have been an excessive use of exclamation marks and a GIF of a man being kneed in the balls that accompanied her message. If only she had kneed Duncan in his balls.

How had she wasted her time with him? There were so many warning signs, present and past, that he wasn't for her. That he wasn't a good guy.

Hell, within seconds of meeting him again, Summer had assessed him as an asshole. The glower in her gaze when her brown eyes studied Duncan in the bakery telegraphed her instant dislike.

Summer: I'll cancel the hitman then.

Me: Where'd you find a hitman in Perry?

Summer: The Penny Saver. It was right next to the ad looking for a new milker at Rice Farms.

Gratitude and humor gentled the ire that still lurked from dealing with Duncan. For so many reasons, she was lucky to have Summer as a friend. This woman had a way of reading people quickly, discovering who they truly were. She saw things that Nat missed or, perhaps, ignored.

"There were signs," she mumbled to herself, rising from the floor.

How had she missed them? In the midday light filtering in from the large kitchen window, the unseen potholes of Duncan's personality were illuminated. Not just who he was now but who he'd been then. The things she ignored. Traits she'd pretended weren't what they really were.

Shuffling to the table, she pulled out her crafting supplies. Creating occupied her hands and her brain. It allowed her to focus on something else, which in turn provided clarity. With each delicious cut of blue cardstock, her mind drifted to Noah's oceanic eyes.

Get out of my head, Noah! She gnawed her lower lip and pushed into decorating the bridal shower scrapbook she was making for Elle and Clayton. The rip of paper drowned out the thoughts of *he who shall not be named* because he already occupied way too much real estate in her head...and heart.

A gentle rap at the door barged into her crafty Zen headspace. Barefoot, she padded across the hardwood floor.

Opening the front door, she almost gasped. "Noah?"

"I don't regret you," he rasped, reaching out and pulling her into his arms. "I only regret waiting this long to do this."

Nat's breath sprinted out of her.

His warm, full lips pressed to hers in an unapologetic kiss. Raising to tiptoes, she encircled his neck. His hands moved to her hips, hoisting her into the air, and her short legs wrapped around his middle like there was no place they'd rather be. The heat of his kisses glided down her jawline to the column of her throat.

Gripping her tight, he strode into the Little Red Barn. His heel connected with the door, and it slammed behind them.

Need and reason wrestled inside her. A conversation needed to happen... But hadn't they done enough talking? They'd had a lifetime of talking and only a moment of kissing. Couldn't she just enjoy the kissing?

"Wait," she whined, pulling her face from his. *Some days she hated her sense of reason!* "We should talk," she breathed, annoyed with herself.

His kiss-swollen lips hung open. "O...kay."

Nat remained in his arms. Heat pulsed in the scant inches between them. Each breath seemed to protest the talking. Legs around him and his hands gripping her ass, she understood the hesitation. It would be far easier to just let her body have control, but her heart and brain were too strong.

If they were going to speak, she needed to dismount Noah. "You should put me down for this convo."

He lowered her to the floor. "Who should start?"

Tugging down her shorts that had ridden up from wrapping around him like a horny Rally Monkey at a baseball game, she mumbled, "Probably me since I suggested it."

He gestured to the couch. Noah sat on one side, body angled toward Nat, who sat with her legs crossed on the other end.

Clutching a green checkered pillow to her middle, she exhaled. "So, you kissed me."

"And you kissed me back." A flirty lilt shaded his tone.

"I've wanted to kiss you since I was ten." She cringed.

Was she saying this aloud? To Noah?

Girl, he had his tongue in your mouth. You can tell him this.

"I've wanted to kiss you since you were eighteen."

Her heart galloped like a racing greyhound.

"What you saw in my eyes the night of Evan's funeral wasn't regret for you. It was disgust for my actions. You were eighteen. You were grieving. I should have been comforting you, but instead, I almost made a move on you. I was twenty-eight. I should have known better," he confessed.

Nat squeezed the pillow closer to her chest. "But you did comfort me. You didn't do anything wrong. You never crossed a line."

"But I had. That entire week I watched you…" He looked away. "It wasn't appropriate."

"Because I'm Clayton's little sister."

"For me, you stopped being Clayton's little sister a long time ago."

She shifted on the couch, folding her legs beneath her.

"I hadn't seen you in person since you were twelve. Between being stationed overseas and my second deployment, I still saw you as that little girl at the other end of those letters and care packages. Five and a half years later, after I got injured in that IED blast, you were the soft voice at the other end of the phone, calling me weekly to check in while I was recovering. A soft voice that no longer sounded like the little girl I remembered. When I came back to Perry after Evan died, you'd become a woman who steadied her family during one of the toughest moments of their lives."

Noah's words from last week echoed. *I see you.*

She could see herself through his eyes. To Noah, she wasn't Chris and Heidi Owen's youngest daughter. She wasn't Evan and Clayton's little sister. She was just Nat. *His Nat.*

Throwing the pillow aside, she crawled onto his lap. His

arms looped around her, pressing her close to his chest. The quiet thump of his heart lulled her in the moment.

"Nat," he murmured, kissing her temple. "I know how strong you are. I know you don't need anyone to protect you...but I want to. Not because of Clayton but because of you."

"Forget talking. Just kiss me."

As bemusement punctuated his grin, he pressed his smile to hers. Nibbling open her mouth, the slick heat of his tongue found hers. His focused kisses drank in every last drop of her. His hands slid down her body, grazing her bare thighs. Liquid desire pooled in her belly and dripped across her bloodstream. Adjusting her position, she straddled him.

"Noah," she giggled with his squeeze of her behind.

"It's such a nice ass." Those dimples popped with the quirk of his lips.

Like an animal in heat, she rubbed her hips against him, feeling his stiffness grow beneath her. It was intoxicating to experience his slow unraveling. The tightened grip on her ass. The deepening kisses. The hungry groans. The press of his hardness against her.

She should slow down. There should be batted eyes and coy comments.

Fuck that! She'd waited long enough to bathe herself in this moment. To have his unbridled kisses and exploring hands set her on fire.

"Noah, take me upstairs," she panted, breaking their kiss.

"Hold on." He held her tight, lifting them off the couch and turning to take the ten steps to the sleeping loft.

"How strong are you?" She mused as he effortlessly carried her up the stairs.

"It helps that you're tiny, Tink," he chuckled.

"*Tink*?"

"You're like Tinkerbelle. Pixie-small but full of spunk."

That big smile on her face would never come off.

Reaching the loft, he placed her on the cream-colored bedspread and then fell atop her. Settled between her legs, his hands skated up her thighs, over the worn denim of her shorts, stopping at the button. A wickedness sparked in his expression as he popped the button and pulled the shorts down.

"I could prolong this, but I think we've waited long enough." The low rumble of his voice scorched her already heated skin.

Noah's fingers were warm as they dipped under the waistband of her cotton boyshorts and yanked them off. Nat, of course, complied. The pads of his fingers crisscrossed up and down her legs, tingling awake every nerve ending in mini explosions of need and desire.

The pulse at her core ached. "Noah, please."

"Do you want me to touch you"—his fingers parted her wet folds—"or kiss you." His tongue flicked over her clit.

Grasping at the silky comforter, she moaned, "Kiss."

Taking her hips, he dragged her to the edge of the bed. Reminiscent of a subject ready to praise their queen, he knelt on the floor and gazed up at her from beneath hooded eyes.

Spreading her wide, he rubbed his nose against that throbbing nub and inhaled deep. "Do you taste as sweet as you smell?"

He licked down her center. Pleasure zinged up her spine.

Eyes dark, he peered up at her with a devilish grin. "A taste of you will never be enough."

Oh, goddess. Her breath hitched.

Gripping her thighs, he raised her to meet his mouth. His playful and indulgent tongue flicks against her clit teased promised pleasure. With a sexy hum, he sucked the sensitive bud between his lips. Like it was a game to see how close to the edge he could get her without tipping over, he alternated between languid licks and hardening sucks. The pressure twined tighter and tighter like thread wrapped around a spindle.

"So close," she moaned, writhing against his working tongue. Reminiscent of a pinata being smashed, spraying candy everywhere, the pleasure built at her core and then... erupted. "Noah!"

"God, you taste so fucking good." His tongue lapped her up, and then he slipped a finger inside her.

He's not done? Perhaps. She was orgasm tipsy. None of her past sexual partners kept going once—or if—she came. If she did come, it somehow computed as time to stop or for them to push inside her. Noah continued to chase her pleasure, not his.

He pushed a second finger inside her.

"Oh...my..." The delicious full feeling stole her ability to speak.

His thick fingers pumped inside her while working her clit with his mouth. That coiled pressure returned. Adjusting and crooking his fingers, he hit something that...*Oh my fucking goddess*...engulfed her in an explosion of ecstasy.

"Fuck!" she cried, squeezing her legs around his head.

The climax rioted through her. Her legs quaked violently. She placed her hand on her sweaty brow, trying to come back to reality. Had that just happened?

She lifted her head, spotting the boyish smile curved into his wickedly proud grin. *Yeah, that happened.*

He stood up, kicked off his shoes, and crawled in on the other side. With a sweet gentleness, he pulled her trembling body into his arms. Tucking her into his nook, he folded the blanket over them.

"You gave me two orgasms," she panted, still trying to steady her breath.

"Yep."

"You found my G-spot."

"Yep."

"You read my notes during Ms. ChaNUT's workshop, didn't you?"

"Yup." Devilment glinted in his expression.

"Now, you're snuggling me." Sleepiness weighed down her eyes, forcing them shut.

"Yep."

"Am I dreaming?" A small yawn escaped.

"Nope." He tightened his hold. "Neither am I."

CHAPTER FIFTEEN

"Such hours are beautiful to live, but very hard to describe."
~Louisa May Alcott, *Little Women*

Nat's eyes blinked open. The quiet sleeping loft was bathed in warm darkness. The bed was empty beside her.

Had it just been a vivid dream? She lifted the blanket to see her *very* naked bottom half.

Settling the blanket at her waist, her lips curved up. "Oh, my goddess," she whispered to herself.

It had happened. Not only had she kissed Noah, but he kissed her back. A lot. There'd been the best oral sex…well, sex, to be honest, of her life. Even better than that, which was pretty damn hard to top, he saw her. Truly saw her. She wasn't Clayton's little sister in his eyes. She was Nat, and he liked Nat.

How long had she slept? She grabbed her phone from the bedstand. It was almost nine p.m. It must have been around six when they fell asleep. Her eyes flicked around the room. "Wait, where is he?"

Had he done a wham-bam-let-me-go-down-on-you-and-run-thank-you-ma'am? Shaking her head, she knew that couldn't be right. Noah was gone, but he wouldn't do that. Even if this was just a one-time thing, he'd not do that to her. Just like the teeter-totter, he'd never let her hit the ground like that.

Pushing the blanket off, she jumped out of bed. After tossing her shirt and bra into the wicker hamper in the corner, she grabbed her blue fluffy cloud robe and wrapped it around her. Then, she padded to the stairs.

With each step, the pungent smell of garlic danced in her nostrils. The soft sound of a cabinet being eased shut drifted from the kitchen.

She bounded down the rest of the stairs, entering the large living room and kitchen area. Noah stood at the island, chopping a bell pepper on a pug-shaped cutting board.

"Are you cooking?" she gaped.

His smile quirked with mischief. "Well, if we counted on your cooking we'd starve or get food poisoning."

"We *never* verified that it wasn't a stomach bug." She crossed her arms over her chest.

There was no proof that the turkey chili she'd made five years ago for a Wilson/Owens Sunday dinner made everyone pray at the altar of the porcelain god. Despite the lack of proof, the two families agreed Nat was no longer allowed to cook.

"So…" She drew out the word as if it would somehow fill in what to say next.

A conversation was needed. What happens next? Was this a one-time thing? Was this more? What did he want? Goddess, what did she want?

"You're spinning, Nat." Noah's warm gaze silenced the many questions wandering inside her.

"Just a bit." She held up her thumb and pointer finger squeezed together. "We do need to talk, though."

Noah tossed the sliced bell pepper into a large salad bowl.

I have a salad bowl? Her forehead puckered.

"What are you cooking?" she asked, leaning against the counter.

"I have a vegetarian lasagna in the oven. I'm making a salad and *unburnt* garlic bread." A cheeky grin covered his face.

"Hardy-har-har," she mocked. "You burn the garlic bread once and they don't let you live it down."

His right brow ticked up.

"Okay, twice." She snagged a slice of bell pepper from the bowl and bit into it. "So, where'd you get the supplies? I survive on takeout, premade salads, and yogurt."

"I noticed," he chuckled. "While you were sleeping, I ran to the store to pick up a few things and grabbed some cooking utensils from my place. I left a note." His head tipped to a piece of notebook paper held on the fridge door with a Sailor Moon magnet. His gaze locked on her. "I didn't want you to think I bailed on you."

"I know you wouldn't."

The intimacy of their gazes pinned both in place. The companionable silence cocooned them in mutual understanding. She saw him as much as he saw her. The idea of seeing and being seen caused happiness to bloom within her.

"Dinner will be ready in twenty-five minutes. It looks like you were about to shower. Why don't you do that? Then we can eat and talk."

"Sounds like a plan, Stan." A goofy lilt coated her words.

Plan Stan? WTF Nat! She bit her lip and pushed off the counter.

"Nat, wait."

"Yup?" She twirled to face him.

He leaned over the counter, capturing her lips in a slow, savoring kiss. Every nerve ending ignited. Her toes curled. All the romantic clichés hit her body with the heat of his kiss.

Pulling back, his dimples popped with a big grin. "I know

we will talk over dinner, but I don't want you to think this is just a one-time thing. At least not for me."

Despite her quickened pulse, a strange easiness relaxed away any whispered rigidness of her body. "It's not a one-time thing for me either."

Showered and changed into a short, green, sunflower-patterned T-shirt dress, she descended from the sleeping loft to find the table set. Her scrapbooking supplies had been tucked back into her bedazzled crafting kit and moved to the desk near the front window. The salad bowl, which he'd clearly brought from home, a glass dish of lasagna, and a platter of unburnt garlic bread sat on the counter. A set of pint glasses and silverware flanked white ceramic plates and bowls trimmed in swirls of bright rainbows on the table.

"This looks great," she said, inhaling the delicious aroma.

Stepping close, Noah brushed a loose tendril of her hair behind her ear. "You look beautiful."

No smile erupted because a permanent one was Gorilla-glued to her face. She fought the urge to pinch herself just to confirm this wasn't a dream, just in case it was.

If it is, let me keep sleeping.

She settled at the table while Noah made their plates. He'd changed from the blue jeans and T-shirt he'd worn earlier into a different pair of jeans and a black T-shirt with *Farmer's Ale* in white block lettering. The shirt molded over his sculpted chest and cut torso.

"What?" Noah's eyebrow cocked, and a smirk pulled at the corners of his mouth.

"Just admiring you in *that* T-shirt." She winked and picked up a fork.

A rumble of laughter skipped out of him. "Nat Owens, do

not objectify me." He bent and kissed her forehead. "I'm going to grab your cider and my beer out of the fridge. Try not to ogle my ass as I do so."

As Noah strode to the fridge, the laughter belted out of her. With a seductive sway of his hips that rivaled Jessica Rabbit, he sauntered to the fridge, opened it, and bent over. Head twisted over his shoulder, he winked with a cheeky smile.

"You're ridiculous," she giggled.

This was the best part about Noah. Well, they were all the best parts. He always made her laugh or smile or both. Even in the darkest of moments, his light shined so bright. Its brightness seemed to almost say it was all only for her. The crush-sick little girl and teenager who had daydreamed about this were floored that their fantasies didn't hold a candle to the reality of Noah.

In his usual stride, he returned to the table and placed the bottles of watermelon cider and pale ale on the table. With the bottle opener from his keychain, he popped each bottle and poured them into their glasses.

"Before we do the *very* adult thing of talking," she said, glass in hand. "A toast to the chef."

They clinked glasses.

"So, you finally went full vegetarian?" She forked up a bite of cheesy lasagna.

"Yeah. I couldn't stomach it anymore. The smell..." His eyes shifted to the darkness outside the window.

Those blue eyes saw so much but had seen even more. Much more than the charming smile and amiable personality showed the world. At times, the unsaid seemed to weigh heavy on him. That heaviness sometimes cast shadows under his eyes after suspected sleepless nights, kidnapped him to a different place while his body remained in the room, and pinned a rigidity to his jaw.

They'd never really spoken about what happened during

his two deployments. What he'd seen. What he'd done. She knew he'd been injured but never pushed. Instead, she just allowed herself to be there in quiet acceptance. After all, she understood the pain of things you could...or wouldn't talk about.

"It's really good," she commented, taking another bite.

Noah's gaze drifted back to her. "Thanks."

"There're so many vegetarian options for things. Even wings. I had some decent cauliflower wings back in Boston."

His face contorted into a grimace. "I draw the line there! Daryl's wings and pizza with Clayton is the exception. Can't break tradition."

Nat nodded.

Once a week since they'd been fourteen, minus the time both lived in different places, Clayton and Noah grabbed takeout from Daryl's Pizzeria. It started as a post-game tradition on Wednesday nights after their JV football games. It was just one of the many traditions they had.

"Clayton," she said, nibbling on her lip.

"Clayton," he repeated.

"If this isn't a one-time thing, that is one six-foot-five hurdle we'll need to get over." Nat's mouth dropped open. Her breath caught. "Oh, my goddess...our fathers...*our mothers.*"

How would their families react to this? How would this impact the dynamic between the attached-at-the-hip Wilson and Owens clans? Nat liked the idea of it pulling them even closer, but her stomach swirled with misgiving that this relationship, if it was that, wouldn't be welcomed. He was ten years older than her. Their families were so close. If this didn't go anywhere or ended badly, it may impact that closeness for everyone.

Noah reached across the table, threading his fingers in hers. "We don't have to tell them. Not right away. We don't have to tell anyone. We can figure *us* out first and then tell others."

"Keep this secret?"

He gently squeezed her hand. "Yes. To allow us to relax into this and find our footing together. The look of sheer panic on your face about our families finding out about us leads me to believe this may be the best thing. For now."

Tightness gripped her shoulders. "What if I want to tell them?"

"Then I'll hold your hand as we tell them together."

That tightness dissolved.

Keeping this secret was the best course of action. It allowed them to figure themselves out as a couple. To figure out if they were a couple.

So much to figure out!

The fact that if she desired to tell their families, that he'd be right beside her as they did, bolstered her resolve to keep this a secret. Her choice wasn't made out of shame or embarrassment. It may seem like this relationship was a dirty little secret, but it wasn't. The only thing dirty about this relationship was the things she planned to do to him once dinner was over.

"And I'd hold yours." She squeezed his hand in hers.

Fresh coolness surrounded them as they walked, hands clasped, to the pond. With Clayton and Elle gone, the two-acre property on the lonely country road played the role of their secret hideaway. A place they could be undiscovered in the glow of the moonlight.

Snuggled in one of the Adirondack chairs on the dock, Noah's arms wrapped around her waist. Back pressed against his firm chest, she inhaled his pine scent. Stars twinkled in the velvet sky.

One of her favorite things about coming home was the nightly star display. Unlike Boston with its city light pollution, in Perry, the sky glowed each night with visible constellations, solo stars, and planets. The out-of-the-world view was fitting for the surreal sensation that enveloped her while in Noah's arms.

"This feels unreal," she murmured.

"It's real." He nuzzled her neck. "We're real."

"So, we're giving this a shot. Does that mean you're not seeing anyone else? If you are, that's fine. I just want to know." A high-pitched tone held her voice at knifepoint.

"I'm not seeing anyone else."

"What about Willa?" She closed her eyes, bracing for the response.

"We kissed once, a year ago, after I'd first met her. We decided we were better as friends."

"Why?"

The hold around her tightened. "Because she wasn't who I wanted. Not then and not now."

"And she knows this?"

The idea of Willa pining for Noah just like Nat had made her heart frown—not with jealousy, but with concern. Unrequited feelings were the truest of heartbreak.

"Yes." He combed his long fingers into her hair. "Willa flirts and kisses men that she knows there's no hope of anything happening with. I was just a diversion for her, nothing more."

"If you were a distraction for her, what was she for you?" She adjusted in his lap, allowing their gazes to meet.

"A friend."

Nat nodded.

The truth shined in his eyes. Only friendship bonded he and Willa. She could trust in that because she could trust in him. If he wanted Willa, he'd have pursued her. He was here with Nat.

The jealousy about Willa had less to do with an actual belief that they were together and more about her not being the one whose fingers skated across his bicep at the brewery. She was woman enough to admit that, even if it was only to herself.

"How about you? Any other assholes-at-law I need to be aware of?" he asked.

Nat frowned. "No."

"I'm sorry. That was careless of me to say." The palm of his right hand cradled her cheek.

"No, it's not what you said. It's the fact that I chose to go out with Duncan…again." She jumped up, needing to move and calm the anxiety jittering along her limbs. With measured steps, she paced the small dock. "There were signs I missed. Even when we dated in high school. My girlfriends went all swoony for how he'd walk me to and from every class, how he'd sit with me at lunch while the other boyfriends sat with their guy friends, and how he'd call or come by my house every day. They'd tell me how lucky I was. So, I thought I was lucky."

With a huffed breath, she spun, facing the pond, keeping Noah behind her. It was too much to look at him. To see the flex of his pupils as she admitted this out loud.

"He was always possessive. He'd get upset if I didn't text back right away or if I had plans with someone else. But then the cruel words or cutting remarks would be washed away with a charming smile, surprise gift, or a romantic gesture."

"Cruel words?"

"He'd say I acted like I was 'better' than him, how selfish I was, or that I didn't know how lucky I was to have him. That everyone says it but me, which always seemed to be reinforced by my friends," she whispered, an acrid taste in her throat with Duncan's remembered jabs.

"Did he ever do more than words?"

She didn't need to turn to take in the storm clouds marring his handsome features. His clenched jaw and balled-up fists were audible in the deliberate cadence of his speech.

Nat moved to the edge of the pond, lowered to the hard plank surface, and slipped her feet into the cool dark water. "No. Today was the first time he got physical. It was like a Jekyll and Hyde switch went off in him. Only I think the Mr. Hyde in him got stronger over the years. When he grabbed my arm, all my unrecognized apprehensions howled." She released a long, stuttered breath. "It shouldn't take someone escalating to that level to realize they're a bad guy. I mean, I still went out with him. I dated him for almost two years in high school and then went out with him…again."

The space beside her filled with Noah's presence. He lowered to a seated position on the edge of the dock beside her, dangling his denim-covered legs in the water.

"First, you broke up with him twice. Both times you realized he was a Grade-A asshole."

The corners of her lips raised into a weak smile at his words.

"Second, there's truth behind the cliché about a wolf in sheep's clothing. Guys like Duncan know how to hide who they are. How to lure people and keep them lured."

"Summer saw it," she sighed.

"Sometimes it's easier to see things when you're on the outside looking in."

"She wasn't the only one. Clayton and Evan never liked him."

"Well, Clayton hasn't liked any of your boyfriends."

Their eyes met in a clumsy stare.

Clayton not liking anyone she dated may soon include his best friend. How would their relationship change a friendship that spanned the entirety of both men's lives?

Weaving their fingers together, Noah lifted their intertwined hands to his mouth and pressed a tender kiss on her knuckles. "I'm not worried about Clayton right now. We'll figure that out. I am worried about you, though. I don't want to be the guy who tells you what to do, but here it goes, guys like Duncan feed on control. On making people so knotted up that he retains power. Blaming yourself for his actions lets him control you from afar. Please don't give him the power to take away your ability to see how strong you are. Even if you didn't know it then, there was something in you that *knew* he was bad news. You broke up with him *twice*."

Closing her eyes, she inhaled deep his words as they floated between them. It was true she'd ended things with Duncan. There'd always been a nibbling concern in her belly about him. How many times had she asked her girlfriends in high school if his behavior was normal? Even the hesitation with this recent dalliance was coated in an unconscious knowing that he was, indeed, a wolf in sheep's clothing.

"You're right. Thank you." She leaned her head against his shoulder. Her feet danced in the cool pond, one bare foot tapping against the leg of his soaked jeans. "Your jeans are wet. You should have rolled them up or taken them off."

"You just want to see my butt in my boxer briefs." He waggled his eyebrows.

With an arched brow, she shoved him into the pond. The splash sprayed cool droplets along her skin.

Emerging from the water, he half-laughed, half-choked. "Oh, you're in trouble now." Raising up in the water, his strong arms encircled her waist, hoisting her up in the air.

"Noah!" she squeaked.

It was only fair. Nose plugged and eyes closed in a preemptive bracing, she readied to be hurled into the water. Only there was no hurling. Instead, he eased them into the water together, his arms wrapped around her as he walked them to the middle of the pond, where he could still touch, but she could not.

Goose pimples bloomed along her skin. Wrapping her legs around his waist and her arms around his neck, she leaned into the anchored floating sensation. Somehow, she was both light in the gravity-defying water and, yet, tethered to safety in his arms.

"Well, this is one way to make me wet," she joked.

He burst into laughter. The blue in his eyes sparkled as if all the stars in the sky had been relocated within them. "Your quick wit is one of my favorite things about you."

"One of your favorite things? What are the others?"

"That may take all night to list."

"Perhaps you should sleep over then," she said, lowering her hand under the water and sliding it beneath his wet T-shirt.

The muscles of his stomach contracted at her touch.

"Perhaps." He took her mouth in a heated kiss.

CHAPTER SIXTEEN

"I'd rather than coffee than compliments just now." ~Louisa May
Alcott, *Little Women*

Nat's wet clothes clung to her body, and her sandals squished with each step. Hands linked, she led Noah to the farmhouse's attached garage, where the washer and dryer were kept. They walked through the door, clicking on the light. A gentle buzz hummed as yellow light flooded the garage.

The garage walls were filled with shelves of neat and organized supplies and storage. A small laundry nook was tucked in the corner. Since Elle moved in, the other half of the two-car garage was home to her vehicle. Of course, Nat's overprotective brother would insist the woman he loved park her car in the garage that he never used for himself. It was just who he was.

"Let's get these in the wash," she said, peeling off the clinging dress. Lifting the lid of the washer, she tossed it in. Then, pulled off her underwear and unclasped her bra.

Her skin thrummed with the relief from the removal of the uncomfortable wet fabric.

She turned to take Noah's clothes but found him motionless. His soaked black T-shirt balled in his fists, his stare heated, and throat bobbing. Nat's breath caught at the rapid rise and fall of his sculpted chest and the darkening of his blue eyes. This is the first time he saw her... all of her. Earlier it was only her lower half he'd seen and feasted upon.

She moved closer, basking in his gaze. The heat of his stare crawled up her legs, to the curve of her hips, up her torso, over her breasts, along the column of her throat, coming to rest on her face.

Being naked in front of someone for the first time often set off a swirl of doubts for her. She'd fixate on how her legs weren't long and toned like other women. Or wish for larger breasts and hips that popped. Regret would surge for not working out enough to tone the softer parts of her body. All those emotions would result in self-conscious nerves and attempts to use her hands or arms to hide her perceived imperfections.

Not tonight. The fire of Noah's gaze boosted her confidence.

"You're perfect," he murmured.

She stepped closer. She was perfect in his eyes and, in that moment, in her own. No second guesses slowed her steps as she closed the distance between them.

"Thank you." She smiled, taking the wet T-shirt from his hand. Twisting, she flung it into the washer as if shooting a ball into a basket. "Nothing but washer."

A deep chuckle belted from him.

Turned back to face Noah, her eyes drank him up. She raised her hand and skated her fingers across his cool, damp skin. His breath grew ragged with each stroke on his muscular shoulders, down his broad chest, and over the ridges of his taut stomach. A small tremor rippled through him along the path of her fingers.

"Someone has school spirit," she teased, using her finger

to outline the yellowjacket tattoo, the Perry School Mascot, on his right peck. "When did you get this?" she asked.

This is the most of him she'd ever seen. There were flashes of memory of him as a teenager in swimming trunks, jumping into the lake from the back of a boat. In the last ten years, though, she couldn't recall seeing him shirtless or in shorts.

"I got it right before I left for basic training." His breath stuttered as her fingers traced down his torso to the dark trail of hair disappearing beneath the top of his jeans.

"Why a yellowjacket?"

"To keep home close even when I was far away."

"Home is important to you."

He placed a hand on her cheek. "As it is to you. We both came back."

She nodded. They had. Both were driven to come back. One to the admiration and respect of the community breathing new life into a once-dying downtown. The other returned to the role of daughter when she craved to be so much more.

Choosing not to dwell on that, she continued her exploration of his body. "Is this okay?" she asked, her hands touching the buckle of his belt.

The rise and fall of his chest quickened. "Nat," he paused. "Nobody has seen me…all of me in almost eleven years."

"Since you were injured." It was part question, part understanding.

"Yes," he swallowed hard.

Nat raised her hand, cupped his cheek, and gently commanded, "Let me see you…all of you."

Noah coiled the fingers around her wrist, guiding it back to his belt buckle. "Okay."

She unbuckled his belt, keeping her gaze intertwined with his. With determined fingers, she unbuttoned his jeans. Noah's eyes remained locked with hers while she guided both his jeans and boxer briefs down. He lifted his right foot and then left to step out of the damp clothes. She rose and swiveled to throw them into the washer.

Facing Noah, she crouched on her haunches on the smooth cement floor. Her eyes dropped to his muscular legs. Her fingers glided along the scars of his right leg and ridges of puckered skin from where he'd been injured.

"You're perfect." She pressed an earnest kiss to the scars.

In her eyes, he was. Each scar represented his story. His loyalty. His sacrifice. His love.

A shuddering breath escaped him. The tight muscles of his legs relaxed with the touch of her lips. "Nat," he rasped, bending to take her by the shoulders and guide her up.

Noah took her in a reverent kiss, tucking her against his firm chest.

Aching need spread within her. "Noah…I want you."

Pulling his working mouth away, he stared at her. "Not here."

Before the words "When?" or "Where?" left her mouth, he scooped her up into his arms. A breathy giggle flew out of her as he strode out of the garage. His bare feet carried them down the stone path towards the Little Red Barn.

"Your feet," she laughed. "They'll get dirty."

"We'll clean them in the shower." His tone was determined.

"Oh, sex in the shower?" she cooed with a sassy lilt.

"After the shower."

Nat skimmed the fingers of her right hand across his chest. "So, we're going to get clean before we get dirty?"

"Yes." He smirked.

He opened the door and carried her inside. Kicking the door shut, he strode across the living room to the bathroom. Deposited to her feet on the cool tiled floor, he turned the shower on and held his hand below the spray until it got to his preferred temperature.

Noah's fingers threaded through her hair. "Do you want this up or down?"

"Up," she said, thankful he'd not dunked her in the pond allowing the shoulder-length strands to remain dry.

It was the most intimate experience of her life. The gentle strokes of the hairbrush through her sandy tresses as he brushed her hair up into a high ponytail.

"How did you know to do that?" she asked, watching him place the brush on the counter.

"My mom." He guided her into the shower and stepped in behind her.

The warm water cascaded across her heated skin.

"But I'd prefer not to talk about her when I am naked with you."

"Your mom doesn't get you whipped up into a lusty frenzy?" she sassed.

Noah squeezed some body wash onto his hand. "Probably about as much as talking about your dad would when I do this." His hands massaged the foamy liquid onto her breasts.

Arching into his firm but tender touch, her breath hitched. "Point made."

Noah's hands crisscrossed her slick skin, rubbing the cucumber-melon scent over her body. With each cleansing swipe, her body hummed, nerves stretching taut. The steam coiled around them as their hands explored one another.

Every muscle in her body contracted with need and then calmed under his caresses. It was the most tantalizing, tension-filled, and relaxing experience of her life.

The shower's glass door was steamed over as they stepped out. Nat grabbed a fluffy blue towel from the rack and patted him dry. Grinning, he reached behind her to grab a second towel and followed her action.

Once both were dry, she took both towels and placed them on the counter. Taking Noah's hand, she led him out the door. Moonlight streamed in through the open blinds, illuminating their way across the living room and up the stairs. With each step, her pulse roared. The anticipation of what was about to happen dripped fire along her veins.

"Noah," she said, breaking the silence as they reached the sleeping loft. The still-unmade bed dared them to mess up the sheets even more. "I am on birth control. My last sexual partner was a year ago. I've been tested, and I'm safe."

He cradled her face. "I'm good."

"I have condoms if you want, but…" She bit her lower lip.

The wise thing to do would be to use a condom. The medical provider in her wagged a cautionary finger. However, the idea of anything between them at this moment felt wrong. She'd never not used protection with someone. Not with any of her boyfriends. Even if they said they had been tested and she was on birth control, a nibbling concern was always there, warning her subconsciously that they couldn't be trusted. With Noah, her heart only knew trust.

"Which would you prefer?" He skated his thumb against her cheek, the rough pad soothed over her smooth skin.

"I don't want anything between us."

"Me either," he murmured, dipping his head to capture her lips.

Noah's hands slid down to her waist, lifted her, and laid her atop the bed. Crawling onto the bed, he hovered above her, caging her between his muscular arms. His strong hands moved down her body to her thighs, the massage slow and erotic. Meeting her mouth in a slow, deep kiss, their tongues danced like long-lost lovers.

Nat's hands moved up his arms and along his chest. A tingling sensation zinged through every inch of her with the lick of his tongue down her throat, to her collarbone, and, at last, at the hard pink peak of her right breast. Covering her nipple with the heat of his mouth, his tongue rolled and flicked.

She moaned as his teeth grazed the taut nub.

"You like that?" he murmured, soothing the sting with a soft kiss.

She arched into the heat of his mouth. "Yes."

Shifting his attention, he repeated the sensual caress on her other nipple. A building tension tightened in her core. As Noah worshipped her breasts, she guided his right hand between her legs, where she was already slick with arousal.

He looked up, eyes smoldering. "You want me to touch you…" he slid his finger, finding her clit "…here."

Melting into his touch, she dug her nails into his shoulder. "Right there." Her hips moved against his ministrations. The almost torturous slowness of his stroking fingers ignited a pleasurable inferno.

Lowering her hand between them, she wrapped her fingers around his impressive length, beads of precum formed at the tip.

"Oh, god…" A pleasure-filled groan burst from him with her slow strokes of his arousal.

As they moved against each other's working hands, the room filled with their panting moans. A familiar contraction of her pelvic muscles announced her coming climax. Closing her eyes, she let the orgasm take her.

"Noah," she whimpered. "I want you inside me."

Releasing him, she opened her legs wider to ready herself for him. Kneeling between her thighs, he raised her hips and placed a pillow beneath her.

"Is this okay?" he asked, positioning himself at her entrance.

Nat's blood pulsed as his penis grazed her entrance. "Yes. Please."

As he slid into her, she bit her lower lip allowing the sensation of stretching to subside.

"So good…nothing has felt so good as you," he rasped.

"Oh!" she gasped.

The sensation of him pushing deeper inside her overwhelmed her other senses. She was both hungry for more and sated at the same time as her body stretched with the fullness.

Placing his hands on her knees, he guided her into a new angle and plunged deeper into her. The position wound delicious tension inside her.

"Oh, my goddess!" Her arms encircled his neck, using the leverage to meet each of his thrusts.

Their tandem movements collided in a tantalizing dance. The pressure built and almost screamed for the sweet relief of climax. Every muscle in her body spooled tight in anticipation. He slipped his hand between them and caressed her throbbing clit.

"Noah!" she cried out.

A tremor seized her legs. Anchoring her to him...to the moment, she folded her legs around his hips, riding out her climax. Using the momentum of her legs, she drew him deeper into her, quickening the chase of his own release.

"Fuck," he grunted, pumping harder.

Those calm ocean eyes raged with desire. His movement grew unfocused and frantic. His fingers bit into her hips. His jaw clenched.

Never had she felt so sexy. She was almost drunk in the knowledge that he was losing himself in her.

He shuddered in release with a string of unintelligible curse words. Still panting, he collapsed onto her. His weight atop her was the coziest of blankets. Nat ran her fingers down his damp spine, listening to the slowing of his breath.

After a few quiet moments, he lifted his head. "Thank you." Their eyes held each other's stare. "Thank you for accepting me."

"Thank you for letting me." She pressed her lips to his sweat-kissed forehead.

CHAPTER SEVENTEEN

"Well, I am happy, and I won't fear, but it does seem as if the more one gets the more one wants." ~Louisa May Alcott, *Little Women*

The aroma of freshly brewed coffee filled Nat's nostrils, coaxing her awake. Still satiated from last night's sex and post-orgasm snuggles with Noah, she rolled over in bed, star-fishing her limbs. They lay intertwined for most of the night. She'd occasionally wake, feel the stroke of his hand along her back or the press of his lips against the corners of her mouth. At some point, she drifted off completely, and he'd disappeared, but his scent still lingered in the sheets and all over her.

As the fragrance of vanilla wafted into the quiet sleeping loft, a giant smile bloomed on her face. "Breakfast!" she cheered, grabbing her robe and heading down.

She didn't stroll, skip, or pad down the stairs. Reminiscent of a child on Christmas morning, she bounded down the stairs toward the six-foot-one Noah-shaped present ready for her to unwrap.

The back of her mind nagged that this wasn't real. That the beyond its expiration date yogurt she'd eaten on Friday had put her in a delusional state over the last twenty-four hours. That any minute, she'd wake up in a bed like a character from a bad eighties TV show and find out it was all a dream.

Noah stood in the kitchen, actually stood there, belying her niggling worry. Sunshine haloed his dark hair as if he were a god from Mount Olympus whose sole purpose was to give her orgasms and feed her.

"So, is this like your thing?" She motioned to the bowl of strawberries and a plate of fluffy pancakes on the kitchen island. "You sex me up, feed me, and then repeat?" She leaned on the counter, resting her elbows against its smooth surface. "I'm not complaining, mind you."

The corners of his lips quirked in a beguiling smile. "Well, I need to keep your strength up."

An oversize grin invaded every inch of her body. Even her toes were smiling. "Sounds like someone has plans."

He leaned across the counter, hovering his lips inches from hers. "Yes, to feed you. Go sit, and I'll make you a plate."

"Tease." Pressing a chaste peck on his lips, she jumped away from the counter and went to the table.

"Almond granola pancakes, fresh berries, and…" He drizzled syrup from a glass bottle atop the two large pancakes. "…hot maple syrup." He placed the plate on the table.

"This looks *so* good, but I don't know if I'm going to be able to finish this all. These pancakes are as big as Fitz," she teased.

"That's for us to share." He placed a carafe of coffee on the table beside a small jug of orange juice. Scooting the chair from the opposite side of the table alongside her, he sat.

"Well, sharing is caring." She forked up a bite and held it out for him to take.

"Yep." He took the bite, licking excess syrup from the corners of his lips.

Next time, I'm going to lick that off.

Nat's eyes closed in yummy pleasure at the first bite. "Oh, my goddess," she moaned. The perfect blend of sweet pancake, crunchy, salty granola, tart strawberry, and sugary syrup. "I love your mom."

"My mom?" he chuckled, picking up a second fork.

"I know she taught you to cook. I have a vivid memory of Clayton and you in butterfly aprons in the kitchen with your mom and my dad teaching you two how to cook."

"They were insistent we learned how to cook before I left for the Marines and Clayton left for Cornell. Mom and your mother had this whole list of everything we needed to learn to do as teenagers to become good men before we left home. Cooking, laundry, grocery budget, regular volunteering, gardening, household repair, and…"

"What?" Her eyebrow ticked up.

A bashful grin danced across his features. "When we were seventeen, our moms made our dads sit Clayton and me down for the most uncomfortable sex talk of our lives that included both of us having to put condoms on a cucumber, sign attestations about always getting consent, and making sure we knew it was important to focus on pleasing our sexual partners." Pink colored his cheeks as he mentioned the last lesson their fathers had bestowed upon them as teenage boys.

"Clearly, you were an excellent student."

Wicked pride glinted in his eyes.

Nat's heart swelled for their parents. The focus they put on ensuring that they raised good men was overwhelming. It made her proud of her parents, as a daughter, for the men her brothers were and thankful to the Wilsons, as a woman benefiting from their hard work, to shape their son into the good man sitting beside her. Not just the stereotypical traits of a good man, like holding open doors, pulling out chairs, or paying for things, but the thoughtful, kind, patient, and respectful men that Clayton and Noah were…and that Evan had just started being before he'd passed.

Even when Noah kissed her for the first time, he took a beat to ask for her permission. The sex they had was driven by her, although he eagerly rode shotgun to their sexcapades. His focus was on her. Her comfort. Her pleasure. He asked her how she wanted to be touched. Hell, he'd snuck a peek at her notes during Ms. ChaNUT's oral sex workshop and had executed that knowledge expertly.

She speared another piece of pancake. "I love that they talked to you about consent. Mom and Dad did the same thing for me. Plus, before I left for college, Dad invited Sheriff Krueger to come by the house to show me self-defense techniques."

"Most of our friends just got the abstinence talk in high school. I think our parents were ahead of their time with everything." He wiped his mouth. "It is amazing how progressive a man in a bow tie and a man who wears bowling shirts can be." Laugh lines crinkled his eyes.

It may be weird to some people, but Nat was comforted by the idea of *our* parents. In so many ways, the Wilsons were second parents to the Owens siblings and vice versa. Scott, Noah's dad, taught her to parallel park because Mom and Dad were hopeless at it. Maura came to all Nat's track meets if Mom and Dad were stuck at the clinic. Dad always baked Noah's favorite strawberry cream cheese cupcakes for his birthday, and Mom commented on all his social media posts with pink heart emojis.

"That's the dichotomy of our parents. In so many ways, they are uber-progressive and in other ways rather old fashioned." She dragged her fork through the syrup mixed with pancake crumbs and bits of berries. "When did you wake up?"

"Around five a.m." He poured coffee into her white ceramic mug and then refilled his.

"Are you an early riser, or do you just not sleep?"

"I don't sleep a lot," he said, shifting his gaze to the open window.

"Do you not sleep *a lot* because you don't need it…or because you can't?"

She followed his gaze to the sun-dipped world outside. Fat, full maple tree branches swayed in a gentle breeze. The sky was as blue as his eyes.

"I used to sleep," he said, his voice was whispery quiet.

All the questions poked around inside her. Like unwanted guests at a party, they vied for her attention. She wanted to ask. Craved the need to fix whatever kept him awake and shadowed his bright smile.

That's what doctors do. They assess. They diagnose. They fix. But she wasn't his doctor.

She was his…whatever they were. This thing they were doing hadn't yet been labeled, but she knew that whatever she was to him, it wasn't her job to fix him. Even with the heaviness that often weighed on him, he was perfect. Her role in this situation was to support, to listen, to just be there with him. Just as he'd held her and told her, "I got you," she could do the same.

"Until the IED…" she started and stopped.

Noah reached across the table, threading their fingers. "Yes."

The muscles in his face were rigid. That charming smile locked in a firm line. Those eyes were still fixed far away. Not from her, but from himself. What does the man who sees so much see in himself? What keeps him awake?

She could push, but something told her to pull. Pull him away from where he'd just wandered. Back to her. "What are you doing today?"

"I'm going to meet my parents at their place to help them mount a new TV and have lunch. You?"

She beamed. "Crafty stuff. I'm working on a gift for Elle's bridal shower in November."

"Is it the scrapbook that was on the table yesterday?" He motioned to Nat's crafting toolkit on the desk in the living room.

"Yup. I'm designing each page to tell their story."

"I peeked a little when I was putting things back into your kit yesterday. It was pretty amazing. I noticed the dried flowers on many of the pages." There was an apologetic yet impressed lilt to his voice.

"You know how Clayton brings her flowers every Friday? I've snagged one from every arrangement for the last few months. I've pressed them to use on each page. I've snagged other things…little tokens of them as a couple, to decorate the pages."

"They're going to love it. You've always been so creative. My mom gets excited about the homemade gifts you give at the holidays and birthdays."

"Thanks." Her smile grew bigger. Was that even possible at this point?

"So, after crafting any other plans for today?" he drawled with almost a searching tone, like a kid trying to figure out if there'd be chocolate cake for dessert.

"Nope." Her mouth slanted into a knowing grin that there would, indeed, be chocolate cake tonight.

"Would you have dinner with me tonight?" That dimple-popping smile was almost boyish.

"Like dinner here and you'd cook or at your place and you'd also cook? The point being, you cook."

Laughter rumbled in his chest. "We could do that, but I was thinking maybe a real date."

"Like where you pick me up and take me out?"

"I could pick you up around six, and we could drive to Canandaigua. It's close enough for us to get there in under an hour, but far enough away that it's unlikely we'll run into anyone. There's this place with great views of the lake."

"Okay."

It was weird to think that after the last twenty-four hours of kissing, seeing each other naked, and having sex, that going to dinner with Noah would quicken her pulse, but there it was; Nat Owens was going on a date with Noah Wilson.

She'd wait until he left before she squealed as if Henry Cavill knocked on her door. Though, Henry had nothing on Noah.

CHAPTER EIGHTEEN

"I've got the key to my castle in the air, but whether I can unlock the door remains to be seen." ~Louisa May Alcott, *Little Women*

For this date, the old oak wardrobe shimmered with possibility. Nat stood, hands on hips, debating which lovely outfit to select. Tonight, she didn't want a little black dress. She didn't need to call Elle in a panic for fashion advice, nor did she wish to be anyone but herself.

You look beautiful. You're perfect. Noah's words waltzed inside her.

It wasn't his approval. It was simply him seeing her…all of her. His brilliant blue eyes were like mirrors, reflecting her back to herself, reminding her who she was. Something the self-doubt that had crept in over the last few months had attempted to snatch away.

A broad smile beamed as she reached for a blue gingham tulle skirt, white silk camisole, and white cropped cardigan. Dolled up, she stood before the gold-framed mirror, admiring her reflection. The youthful and flirty outfit melded perfectly with the loose waves she styled her hair into. Grabbing a pair of white ballet flats, she headed downstairs.

A confident knock tapped at the door. She bounded down the remaining steps and skipped to the entryway.

"Hey, stranger," she purred, opening the door.

Like a firework explosion, a big smile blasted across his face, bathing every feature in bright happiness. His dimple popped. Those eyes sparkled with tiny crinkles that kissed their edges.

"Hey, gorgeous." He winked.

Not cute, but gorgeous. Smelling salts were needed, stat! The butterflies swooped in her belly.

"Look who's talking." Her eyes dragged down him in appraisal.

Tanned skin peeked out at the vee of his untucked, mint-green button-up shirt. His corded forearms on full display in his short-sleeves, reminding her of how those strong arms held her. Dark jeans wrapped themselves around his muscular legs in the exact same way she wanted to.

He closed the distance between them and kissed her. "I brought you something." He held up a fluorescent pink gift bag.

"You brought me a gift?" Taking the bag, she stepped back and ushered him inside.

"I know it's customary to bring flowers for a first date, but I thought this was more you."

She tilted her head to the right and set the bag on the desk. "Customary? Noah Wilson, are you courting me?"

He grinned. "Perhaps."

Opening the bag, she pulled out something wrapped in glittery silver tissue paper. "Oh my…" Her breath was stolen by a pair of ruby-red ballet flats. The same pair she'd eyed at one of the artisan tables at the farmer's market. *How did he know?*

Noah stepped close again. The scent of pine wafted off him, enveloping her in his aroma. "After we kissed behind the Wine Down and you left, I walked around downtown to clear my head. I wandered past the farmer's market and saw these on one of the tables. They made me think of you."

Her brow creased. "Why?"

"They sparkle." Raising his hand, he caressed her cheek. "Just like you."

"Phew, I thought you were going to say because they are obnoxious and childish."

His brow wrinkled. "Why would you say that?"

She blew out a long breath. "It's something Duncan said about me needing to act the part to be taken seriously. He talked about dressing the part, which made me rethink my entire wardrobe. Well, my entire self." She ran her fingers along the sparkled sequins lining the shoes. "In Boston, I was Dr. Owens. Here I'm Dr. Owens' daughter."

"Why do you have to be one or the other?"

Her lips pursed. "Because people don't take me seriously when they only see me as Dr. Owens' daughter."

"That's bullshit." He raised his right hand as she opened her mouth. "Not what you said nor how you feel, but that people are so narrowminded that they don't see that you can be both. You *can* be both a badass doctor and an amazing daughter. You can wear both a lab coat and sparkly shoes. That you can both be serious and goofy."

Nat nodded. An all-consuming warmth spread through her. Unlike Duncan, Noah didn't tell her to be something she wasn't, to play a part. He didn't tell her to do anything, just talked about the failing of others to see her. In his eyes she wasn't a square peg that needed to be cut and sanded to fit into a round hole. To him, it wasn't about her changing to fit, but them making space for her as she was.

"I don't see why you have to deny who you are to be what you are," he said, skating the pads of his fingers across her hands clenched around the ballet flats.

Her eyes shifted to the shoes. "I like who I am."

"I like who you are too…very much." He rested his hands on her waist.

In Noah's presence, she was perfect and could face any storm, but she knew once away from this little bubble they'd created those self-doubts would re-emerge. They had been so loud since coming home. She just needed to learn how to drown them out on her own.

"How do I get people to take me seriously, though?" It was one thing to embrace who she was but another thing to get others to do the same.

"By being who you are…who you really are. Not what other people expect you to be. Not some pretend role that fucking Duncan thinks you should play." His nostrils flared.

"Fuck them." She smiled, repeating his words from the previous week.

It wasn't just his belief in her that bolstered her but the reminder of who she was…of who she'd been before coming home. In Boston, Nat had tapped into her feisty and some-times goofy core self. Seedlings of her take-no-prisoners spunkiness had blossomed in undergrad and medical school. Evan used to tease her it was her bratty little sister power. Then, he'd wrap his arms around her shoulders, telling her it was just that she was a badass and that she should never forget it.

"Damn right… Fuck them." Noah dipped his head, sealing his mouth to hers.

After a thorough kissing session, Nat slipped on the ruby-red shoes. After all, gifts this cute were meant to be worn. Linking their fingers, they left for their date.

For the next forty minutes, she settled fully into just being with Noah. Between effortless conversation and his periodic squeezes of her knee from across the console, the daydream quality of being with him dissolved to a rightness. As they walked into Zambito's, an Italian restaurant nestled against the lakeshore, her hand rested so nicely in his like it was always meant to be there.

The hostess led them to a large wraparound deck. Olive trees in red clay pots lined the white lattice fence bordering the outdoor dining area. Dark walnut tables, bedecked with a single white lily, offered a perfect view of Lake Canandaigua's calm waters. String lights crisscrossed the above lattice awning, and Nat knew they'd be magical once they turned on at dusk. A soft orangey-purple hue crawled across the sky, whispering the coming of sunset.

"This place is adorable," she gushed, taking her seat as Noah held her chair out for her.

"I take zero credit," he chuckled, pushing in her chair.

"I'll take all the credit," the hostess boasted, handing Nat a menu. "Speaking of adorable, those shoes are on point." She gestured to Nat's feet.

"They were a gift." Nat kicked her right leg out, wiggling her foot in the sassy shoe. It wasn't that the shoes had been a gift from Noah, but what they represented. The petite ruby red shoe covered in sparkles was unapologetically Nat. At least who she wanted to be...to be her again. To let go of the self-doubt that had slithered in since coming home.

"Now, *that* I can take credit for." A playful smugness curved his lips.

"A man who gives cute shoes like that as a gift is a keeper!" The hostess winked, snapping her fingers.

"He also cooks." Nat grinned, winking back at the hostess.

"Now, you're just being boastful," the hostess teased. "Your server will be by shortly."

Nat leaned over the table, whispering, "Imagine if I told her about the multiple orgasms you give."

A ruddy flush crawled up his neck. "Speaking of telling

people things…" His mouth closed as if considering his next words. "I spoke to Todd."

Todd. She leaned back. In the haze of the little Noah/Nat bubble she'd lived in over the last twenty-four hours, she'd forgotten that Todd had caught them kissing. Well, more like he'd caught them making out like a pair of horny teenagers.

"The guy is a vault. For as much shit as he gives me, he's loyal. He'll say nothing. Although, he did threaten to kick my ass if I fuck this up," Noah explained.

She shouldn't smile when someone she cared about was threatened, but Nat did. It was weirdly heartwarming how Todd had both their backs. Of course he'd keep their secret. Above all he was a good friend to Noah. He'd also been good to Nat. That cocksure confidence that radiated off Todd reminded her of Evan and endeared the sometimes surly brewmaster to her.

"Since Todd knows," he continued. "I wanted to let you know if you wanted to tell Summer, I am okay with that. I know we want to wait to tell people, but I want you to have someone to talk to about us. I know you like to craft things out, but I also know Summer has become one of your closest friends. I like the idea of you having someone to talk to if you want it."

Noah's thoughtfulness was like sinking into a hot bubble bath. The calming steam enfolded around her. The catalog of the last week and the many years of Noah in her life flipped to how those watchful eyes not just saw but anticipated.

"You really do see me, don't you?"

"You can't help but see what sparkles."

Heart thumping, she picked up the silverware setting, unwrapped the red cloth napkin, and tossed it at him. "That was cheesy."

Catching the napkin, he smirked. "You *loved* it."

She did. She fucking did.

CHAPTER NINETEEN

"Seldom except in books do the dying utter memorable words...."
~Louisa May Alcott, *Little Women*

There'd be no *maybe* expired yogurt consumed while charting today. The smell of leftover vegetarian lasagna from Saturday filled Nat's office. Between bites of the cheesy pasta, she waged an internal debate on whether Noah was better at cooking or sexing her until her toes curled...it was a tie, and as she completed paperwork requests for patients, she reveled in being her again. After waking up this morning to find Noah brewing coffee and making avocado toast in her kitchen, she'd resolved to wear her new red shoes. Paired with a navy pinstripe pencil skirt and red blouse, she was embracing both Dr. Owens and Nat.

Why deny who you are to be what you are? Noah's words from last night hummed within her.

"That smells delicious." Mom appeared at the open office door, inhaling deeply. "Did Elle and Clayton leave you food for the week?"

Nat swiveled to face her mom. "Uh..." Her mouth closed as soon as it opened.

She'd almost said Noah made it for me, but then that may or may not lead to more questions. Clayton had asked Noah to check in on her. It wouldn't be out of character for him to drop dinner off. Everyone knew the pinnacle of Nat's culinary expertise was ordering takeout or making almost burnt frozen pizza. But what if Mom used her maternal superpowers and sniffed out that this wasn't regular lasagna, but sex lasagna?

Ah! You've been quiet too long!

"Zambito's," she blurted.

Eyebrows knitted, her mom's head tilted. "Zambito's?"

"It's a place on Lake Canandaigua. It's Italian. I went there for dinner last night… By myself. Solo date," she sputtered.

"Not with Duncan?"

She made a disgusted noise to cover her discomfort with the conversation. This was Mom. Lying to her had never been easy. At least this was true. "I'm not seeing him ever again."

"Well, I'm glad you came to that conclusion yourself. I never liked Duncan. He had a weak handshake," Mom said, combing her fingers through her long silvery-blonde strands.

Unlike Nat, everything about Mom was long and lean. If Nat was built like a compact car, then Mom was a stretch limo. Like Dad and Clayton, she was tall but with a slender frame. Silver shimmered along her blondish strands that hung loose past her shoulders. A regal approachability oozed from her mom. At sixty-two, she was still one of the most beautiful women in any room.

"Clayton and Evan didn't care for him either," she said.

"Yup." Mom's jaw clenched, and her gray eyes lifted to the fluorescent ceiling lights.

Nat fiddled with the hem of her skirt. "Ev…" she stopped.

Her stare zeroed in on the fingers of Mom's right hand pulling at the cuticles of her left. An image of nails bitten past the quick and ragged red cuticles flashed in her vision. They never talked about Evan, especially with Mom. Why had she mentioned him?

"Everything at Zambito's is good. Dad and you should go on a date night." She reached for a distraction from the ghost of Evan swirling between them.

Mom's gaze flicked to the picture frames on Nat's desk. That gaze narrowed in on the one from Nat's eighteenth birthday, the last "Complete Owens Family" picture with Evan.

"Mrs. Owens." LeAnne appeared at the door, her dark brows linked in frustration. "I'm having issues with one of the insurance companies. Can you come work your magic?"

"Of course," Mom said, tearing her gaze from the photo and shifting away with LeAnne.

Nat picked up the picture and stared at it. The last captured moment of all of them. The last time when mentioning Evan's name didn't send Mom into a tailspin. Opening her top drawer, she slid the picture inside and with a sigh shut the drawer.

CHAPTER TWENTY

*"I don't pretend to be wise, but I am observing, and I see a great deal more than you'd imagine." ~*Louisa May Alcott, *Little Women*

"**T**his sex lasagna is pretty tasty," Summer teased, pitching her voice in a low, seductive tone.

"There are *multiple* layers." Nat winked, not being the least bit embarrassed by the teasing from her friend, with whom she'd shared the entire story the moment she walked into the Little Red Barn.

Both were too tired from long workdays to venture far for their dinner date. Nat reheated the leftover lasagna, while Summer brought a salad and a piece of chocolate peanut butter pie to share from the café.

"God, I miss *multiple* layers," Summer whined with the fury of a five-year-old forced to eat spinach.

"I'm sure Todd would offer to assist you with that."

Summer kicked Nat's calf. The two sat on the couch, bare feet up on the coffee table and plates balanced on their laps.

"He's *so* into you." Nat pointed her fork at Summer. "He's

got that whole sexy Prince Harry thing going on. Is it because he's a ginger? Are you a gingeriest?"

"The only man in my life is Liam." She waved her off. "So, will Stud Muffin be coming over tonight?"

"We didn't plan on it." Nat sat up, placing the plate on the coffee table before her and shifting her legs underneath her.

"You mean you're *not* taking full advantage of this little love nest for the next five and a half days before Clayton and Elle come home?"

Face scrunched, Nat's head tilted to the right. "Fair point."

"So, I know this is a secret, but why? Clayton doesn't seem the unreasonable type." She forked her last bite of pasta.

"You've not experienced him when I have a boyfriend. He's never liked any of them."

"Well, after meeting Duncan, I can understand."

It was beneath a very mature doctor, but Nat pinched her side.

"Asshole," Summer giggled.

"They weren't *all* like Duncan. I only had two other boyfriends. One in college for two years and one in the first year of medical school. They were nice guys, just not..."

"Noah," Summer finished the sentence, her expression smug.

"Fuck," Nat gasped. "Duncan said I never gave him a chance."

"That's because he's a dick."

"True, but the other two boyfriends I dated said the same thing. They both complained that I always had one foot out of the relationship."

"That's because you're in love with Noah. It's hard to give your heart away when it already belongs to someone else." Summer shifted, placing her empty plate on the table and sitting crossed leg.

"That's ridiculous. I'm not in love with Noah. I know I can be a little fanciful at times but I'm not naïve enough to think I fell in love with him. Yes, I care about him. I've crushed on him for far longer than is appropriate outside of a Brontë novel, but I'm not in love with him. I mean, we only just started seeing each other."

Summer gave her a "Sure, tell yourself that" look.

"Fine, if I'm in love with Noah, then you admit that you like Todd," Nat said in a tone equivalent to a three-year-old sticking their tongue out.

Summer narrowed her chocolaty eyes. "Back to my original point. I don't think Clayton will be angry. It may be an adjustment, but he already knows what a great guy Noah is. Also, I think your parents would be happy. Everybody loves him. Liam is very picky with new people and he took to Noah like a fish to water."

"It's complicated."

If you only knew how complicated. Eyes closed, the memories blew through her like a howling wind. Each swirled and nipped with the icy breath of regret. Tension shivered down her spine and sputtered across each muscle.

Summer linked their fingers. "I'm a good listener."

"I…"

It was as if she'd forgotten how to speak. The story was there, but the words couldn't or wouldn't form. There's such a thin line between couldn't and wouldn't.

Summer squeezed her hand. "When you're ready, I'm here."

She leaned her head on Summer's shoulder. "And when you're ready to admit you're hot for the Prince Harry of Perry, I'm here."

"Asshole." Summer chuckled, wrapping her arm around Nat.

CHAPTER TWENTY-ONE

*"Watch and pray, dear, never get tired of trying, and never think it is impossible to conquer your faults." ~*Louisa May Alcott, *Little Women*

Three days in a row with breakfast made by a very sexy man. Nat could get used to this. Perched on the kitchen island, her short legs dangling, she watched as Noah made them vegetarian breakfast burritos. After Summer left last night, she'd exchanged a series of flirty texts with Noah that resulted in him arriving and bending her over the desk in the living room.

He'd slept over again, but she'd woken up alone. When she woke, she knew he wasn't gone. Nonetheless, the loss of his arms chilled her.

"This is nice." She sighed.

"Agreed." His lips lifted, forming happy crinkles about his eyes.

"I'd like to propose something," she said, taking the plate he handed her.

"Okay." He leaned against the counter beside her.

"Clayton and Elle return Saturday afternoon, which may make these sleepovers challenging."

Noah nodded.

"I say we take advantage of this time, and you sleep here for the rest of the week. It will give us more time to settle into this and figure out the next steps."

"You mean you just want a week of uninterrupted orgasms and homecooked food." A wicked gleam sparked in his eyes.

"I wouldn't be the only one benefiting."

Noah arched an eyebrow.

"I mean, you'd have the pleasure of providing said orgasms and homecooked food."

"Your benevolence knows no boundaries," he deadpanned.

"Oh." She placed her plate on the counter behind her and jumped to the floor. Moving in front of him, she took his plate and set it aside. "I can be very benevolent." Her voice was a husky whisper as she popped the top button of his jeans and dragged the zipper down.

His pupils dilated, and his breath grew ragged.

Wicked mischief swirled in her, curling her lips into a seductive smile. She lowered to her knees, pulling down his jeans and boxer briefs. Her hands grazed up the muscles of his legs to his growing arousal, wrapping her hand around it.

"Let me show you how benevolent I can be," she purred, pumping him twice with her hand.

"So fucking benevolent." A throaty groan escaped Noah with her first slow lick up his length.

An hour later, they kissed goodbye. Noah headed to the bakery, and she drove to the clinic. Two orgasms really were the breakfast of champions. With an extra sated pep in her step, she glided through the clinic, her ruby red ballet flats paired with a white pencil skirt and red blouse.

"You seem extra chipper this morning," Mom said, meeting Nat at the reception desk after she'd said goodbye to her patient.

"I had a good workout this morning." Breathiness shook her voice as she recalled this morning's *workout*.

The tug of Noah's long fingers into her hair while she wrapped her lips around his cock and undid him. The loss of his measured control when he pulled her from her knees and took her against the fridge. His deepening thrusts driving her into bliss. All while whispering that she was fucking perfect.

"You look flushed. Are you feeling okay?" Mom stepped closer; her brows knitted together in assessment.

"I'm fine. It's warm in here today."

"Are you sure?" She placed her palm on Nat's forehead.

"If only there were someone in this room with a medical degree to assess if someone is fine...oh wait, there is," Nat sassed, batting her away.

"I'm still your mother," she *tsked*.

"Is Dr. Owens here?" A voice cleared.

Nat turned to find Mrs. Lewis at the counter being greeted by LeAnne.

"Sorry, Dr. Owens is at the hospital doing rounds and hasn't returned yet," LeAnne explained.

"Will he be back soon?" Annoyance creased Mrs. Lewis's wrinkled face.

Nat opened the half door and stepped into the patient check-in area. "Hello, Mrs. Lewis. May I assist you?"

Mrs. Lewis's brown eyes narrowed. Her judgy gaze swept down Nat, reaching the ballet flats. Her lips pursed. "I'll wait for Dr. Owens."

Nat sucked in a breath. "Mrs. Lewis, I am Dr. Owens."

"I want the *real* Doc—"

"I am a real doctor," Nat sniped through clenched teeth.

Mrs. Lewis bristled. Her features fixed into a disapproving frown.

Nat waved her hands. "I know…I know…my father."

"Mrs. Lewis." Mom beamed a warm smile at the cranky woman as she stepped beside Nat. "So lovely to see you. Chris will be back from the hospital any minute now. Would you like to have a seat? I'll have LeAnne bring you a cup of tea?"

Mrs. Lewis's expression softened. "Some of that delicious lavender tea?"

"Of course," she said, escorting the older woman to a seat in the waiting room.

Nat balled up her fists and shoved them in her lab coat pocket. *I am Dr. Owens. I am Dr. Owens. Don't slap Mrs. Lewis!*

"Dr. Owens," Dad greeted her as he walked into the clinic. His blue eyes shimmered with playful pride.

She frowned. "Hey, how was the hospital?" Her voice was soft, like a delicate sheet of parchment that could easily be torn.

"Good. Mrs. Jarvis and the baby are doing well." His warm stare focused on her. "Are you okay?"

"Mrs. Lewis is here." She motioned to where Mrs. Lewis sat with an oversized tan leather purse in her lap, waiting for her cup of tea. "She wants you…the real Dr. Owens."

His grin flattened. "Natalie…" His eyes flicked to Mrs. Lewis and back to her. "…it will take time, but it will get better. I promise."

With a tender squeeze of her shoulder, he turned and walked to Mrs. Lewis. Nat stood, watching Mrs. Lewis light up with his approach.

"Oh, thank goodness Dr. Owens is back." LeAnne let out a long breath as she shuffled past with a cup of tea.

Nat dug her fingernails into her palms, pivoted, and walked away.

CHAPTER TWENTY-TWO

"When we make little sacrifices, we like to have them appreciated, at least." ~Louisa May Alcott, *Little Women*

The crafting Zen cocooned Nat. She sat, crossed-legged, in front of the coffee table, scrapbooking supplies sprawled over the surface. The rainbow bedazzled crafting kit sat beside her like a trusty sidekick on all her adventures. In so many ways, it was. It was with her each time the swirl of feelings and thoughts rippled through her like a frenzied storm.

She lost herself in it. The sound of paper being cut replaced the echoed voice of Mrs. Lewis's *the real Dr. Owens.* The squish of cardstock placed on hot glue replaced LeAnne's sigh of *Thank goodness, Dr. Owens is back.* The sensation of stray glitter clinging to her fingertips could not replace the truth.

I am not Dr. Owens.

Tears stung in her eyes. Even crafty time lacked the power to erase the truth. The attempt to blink away the tears failed. Each salty droplet taunted her.

"Hey." Noah's soft baritone filtered into the room.

Nat looked up. Through tear-fuzzed vision, she saw him standing at the open door, takeout from Daryl's Pizzeria in hand, concern sketched on his face.

Placing the takeout on the desk by the front window, he moved to her. "What's wrong?" He lowered, sitting next to her.

"I'm not Dr. Owens," she whimpered, falling into his waiting arms.

She offered no words, just tears. Noah held her tight, rubbing soothing circles along her back. He offered no whispered commands to "Don't cry" or "None of that." Just like that morning at the park, he embraced her sadness. She buried herself in his open arms.

"I'm here." He pressed a gentle kiss against her temple.

As her tears ceased, she remained nestled in his embrace. The quiet evening enveloped them, freeing her to let this go into its secret darkness. The sun that once streamed in from the open windows was swallowed by the velvet night. In the light, she'd smile, but here in the shadows of the dimly lit room and safety of his arms, she'd let the sadness out. If only for a moment.

"I'm sorry," she whispered.

"Why?"

She sat up, dashing away the tears with her hands. "Ugh," she groaned, pulling her hands away and noticing the pieces of glitter on her fingertips that were no doubt all over her face. "I'm a mess."

Noah cupped her cheeks, and the warmth of his palms cascaded through her body. "You're my beautiful mess. What happened?"

"They don't take me seriously at the clinic…the patients… the staff. They always ask for my dad. When I give directions, the staff say, 'Let me check with Dr. Owens' because I'm *not* Dr. Owens…I'm just his daughter."

"What do your parents say about it?"

Nat closed her eyes. "They're part of the problem." The quiet response was almost drowned out by the chorus of crickets chirping outside the open window.

It was the first time she said it out loud. In so many ways, her parents' words and actions told her over and over again that she was just Natalie, their daughter, and not Dr. Nat Owens, their colleague.

"Have you talked to them?" His right hand moved to her hand, intertwining their fingers.

"No," She sighed and looked away. "I don't want to upset them. They've been through enough."

Because of me. A hard lump choked in her throat.

Noah guided their threaded fingers to his lips, kissing her knuckles. "But what about you? You're upset…you're hurt."

"I'll get over it. It will be fine. It's just a bad day. I'm fine."

"You've had a lot of bad days since coming home," he murmured.

Nat twisted her gaze to him.

That charming smile was fixed in a firm line. Those blue eyes were shaded with a blend of sadness and anger. Not at her but *for* her.

"Your brightness is too special to be darkened by anyone, even by yourself in an effort to spare the feelings of others. It's like when Evan died. When your mom broke down at the calling hours, you stood beside your dad greeting mourners. At the funeral, when Clayton trembled in his chair about giving the eulogy, you turned to me and mouthed *help him.* After the funeral, when grieving friends and family left, you cleaned everything up. I remember sitting on the back porch trying to get a stone-faced Clayton to talk and watching you through the window. Everyone else broke, but you smiled. Even though your heart was broken, it was still big enough to take care of everyone else."

"Noah…" she cleared her throat, not sure of what to say.

He reached for her, scooping her up into his lap and wrapping his arms around her. The gesture seemed a little for him as much as for her. As if they both needed the closeness. Like her bad day was his.

"I just want you to remember that it's okay for that big heart of yours to take care of yourself, not just everyone else." The pads of his fingers glided up and down her spine.

She leaned her head on his shoulder, soaking in his supportive strength. "Okay."

She wanted to say so much but couldn't. All the reasons stacked up inside her, trapping the words.

Instead, she asked, "Noah, can we have sex and eat pizza?"

An unexpected laugh fell out of him. "In which order?"

"Sex first, please." Twisting on his lap, she straddled him, sealing their mouths together. She wanted to feel him…to feel *them* instead of the ache in her chest.

CHAPTER TWENTY-THREE

"Dear me, how happy and good we be, if we had no worries!"
~Louisa May Alcott, *Little Women*

Hallelujah! Six days in a row of waking up sated and breathing in the aroma of freshly brewed coffee. It was the last morning of their undisturbed romantic bubble at the Little Red Barn. Elle and Clayton returned today. Now they'd have to figure out how to see each other when she lived on her brother's property and Noah's house was around the corner from her parents.

"Small towns." Nat sloshed a breath, slipping out of bed.

"Good morning." Noah greeted her with a cup of coffee and a kiss when she walked into the kitchen.

"I see you've been busy this morning." She motioned to the bowl of freshly cut melon and plates of pancakes and vegan sausage on the counter.

Looping his arms around her middle, he pulled her in close. "I also replaced your expired yogurt with fresh ones and picked you up some salads for the week. I don't want you starving without me here to cook for you."

She pouted about that. Tomorrow when she woke, there'd be no Noah in her kitchen. He'd be in his kitchen, and she'd be here eating the yogurt he'd bought her.

"Hey." He dipped his head, capturing her bottom lip in a reassuring kiss. "We'll figure it out. Although, if you want to—"

"Nope," she interrupted, knowing what he was going to suggest. "I still want to keep this between us...for now."

"Alright. We'll work it out." He leaned back, nibbling on his lips. The sudden arch of his eyebrow was reminiscent of a light bulb turning on. "Are you working at the clinic next Saturday?"

"No. It's Dad's week for Saturday clinic."

"I have to go to Syracuse to speak at a rural business conference—"

"What?" Her bounce-filled exclamation cut him off. "That's amazing! You really are the Mark Cuban of Western New York. Will it be videoed? Can I see it?"

A bemused grin flooded his face. "Even better. How would you like to see it in person? We could leave Friday night after you're done at the clinic. Originally, I just planned on going up Friday and coming back Saturday after the conference, but we could come back Sunday. We could go out to dinner. We could—"

"Have dirty hotel sex." She wiggled her hips.

"I'll take that as a yes."

"It's a hell yes." She beamed. "You just gave me an excuse to go shopping after I'm done at the clinic today."

"Speaking of..." His eyes dropped to the microwave clock. "...You have to leave in an hour, which doesn't give me much time to eat."

"That's plenty of..." Her words faltered as he untied her robe, allowing the fluffy fabric to hit the hardwood. Her breath caught. "Oh!"

Noah lifted her, setting her on the edge of the counter. "I need to get my fill. I'll be on a diet for the next six days." He lowered to his knees. The rough pads of his fingers skated along her thighs, guiding her legs open.

"I would never deny you a last meal," she moaned with the first flick of his tongue across her sex.

CHAPTER TWENTY-FOUR

"But like all happiness, it did not last long…" ~Louisa May
Alcott, *Little Women*

Birthdays were always special in the Owens' house. There'd be birthday cupcakes for breakfast. Dad made a special meal. The Wilsons always joined. Mom and Maura had been besties since they were teenagers, so it was not unusual for their birthdays to include both families.

Nat sank onto the plush chair in the sitting room. The old Victorian where she'd grown up featured a front sitting room, where entertaining happened, and a back living room that her parents called the TV room like they were Mr. and Mrs. Brady.

The ladies and Fitz lounged in the front sitting room. The humans sipped wine and munched on the contents of the cheeseboard Elle supplied. The pudgy pug snored on Nat's lap while Lizzie used her big brown puppy eyes to implore her human grandma to drop the piece of cheese she waved in the air as she talked.

"I kind of love that in this family the men are in the

kitchen while the ladies drink wine." Elle grinned, sipping her glass of rosé.

Unlike Nat, the other three women in the room had serious culinary chops. Mom was the queen of the casserole. Maura never met a recipe she couldn't make even better. Elle had some *Great British Bake Off*-level baking skills.

Nat aced her MCATs. She'd carried a 4.0 GPA during undergrad. She could speak Spanish and knew American Sign Language. She was in the top of her class in medical school but not burning the garlic bread and not giving the family food poisoning–*Allegedly*–was beyond her.

"Ladies," Noah drawled as he sauntered into the room with a blue vase of yellow chrysanthemums. "Happy birthday, Heidi." He bent to kiss Mom on the cheek and handed her the flowers.

Nat's heart squeezed at the gesture. As weird as the entanglement of the two families made this situation with Noah, warmth spread at how sweet he was to her parents. He always brought gifts when he came to the house, and not just on special occasions. Dad hadn't shoveled his front walkway or driveway since Noah moved back to Perry. Noah, who lived around the corner from them, woke early after any snow, no matter how tiny the accumulation, and not just shoveled for her parents but salted their walkways.

"Perfect choice of flower for a birthday." Elle tipped her wine glass toward him. "They mean joy and longevity."

"I see all the flower talk with Janet for the wedding is paying off," Maura teased, taking a cracker from the cheeseboard on the coffee table.

As Elle explained all she learned from her florist aunt, Nat watched Noah move around the room. First, he kissed his mom on the cheek. Then moved to Lizzie, scratching her ears. Much like Nat, the pit bull had a crush on him. Within the first few pets, she rolled onto her back, letting him know she was open for all the belly rubs business.

Lizzie melted into his touch, groaning with canine pleasure.

As his hands stroked along her soft underbelly, his blue eyes drifted to Nat. Never had she been so jealous of a dog. Goddess, she wanted to push Lizzie aside and lay there, allowing his magic fingers to have their way with her.

"Natalie, are you okay? You look rosy. I'm worried you're getting sick. You've looked like that most of the week," her mom said.

Nat placed a hand on her heated cheek. "I think it's the wine. Need to eat more."

"Here." Noah grabbed the cheeseboard off the coffee table and held it up to her.

Nat took a piece of gouda with far more sensual slowness than was appropriate. "Thank you." She bit into the cheese, enjoying the slideshow of his throat muscles working and the dilation of his eyes with the languid lick of her tongue across her lips.

"Do you want more?" he murmured, a slight catch in his tone.

Goddess, did she. It was a little more than twenty-four hours since they'd feasted upon each other before saying goodbye.

"I'm saving my appetite for what I really want." She bit her lower lip, tamping down the breathless quality of her voice.

"Noah looks a little flushed, too," Maura said. "Maybe it's too hot in here."

Smirking, Noah placed the cheeseboard back on the table. "I'll be fine, mom." He stood up and dusted off his hands. "Are the guys in the kitchen?"

"Except for Fitz. He's hanging with the ladies." Mom beamed at her sleeping pug grandbaby.

It was looking more likely that the four-legged variety would be the only grandchildren for her parents. At least for now. Elle and Clayton didn't want kids and Nat... Well, she wanted them but wasn't sure if Noah did. That was too soon of a thought to have let alone a conversation to have with him.

"It is a good spot to be in." Noah stared at Fitz where he'd curled up on Nat's lap.

Maybe someone else is jealous of a dog.

He turned toward the entryway. "I should probably go check on them."

"Elle, what do yellow gardenias mean?" Nat asked, stopping Noah's steps.

He twisted, facing her, a lopsided grin kicked across his face.

Their eyes locked, waiting for Elle to share the meaning behind the flowers he'd brought her. The idea of the flowers meaning more than just an apology never dawned on her until he brought flowers symbolizing long life for Mom's birthday. Nat was dying to know not just what they meant but also, if he knew and had picked them specially for her because of that meaning.

Elle clicked her tongue. "They're the flowers for secret crushes or love."

Busted! Her eyebrow arched.

Bashful pride lit his face. Those blue eyes twinkled with playful mirth, like a kid getting caught stealing a cookie. "I'm going to go set the table since the other guys are cooking. Nat, you want to help?"

"Sure. Mom, you want the pudge monster?" Nat lifted a now perturbed Fitz.

"Don't fat shame my grandbaby," she cooed, taking Fitz, who nuzzled into her chest.

"Wash your hands. You've both been petting the dogs," Maura called as they started to walk away.

Noah shook his head and rolled his eyes, mouthing *moms*. His mom hadn't stopped mothering him just because he was thirty-eight. Just another thing Nat and he had in common.

"Use the upstairs bathroom. The one downstairs is out of commission until the plumber comes tomorrow," Mom shouted.

They ran up the steps to the bathroom. As soon as she slipped inside, he peeked down the stairs and ducked in after her. Keeping the door ajar to listen for footsteps, he pulled her into his arms.

"This is torture," he breathed. "When I walked in, all I wanted to do was kiss you."

She raised to her tiptoes, encircling the nape of his neck. "I was thinking *very* naughty things when you were petting Lizzie."

His mouth quirked. "Yeah?" Those lips of his found hers in a savoring kiss.

Movement from downstairs halted their kisses.

Noah poked his head out the door. "It's Lizzie," he said, the tight muscles in his jaw relaxing.

Seconds later, the pit bull bounded into the small room. Her long tail slapped against the door frame and Noah as she pushed into the bathroom.

"Looks like your Owens ladies' fan club is all present."

"Ha!" he laughed, turning on the faucet for them to wash their hands.

"So, secret crush flowers?" She hip-checked him, lathering the lavender-scented soap on her hands.

"I told you I've wanted to kiss you for a long time. I've wanted you...this..." he motioned between them with his wet, foamy hands. "...for a while. I know we're still figuring this out, but whatever is happening between us, I want you to know that I'm in this."

Her pulse ticked up.

He was in this. Whatever this was, he was in it. Noah's assurances offered a promise for more. For the dream of the shared meals from last week, watching him cook in her kitchen, going to bed together, hands clasped as they walked into restaurants, Noah holding her when she was sad or happy, and so much more could be their lives.

"I thought you said Noah was here." Clayton's voice crept upstairs, bursting their bubble.

"They're washing their hands before setting the table," Mom shouted from the living room.

"Why are they upstairs?"

"The downstairs bathroom is out of order."

"What? It's not—"

"Keep your pants on," Noah yelled down the stairs, cutting Clayton off. "I had to wash my hands again, because Lizzie found me and demanded more pets." He glanced down at the dog, who tilted a pouting face up at him, having not received the aforementioned additional pets. "I'll sneak you a piece of turkey if you play along," he whispered to her.

After washing their hands and sharing one last kiss, they headed back down.

Clayton stole Noah for some secret groom/best man conversation. Nat and Elle set the table.

Each year for Mom's birthday, Dad did a Thanksgiving-themed dinner. It was Mom's favorite holiday. Plus, he liked the idea of a day dedicated to things he was thankful for being the theme for celebrating his wife.

Grandma Owens' antique lace tablecloth was draped over the table laden with the mini feast. Savory scents mingled with the floral aroma of the chrysanthemums now located on the sideboard. Light flickered from two long white candles flanking the platter of freshly carved turkey.

Their seats weren't assigned but each family dinner they sat in the same spots. Noah, Maura, and Scott sat on one side of the eight-person table, with Nat, Elle, and Clayton on the other side. Her parents sat at the opposite ends of the oval-shaped table.

Noah sat, his jaw clicking. His eyes flipped to the cooked meat at the center of the table and then to Nat, who stood holding a giant bowl of butternut squash. Instead of placing it at her side, she switched it with the bowl of cornbread and sausage dressing.

It wouldn't make much of a difference, but the idea of Noah being assaulted by the smell of cooked meat was too much to bear. She rearranged the table, moving anything not containing meat to where Noah sat and moving the meat dishes away from him.

"Nat, what are you doing?" Dad asked, forehead puckered in puzzlement.

"I like this configuration better. It separates it into food groups. Veggies. Meats. Carbs." She motioned around the table.

Elle beamed. "Love it! I'll be avoiding that section." She pointed to the carbs located near Dad's end of the table. "I have a wedding dress to fit in to."

Nat felt a brief brush against her leg from beneath the table where she stood.

Noah looked up with a thankful smile.

"This smells amazing!" Mom gushed, strolling into the dining room, followed by Noah's parents and Clayton.

Nat stepped away from Noah and took her regular seat directly across from him. Dinner was delicious. As always, Dad threw it down in the kitchen.

"So, Nat, are you keeping your dad on his toes at the clinic?" Scott asked, spooning up a bite of mashed potatoes.

"She sure is." Dad smiled.

Nat shrugged. "More like I'm riding his coattails." It came out snarkier than she intended.

"Hardly. That electronic charting system and tablet process you had us implement in July has saved us so much time." He placed his warm palm atop her hand. "She's helped us innovate."

"Good. You'll be able to join us in retirement soon. Then we can plan that European cruise the four of us have talked about going on for years." Scott pointed at Dad with his spoon.

"I don't know about retirement yet. Not at least for another year or so," Mom said, then sipped her red wine.

"Why not?" His face scrunched. "You have Natalie to run the clinic. Plus, you've got the business side running like a well-oiled machine. I'm sure if Natalie needs guidance in that area, Noah can give her some tips."

"We just want to give Natalie time to settle in before we run off." Dad chuckled, patting Nat's hand.

The gesture was less sweet and more like twelve-year-old Nat being told she still needed a babysitter. She cast her gaze down to her plate, picking up her fork, and spearing a piece of squash.

"I think Nat's ready now," Noah said, his tone was resolute.

Nat's eyes shot over to him.

"I mean, it's one thing if you're not ready to retire because you enjoy the work you're doing, but if it's out of concern for Nat…she's got this."

"I second that." Elle raised her glass.

Nat gave them both a small smile.

"That reminds me. Nat, I ran into Laura Ellis at the market last Friday. She mentioned that you and Duncan are seeing each other again." Scott lifted his eyebrows a couple times.

Nat cringed. Scott's waggled eyebrows when he mentioned Duncan deeply disturbed her.

"She mentioned he's an attorney now. A doctor and a lawyer. Imagine if they got married." Scott nudged Dad. "You're hitting the jackpot with who your kids end up with."

"You're dating Duncan? From high school?" Dad blinked rapidly. "When did this start?"

What the actual fuck is happening? Nat's heart raced. Since when had her love life become a topic for dinner conversation?

Noah's jaw clenched. "They're not seeing each other."

"What?" Clayton's head ping-ponged between Noah and Nat.

"We went on a few dates, but we ended things," she offered.

Mom and Maura shot knowing looks between themselves. No doubt, Maura knew but hadn't informed Scott. The dads were always the last to know.

"Aw, Nat." Scott frowned. "If I had known, I wouldn't have brought it up. I am so sorry."

"It's okay. I'm totally fine with it." She hoped her smile was reassuring.

"Duncan's a dick," Noah muttered.

"Language! You're not in the Marines anymore," Maura half-heartedly chastised her son.

"Sorry, Mom." He flashed her an apologetic smile. "Nat's too good for Duncan."

"Agreed. I didn't like it when Elle told me they went out." Clayton picked up his beer. "How'd you know they weren't seeing each other?"

"You told him to check in on Nat, remember?" Elle elbowed him. "Noah takes his job as the Owens family protector seriously."

Noah nodded, his eyes lingering on Nat from across the table.

Stop looking at me like that! They'll notice. Nat crossed and uncrossed her legs. This was far too much attention on her to be comfortable.

"Well, thanks for checking in on Nat." Clayton picked up his fork. "I never liked Duncan."

"You never liked any of her boyfriends," Mom teased.

"It was more than that. There was something about the

guy that Evan really disliked. He didn't trust him. He said…" he stopped speaking, his eyes dropping on Mom.

The white of her knuckles was on full display where she gripped her fork. A tiny tremor wobbled in her hands, tears welled in her eyes, and her lips quivered.

It was like the ghost of Evan had walked into the dining room, and taken a seat at the table, to remind them that he was still there. His presence did not feel like the warmth of a remembered sunny afternoon but the chilled breath of a barren winter night.

The guilty swirl in Nat's belly crept up her throat. Stinging bile threatened to choke her.

"Heidi." Dad opened his mouth but closed it as Clayton started to speak.

"Mom…I'm—"

"Heidi," Noah interrupted, turning to her. "Did I tell you we're launching a new cider in the fall? It's an apple cider aged in a whisky barrel, and we serve it warm."

"That sounds lovely, dear," Mom said, but her voice was laced with a shaky quality, like a baby deer using its legs for the first time.

"Yep, we're calling it the Boss…it's named after you."

Mom turned to him with wide eyes. "Really?"

"We were going to announce it during Fall Fest in September, but since it's your birthday, I wanted to share the good news with you."

Nat's heart swelled.

"Oh, Noah, that is so sweet!" Mom gushed as she rose and walked over and hugged him.

"Way to show us up on the gifts, son." Scott laughed.

After dinner, Nat helped clean the kitchen. It was the only time her help in the kitchen was welcomed. Standing at the sink, she rinsed the plates. Dad brewed coffee and tea while Noah carried dishes into the kitchen. Everyone else sat on the back porch digesting before digging into the birthday cake. The last item was loaded into the dishwasher, and Nat filled the sink for the pots and pans, allowing the hot soapy water to wash over her hands.

"I'm going to take this out," Dad said, carrying the tray with the coffee carafe, teapot, and cups.

"I'll finish the dishes and then bring the cake out." Her stare remained fixed on the gazebo in the backyard.

How often had she sat out there with Evan? Their last conversation took place there.

You're making a mistake. Evan's voice hissed in her ears.

She closed her eyes tight, losing herself in that memory. Her eyes shot open at the gentle touch of a hand around hers in the water. Twisting her head, her eyes met Noah's.

"Are you okay?" he asked, squeezing her hand beneath the sudsy water.

"I...I'm fine."

"Please, don't lie to me." His firm fingers massaged her palm. "We don't have to talk about it...not 'til you're ready, but please don't hide how you're feeling from me. I can't do my job if I don't know how you're really doing." His tender tone coaxed.

"You mean as the Owens family protector?"

"As your..."

Nat's breath stuttered. "My what?"

"Whatever you want to call me...call us...my job is to be there with you. To stand beside you." He nudged her with his elbow. "So, please answer me honestly...are you okay?"

"No." Her voice cracked.

After cake, everyone drifted back to their own homes. Noah and his parents left, then Elle, Clayton, and the puppies. Nat sat with her parents for a bit before jumping into her Jeep to head home.

She drove toward the Little Red Barn. Across the yard, Clayton's pickup was parked in the driveway. Instead of slowing down to turn into the driveway, she drove past, made a U-turn, and headed back to town. Like iron filings to a magnet, she was pulled back to Noah.

Parking her recognizable yellow vehicle was problematic. It never seemed obnoxious until she was trying to sneak around with Noah. Again, she drove past her destination.

The park didn't close until eleven, and it was only eight, so she drove in and parked by the tennis courts. The sky darkened with sunset, but the park was still full of families playing and softball teams practicing. She walked through the greenspace toward Noah's house.

Walking up the steps of the blue Victorian, her rapid intake and exhale kept cadence with each step. She stood, tugging the hem of her dress. Holding her breath, she knocked.

Noah opened the door. Changed out of the button-up and jeans from dinner, he wore a fitted grey T-shirt and black track pants. His feet were bare.

"God, I hoped you'd show up," he murmured, reaching out and pulling her into him.

Collapsing against his firm chest, she croaked. "Evan's dead because of me."

CHAPTER TWENTY-FIVE

"I am not afraid of storms, for I am learning how to sail my ship."
~Louisa May Alcott, *Little Women*

The words fell out and they couldn't be put back in.

"It's my fault. Evan is dead because of me." Like a record on repeat, it just kept coming out of Nat, along with her tears.

For ten years, she'd held onto this secret. For ten years, guilt had been her constant companion, a noxious swirl in her stomach threatening to choke her.

Noah drew her into the house and closed the door. Keeping her tucked into his chest, he guided her to the couch and then down onto the cushions. He squeezed in right next to her, never withdrawing his arm, or his hand, or his concern.

With quiet patience, he held her, not asking...not demanding more.

Nat twisted her gaze away from his watchful eyes. It was too much to look at him as she confessed. "The night Evan died, we were supposed to go on a run together. We had planned it earlier in the day but..."

He linked their hands and squeezed gently coaxing her to continue.

"Before we went, we got in a fight. Duncan was pressuring me to go to NYU with him, instead of Boston College. I told Evan I was thinking about it. He said I was making a huge mistake… He was right." The words were a quiet croak.

She focused on a watercolor painting of an elderly couple in a rowboat hung on the wall. The man's blue eyes, rimmed in happy crinkles, looked at a silver-haired woman. Their joined hands clasped around the oar, working in tandem to row the boat. The picture could be of her mom and dad, or even a glimpse into a future that she worried was too soon to wish for.

You're not that rainbow-sprinkled single scoop any more.

She swallowed hard. "I told him I didn't want to run with him. I called him a jerk. That was the last thing I said to him. Then he died, and it was my fault."

"Nat, it was an accident."

"It wouldn't have happened if I had been with him."

Noah cupped her chin, turning her to face him, his eyes the color of a stormy sea. "If you had been with him, the truck would have hit both of you."

"He *never* ran on the country roads when I was with him. If I had gone, we would have been at the park. Evan would be alive. He'd be here. We'd have the complete Owens family instead of the one I broke. I broke them…I broke us." Hot tears coursed down her cheeks.

"It was an accident, baby…a terrible fucking accident." His strong arms held her as if they'd never let her go.

As if her confession changed nothing in his eyes. As if she was still special. Still perfect.

Burying herself in his embrace, the tears raged. Each tick of the last precious moments with Evan salted every tear. The regret in his eyes. His usually carefree smile just a firm disappointed line. The frustrated tug of his strawberry-blond hair. The exasperated rasped mutter for her to be reasonable. The knock on her door that she'd ignored, knowing it was him.

"I've got you," Noah soothed, running his hands along her spine.

Raising her head, her eyes met his. His stare crawled into her. Seeming to not look *at* her but *into* her.

Closing her eyes, she buried her face against his chest once more, finding shelter in his strength. It felt like days later, but it was only moments when the storm of tears tapered to a mere drizzle. She remained pressed tight to him. The front of his soft T-shirt was damp from her emotional torrent.

"I'm sorry I used your T-shirt as a tissue…again," she sniffled, her voice muffled in his embrace.

His hand swept soothing strokes up and down her back. "That's why I buy such soft T-shirts. They make the best tissues."

She met his gaze. "What do you see when you look at me now?"

Over the last few weeks, she'd seen glimpses of how she looked in his eyes. *You're perfect.* His words whispered to her fearful heart. How would she look to him now that he knew the truth about her? About what she'd done. About who she was. She wasn't who he thought…who anyone thought…she was. She wasn't a good daughter. She was the destroyer, not the caregiver. She was an imposter.

"You're still my Nat… My perfect Nat." Sincerity glimmered in his gaze.

"But—"

The press of his lips stole her protest.

Nat didn't fight it. Pushing away the voices telling her to stop, the voices hissing that she didn't deserve this. Her arms encircled his neck and she melted into their hungry kisses.

Emotions collided in a riot within her; sadness, anger, self-loathing, belonging, desire. And above all else, something she was not yet willing to name fought for control. Once you name something you own it. It was too soon to own that emotion. So much swirled within her.

"I need you… Please."

He stood up and scooped her into his arms, carrying her upstairs. Their mouths locked in devouring kisses with each step. Noah laid her upon the wine-red bedspread. The satiny softness cushioned her. Crawling over her, his ravenous mouth pressed kisses everywhere. Her mouth. Neck. Collarbones. Breasts. And down her torso over the smooth fabric of her sundress.

Strong hands glided up her thighs, pushing up her dress until it bunched at her waist. Like an acolyte worshipping her, he placed a soft kiss over the lacy fabric of her panties. The touch of his lips scorched through the thin barrier.

All she wanted was to get lost in this. In the touch of him…of them. Drowning in the ocean of them, warm waters lapping over her to wash away all other thoughts or feelings.

Impatience crested and she pushed him away. Pulling the sundress over her head, she tossed it to the carpeted floor. Noah followed her lead, yanking off his T-shirt. Then, she unclasped her bra and pulled off her own panties. He stood, shoving his track pants and underwear off. This felt like a race, where both of them panted toward the naked finish line.

No preamble. No slow seduction. Just a need for connection. To have the only sensation inside her be him. Rising to her knees, she pushed him onto his back. She crawled on top of him and notched his tip at her entrance.

As she sank onto his firm shaft, every single one of her nerve endings screamed with relief.

"Noah." She uttered his name like a thankful prayer as the delicious twinge of almost-too-full pushed away anything but this. But them.

Noah grasped her waist, rocking her hips in a slow, tantalizing pace. Wantonness surged inside her. She wanted… needed more. The quickening pace of their rhythm built a pleasurable pressure at her core.

"More… I need more," she whimpered her demand.

Wrapping his arms around her waist, Noah flipped them, pressing her into the soft mattress. "I've got you, baby," he growled, thrusting deeper inside her.

"Fuck!" she gasped, combusting with the fire that burned along her veins.

He gripped the backs of her knees, widening her legs and finding an angle that sent an achingly sweet tremor across her entire body. Noah sheathed himself up to the hilt, thrusting more forcefully. Driving her mad with his body.

"Come for me, baby," he grunted, moving his hand just where she needed him.

"Yes!" she cried.

Her sex clenched around him as the first waves of release crashed over her. She was destroyed. Her limbs were almost liquified by the pleasure slamming through her. She clung tight to his shoulders.

The muscles in his back grew rigid. He gritted his teeth. His hands dug into her hips, pumping hard. "Nat," he grunted, slamming into her before his body convulsed with release.

They lay still, panting hard.

When she rolled her head toward him, she found Noah studying her. He caressed her cheek. "You're still perfect to me, baby. The only thing that changed with you telling me about what happened with Evan is that I feel closer to you… something I didn't think was possible."

Nat didn't know how to respond, so she merely lay quietly in his arms.

Pulling out of her, he rolled over onto his back, tucking her under his arm close to his chest.

Eyes closed, she melted into his embrace. Every thought,

feeling, and tension that lingered dissipated in his arms. In the soothing cocoon of silence broken only by the beating of his heart, everything disappeared but him and her.

"When I was in Iraq, one of my closest friends in my unit was this guy named Seth."

Nat traced the outline of his yellowjacket tattoo with her finger. "The surfer from San Diego?"

"Yeah." She opened her eyes to find a tiny smile on his lips. "You remember from my letters?"

"I remember everything you wrote me."

He kissed her forehead. "Seth was supposed to be in the last truck in the convoy with this Navy Corpsman named Martin, who talked nonstop about golf. We'd done rock, paper, scissors, and I let him win. Seth always picked rock. Our CO let us switch vehicles since our jobs within the convoy were identical."

She pressed harder into him, instinct telling her he needed it or, maybe, it was just for herself.

"We ran across a series of IEDs." He swallowed hard. "There were no survivors in the first few vehicles."

"Was this how you were injured?"

He nodded and swallowed hard. "I woke up on the road-side, a searing pain in my leg and the smell of burning…"

Nat placed her hand on his heart. Something pulsed in her to remind him that, at this moment, his heart was safe in her hands. That she was there to carry his story…his pain, just as he'd done for her.

"Martin was there. The Navy Corpsman that nobody wanted to sit by patched us up and got us out of there…those of us who were still alive. Ten of us made it."

"How many…"

"There were thirty in the convoy." He sucked in a deep breath. "I didn't find out about Seth until I was transported from the field hospital to Germany. If I had let him lose…" His voice cracked, and he coughed to cover the emotion. "If

I'd let him lose, he'd have been on that flight to Germany. He'd be alive."

"But you'd be gone." The words flew out of her, almost like a scolding.

Quiet fury boiled inside her. How dare he think that! How dare he even consider a world where he wasn't here?

Noah pressed a hand to her cheek. "Not like that. I don't regret surviving. I don't regret the gift I have to live, but I do feel guilt that my gift came at the expense of someone else."

"You were just helping a friend. There's no way you could have known that would happen."

His fingers traced along her hairline. "Just like you didn't know that would happen to Evan when he left for his run."

"It's not the same...I made a decision that cost him his life." She sat up.

Noah followed, pulling her back into his arms. "So did I. We both made choices. Baby, we both feel guilty for our choices, but we didn't make it happen. I didn't cause the road to be lined with IEDs. You weren't the reason that over-worked truck driver dozed off at the wheel. You didn't make Evan run on the country roads instead of at the park. Evan ran those roads all the time despite your parents telling him not to."

The tears fell again. Tears for Evan. Tears for Noah. For Seth and the nineteen other Marines lost, and the semi-truck driver who had to live with what he'd not meant to do. Tears for her parents and Clayton. Tears for herself.

"Evan loved you so much. Clayton was already a big brother when you were born, but Evan became one because of you. It was like you fulfilled all his dreams. I remember him being so excited to have a little sister. He'd annoy Clayton, saying he would be a better big brother than him."

"He was a really good big brother," she sniffled.

"I know Evan wouldn't want you to blame yourself. I know people say things like that, but I am confident about this because I knew Evan. All he ever wanted for you was for you to be happy. To be all that he knew you could be. All that you are."

Nat swiped away her tears, allowing the memories to wash over her like a cleansing shower. Evan helping her study for the SATs, laughing about how they'd be the Dr. Owens duo of Perry. His twenty-first birthday where he snuck her a hard cider, and they sat in the gazebo after Mom and Dad went to bed, toasting to his first legal drink and her first illegal one. The morning before the accident when Evan tried to teach her how to make pancakes and, of course, she burnt them, so they toasted Pop-tarts and drizzled syrup on them.

"Guilt is a powerful master. It not only keeps us locked in, but when we finally escape, it pulls us back in time and time again," he murmured, skimming his fingers along her back. "I wish I could take the pain away from you so you didn't hurt like this anymore, but I can't...What I can do is share it with you. Let me share your sadness, your struggles, your happiness, your laughter...let me be here with you and for you."

"My warrior," she whispered, pressing her hand on his cheek.

"Your everything." He took her hand, placing it back on his heart.

The cadence of his heartbeat roared like a bass drum, loud and commanding in its declaring beat. The air exited her lungs in a swift jolt. Noah wasn't promising everything, he was offering it. He was offering himself. All of him for her... only for her.

"My everything? So, you're the Swiss Army knife of boyfriends then." Her lips curled in a teasing smile.

"Boyfriend?" His right eyebrow arched.

"Well, it stands to reason that if you are my *everything* that would include boyfriend." She tapped her chin in mock thought. "Personal chef. Snowplow guy in the winter. Giver of orgasms year-round."

Laughter pulsed through him. "Yes. All of those things and much more." He dipped his head, sealing their mouths in a reverent kiss.

"Sorry. Not to be like a teenager handing you a check 'Yes' or 'No' note in study hall, but we are saying that I"–she motioned to herself—"am your girlfriend and you"—she motioned to him—"are my boyfriend. Correct?"

"Yes." He raised his hand as if taking an oath. "I, Noah James Wilson, do solemnly swear that I am the sole boyfriend of Dr. Natalie Joan Owens."

She giggled, "You middle-named us both."

"I take this being your boyfriend thing very seriously." He snuggled her closer. "Next question: are we telling people we are boyfriend/girlfriend?" His nose scrunched. "Now I sound like a teenager."

Nat bit her lip. Hesitation tiptoed inside her. Dating Noah wasn't like dating anyone else. If today reinforced anything, it was that their families were so enmeshed that if this wasn't handled just right, it could rip lifelong relationships apart. She'd lost one brother; she couldn't lose another nor see him lose the surrogate brother he had in Noah.

"Not yet." Her fingers threaded through the silky dark hair dusting his chest. "I want to just give us more time before we let others in. I promise it won't be forever…I just need more time. If this is a deal breaker…" The words refused to come out.

"I understand." He traced her lips. "Sometimes warriors need to be patient."

"Well, patience is something that should always be rewarded." She pressed him backward until his back hit the mattress.

Nat's eyes flicked to the alarm clock on the bedstand. "I'm going to reserve the right to harass you about having an alarm clock like the geriatric millennial that you are for later because I only have forty-five minutes to sex you up before I have to grab my Jeep from the park and head back home."

Noah flipped her onto her back, kissing down her body. "Forty-five minutes? I need to get to work then...I have a girl-friend to please."

CHAPTER TWENTY-SIX

"There are many Beths in the world, shy and quiet, sitting in corners till needed, and living for others so cheerfully that no one sees the sacrifices till the little cricket on the hearth stops chirping…" ~Louisa May Alcott, *Little Women*

"Tater tots are truly the food of the gods!" Nat dipped a crispy potato round into ketchup. "I *love* it when you have morning shifts at the café," she groaned with happy pleasure.

"I supply free lunch, and you give me free medical advice. It's a quid pro quo relationship," Summer teased, stabbing a piece of salmon from their shared salad.

Whenever Summer worked the breakfast shift at the café, she'd get a to-go salad and an order of tater tots for lunch and stop by the clinic to eat with Nat. These lunch dates were contingent on Liam's schedule or on Summer not having to see a client for her growing event planning business.

Today, Liam, the mini-Clayton, was spending the afternoon at the vet clinic. Most of the time, he'd be in the reception area eating too many cookies, greeting the animal patients, and playing with Fitz and Lizzie, who went to the clinic whenever he was there or Elle was out of town for work.

Lunch dates with her bestie were better than ice cream for dinner. Since last Monday's dinner date, too much of their interaction with each other had been via text messages, and that had been dominated by Nat's relationship with Noah. Since then, Summer had been busy with work and had an initial telephone interview with the behavioral therapist in preparation of Liam starting therapy in the fall.

"How'd your chat with the therapist go?" She lifted her iced tea.

Summer pulled her long hair into a low ponytail. "It went well. We just went over some insurance, logistical, and background info. She made some suggestions, including joining a support group for parents with kids on the spectrum."

"That's great." Her excitement was soon dulled by Summer's pinched expression. "Let me guess...it's in Buffalo."

"Yup," Summer sighed, setting her fork down. "She did suggest some online resources, though. Message boards, Facebook groups, and websites. That kind of thing."

Nat leaned back in her chair, gnawing on her lip. It was ridiculous how few resources were available in rural communities. In Boston, if she had a parent in the same situation, there'd be an entire list of organizations to connect with.

"Is there a way to reach out to other parents in the county and put together a group?" she suggested.

"I thought about that, but the group in Buffalo is facilitated by a trained psychologist. We'd need to find one with the expertise in Autism to run our group, and there's no one outside of Buffalo or Rochester. As it is, we barely have any mental health services in the area. I remember when I first moved back..." Summer shifted in her seat. Her worry-filled eyes flicked to the open office door.

Summer's gap years, between leaving Perry at eighteen

and returning at twenty-nine, were a mystery. She'd offered small glimpses but not much.

Nat's vision moved to the doorway. Without saying a word, she stood, walked over, shut the door, and sat back down.

Summer offered a thankful smile. "Liam's dad, Max, and I dated for four years. I thought he was everything. Good looking. Sophisticated. Rich. He was the opposite of Perry…of me. I felt so lucky to be with him and…" Her voice quaked. "If I forgot that, then he reminded me with…" She shook her head. "For four years, I lost myself in the relationship…no, I lost myself to him."

Nat reached across the space between them, linking their hands.

"I tried so hard to make him happy. To make him not…"

So much was said in the unspoken words. Nat squeezed her hand, reminding Summer that she was there. That even if Nat hadn't been there then, she was there now. And she'd be there after.

"I thought it was what I deserved, and I stayed until I found out I was pregnant. Max was in London on business. It wasn't just about me anymore…and I left. I came back home. Max had only met my parents when they came to New York City to visit. He'd never been to Perry. I changed my cell phone number. I deleted social media. I didn't talk to anyone from my life there. I went back to my natural hair color. When I came back, I was a mess, and my parents thought it would be good for me to talk to someone, but it was so difficult to find a therapist in the area. Especially one that was affordable. I didn't have insurance until Cassie hired me full-time."

"Did you eventually find someone?" she asked.

Summer shook her head. "I talked to the pastor at my parents' church for a while and…" An embarrassed laugh slipped out of her. "…remember Mrs. Anwar, the school guidance counselor?"

She nodded. "Yeah. I talked to her after Evan died."

"She's friends with my mom, and she'd have me over for tea once a week to talk." Summer made air quotes. "It was like secret therapy, but it helped. Although, she kept recommending lots of career suggestions."

They both chuckled.

Nat remembered Mrs. Anwar listening attentively after Evan had died, but most of their conversation drifted to what she'd major in at Boston College. That was probably because each time Mrs. Anwar asked how she was doing, Nat responded that she was fine, even though she wasn't.

"I wish there were more resources here." Nat blew out a heavy breath, tapping her glittered pink fingernails against the desk. "I know my parents tried to get a psychologist to join the practice about five years ago, but they had zero luck with attracting one. Even the ones who live in the county prefer driving to Buffalo or Rochester to work where they can make more money."

"What about Sloan-Whitney? Doesn't Elle oversee their telehealth network?" Summer grabbed her fork and speared a tater tot.

"Elle tried to convince my parents last year, but it means giving up our clinic's independence. We'd no longer be the Owens Family Clinic but a Sloan-Whitney Clinic. It means giving up a lot of control with the practice. Mom and Dad aren't willing to do that," she explained.

"Elle's their Deputy Chief Operating Officer; wouldn't she be able to stop that? Make some sort of deal to keep your independence while getting the additional resources?"

Nat shook her head. "No. She'd have to keep herself completely away from any decisions related to the clinic. With her marrying my brother, it would be seen as a conflict of interest. Even if Elle wasn't so ethical, my parents would never let her risk her professional reputation like that."

"Adulting blows," Summer groaned.

"Tell me about it."

"Speaking of adulting…" She shimmied her upper body in a suggestive manner. "…now that the door is shut, can we dish about the adulting you're doing with Noah? Have we packed all our *sexy* panties for this weekend?"

"Panties are unnecessary for what I have planned." Batted lashes accompanied her low sultry voice.

"Get it, girl!" Summer grinned.

CHAPTER TWENTY-SEVEN

"Love is a great beautifier." ~Louisa May Alcott, *Little Women*

Their hands clasped, Nat and Noah walked across the lobby of the Hotel Skyler Syracuse. The heels of her gold sandals clacked against the marble floor as they made their way toward the elevators. The small boutique hotel was tucked in the University Hill neighborhood, a short walk from the University of Syracuse campus where the conference was being held.

A light floral scent greeted them when they entered their room. Slipping off her sandals, her toes sank into the sumptuous carpet. Sunshine streamed in through a large window that took up much of the room's outfacing wall. The open curtains offered a breathtaking view of the bustling neighborhood.

"This is adorable!" she gushed, depositing her suitcase in front of the dark wood dresser.

Noah's arms looped around her middle, and he pulled her into his chest. "Do you want to leave our things and go to dinner or unpack first?"

She twirled to face him. "Do they have room service?" she purred in a buttery voice.

Amusement lit his features. "As much as I'd love to stay locked in the room with you, I really would like to take you out. I've only gotten to go on one actual date with my girlfriend. I'd like to wine and dine you a bit. You know, the whole romance thing?"

I'm Noah Wilson's girlfriend. Goddess, he is my boyfriend. Happiness fluttered in her chest.

As much as she'd enjoy putting the *Do Not Disturb* sign on the door for the next forty-eight hours, the idea of walking, fingers intertwined, in the world with him was far too intoxicating. True, the secret nature of their relationship was her idea. It was still the best way to proceed, but the enticement of a weekend of just being a couple living in the light was too precious to give up. To just be his girlfriend and let him be her boyfriend without having to think of the impact on their families would offer them time to settle into this relationship.

Despite the years of daydreaming about this, it was all still so new and a little scary. She'd spent eighteen years fantasizing about what it would be like to call him her boyfriend. In the last two weeks, the reality had already surpassed any of her girlish musings.

She raised to her tiptoes, nuzzling his nose with hers. "Let's go to dinner but bring dessert back here."

"Maybe you should speak to the Rural Business Conference, you're a cutthroat negotiator." The low timbre of his voice zinged directly to her core.

How fast can we eat?

They sat on the fairy-light-draped outdoor patio of a small café, her right hand clasped in his left one, both their arms resting on the bistro table. Conversation flowed effortlessly between them. Nat talked about her friend from college, Preeti, whom she'd be meeting for breakfast in the morning. She was happy to meet up with her friend who'd unwittingly served as part of Nat's cover story for the trip. Noah showed her some of his favorite TikTok puppy videos, and she taunted him about getting a dog. He listened intently when she sputtered down a rabbit hole about the need for more mental health services in the county.

The soft glow of candlelight illuminated his dimpled smile. The dusting of dark stubble kissed his strong jawline. His blue eyes shimmered with each word she spoke.

"I know your parents aren't open to partnering with Sloan-Whitney, but how do you feel?" His thumb caressed her palm.

"I wish there was a way to do both. Having the tele mental health services would be a huge resource for our patients, but I don't want to lose our autonomy. I like the idea of one day my kids taking over the clinic. Well, if my parents ever retire."

"Have you told them you're ready to take over?"

She let out a heavy sigh. "I don't know if I am."

"What makes you think you're not ready to run the clinic yourself?"

Her forehead puckered. "We've talked about this. The staff second-guess me all the time, and many of the patients prefer seeing my dad."

"I know, but that's other people, not you. Do *you* think you're ready? Do you think you have the skills needed to do the job?"

Nat closed her eyes and chewed on the question. Did she have the skills needed? She was half her mom, the business side of the clinic, and her dad, the clinical side. She grew up in the clinic, learning the everyday ins and outs. She worked in the reception area throughout high school. Not to mention, she was top of her class in medical school and dominated her residency program.

"Yes," she replied with steely certainty.

"That's my girl." Prideful amusement filled his features.

"I like being your girl." She leaned across the table and pressed her smile against his.

Noah believed in her because she believed in herself. It was less about him voicing confidence that she could do it than reminding her to ask herself. The answer was clear. She had what it took to be *the* Dr. Owens. In the last few months, she'd just forgotten. She'd lost sight of who she was, but he reminded her.

A throat cleared, breaking their kiss. "Sorry. Your food," the apologetic server said, presenting their meals.

"Sorry," she giggled.

"Oh, I get it. He's too cute not to kiss." The server winked.

"You should try getting through a meal without kissing her." Noah's grin was devilish yet endearing.

The server placed a hand on his heart. "Stop! He's like a leading man from a rom-com."

"Tell me about it!" Those butterflies in her belly had drunk one too many Red Bulls, resulting in their overactive antics. At what point would her body no longer react to him like this? She hoped the answer was never.

"Can I get you anything else?" After they both shook their heads, the server walked away

Picking up a knife, Noah cut his veggie burger in half. "So, you mentioned kids. You want them?"

"Yes, I do. Not right now, but in a few years." She cut a piece of her orange-glazed salmon. "You?"

"I do," he said.

Seeing how Noah was with Liam and the interactions he had with other kids through the years, it was easy to see he'd be an amazing father. It was odd to think that he wasn't already a dad.

It was odder to think that he'd been single this whole time. Other than the flirtation with Willa, there was no sign of him having dated anyone in the last eleven years.

"In the garage, you said nobody had seen all of you since your injury." Her eyes locked on his. "Does that mean that, before me, you hadn't had sex since you were injured?"

"Correct."

She tried not to physically react to his admission. "What about dating? Has there been anyone?"

"Outside of the kiss with Willa, I've not dated nor had sex since before I was injured."

"I don't know how to ask this without sounding rude… but why? You have so much to offer."

He let out a heavy breath. "I didn't always. After my injury, I wasn't…" His eyes flicked to the street and then back to her. "…me. Not really. At first, I had no interest in dating because I needed to get my head straight. After I was medically discharged from the Marines, I focused on getting healthy. I did my PT and went to see a counselor at the VA. I wasn't in the right headspace to date anyone."

"Do you still see your VA Counselor?" she asked.

"Every two weeks." He leaned back in his chair. "PTSD will always be something I have to deal with. I think that was a big reason why I didn't date. PTSD is part of my life, and that means it will be part of my partner's life. For a long time, I was scared of laying that on someone else."

"Did that concern also hold you back when you almost kissed me after Evan died?" Nat bit her lip, thinking of the regret that swam in his eyes that day.

He'd said it was because her brother had just died and he felt like he was taking advantage, but she wondered if it was more. If all that he'd been battling since his injury held him back. It had only been ten months after his accident when he almost kissed her.

"It wouldn't have been fair to put that on you then. You already had so much to deal with."

Her heartbeat galloped as she replayed all the moments with Noah over the last ten years. "But you wanted to…even if you didn't do it, you wanted to kiss me, and not just *that* night."

"Yes."

Nat closed her eyes. The image of the yellowjacket tattoo on his right pec flooded her vision. Home was so important to him. Why had he stayed away for so long after he'd gotten out of the Marines?

"Why didn't you come back after you were discharged? You'd just got out when Evan died. The plan was for you to come home. Why did you stay in San Diego for five years?"

"I needed to get to a good place mentally before coming back."

What he didn't say aloud, despite the words dancing between them, was, "to you." There was no reason she should think that, but she did.

"Did you stay away because of me?" she breathed, her steady gaze locked with his despite the anxious twist in her belly.

"Yes."

Her heart raced. "Did you come back because of me?"

"Yes."

"Noah, why?"

"When I was injured and came back to Walter Reed for my recovery, you called every Friday night. You were the only person to talk to me like I was…well, like I was still me. Everyone else was so tentative around me. You talked to me about everyday things, like about a crafting project you were doing or *The Gilmore Girls*. You even called me names and picked on me. I don't think you know how much you helped me. When you called me after Evan died, I got on the next plane. I know you thought it was because of Clayton, but it was also for you. I wanted to be there for you in the same way you'd been there for me."

Nat reached across the table, linking their hands. "You were. You were the first person I called after the police told us what happened. You were the only person I could let myself fall apart with because I knew you had me."

"And you had me," he murmured. "You brought me back from the darkness I was in after the injury. Those calls from you were like a lighthouse leading me home. When I came home for Evan's funeral, I was expecting to find that twelve-year-old girl I had last seen, not the eighteen-year-old woman I found. It threw me. It wouldn't have been right then. I wasn't who I needed to be, not then. I left to become him and came back when I felt like I was him." He swallowed hard. "Although, I don't think I'm him. Not completely. I still have my demons…they'll never be gone. There's no magic pill to take them away."

"You're still my Noah. You're still perfect." She smiled as she repeated his words from the night she told him about her guilt over Evan's death. "Our broken pieces are parts of who we are. You never stopped being Noah. When we'd talk while you were recovering, there was a shade of something different in your voice. The charming carefreeness that had been there was dulled, but you were still Noah. You've always been that man you say you want to be. Even if you don't see it, I did…I do. If you weren't, you wouldn't have stomached thirty-minute conversations about why Rory should have never dated Dean and listened to my pro/con list about which colleges to apply to."

He chuckled.

"So, when you came back…why didn't you make your move?"

"Your life was in Boston. We'd talk and see each other when you were visiting. I used that as an excuse, though. Then, I told myself that you could do better. I found so many excuses to hide the fact that I was scared. Scared that you didn't feel the same way. Scared that it was all one-sided. Scared of hurting you. I'm still scared. When you came back... all those excuses fuzzed in the reality of you being there. When we got into that argument the night of the engagement party, the only thing that scared me was the possibility of losing you. Nat, I care about you so much. I can't imagine a life where you're not in it. When you started seeing Duncan again, I told myself to not get in the way of your happiness, to be content with you in my life as a friend."

"You didn't do that very well now, did you," she teased.

"No." He smirked. "I know it's still early with us, but I don't think I could ever be content with just being your friend."

"Me either."

CHAPTER TWENTY-EIGHT

"Don't try to make me grow up before my time..." ~Louisa May
Alcott, *Little Women*

The soft click of the door shutting broke into Nat's
dreams. Blinking her eyes open, she stretched. Streaks
of early morning light peeked into the hotel room through a
small gap between the drawn curtains. She reached, finding
only emptiness beside her.

Where is he? She sat up in the bed. The sheet slid to her
waist, exposing her very naked top half, which matched her
very naked bottom half. Why had she wasted space in her
suitcase for pajamas?

The only thing better than going to bed with Noah would
be waking up with him. It still hadn't happened, but she
wouldn't push. Sleep was difficult for him. The memories of
what happened on that roadside in Iraq seemed to visit him
most nights.

"Noah?" she called, hearing the shower turn on.

After no answer came, she slipped out of bed. The
running water may have drowned out her voice. The sound

of the shutting door must have been him returning rather than leaving.

Nat tiptoed to the bathroom, easing the door open. Tendrils of steam filled the bathroom, warming her body, which was both cold from leaving the bed and heated with the sight of Noah's muscular back and ass facing her.

He stood underneath the showerhead as hot water rained down on him. The droplets cascaded across his defined physique.

Nat's eyes fixed on the small Marine bulldog tattoo on his right shoulder blade. She'd never really seen it before. Her fingernails had skated across it or dug into it when he drove into her, but she'd never gotten a good look at his backside. The white bulldog outlined in blue appeared both fierce protector and an adorable playmate. Just like the man it was inked on.

Goddess, he's beautiful. Licking her lips, she stepped over the small pile of workout clothes on the white tile floor and opened the glass door.

Noah turned. "Good morning, gorgeous," he said with an almost wicked grin.

"Good morning, handsome," she said with very wicked intentions.

"Care to join me?"

"Well, I am undressed for it."

With a sated ache between her legs, Nat sat in the brown armchair, a fluffy white towel wrapped around her. The coffee she sipped was hot and rich. Noah, who would be heading down for the conference, was getting dressed in the bathroom.

She was going to meet Preeti for breakfast. It would make

that story she'd told her family about visiting a friend from college the tiniest of white lies. After breakfast, she'd attend Noah's speech. He secured a pass for her to visit the conference's vendor area and attend his keynote speech at the end of the day.

Noah stepped out of the bathroom dressed in a fitted navy suit. As he turned to Nat, her breath hitched. The sight of Noah dressed like that, so fine and fit, was knee-wobbling. She resisted the urge to fan herself. Some men wore suits. Some suits wore men. What Noah did to that suit defied all laws of fashion.

"Good goddess," she gasped. "Have you seen yourself in a suit?"

"I think you're biased," he said, walking over to her.

"I have half a mind to lock you in this room. You may cause a hormonal riot in that suit."

Nat's gaze swept over the perfect fit of the fabric on his broad shoulders and cut body. The color made his eyes shimmer like the Caribbean Sea. The combination of his boyishly dimpled smile, strong jawline, and that suit melded into a sexy boy next door package. A sexy boy next door that not thirty minutes ago pressed her against the tiled wall of the shower, driving into her and causing her to scream his name so loud that they feared someone would call hotel security.

Oh, goddess. The memory pooled liquid heat between her legs.

She was acting like a teenager. Although, she'd not acted like this as an actual teenager. Nobody had ever set her entire body on fire sexually while capturing her heart at the same time the way he did. Whether having sex or just being together talking, she burned for this man.

Noah bent and kissed her. "They'll have your pass at the check-in desk at the conference. Have fun at your breakfast, and I'll see you after my speech," he said, starting to straighten up.

Nat grabbed his emerald tie, pulling him back to her lips. "Kick ass today, baby."

A huge smile erupted on his face. "You called me baby."

"Sure did," she crooned. "You said baby first, so I thought I'd return it. It's only fair, after all."

With one last kiss and a big grin, Noah left. After she lounged in the memory of him in that suit and plotted to peel it off him later, she got ready to leave for breakfast with Preeti, her undergrad roommate and fellow primary care physician, who lived in Syracuse.

After breakfast and lots of "I can't believe we did that" stories from her undergrad days, Nat went to the room to change from her casual sundress to something a little sexy business casual. After Noah's speech, they'd be attending a cocktail hour and then head out for a romantic dinner.

Nat pushed into a pair of rose gold heels and then stepped in front of the full-length mirror in the hotel room's small entryway. Twirling, she admired herself. The light green sheath dress fell just above her knees and hugged her petite frame. She may not have luscious curves like Summer, but this dress perfectly punctuated what she did have. She pulled on a fitted navy blazer and finished the outfit with a pair of rose gold hoops that popped out of her blown-out sandy locks.

"Look at you," she said, wiggling her hips in the mirror. Grabbing her purse, she headed out.

Nat zigzagged through the vendor tables outside the large auditorium where Noah would speak. Each table highlighted different rural business resources. Business consultants, social media/marketing experts, and various small business organizations filled tables lining the long stretch of hallway. She wandered, grabbing pamphlets, cards, and free swag to share with Noah and for Summer's growing event planning business.

"Yes, the grant can be used to fund equipment for expansion." A husky man with gray-streaked dark hair addressed a young woman.

Nat turned from the table she was in front of and listened to the man go on. His deep voice commanded attention. The man picked up a laminated postcard from the table draped in a blue tablecloth embossed with *The Clark Foundation*.

"Thank you," a young woman said, taking the advertisement and walking away.

Nat stepped up to the table, picked up the advertisement, and read it. "What is the Clark Foundation?" she asked.

"We're a nonprofit focused on supporting rural community development. We offer grants, business coaching, and resources to support rural communities."

Her brow wrinkled. "Have you ever worked with rural medical clinics?"

The man cocked his head to the right. "We haven't, but there's always a first time. I'm Caleb Walters." He reached out his hand.

Nat took it. "Dr. Nat Owens. I work with a small clinic in Wyoming County."

"Nice to meet you, Dr. Owens."

A giddiness rippled through her. *Dr. Owens.* She was Dr. Owens, goddess damn it. Time to not just say it but be it.

After a lengthy discussion with Caleb, she found her way to the fourth row of the auditorium. The room was filled with whispering people in white dress shirts, suits, and business casual attire. A blue wooden lectern stood in the center of the raised stage with four chairs flanking each side.

Two men in black suits and a woman in a gray dress walked onto the stage, followed by Noah. Each took a seat beside the lectern. Noah's gaze drifted around the room.

She stood up pretending to adjust her blazer, but in hopes he would see her. The pop of that dimple in a big grin told her that he'd seen her.

With an equally big grin on her face, she mouthed, *Kick butt, baby.*

Those butterflies jigged as he mouthed back, *Thanks, baby.*

The woman in the gray dress strode to the lectern, calling everyone's attention. "Ladies and gentlemen, welcome to the Annual Rural Business Conference. I have the distinct pleasure of introducing this year's Keynote Speaker, Mr. Noah Wilson. Noah is not only the owner of three successful businesses, helping revive the Main Street of Perry, New York, but serves as a coach through the New York State Rural Business Association and mentors future entrepreneurs as an advisor to the Perry Central School's Future Businesspeople of America club. Please help me welcome Mr. Noah Wilson," she announced.

Nat clapped as loudly as she could, just skirting obnoxious. She had no idea he was coaching fellow businesses and mentoring students at the school, but she was unsurprised. There were so many things around the community that he did without people noticing. He quietly cross-promoted other businesses in town by, along with his staff wearing T-shirts with their business's names, having their advertisements at his businesses, or doing joint events. Each Saturday, he brought free cookies to Cow Tales for their weekly children's story hour. He volunteered for most of the village's events. Summer shared that he'd even rocked the pink Easter Bunny costume the last three years for the VFW's Annual Easter Egg hunt.

Noah strode to the lectern. "Thank you, Madam Chairwoman. I'm here this weekend because of love—"

What!? Nat's freaked-out internal monologue cut Noah off. He couldn't be talking about her. This was *too* new for love. Also, was he proclaiming his love in front of two hundred people? Nope, this was not happening.

"—Love is what drives me to do the work I'm doing. The love for my community and the people there." Noah went on, interrupting her internal freakout.

Thank the goddess. She exhaled.

The tense muscles in her body melted as Noah spoke. With rapt attention, the attendees listened as he explained his professional philosophy about the importance of staying anchored in the why. That success is more than profit. If a business owner is focused on taking care of their staff, they'll take care of your business. That supporting a community results in thriving businesses.

Noah talked about his first business, the Farmer's Wife, that he hadn't bought to get rich. The bakery had struggled for years, but he knew that there was still a need for it. People doubted that a man with a recent business degree from UC San Diego and four years of experience managing a sports bar after getting out of the Marines could turn around a bakery. By focusing on his community's needs, allowing the bakery to meet those needs, and becoming an essential part of the village, he'd done what he set out to do.

Admiration fluttered throughout Nat's entire body as she listened to Noah speak. He was everything she knew he was and so much more. Her heart burst with affection and pride.

After the speech, she followed the crowd into a large banquet room. Two bars were set up on either side of the room. Servers in black shirts wandered through the clusters of networking people, offering different hors d'oeuvres.

Nat stood at a high top in the front of the room. Noah had been surrounded by people offering congratulations and picking his brain, so she'd slipped away to let him mingle. She was content sipping her glass of rosé and nibbling on a bacon-wrapped date. She used the time to pull up the Clark Foundation's website on her phone. The more she read on the website and thought of the conversation with Caleb, she knew with certainty that this was her answer.

"Hey, gorgeous." Noah sauntered over, resting his hand on the small of her back and pressing a kiss to her cheek.

"Hey, tall, blue-eyed, and handsome." She winked.

He chuckled. "Are you drinking rosé? Elle would be so proud of you."

"They didn't have cider," she pouted.

Rosé wasn't her favorite. Ever since her first illegal sip of alcohol when she was fourteen, she had been a cider girl. Just don't tell her soon-to-be sister-in-law, who, no doubt, would require the entire wedding party to drink tea or rosé. Since Elle had joined the family there was always a bottle chilling in Clayton and their parents' respective fridges, standing ready for Elle.

"Your speech was wonderful. I'm so proud! I wish I had recorded it. Your mom and dad would burst with parental pride." She almost squealed from her own sense of pride.

It wasn't just his story that captured the room, but how he spoke. Confidence, humility, inspiration, and sincerity were woven seamlessly into the fabric of his speech.

"The conference organizers recorded it, so it will be available on their website on Monday. I'll send my parents the link," he offered.

Nat's heart squeezed. "You're such a good son." Her face scrunched. "You're such a good everything."

Bemusement curled his lips. "Well, I'm failing as a boyfriend because my beautiful girlfriend has been reduced to rosé. I need to rectify that immediately. Ready to head to dinner? We're going to the Cider Mill, so I know for a fact they have cider for..." He paused and then winked. "...my baby."

A big laugh sprinted out of her. "Lead the way, baby."

Fifteen minutes later, she jumped out of Noah's SUV. She slipped her blazer off and tossed it onto the front seat before shutting the door. The evening was still warm, so the jacket wasn't necessary. Also, the full effect of the dress needed to be experienced.

Noah rounded the vehicle. Stopping as he reached her, his throat bobbing and eyes raking down her figure. "You're stunning."

"Oh, this old thing?" she said with sassiness, shaking her hips. She'd only bought the dress the previous Saturday just for this trip.

He stepped close, settling his hands on her waist. "You worried about me causing a hormonal riot in this suit, but you in that dress…" He hummed his appreciation.

She lifted to her tiptoes, snaking her arms around his neck. "Good thing I have my warrior to protect me from horny rioters."

"I do enjoy your wit." He dipped his head, kissing her. "I have something for you." He released her and stepped back.

Nat arched an eyebrow, and a salacious smile kicked across her face.

"Not that." With a teasing smirk, he slipped his right hand into the pocket of his jacket and pulled out a rectangular purple velvet box.

Nat took it, biting her lip as she opened it. A delicate rose gold gardenia pendant necklace was inside. "Noah." Her words and breath both hitched.

"Do you like it?" The playfulness of his tone was replaced with a nervous hopefulness.

"I love it. A gardenia."

It was just like the flowers he'd given her. The ones that meant secret affection.

Noah took the box from her. "May I?" he asked, removing the necklace.

She nodded, turning her back to him. The heat from his body enveloped her as he stood behind her. Goosebumps bloomed across her skin. His hands were gentle as he placed the necklace around her neck.

Nat raised her fingers to the pendant, tracing its smooth edges. "It's lovely."

"I saw it and thought of you." He cupped her upper arms. "Besides the obvious, gardenias are both beautiful and strong, they have an intoxicating fragrance that lingers, and they aren't every day. They're special."

"Baby," she crooned, twisting to face him. "Thank you for seeing me. For reminding me who I am and not expecting me to be anything else but that." She wrapped her fingers around the necklace.

The gift wasn't just about the secret romance they had, but it represented her. Since coming home, she lost herself. So much of the spunky Nat had been tamped down by self-doubt.

Noah caressed her cheek. "Who you are is far too special to be marred by being anybody else. A rose can never be a gardenia."

"And a gardenia can never be a rose, and that's okay." She smiled.

It was a ridiculous metaphor, but it made sense to her. So, what if she wasn't *the* Dr. Owens. She was *a* Dr. Owens. Better than that, she was Dr. Nat Owens. She didn't need to be her father. She could be herself and win them over, just as she'd done with classmates in medical school and fellow residents in her residency program. Whoever didn't get on the Dr. Nat Owens train, well...*Fuck them!*

"I have an idea that I'm really excited about. Can I pick your sexy business brain during dinner?" She pitched her voice low and seductive. "I'll let you bend me over the desk in the hotel room in return for your business god knowledge."

"There's that cutthroat negotiating mind of yours at work again."

CHAPTER TWENTY-NINE

"…I can't help but see that you are very lonely, and that sometimes there is a hungry look in your eyes that goes to my heart." ~Louisa May Alcott, *Little Women*

A chill shivered along Nat's spine, startling her awake. The energy in the room had shifted. Something foul crackled in the air. Noah's arms were no longer folded around her. Beside her was only emptiness where he'd once been. Clicking the lamp, the inky darkness dissolved in the dim light.

Her eyes moved to Noah's hunched figure perched at the end of the bed. The muscles of his back contracted and restricted with the rapid intake of breath.

Tension coiled in her body. "Noah?" she asked with tentative gentleness.

There was no response outside of his ragged breath.

Jumping up, she rounded the bed. Her footsteps halted in front of him. Rigidity gripped Noah. The muscles and tendons of his body appeared to be wound so tight that they'd burst. The handsome features of his face were contorted and twisted in a pained, fearful expression. A fog glazed his blue eyes. They looked at her, but there was no recognition in them.

"Noah," she repeated his name with a soft but firm voice.

Eyes unfocused, he shook his head as if unsure of his own name. His hands gripped his bare knees. The tanned knuckles were almost white. Red spots formed on his thighs from where his fingernails dug into his legs.

Fear slithered through her. She'd never seen him like this. Confusion and terror wafted off him.

Stay calm. She slipped from girlfriend to doctor mode. *Assess. Prescribe. Treat.*

Nat searched her mental database about what to do when a patient experienced a panic attack, which this clearly was. When panic clutched at a person's throat, all reality was ripped away. The seized were immersed in their fear. The world distorted into a nightmare.

She needed to pull him away from the nightmare that had snatched him from her. She needed to bring him back to the here and now, where he was safe and with her.

"Noah Wilson." His name was a stern but tender command.

His gaze was foggy when he looked up at her. Confusion etched across his features.

"You are in a hotel room. Feel the soft sheets beneath you. See the white walls with the framed landscape pictures."

Noah nodded.

"Noah, tell me what you see."

He blinked.

"Do you see the bedstand?"

His slow blinks were a response to her question.

"What's on the bedstand?" She kept her voice steady despite the chaotic cadence of her pulse.

"Lamp." His voice was shaky.

Nat moved closer. "Do you feel the carpet beneath your

feet?" Her eyes moved to the ground, watching his feet brush across the plush carpet. "What else do you see?"

The fog started to lift. Noah's head turned, and he listed items in the room: TV, dresser, desk, picture, alarm clock, chair, phone, suitcase.

Then his eyes stopped at her. "Nat," he said, hoarsely as if he'd just woken up.

As if approaching a scared animal, she crouched in front of him. "Yes. I'm here. I'm in front of you in our hotel room in Syracuse."

She repeated the location to help anchor him. To pull him from wherever he'd been taken to. Not exactly accurate. She knew where he'd been; on that roadside in Iraq.

"Nat," he rasped, reaching for her.

His hands trembled as he caressed her face. The tender and tentative movement seemed like he was confirming that she was real and not a mirage. His fingers trailed down to her necklace. The moment he touched the gardenia pendant, every muscle in his body loosened its gripping tension.

Tears flooded his eyes. "I'm sorry. I'm so sorry."

"Why are you sorry?" she murmured.

"For this." He hid his eyes behind one hand.

"Should I apologize for the three times in the last three weeks that you've been there for me when I wobbled?"

He shook his head.

"Then don't apologize for this." She sat beside him on the bed. "There are going to be times when I wobble and times when you do."

He nodded.

Nat crawled around him to the top of the bed. "Come here." Her command was soft.

He turned. His weary eyes met hers. Exhaustion sighed across every muscle. He crawled into her waiting arms, lying his head against her chest.

"I thought I was back there. The dream was so vivid. I..." he trailed off.

Nat stroked his short dark hair. "I'm here. You're safe. You're with me."

His hand tightened on her ribcage. "I'm with you."

With each sweep of her fingers, his tense muscles eased. His breath slowed. His eyes closed. Soon he slept. Nat continued her soothing touches until sleep took her as well.

CHAPTER THIRTY

"Into each life some rain must fall..." ~Louisa May Alcott, *Little Women*

The weight of Noah asleep atop her was as cozy as a down comforter. They'd remained intertwined with each other since falling asleep. His arms draped over her waist, and his head rested on her chest.

"Good morning," he murmured.

"You're awake?"

Raising his head, he looked at her. "I woke up a few minutes ago, but I didn't want to move."

"I like waking up with you." She sighed with happy contentment. As much as she hated what he experienced last night, she loved waking up in his arms.

A sweet smile bloomed across his face. "I like waking up with you too."

"How are you feeling?" She brushed her fingers into his sleep-rumpled hair.

"I'm okay... Thank you." Gratitude shaded his blue eyes. "I'm sorry about last night."

"There's no need to apologize." She combed through his hair.

He nodded. "I just wish it wasn't part of being with me."

"I hate that you went through what you did in the service and that it pulls you back at times. I can't take away what happened to you, or its power to steal you away, but never doubt my ability to be there with you just as you are for me."

An almost painful fullness clogged her chest. It hurt as much as it offered a sense of completeness. She'd never felt like this with, or for, anyone. The realization of how deeply she cared for this man trembled within her.

"You are so strong." He shifted in the bed, pressing his lips against hers.

"I'm your warrior, and you're mine," she said between seeking kisses.

She couldn't get enough of him. It was like being pulled in different directions. Both longing for and achieving the completeness of them. It terrified and exhilarated her...as if she soared in the sky, the vast view below, but the fear of falling still loomed.

She knew that as Noah would never let her fall, she'd never let him. Even if there was a part of her that knew she'd already fallen and there was no way she'd ever be able to get back up.

"Noah," she said with breathless want. The words were trapped inside her, not ready to come out. But her body could express every syllable. Every unsaid feeling that filled her chest.

"I know, baby. I know what you need. What I need," he rasped, trailing kisses down her neck.

She submerged herself into his exploring mouth. Its heat raked down her, licking down her breasts to her belly button and lower. Her back arched. Every inch of her pulsed awake, yearning for more.

Threading her fingers in his silken hair, she guided him to where she wanted him. A greedy shiver slid through her with the first lick against her clit. With every flick of tongue, and hard suck, wildfire blazed within her. The delicious pressure spooled tighter and tighter…until she exploded.

Aftershocks still rolled through her as he plunged deep inside her. She dug her nails into his back. The satisfying fullness of him inside her engulfed her. He pulled back out, stealing away that fullness she craved. Just as she opened her mouth to protest, he drove back into her.

She gasped an unintelligible stream of curses. Tension-filled pleasure seized her.

"You like that, baby?" he growled.

"Yes," she whimpered as he did it again.

With a relentless rhythm, he tipped her closer to the edge. Shifting their position, he draped her legs over his shoulders, seating himself completely in her.

The coiled pleasure was almost too much…*Almost.*

"Noah!" she screamed, her limp arms and legs clung to him, fearing that if she let go, she'd be lost.

"Fuck," he grunted and collapsed in a sated heap atop her.

Uncurling her legs from his shoulders, he pulled out of her. Cradled close, his fingers soothed along her spine. Despite the settling breaths, emotions thrummed within her. This man was becoming both the anchor that kept her grounded and the balloon that allowed her to fly. He'd always been there, but now it was so much more than it had been and what she'd dreamed it could be.

"You always have me," she murmured, caressing his cheek

His piercing gaze bore into her. "And I always will. Just as you'll always have me" A reverent kiss sealed their joint declaration.

He had her, and she had him. They had each other.

Satiated and quiet, they lay in each other's arms. The pads of his fingers skated along her spine. Each stroke punctuated their mutual belonging; her with him and he with her.

"The dreams don't come every night," Noah whispered, breaking their silent post-sex cocoon.

His gaze shifted to the ceiling. She followed, allowing her stare to meander along the white crown molding. Streaks of light from the half-closed curtains crisscrossed with the lingering shadows of the dim room.

"Most nights, I don't sleep. I think because I'm trying to avoid the dreams from coming. I'm never sure when they'll come. There are things that trigger panic attacks or nightmares. Certain smells...campfires and cooking meat..." He swallowed hard, cutting himself off.

She wove her fingers into the dark hair peppering his chest. "You don't have to say it if you don't want to, but I can handle it if you want to tell me about it."

He turned his head, looking at her. "I know you can. You're my warrior."

They lay there for another hour talking. Noah shared his burdens with her. How the dreams would sneak in like a thief in the night, stealing away restful peace. How certain triggers, stressful events, or anniversaries caused his symptoms to flare. There were tricks and exercises he used to cope with his PTSD. How he'd never been able to fall into a restful sleep after a panic attack like he'd done last night.

"Why do you think you were able to sleep last night?" she asked.

His fingers traced along her hairline. "You. I told you... you're my lighthouse, guiding me out of the darkness. Once I found you, I knew I was safe."

The proclamation stole her breath. He said he wanted to be her everything, but at that moment, she realized that she was his everything. Nat snuggled in tight. If she could have crawled inside Noah, she would have. But she also knew that she couldn't save him from this.

"I don't think it was just me. I helped, but I didn't—"

He stole her words with a tender kiss. "I know. As much as I feel safe with you, I know that our relationship won't cure my PTSD. I still need to do the work to manage it. I have an appointment with my VA counselor this week. I never miss my appointments."

"When did you first start seeing a counselor?"

A soft laugh left his lips. "After Clayton told me to get my shit together."

"What?" she guffawed. "Clayton told you to get your shit together? When? Why?"

The idea of her brother telling anyone to get their shit together was astounding. In her twenty-eight years, he'd teased her but never been so harsh or frank. Clayton seemed to have an endless supply of quiet patience for the people he loved. The only time she'd seen him be curt was with the guys she'd dated.

"After I was discharged from Walter Reed and transferred back to Camp Pendleton, your brother flew out to San Diego to see me. We went to a bar and some guy bumped into him, spilling Clayton's drink. The guy didn't apologize. My fuse was so short then. I lost it and grabbed the guy by the collar and slammed him against the wall."

Nat's eyes closed, remembering Noah slamming Duncan against the building. If provoked, the beast inside this gentle, kind man would come out. A fierce protectiveness rested just below the surface, but it seldom came out like that. What he'd described was as if his protective nature was on hyperdrive.

"Clayton pulled me off the guy. When your brother grabbed me, I shoved him to the ground. I didn't realize what I was doing. He and a bouncer at the bar dragged me outside. I don't know how, but Clayton convinced them not to call the police. After, we sat on a curb, and your brother told me I needed to get my shit together. That I wasn't the man I wanted to be. He was right."

"You went after that?"

Noah shook his head. "No. I still thought I could just get over it. I was a Marine. I'm still a Marine. Once a Marine always… well, you know. My dad was in the corps too, so I grew up in a house where we didn't do the touchy-feely thing."

"What finally pushed you?"

Their gazes weaved together. "You. That Friday, you called for our weekly check-in. I just kept thinking about how I shoved your brother to the ground and…" Concern creased his brow "…What if I'd done that to you? What if it was my mom? I hadn't hurt Clayton, but I could have."

It seemed preposterous to her that Noah could lose control. When she placed her hand on Noah to release Duncan, he relented. Rage hadn't overpowered him. As angry as Noah was, he still had control. The only danger Nat was in was from Duncan, never from Noah.

"I didn't want to hurt the people I care about because I was too stubborn to get help. So, I started seeing a counselor on base, and when I was discharged, I went to the VA."

She leaned in, pressing a gentle kiss to the center of his chest. "I'm in awe of you. Most people wouldn't tackle things so head on."

Most people included her. Besides a few sessions with the school guidance counselor after Evan died, she'd never talked about it. Those sessions were spent smiling and saying, "It's all good." She'd never dealt with the grief and guilt outside of her confession to Noah.

Nobody in her family had. They never brought Evan up in front of their parents out of fear of their mom's reaction. Hell, Clayton and Nat barely spoke about Evan with each other.

She sighed. "I wish I was as brave as you."

He ran his fingers through her messy tendrils. "You are. You just need to let yourself be."

"I worry that even if I'm brave enough to talk to someone about Evan, that my parents...well, my mom isn't ready."

Noah shifted in bed, lying on his side so that they faced each other. "My mom says your mom hasn't talked about him since he died."

"I had a picture on my desk of the entire family on my eighteenth birthday. Clayton had driven down from Ithaca and Evan from Buffalo. It was the last time we were all together. It was our last complete Owens' Family picture."

Nat closed her eyes, picturing Evan's full-faced grin as he stood next to her in the photo. Frowns, firm lines, and even grimaces were such a rare thing on his face which always had a beaming smile.

Opening her eyes, she whispered, "I put the picture in my desk drawer the other day."

"To protect your mom?"

"You saw her on Sunday. Evan's name was mentioned, and she..."

It was hard to describe what happened to her mom when Evan was brought up. It was like someone else took over her body. The warmth in her gray eyes and the lightness in her smile disappeared.

"When Evan died, she fell apart. She only got out of bed to attend his funeral. She spent weeks in bed. It wasn't until my graduation that she finally started living again. I remember she was upstairs getting ready. Clayton and I were downstairs. Dad came into the living room and asked us to not bring Evan up, so we didn't. We never spoke of him again. When Clayton mentioned him last Sunday, it was the first time in ten years he was brought up. Clayton and I hardly speak of Evan. It's like he never existed, but at the same time, he's everywhere."

"You deserve to talk about your brother. Evan deserves to be talked about. Hell, he would have insisted on it."

A watery laugh escaped her. "He did like being the center of attention."

"He did." Wistfulness glinted in his eyes.

The only other people in the world who knew Evan as well as Nat, her parents, and Clayton, were Noah and his parents. Evan was three years younger than Noah and Clayton. He was the little brother who tagged along with them. It warmed her heart that she could talk to someone who knew Evan as well as she did. She didn't need to introduce Evan to Noah like with others. It made it easier to be open with her feelings.

Although, so many of her unspoken emotions seemed to be said with Noah. His presence was like coming home. With him, she was safe. She could be her. The woman who came out behind the closed door of her home. The home where she could be unapologetically Nat. Messy. Sassy. Sad. Happy. Goofy. Grieving. Self-doubting. He didn't seem to just accept her but revel in all that she was and wasn't.

"Did you know when I turned sixteen, he drove down from Buffalo to surprise me at school? I was in the cafeteria when he showed up with sixteen balloons, all different colors, and a car-shaped cake. He sang 'Happy Birthday' at the top of his lungs in the middle of the lunchroom. I was *so* embarrassed, but my girlfriends went gaga for him."

Noah laughed. "He was such a ham."

"It was sweet, though. He sat there eating cake with me and my friends during lunch. After school, he picked me up, and we shoved all those balloons into his Chevy Cobalt." Her entire body rumbled with the memory of the balloons slapping against their heads as they pulled out of the school's parking lot.

"You know the first Christmas I came back on leave from the Marines, he gave me a signed, framed picture of himself?"

She snorted. "I forgot about that!"

Noah's hand moved to her mouth, tracing her lips. "I know you worry about your mom, but if this smile is any indication, you need to talk about Evan. The good memories..." His hand trailed down to her heart, placing his warm palm on it. "...and the sadness and loss in here. You deserve to grieve properly."

CHAPTER THIRTY-ONE

"I want to be great or nothing." ~Louisa May Alcott, *Little Women*

After several long goodbye kisses in the hotel parking lot, Nat slipped into her Jeep while Noah climbed into his SUV. It was odd to think they'd be driving back to almost the same destination but in separate vehicles. As she drove down the interstate, music blasted through her speakers. She lost herself in the idea of what it would be like to drive back with Noah riding shotgun. No doubt he'd tease her for her bad singing voice but join right in with her version of carpool karaoke. There'd be stolen kisses across the console, and hands clenched together. What would it be like to head to his place…their place?… instead of the Little Red Barn?

"You're being ridiculous," she chided herself with an exaggerated eye roll.

Cranking the music, she sang along with Taylor Swift's "Love Story." The song made her think of Noah. It was going to be a long ninety-minute drive. Hell, it was going to be a… however long until she got to see him again.

"Goddess, you have it bad." Laughter belted out of her.

The pop music sing-along was soon interrupted by an incoming call from Summer. Nat hit answer.

"Are you alone?" Summer's voice filled the Jeep.

"Yes. I'm on my way back. Why?"

"How was your sexcation?"

That's why she wondered if I was alone. More laughter vibrated through her. "It wasn't..." she scrunched her nose. "Exactly how much sex does one have to have in order for it to meet the definition of a sexcation?"

"The fact that you even have to ponder that tells me it was a sexcation." Her laugh was somehow both buoyant and salacious. "Can you even walk?"

"Yes, I can walk, but I am a little sore."

Delicious tenderness ached between her legs. In the ten years she'd been sexually active, this was the most *active* she'd ever been. She wasn't a prude; she'd had plenty of sex with past boyfriends and a few regrettable one-night stands, but nobody who left her in an almost constant state of physical, emotional, and intellectual arousal like Noah did.

"Sex aside, how was the weekend?" Summer asked.

The sound of children playing in the background told her that Summer was at the park with Liam. The image of Summer relaxing on one of the worn wooden benches of the village's park while Liam played on the swings filled her imagination.

"Amazing!" She couldn't describe the sound she made. It was half-elation, half-wistful longing for more time with Noah.

"Girl, I can hear the Cheshire Cat grin in your voice. Oh, you're a goner for him."

Nat bit her lip. She could hear the question coming. She knew Summer well enough. She'd ask if there was a plan for them to disclose themselves as a couple. Nat still wasn't ready for that. So much needed to be discussed with her parents and Clayton. Adding Noah to that equation may be too much. As much as she longed for the idea of parking her rather conspicuous yellow Jeep in his driveway during a very adult sleepover, there were too many wrinkles to smooth out first.

"Hey, so I grabbed a bunch of swag for you and some possible resources for your event planning business," she said, changing the subject before Summer could pounce.

"It's hardly a business." The dismissive wave of her hand was audible in her voice.

"Whatever, Modest Mary," Nat *tsked*. "You're a badass boss! Besides Elle's wedding, you're planning four other parties *and* the upcoming Fall Fest at the end of September. Anyway, I have lots of stuff for you. Also, I need your help with an idea I have."

"Is it how to tell your family that you're dating Noah so you can stop sneaking around like a pair of horny teenagers in a bad melodrama?"

Can't distract supermom. Nat's brows knitted in mild annoyance. "No. It's about how we can offer mental health services at the clinic."

"Oh, you have your determined Nat voice on."

Nat's grin couldn't be contained. "Sure do, because who runs the world?"

"Girls!" Summer cheered.

They sure fucking do! Dr. Nat Owens was in the house, and her prescription pad was ready to take charge.

CHAPTER THIRTY-TWO

"Your father, Jo. He never loses patience, never doubts, or complains, but always hopes and waits so cheerfully that one is ashamed to do otherwise in front of him." ~Louisa May Alcott, Little Women

Nat tapped her leopard print ballet flat against the leg of her office chair, reviewing the grant application for the Clark Foundation. It had been four days since she sat at the Cider House excitedly telling Noah about her idea. Since then, minus the stolen moments with Noah, she'd used her free time to compile everything needed for the application and to develop her plan. The next step was to talk to her parents about it.

Nat picked up her phone from beside her laptop and texted Noah.

Me: Hey Baby. *Kissy Face Emoji.* **If I email you my draft business plan and grant proposal later this week, would you give me your business-god opinion? In exchange, I'll let you play doctor and I'll be the patient.** *Doctor Emoji.*

Noah: Hey baby. *Winky Face Emoji.* **Of course, I'll review**

it. Also, you don't have to offer sexual favors for me to help you. I'm your boyfriend, I'll do it for free.

Me: So, you don't want to play doctor with me then?

Noah: I didn't say that...

Giggling, Nat placed her phone back on the desk. She clicked on the foundation's mission statement to help guide the points she'd make in her proposal and show why her plan fit with the organization's overall mission to support thriving rural communities. Her Boston friends never understood why she'd wanted to move back to the small farm town where she'd grown up. Boston offered so much, especially for a young doctor. There were ample supplies of hospitals and clinics to work at. Not to mention the many neighborhoods full of restaurants, bars, and clubs for the rare night off versus a downtown with just a few spots open after eight.

Although, two of those spots were owned by her boyfriend, a fact that trumped anything Boston offered. That's what pulled Nat back to Perry. Yes, here she was seen by so many as the youngest child of Dr. and Mrs. Owens, but the town was filled with her people. In Boston, she was just a nameless face in an ocean of people, but in Perry, she was Nat, Natalie, and to some Dr. Owens.

Here she was a part of the fabric of the community, not just another person drowning under an oversize blanket. Some people adored big cities, but Nat loved her small town and she wanted to support it. To ensure the people in Perry had what they needed not just to survive but to thrive.

"Dr. Owens," Dad's gentle voice filtered into her office.

Nat minimized the Clark Foundation's website and swiveled in the chair to face him. "Dr. Owens."

Happiness quirked his lips. "I was heading over to the hospital to round with some of our admitted patients during the long lunch break. I thought..." He paused, adjusting his red polka dot bow tie.

Nat straightened. Was he inviting her to come? Since she'd

returned, he'd primarily rounded at the hospitals without her.

"I thought you'd like to head out for lunch. You usually just eat here and catch up on charting. Remember, it's important to have balance," he said.

Nat shook her head. "No."

Dad's hand rose to the back of his neck, his eyes squinted in confusion. "I'm sorry?"

"I should be going on hospital rounds with you." She stood up. She wasn't sure why, but it felt important to be standing when she said this. "In fact, we should set up a schedule to rotate who goes on the visits."

If she waited for her parents to treat her like a colleague instead of a daughter, she'd wait forever. For twenty-eight years, she'd only ever been a daughter to them. It was too naïve to think they could just flip the label without some prompting from her.

Nodding, Dad tapped his fingers against the breast pocket of his lab coat. Each tap seemed to consider her suggestion.

"That sounds good. We only have two patients at the county hospital today. How about we visit them for an hour and then grab lunch before coming back? We can discuss the schedule," he said, slipping his hands into his coat pockets.

Joy slid over her, causing a large smile to spread. "Sounds like a sound plan, Dr. Owens."

"Why, thank you, Dr. Owens." He grinned.

They rode to the county hospital in Warsaw, the next town over. Nat couldn't help but giggle as Dad sang along to Taylor Swift on the radio. He was just as much of a Swiftie as she was. The selfie of them at a T-Swift concert, her in a home-made *Shake it Off* glittery T-shirt, and Dad, wearing a bow tie with tiny guitars, sat framed on the bedstand in the Little Red Barn.

This was one of the best parts of Dad. He was like a many-layered, jam-filled cake. On the outside, he appeared the stoic formal doctor, but with his family, he'd let out a hidden goofiness. Most people thought Nat was like her mom, but in moments like this when Dad belted his off-key version of T-Swift music from the passenger seat of her Jeep, she knew she was a lot like him.

After seeing their patients, they stopped at a small pizzeria on Main Street in Warsaw. A basket of wings and a large antipasto salad sat in the center of the red table for them to share.

Smiling, Nat scooped salad onto a small yellow plate. "It's been ages since we've had a solo lunch date."

"Too long." He stirred his iced tea with his straw. "Maybe we can make this a thing with the schedule. We can rotate, but maybe we should have one day when we do together. I enjoyed rounding with you today."

"That would be nice." Nat speared the lettuce with her fork. "Thanks for agreeing to let me come and to the schedule."

"Agreeing?" he chuckled. "You make it sound like an imposition. I've been hoping you'd ask to come."

Placing her fork down, she leaned against the black leather seat. "Waiting? How come you just didn't ask me to come?"

"I didn't want to push you. I wanted to give you time to settle in."

"Why?" The questions buzzed through her. *Was it because you worried that I wasn't ready? Was it because you weren't ready?* Each remained inside her as he went on.

A heavy sigh fell out of him. "I had pushed Clayton to be pre-med at Cornell. I was so excited about sharing this with one of my children." He motioned around them as if they sat in the clinic, not a pizzeria. "When he'd chose not to go to medical school, I had felt rejected, and it strained our relationship for a long time."

Nat nodded. For years, there had been tension between

father and son. Clayton thought he'd disappointed their dad when he'd chose to become a veterinarian instead of a family medicine doctor like their father. Dad thought Clayton's choice was a rejection of a relationship with him. It wasn't until last year that the two had finally talked. Sharing their truths had formed a stronger bond between them.

"I was so happy when you said you wanted to become a doctor, but I didn't want to push you. I didn't want you to think my pride...my love for you was contingent on you becoming a doctor."

"I worried it was because I wasn't Evan." The confession was so quiet that she feared he'd not heard and feared even more that he had.

"What?" Regret shimmered in his blue eyes.

"I'm sorry..." she started and then stopped herself. How often had she apologized for mentioning Evan and then changed the subject? How often had she said things were fine when they weren't? How frequently had she wished to be brave?

You are *brave. You just need to let yourself be.* Noah's words whispered in her ear as if encouraging her to keep going.

"No, I am not sorry." She shook her head. "When Evan was alive, the two of you would talk for hours about his medical school courses and plans for the clinic after he came back. Mom and you would talk about early retirement, but with me, you did none of that. When Noah's dad mentioned the idea of retirement, Mom and you squashed it quickly. Is it because you don't think I can do it? Is it because I'm not Evan?"

The words choked her as they came out, but she kept her gaze fixed on him. Gray clouds rolled in his eyes, and his smile wobbled.

"No." His voice came out low and hoarse. "I lost one child and felt like I was losing another. I was not going to risk you." Tears welled in his eyes.

"Dad...I'm sorry...I—"

He reached for her hand, grasping it. "Do not apologize. I'm the one who's sorry. I never want you to ever feel like that. You are not Evan, but Evan was not you. I was blessed with three amazing children. Each of you is so different from one another, yet all three are equal in the gifts you've given your mother and me. Clayton is so stoic, thoughtful, and protective. Evan was charming and effervescent. You are all those things. You are love in motion. Everything you do is anchored by love and you spread that love to everyone around you."

Nat swiped at the tears pricking her eyes. "I didn't know you were worried about losing me."

He inhaled deeply and then pinned his gaze on her. "I never said anything. Just like with Clayton."

"Why don't we talk about things?"

"Your mom and I came from families that didn't talk about ...emotional...things. We kept everything inside. It's not an excuse...it's just how we were raised, and I think we raised you kids the same way. Clayton and I went fifteen years without really talking about important things, and now you and I have gone ten years. I don't want unsaid things to keep coming between me and my children. I don't want to be the reason I lose one of my children. It hurt so much to lose Evan. If I lost Clayton or you..." His voice quaked, and his words trailed off.

"We do need to talk more...and we need to talk about Evan," she said.

His confession fueled her bravery. It was time to take off the Band-Aids and let the wounds heal in honesty's fresh air.

"At my graduation, you'd asked us not to mention Evan so we wouldn't upset Mom. We've obeyed for the last ten years, but it hasn't helped. Mom may be out of bed. She may be smiling. She may be laughing. She may be doing all the things that make someone seem fine, but she's not fine. None of us are. Until we truly grieve Evan, we never will be." Steely resolve punctuated her words.

"I know," he whispered, his eyes downcast to his lap.

"Hey." She tugged at his hand, pulling his gaze back to her. "How about we start with us? Maybe we can talk about Evan during our father/daughter lunch dates...really talk. We can figure out together how best to help Mom...to help ourselves."

Mom wasn't the only Owens who needed to grieve. Evan's death had haunted them all in different ways, beyond just the missing of a son or brother.

He shook his head *No*. Her heart plummeted to her feet. They'd just discussed how important it was to talk.

"I'd like to have our father/daughter lunch dates, but I think we need to include Clayton in this discussion about Evan and how best to approach your Mom to move forward as a family. I need both my children's strengths and good hearts to help guide us on this." He squeezed her hand.

"Plus, Clayton has the puppies, and that always softens Mom up," she joked.

He chuckled. "She does love being a grandma to those fur babies."

"Imagine how she'd be with human grandbabies." Nat grabbed her iced tea and sipped.

"Well, since Clayton and Elle don't want human children...maybe Noah and you will give her some grandbabies soon."

Nat spat out her iced tea. The cool liquid dribbled down her chin and splatted onto the table. "Excuse me?" She coughed, blotting her face with a paper napkin.

Is he joking? This had to be a weird new form of a Dad Joke. Nat's pulse sped up as she dabbed at the table.

The corners of his mouth flexed into a knowing grin. "So, Noah and you are together?"

She waved her hands in the air. "What are you talking

about, old man? I think you're having a stroke. Do you smell burnt toast? I smell burnt toast!" she sputtered, flicking her gaze around the empty pizzeria.

"Natalie Joan Owens." He arched an accusing right brow.

Oh, fuck, I've been full-named.

"If we're honestly going to talk about things, I assumed Noah would be one of those topics. I mean, the two of you aren't planning to keep your relationship secret forever, are you?" His tone was warm, but a little scolding.

"How do you know? Is this like fatherly intuition?" She motioned to him.

"I drove out to the Little Red Barn to check on you while Clayton and Elle were gone. I saw Noah's SUV parked there."

She tossed her hands up. "That means nothing. He just stopped by…"

"Four nights in a row," he interrupted, holding up four fingers. "Then, this weekend you said you were going to Syracuse to see a friend, and Scott mentioned Noah was speaking at the Rural Business Conference in…" he paused with a gleefulness that was reserved for men not prone to formal bow ties. "…Syracuse."

Busted. She raised her hands to her heated face.

"Does Mom know? Oh goddess, does Clayton know?" Her questions were muffled behind her hands.

He pulled her hands down. "Nope. Only me. I didn't say anything."

"This is the one time I'm grateful for our family *not* talking about things."

"Curses can be blessings, and blessings can be cursed," he said with a shrug.

"Are you upset?" She fiddled with the gardenia necklace Noah had given her. For a moment, its smoothness felt as soft as Noah's hand holding hers. He'd promised he'd hold her hand when they told their families and in a way he was.

"Absolutely not. I love Noah. He's a good man." He

leaned back, his face scrunched in thought. "Over the last few years, I've suspected something brewing between the two of you. The way his eyes always seemed to follow you. The way your face would light up when he entered a room."

"You and your love of detective novels figured this one out before anyone else. I think even before Noah and me."

Amusement played in his expression. "Yup."

"I know this is counter to everything we've talked about, but I'm not ready to tell Clayton and Mom yet."

"Mainly Clayton?" It was a question, but they both knew the answer.

"They've been best friends since they were in their mom's wombs. This could change their relationship. I don't know how Clayton would react to this. He's never liked anybody I've ever dated. I don't want this to end their friendship."

"I think your brother would be happy with this."

"Now I know you're having a stroke," she guffawed. "Think about how he interacted with all my boyfriends through the years."

"Perhaps he didn't like them because none of them were Noah."

Nat rolled her eyes. "If only that were the case."

Dad opened his mouth, shut it, and then furrowed his brows. "I know he didn't like Duncan."

She pointed at him. "That one he was spot on about. Duncan was an asshole."

"Do I need to speak with Duncan? Was he not a gentleman?" Eyes narrowed, his jaw clenched.

"He's a dick, but I took care of him and I'm okay. Plus, Noah put the fear of the goddess into him."

Like a proud peacock, he puffed up at that. "That's my Noah."

She fought the urge to correct him that he was *her* Noah and not his, but the warm feeling spreading within her with that statement was too intoxicating. Her concern about telling her family had very little to do with Dad. Deep down, she knew he'd be the one to embrace her relationship with Noah. It was Clayton she was most concerned about.

"Dad, it wasn't just Duncan. When I dated Tim in undergrad, Clayton called him Tom for two years and said two words to him when they met. Then there was Jacob when I was in medical school. I believe Clayton threatened to grind him into dog food. Anytime I've mentioned going on dates, he's lectured me. Hell, at the engagement party, he told me to put a jacket on, because he thought my dress was too short."

Dad frowned. "That dress was a little short."

She rolled her eyes.

"I know…not the point." He raised his hands in defense.

She smiled.

"You're right. Clayton is a tad overprotective. It may be best to strategize how best to tell him this." He tapped the fingers of his right hand on the table and then raised his hand, presenting his pinky to her. "I promise to keep it between us 'til you're ready."

A soft laugh escaped her. It was just like when she was a little girl, and she'd make him pinky swear not to spill the beans about a crafting project she was making to surprise Mom or one of her brothers.

"It's a deal," she said, linking their little fingers.

CHAPTER THIRTY-THREE

"I know I shall be homesick for you…Even from heaven." ~Louisa May Alcott, *Little Women*

The night air caressed Nat's exposed arms, its cool kiss causing goosebumps to bloom. It had been warmer when she'd first come out to sit on the dock. The Boston College hoodie she'd worn with her shorts was draped over her legs as she lounged in the white Adirondack chair, sipping from a bottle of cider. She should go inside, but the serenity of the stars scattered across the velvety sky and the hum of acoustic music from her phone kept her in place.

It was needed respite after the good but emotional talk with Dad earlier today. Eyes closed, Nat leaned back in the chair as the music thrummed through her, easing the tension that had tightened her muscles.

Talking to Dad had been a huge step, but there were so many more steps to go. Goddess, there was a whole staircase. They needed to talk to Clayton and figure out a strategy to approach Mom about Evan. It wouldn't be enough for just Dad and her to talk about Evan. The only way for them to move forward was as a family. Evan wasn't just her loss but their whole family's loss. Therefore, the entire family needed to handle it together. None of them would be free if one of them remained imprisoned by grief.

"You look cold," Noah's deep baritone called Nat away from her thoughts.

Nat blinked her eyes open. Noah stood, hands in pockets, at the edge of the dock on the stone path. With Elle out of town for the week for work, Clayton and he had hung out. When Nat had returned home from dinner with Summer she'd found Noah's SUV parked in front of the farmhouse.

She waved to her lap. "I'm using my sweatshirt as a blanket."

The heat of his gaze dragged along her bare arms and shoulders in her pink tank top.

"I was too wiped to get up and get a blanket." Exhaustion dragged down her tone.

"Are you okay?" he asked, seeming to study her with shrewd, assessing eyes.

"Yeah. Dad and I had a heart-to-heart at lunch. It was good, but it was a lot. We talked about Evan and about how I've been feeling at the clinic."

"That's great, baby."

Baby. The endearment ignited a sensation of being wrapped up in a fluffy warm blanket. Any lingering tension dissolved with Noah's proximity.

"Did you also talk to your mom?"

"No. I'd need more than this cider after *that* conversation." She tipped her almost empty bottle to him. "We're going to strategize that convo. Dad suggested Clayton, he, and I figure it out together."

He stepped closer, halted, and looked toward the farmhouse.

"You want to kiss me *so* bad right now, don't you?" she teased.

"So bad." His throat bobbed.

"Oh, my dad knows about us." The cider and exhaustion loosened her lips. Tipsiness dripped through her from the emotional talk with Dad, along with the bottle of cider. Goddess, she was a lightweight.

"You told him?" Bewilderment twisted his expression.

"No. You know how he fancies himself an amateur sleuth with all those detective novels he reads? He figured it out and confronted me at lunch with a joke about us giving him human grandbabies. Well, giving Mom grandbabies, but I guess they'd be his too."

A cautious huff of laughter slipped past Noah's lopsided grin.

"He approves, by the way." She drained her cider. "He says you're a good man and he suspected we were into each other for a while."

Noah shook his head. "Your dad never ceases to surprise me. So, how do you feel about him knowing?"

Placing the empty bottle on the dock, she decided she was too cold. Grabbing her sweatshirt, she tugged it over her head. "I'm okay with it. Dad was never my concern."

Noah nodded.

Nat adjusted in the chair, sitting cross-legged, her short legs exposed to the chilled air. "How was boys' night with Clayton?"

"Good. We got Daryl's and watched a baseball game." Noah stepped to the chair, placing his firm hand on her shoulder. "I'm so proud of you, my brave girl."

She moved her hand to his and leaned her head against the warmth of his arm. She had been brave. Noah didn't make her brave but reminded her she already was. It bolstered her for having the conversation with her dad today.

"Thank you for reminding me who I am when I forget." She closed her eyes, letting his soothing presence fold around her.

"I thought you were leaving." Clayton's voice called in the distance.

Nat's head jolted up, and she released Noah's hand. Noah stepped away from the chair, turning toward the sound of shuffling feet.

"I am. I saw Nat and was just saying hi," Noah offered.

Nat adjusted in the chair, crossing her legs in front of her. "Hey, Clay Pigeon, how was boys' night?"

"Ugh," he grumbled at the nickname. "Good. How was your night?" Clayton reached the dock, stepping to its center.

"Good. I had dinner with Summer, and now I'm just decompressing with the stars and cider." She waved to the sky and then to the empty bottle sitting next to the leg of the chair.

Clayton's eyes narrowed. "Shouldn't you have pants on?"

Nat looked at her bare legs. "I'm wearing shorts. They're pants-lite."

Clayton took off the Cornell hoodie he wore and draped it over her legs.

"Seriously? I'm not a little girl!" she muttered.

Noah's eyes flashed with an apology as he looked at Nat. She wasn't sure if the apology was for him not wearing a sweatshirt to offer her or if it was for Clayton's protective yet Victorian instincts. It could be for both.

"It's a casualty of having a big brother." Clayton shrugged. "Are you still stopping by the brewery tonight?" He turned to Noah.

Noah nodded. "Yeah. I'm going to help Todd with closing. I should get going."

"Good night, Noah," Nat said.

How she wanted to stand up and wrap her arms around him. To kiss him goodnight and beg him to come back after closing. But the sweatshirt draped on her lap stopped her as if it was an anchor holding her down.

"Night." Noah tipped his head to Nat and then to Clayton.

As Noah walked away, Clayton crossed the dock taking the chair opposite of her. "It's been a while since I sat out here. It's been such a busy summer that Elle and I haven't spent much time out here."

"Yeah. I come out here at least once or twice a week to sit after dinner."

"I noticed." He leaned back in the chair and stretched his long legs in front of him. "It's been a while since we've hung out too. I know since Elle and I got engaged, we've been busy. I'm sorry about that. Maybe we can schedule a weekly thing."

Nat arched a brow. "What's causing this brotherly guilt?"

"I mentioned to Noah I hadn't seen much of you this summer, and he asked if I'd scheduled anything with you. I realized that I hadn't asked you to hang out in a while. I don't know...I don't like that you live on the same property as me, and I never see you unless it's at family dinners at Mom and Dad's."

It had been a while since they'd spent any brother/sister time. Since coming home, Nat had been focused on the clinic and building her new life back home, while Clayton had been focused on his engagement to Elle. They'd not intentionally pulled back from each other. It was just the casual result of life taking over.

"Yeah." She sighed a heavy breath. "I've missed hanging out with you too. I agree...let's set up weekly dinner dates."

He grinned. "Great. As long as you're not cooking, I'm game."

She flipped him off.

Teasing laughter glinted in his gray eyes. "Manners."

Affection swirled with her tipsy exhaustion. "Do you remember when you'd come home on weekends when you were at Cornell, and you'd take Evan and me to Daryl's for pizza and pinball?"

Clayton nodded, his gaze staring into the inky darkness. "Evan always got the high score."

Nat could almost hear the ding of the pinball machine and Evan's cheering as he crushed Clayton's score. Her once-girlish hoots of, "Go Evan!" filled her ears. The image of the three of them huddled around the flashing and pinging pinball machine broke loose a tiny tear that rolled down her cheek.

She dashed the tear away. "Dad and I talked about Evan today."

Clayton's head turned. "Wh...wh...what?" he stuttered.

Nat bit her lip, trying not to react. Clayton's childhood stutter came out when he was tired or too many emotions tripped his words as he tried to speak around them. The last time she'd heard him stutter was at Evan's funeral. He'd stumbled over his words as people approached the family in the church to offer their condolences. It was why she'd turned to Noah, mouthing a request for help and to deliver the eulogy instead of Clayton.

"We talked about how we need to well...talk. None of us can move on if we don't. We talked about Mom. I'm worried about her," she admitted.

"I am, too," he murmured.

The truth settled between them.

"I think we need to talk to Mom, and I think we need to talk to a professional about our grief...and I think I need to talk to someone on my own, as well." The unrestrained tears fell from her eyes. "I miss him so much. I feel so guilty that he's not here. That he's not at the clinic. That he's not here with us now. That he's not going to be at your wedding."

Clayton stood and dropped to his haunches in front of her. "Why do you feel guilty?"

"I was supposed to go running with him that night, and I didn't because we got into a fight over Duncan."

Clayton closed his eyes, seeming to take in her words. "We only ever ran with you at the park."

She nodded. Falling tears fuzzed her vision.

"Evan's accident was not your fault." Each word came with a deliberate slowness, as if he wanted her to not just hear each syllable, but to let the truth absolve her.

"I know that, but I don't feel that." It was her truth. Intellectually, she knew that Evan died as a result of an accident, but her feelings weren't logical. In her heart, she still believed that if she hadn't argued with her brother, Evan would still be here. That this sibling moment would be the three of them. Not just a triangle missing its vital side.

Clayton folded his arms around her. Nat melted into his embrace, allowing one brother to comfort her for the loss of the other.

"You know, Elle talks to someone every two weeks. It's helped her to deal with a lot of things. I can ask her for their contact info." He rubbed soothing circles across her back.

"That would be great," she sniffled.

He pulled back and looked at her. "I'm so sorry we stopped talking about Evan. That I left you alone with this. I didn't do my job as your big brother." He cleared his throat. "I should have been there for you."

"We should have been there for each other."

"It's not too late for us to do that now. To be there for each other and for Mom and Dad."

"It's not too late." She wrapped her arms around him, squeezing tight.

CHAPTER THIRTY-FOUR

"It's my dreadful temper! I try to cure it, I think I have and then it breaks out worse than ever." ~Louisa May Alcott, *Little Women*

Nat dipped her grilled cheese into the creamy homemade tomato soup. It was a drizzly mid-September day. The heat of summer had dulled with the cool breath of autumn. The meal was a perfect pairing for the first crisp day of approaching fall. Even better was the pairing with her lunch date for today, Noah. In the quiet confines of his back office at the brewery, they sat opposite each other, his walnut desk serving as their table.

In the last two weeks since she'd talked to Dad and Clayton, she and Noah found or, frankly, created stolen moments with each other. Today was Dad's turn on the hospital rotation schedule, so Nat took his work/life balance advice to heart and snuck away for lunch with Noah. The brewery didn't open until four. It was only noon, so staff wouldn't arrive until three to prep for opening. It was just them in their little secret romance bubble.

"So good," she groaned with pleasure, tilting her head

back as she bit into the gooey Gruyere spilling over the sand-wich's edges.

An amused expression covered his face. "I don't think I'll ever tire of feeding you. You're adorable when you eat my food."

She pointed her half-eaten sandwich at him. "You think I'm adorable, period."

"Very true." He leaned over the desk and bit off a piece of her sandwich.

She gaped. It was both very sexy when he did that and also frustrating. How dare he eat the food he'd prepared for her? Although, the playful glint in his eyes dissolved any inclination to be annoyed with him. She could never be angry with this man.

He wiped his mouth. "The way you're looking at me tells me you think I'm also adorable."

"You are adorable. I've even told my therapist how adorbs you are." She dunked the last bit of the sandwich into the remaining soup.

After the talk with Clayton, he'd texted Elle to get the name of her therapist. Dr. Horin was a psychologist located at Sloan-Whitney's Manhattan Hospital but offered virtual appointments. Nat's first session was last week, and her second session was scheduled for after work today. The first session had been tough but good. Elle had warned her that sometimes Nat would leave a session feeling wrung out like a dishrag, but she'd encouraged Nat to stick with it because a wet rag needed to be wrung from time to time to make it work.

"I've also told my therapist about how adorable you are." Noah winked.

"Aren't we just the enlightened, emotionally healthy couple talking about our therapy sessions over grilled cheese and soup."

His lips kicked up into a smirk. "So, the application deadline is coming up for that grant. Have you spoken to your parents about it, yet?"

"Tomorrow. I asked them if we could have lunch at the house after the clinic closes."

The clinic closed at noon on Friday to accommodate the schedule to be open on Saturdays. Most Fridays, Dad rounded at the hospital or spent it shadowing Clayton at the veterinarian clinic, but this Friday, he'd agreed to their lunch meeting instead. Dad had started going to Clayton's clinic last year after the two had reinvented their relationship. It was one of the ways that Dad wanted Clayton to know how proud he was. It was just another reason she loved and looked up to her dad.

"You got this, baby," he assured, picking up his bottled water.

Nat leaned back in the red Windsor chair. "Thanks. I'm really excited about this. So is Summer. I hope they go for it. Although, if they don't, I think I may do it anyway. I mean, the clinic will be mine one day. I'd prefer to do this with their support, but if they're not on board, I'm going to submit the proposal either way."

"Do you think they'd not get on board?" He scooped up their empty paper plates and bowls to toss into the bin beside the desk.

She unwrapped a moist towelette, then cleaned her hands. "Not anymore. I think Dad will be on board. Mom may get a little fussy that I didn't bring her in before I pulled together the application, but I want her to see that I can handle both the clinical and administrative side of the clinic. At the end of the day, I know they'll be supportive because this is what's best for our patients."

The self-doubts that had nipped at her after first coming home had dissolved over the last few weeks. No longer was she trying to be Dr. Owens. She was Dr. Owens. Her version of it.

"You're a badass, baby." He bent to kiss her.

The delicious taste of tomato soup lingered on his lips. Deepening their kiss, a tingle spread through her body. Nat rose to her feet and stepped into his arms. His hands were strong and gentle as they wrapped around her waist, pulling her against his firm chest.

"Does your office door have a lock?" she panted as they broke their kiss. Thanks to her period last week, it had been several days since they'd had sex. *Unacceptable!* She was leaning into this horny teenager phase they were in.

Noah lifted her onto the desk. Pivoting, he walked to the door and locked it. Hunger darkened his blue eyes as he prowled across the office to her. A starving wolf ready to devour a helpless doe. Although, she wasn't helpless, and the way her nails left the imprint of her passion in his skin showed she was more she-wolf than docile doe. Heat crawled up her body with each step he took.

"We're alone," he nipped her lower lip, the delicious sting coursing through her. "No need to be quiet."

She was not quiet. Neither was he.

Sated and giggling, they walked out of the office. Nat smoothed her ponytail, which had come undone during their rather athletic office sexcapades. *The desk and wall will never be the same.* Noah's button-up was untucked and wrinkled from where she'd pulled it off him and tossed it to the floor. As they headed down the short hallway coming into the main front of the bar, clapping halted their steps.

Todd leaned against the bar, a giant grin on his face, as he clapped. "Nicely done, you two."

Nat's cheeks flamed. "Oh, my goddess!" she squeaked, burying her face against Noah's chest.

"I thought you weren't coming in until three," Noah grumbled, running soothing strokes down Nat's back.

"I came in early to work on the pumpkin ale for Fall Fest next weekend. I was in the basement."

"I'm mortified." Her voice was muffled against Noah's chest.

Getting caught by Todd making out was one thing, but getting caught post-coitus at his place of business was quite another thing.

"Don't be embarrassed, Nat." Todd's default snarky tone turned tender and comforting. "I barely heard anything. Although, what I did hear was rather impressive."

"Dude!" Noah snapped, his tone warning. He tightened his arms around her.

Nat poked her head up, twisting to Todd.

His lips turned down in a frown as he looked at her face. "Sorry, Nat. I'm a dick. If it makes things even, I haven't had sex with anyone but my left hand in two years."

Strangely, that did make her feel a little better.

"Why the left hand?" she blurted.

"Because I'm right-handed, so it's like I'm having sex with someone else."

"Ha!" she barked.

"Dude." Noah vibrated with embarrassed laughter for his friend.

Todd shrugged. Not a twinge of mortification tinted his green eyes nor his smirk.

Nat faced Todd while Noah's arms remained draped around her shoulders. "Todd, we need to get you a girlfriend."

"I don't want *a* girlfriend. I'd like *the* girlfriend." Wistfulness shaded his voice.

Nat knew who *the* girlfriend was. At least, she suspected who it was. Maybe it was a kinship with a fellow crusher, but she could never be annoyed with Todd. For years she'd crushed on Noah with no hope of the feelings being returned. She hadn't been brave enough to put her desires out there. Todd's advances and flirtations had been batted away by Summer countless times. Nat believed the rejection had nothing to do with Todd and everything to do with Summer's past.

Noah kissed Nat's cheek. "I highly recommend *the* girlfriend."

Her pulse ticked up. *The girlfriend.* It had been just over a month since Todd had first caught them kissing behind the Wine Down. Like a boiling pot of water, her feelings had only intensified. She toggled between a lightness that almost lifted her off the ground and the too-full sensation within her heart.

Thoughtfulness lit Todd's features. "I'm glad Prince Charming finally found his queen."

"Thanks, Todd." She smiled. *I am a queen, not a princess. Suck it, Duncan!*

"I'm assuming we're still *hush-hush* about this." Todd gestured between them.

They nodded.

Shaking his head, he said, "Okay. Well, on that note, I'm going to head out to run an errand. I'll be back at three. From now on, I'll text you before I come in, just to be on the safe side."

After Todd slipped out the front door, Noah locked it. He turned, and they both burst out into unbridled laughter.

"Well, at least he'd only heard us and didn't see us," Noah said, walking to her.

"Are we as *bad* as Elle and Clayton?" she lamented.

"Never! Again, he only heard us. They've been caught in person having sex by at least three members of their wedding party." He kissed her forehead. "But he does bring up a valid point. It's been a month of sneaking around. I know you've told Summer, and your dad knows. By the way, does he know that I know that he knows? I only ask because he kept calling me son and giving me these almost salacious looks during dinner last Sunday."

She shook her head. "I didn't tell him that you know that he knows. By the way, that question sounds like a line from *Friends* when Monica and Chandler were sneaking around."

His lips quirked. "Your dad aside, I think we should tell people. Fall Fest is coming up, and I'd like to take my girl-friend. I'd like to hold her hand while I buy her an apple dumpling. I'd like to kiss her in public. I'd like to stop sneaking around." Determination glinted in his eyes.

All of that sounded wonderfully tempting. To step into the light with Noah. The only time they held hands in public was when they'd drive to Rochester or Buffalo for a date. It would be nice to not have to drive an hour to hold her boyfriend's hand.

Nat's gaze flicked to the picture behind the bar. It was from the grand opening. Noah and Clayton beamed as they toasted with bottles of Doc Owens beer. A vision of that picture torn in half flashed through her brain.

She shook her head. "I'm not ready."

"Nat." His exhale was loud and heavy. "When do you think you'll be ready?"

She stepped out of his arms. "I don't know. I don't know."

"I know you're scared to tell Clayton, but if your dad is any indication, I think he'll be okay with us."

"You think Clayton will be okay that you're fucking his little sister?" The harshness in the words left a bitter taste in her mouth.

Noah blanched. "How could you say that? That's not what we're doing, and you know it. We're more than that."

She threw her hands up. "I know that's not what we're doing, but that's where Clayton will go. Besides Elle, you probably know Clayton best. Can you look at me and honestly say he's going to jump for joy that you are screwing his sister?"

Anger flashed in his expression. "I wish you'd stop putting it in those terms."

"That's how Clayton's going to see it!" she shouted.

"Not if we explain things," he shouted back.

Nat stepped back. "Stop pushing, Noah."

He closed his eyes. "I don't want to be your dirty little secret anymore."

The words stung like a slap to the face. "Then don't be," she hissed, walking towards the back door.

"Nat, wait," he called.

"No. I need to get back to the clinic. I have patients," she said, slamming the door behind her as she left.

CHAPTER THIRTY-FIVE

"The sincere wish to be good is half the battle." ~Louisa May
Alcott, *Little Women*

Dr. Horin's angular features filled the screen as Nat sat crossed-legged on the floor, back pressed against the couch, her laptop perched on the coffee table. The tightness in Nat's shoulder blades and jitteriness in her limbs made her shift her position for the third time in ten minutes. Her legs were now bent beneath her. They'd spent the first part of the session discussing the day Evan died.

"So, you called Noah before you called your older brother?" Dr. Horin asked, or perhaps stated. Questions seemed to be statements, and statements seemed to be questions coming out of her red lips.

Nat nodded. After the police left that night, Dad held his wailing wife in his arms while Nat had stood motionless and disbelieving on the bottom step in the entry hall. Without thinking, she'd turned, walked upstairs to her room, and collapsed onto the floor. Holding her cell phone in a death grip, she'd called Noah. Her voice was soggy with not-yet-shed tears as she'd told him Evan had died.

"Were the two of you dating then?" Dr. Horin clicked her pen.

She shook her head. "No."

Were they still together? After today's fight and her cutting words as she walked out of the brewery, she wasn't sure. Neither had texted nor called since this afternoon.

"Why was he your first call?"

Nat pulled at the string of her Boston College hoodie. "I needed him." It sounded more like a question than an actual answer.

Dr. Horin's face remained thoughtful as she sat quietly.

After a few silent moments, Nat inhaled a long breath. "I called because I needed Noah to be there for Clayton. I knew Clayton would need him. They've been best friends since they were zygotes."

Dr. Horin clicked her pen again. "It's good that you had such a supportive friend in Noah."

Nat just twined the gray string around her finger, allowing the movement to steady her jittering nerves. Every piece of her wanted to end this conversation. To do what she had always done, just smile and say, "It's fine." But those days were over.

At least, she hoped.

"You mentioned during our last session that it was best that Noah was the one to tell Clayton that Evan died. Why was that? What made him best?"

"As I said, they're best friends." Nat shifted her legs, stretching them under the coffee table, grounding herself with the cool hardwood floor against her heels.

Dr. Horin nodded. "True, but why not you? You're Clayton's sister. The two of you shared Evan as a sibling."

Guilt jackhammered inside her, provoking a sharp pain in her chest. This is why she was here. To air this out. It was so much easier to talk about talking than to actually do it. It was time to unravel the cluster of emotions writhing inside her.

Sucking in a deep breath, she spoke, "Because it's my fault that Evan died."

Nat rushed on to explain everything to Dr. Horin, who sat with a placid smile on her face. No judgment sparked in her eyes. No quick words were uttered telling Nat she was foolish to think or feel that she was responsible for Evan's death. She just listened.

"I know that Evan's death isn't my fault. Like I know that here." She pointed to her head. "But I don't feel that here." She pointed to her heart. "I know it's stupid and probably a little narcissistic to feel this, but I do."

"Well, most feelings are narcissistic because they're our feelings, nobody else's. If they weren't a little narcissistic, then they wouldn't be ours."

Nat allowed a small smile to tick up.

Dr. Horin went on, "Therapy isn't going to take away these feelings, but our sessions will help you better understand and deal with them."

"That's what Noah has told me," she said, her voice soft and sad.

"It sounds like you have a very understanding partner in Noah." Dr. Horin grinned, adjusting her red-framed glasses.

"I had."

"*Had?*" A dark brow arched.

Tears gathered in the corner of Nat's eyes. "I may have broken up with him. I'm not sure, but I think I did."

Nat swiped at her tears with the end of her sweatshirt sleeve coating the soft cotton with salty wetness. It all spilled out of her. The secret nature of their relationship. Dad figuring it out. Noah pushing for them to declare themselves as a couple and her insistence that they wait.

"Why do you think you are hesitant to tell people you are a couple?" Dr. Horin asked.

Was she *not* listening to Nat? It was what Nat was paying her to do...listen. This was very black and white.

An exasperated breath puffed out of Nat. "Like I said, I'm concerned about the impact on Noah and Clayton's friendship. Clayton has hated all my boyfriends. I don't want to be the reason they aren't friends anymore."

Dr. Horin nodded, but her nod seemed to display assessment rather than agreement. "How do you think telling your brother about your relationship with Noah would impact your relationship with him?"

Nat's gaze flicked to the desk pressed up against the front window. A framed picture of her with Clayton, Elle, and Noah from this past Christmas sat on the corner. The picture soothed and mocked. Both a glimpse of the possible future for the two couples and what would be at risk if this didn't go well.

"That I could lose him." A tiny tremor shook her words.

"Which him do you fear losing most?"

"What?" she gulped. Her heart jumped in her throat, choking her ability to speak.

"You don't have to answer it now, but it may be good to really look at your fear about telling your brother and ask yourself what you are *truly* afraid of losing. Then, ask yourself what impact that fear is having on you? How is that fear's hold on you helping make what you fear could happen… happen?"

CHAPTER THIRTY-SIX

"To be loved and chosen by a good man..." ~Louisa May Alcott,
Little Women

After the session with Dr. Horin, Nat lounged on the couch, her acoustic chill playlist her only companion. Exhaustion melded with all the feelings roaming aimlessly within her. Sadness for what happened with Noah. Anger at herself for causing it. Regret that she'd lost him. Fear that she was destined to lose everyone she cared about.

"You're being melodramatic," she scolded as she sat up on the couch, allowing the patchwork blanket to fall to her waist.

In so many ways, when Evan died she'd lost the people she loved most in the world. Even if they were still there physically, a barrier existed between them. With her family, it was Evan. His ghost not only haunted them but seemed to hold them at a distance from one another. By not grieving, they'd erected invisible walls between them, but brick by brick, they could dismantle those barriers. Dad, Clayton, and she had started. Soon, they'd figure out how to get Mom to pull down her wall, the stoutest of them all.

It wasn't just her family she'd built barriers against.

Duncan had said that Nat had never given him a chance. Not that he deserved a chance, but he was right. Her heart had been closed to him. In her heart, she knew that to be true. Her other two boyfriends had said the same thing. Summer thought it was because Nat was so enamored with Noah that she didn't let past boyfriends in.

"It's not Noah...it's me." Nat nibbled on her bottom lip and considered her racing thoughts.

She had held those previous boyfriends at a distance. Not allowing herself to be...well, herself. She'd never opened herself up to any of them like she had with Noah. She'd shared *almost* all her truths, fears, joys, flaws, strengths, and all the things that defined her. As much as she'd given over herself to Noah, she'd still held back pieces. Not standing fully in the light with him, remaining on the edge of shadow and light. That hesitance had cost her Noah. The one man she wanted to not only break down her walls but snuggle with her within them. Letting him in as she took them down as she healed.

A soft knock interrupted Nat's introspection. Jerking her head toward the door, she shouted she was coming. Tossing the blanket to the side, she stood up and shuffled to the door.

It was Thursday night. Clayton played darts at the VFW. Nat would often join him and Elle, but she'd texted earlier that she was wiped and was bowing out tonight. It was just after seven. The two should have left already, but maybe they were checking in on her before they left. It would be a very Clayton thing to do, after all.

She opened the door. "Noah." Her heart both ached and sighed with sweet relief at his presence.

Noah stood, hands at his sides. Regret etched his handsome face. Was it regret for her? About her? Because of her?

What have I done? "I am so sorry," she said, tears brimming in her eyes.

Noah stepped close, pulling her into his embrace. Burying

her face against his chest, she let the tears fall onto the softness of his T-shirt.

"I didn't mean it...I didn't mean it." The words tumbled out of her in hiccupping sobs.

"I know, baby," he soothed, pressing her closer to him. "I'm sorry I pushed you."

Nat tilted her face up to him, meeting his eyes. "You aren't my dirty little secret. I'm not scared to tell Clayton because of you..." The icy truth shivered up her spine. "I lost one brother. I don't want to lose another, but if I have to choose between Clayton and you, I'd choose you." She closed her eyes. "The reason why I'm scared is that if it came to you choosing between Clayton and me, I fear you'd choose him."

As soon as the words left her lips, the rigidity holding her muscles captive released its hold. Weakened by her confession, she swayed. Only his strong grip on her kept her upright, even though every muscle cried out to collapse. As if they had no more strength after holding onto her truth for so long.

Noah cradled her face, his gaze capturing hers. "I choose you."

The pounding of her heart almost drowned out his words. *Almost.*

"I choose us." His lips met hers.

"Will you hold me?" she whispered between their kisses.

Scooping her up in his arms, he carried her through the living room, up the stairs to the sleeping loft, and laid her on the bed. Slipping his sneakers off, he scooted in beside her, tucking her into his chest. Snuggling into his nook, she closed her eyes, allowing his soothing pine scent to wash over her like a gentle spring rainstorm nourishing her.

"I can wait. I can be patient," he murmured, the pads of his fingers slipping beneath her sweatshirt, caressing up and down her spine. "I can do that. What I can't do is lose you. I can't—I *won't* lose you. When you walked out today, it was like my heart was ripped out of my chest." His voice cracked.

She shifted up, placing her hands on his face. "I am so sorry. I was being selfish and stupid. I was—"

"You were scared." He filled in the words for her. "I'm scared too, baby. I've never felt like this about anyone."

"Neither have I."

The words hid in her heart. Scared to come out to the light. She wanted to be brave and say what she'd never said to anyone else. Three tiny words that were the Kilimanjaro of feelings. As with many of the tentative steps she'd taken into the world of being brave today, she wasn't ready to scale that mountain of truth.

Not yet.

Even with Noah's proclamation that if he had to choose, he'd choose her, it was a risk her brain wouldn't allow her heart to take.

The photograph on the desk played in her vision. Noah and she alongside Elle and Clayton. What that picture represented was at risk. All their relationships.

What if that picture is the future? Am I willing to give that up? Was there hope for a world where that picture was of two couples, not just four friends?

Her words rushed out. "Noah, Fall Fest is next weekend. Will you take me, hold my hand, buy me an apple dumpling, and kiss me as we wander around?"

They were worth the risk. Even if her voice shook as she asked, she knew the truth with every fiber of her being. As sure as she knew the sun would rise tomorrow. So much more was at risk if she allowed fear, guilt, and grief to continue its relentless hold on her. Maybe there wasn't a guarantee of a happily ever after, but if she didn't try, an unhappily ever after was certain.

"Yes." He pulled her to his lips, consuming her in hungry kisses. After their kisses subsided, he caressed her cheek. "So, are we going to tell them or just surprise them at Fall Fest?" The corners of his lips flexed into a lopsided grin.

"Sunday dinner. I know you and your parents are coming to Mom and Dad's this Sunday. Clayton and Elle will be there. We can tell them then."

"Are you sure?"

She was. Even as uncertainty nipped at her. "Yes."

He threaded his hand in hers, bringing it to his lips in a tender kiss. "We'll do it Sunday…together."

Together.

CHAPTER THIRTY-SEVEN

"I like good strong words that mean something…" ~Louisa May Alcott, *Little Women*

"Dr. Nat!" Sally squealed, bounding toward Nat, her cherub cheeks flushed with pink.

Nat bent down to accept the little girl's hug. "Sally, so nice to see you."

The four-year-old wasn't Nat's patient for today. Her grandmother was, but Sally must have come along for the appointment. Mrs. Greene, Sally's grandmother, would be Nat's second-to-last patient of the day before heading to Mom and Dad's to pitch them on her idea of expanding their clinic to offer mental health services and her application for the Clark Foundation Grant to support it. She vibrated with nervous and excited energy.

After this hurdle, the next one she'd jump would be done hand-in-hand with Noah as they told their families they were a couple. Of course, the queasy sensation in her stomach wasn't about telling their parents. She already knew her dad was on board, and she was almost certain her mom and Noah's parents would be thrilled. But Clayton remained an unknown. For a woman of science, that was the scariest concept.

At least Elle would be there on Sunday. There was a strong probability she'd prove an ally. Elle may be marrying Clayton, but the girl code ran deep in her soon-to-be sister-in-law.

Nat released Sally and stepped back. "It was so sweet of you to come with your grandma to her doctor's visit."

"She's a good girl." Mrs. Greene patted Sally's head.

"You have your fun doctor shoes on today." Sally pointed down to Nat's ruby-red ballet flats.

"Thank you for noticing." She preened just enough to make RuPaul proud. "Look at your cute shoes." Nat motioned to Sally's pair of gold butterfly-encrusted flats.

She beamed. "Grandma got them for me. They're my doctor shoes."

"Yep. My Sally wants to be a doctor just like you, Dr. Owens. She's gone on and on about you. She wants to help people and wear cute shoes when she grows up. Just like you." Mrs. Green's dark brown eyes sparkled as she looked between her granddaughter and Nat.

Pride lifted Nat's lips into a giant grin, and her heart squeezed with affection. Unwrapping her stethoscope from her neck, she held it up. "Maybe we should start your doctor training now. You have the cute shoes, after all. Do you want to learn how to use this? We can listen to your grandma's heart."

Sally's face lit like a lamp as she reached for the stethoscope. "Oh! Mommy says Grandma has an extra big heart."

"Those are the rarest of hearts, so it's good we're practicing on her." Nat winked.

"Mommy said you have a big heart too! Can I practice on you too?"

"Of course." That extra big heart squeezed tighter with joy.

After Sally and Mrs. Greene left, Nat stood behind the

reception desk, reviewing her orders for the day on her tablet. Once signed, they went directly into the patient's chart and automatically to the nurse to call in any prescription, lab tests, or consultation orders. With Elle's guidance, and Nat's pushing, they'd implemented the automated system in July. It streamlined things for both the staff and patients.

"Oh, Dr. Owens, there you are," LeAnne said, walking past Nat.

Nat looked up seeing her dad leaning on the front of the reception counter, face wrinkled as he looked at his tablet. LeAnne shuffled up to the counter, plopping a clipboard in front of him. The medical assistant had worked at the clinic since before Nat was born. Despite most of the staff loving the tablet, LeAnne had clung to her clipboard. She would use the tablet and the computer, but after writing everything by hand first. Nat had even seen LeAnne write text messages on Post Its and then type them into her phone.

"What can I do for you, LeAnne?" Dad said, lifting his head to face her.

LeAnne yanked a pen from behind her ear and used it to point to the sheet of paper on the clipboard. "I'm getting the list of supplies for our upcoming flu vaccine campaign. I wanted you to go over it before I gave it to Mrs. Owens to order."

Dad's brows knitted as he glanced at the list. "Did you have Dr. Owens look at this?" he asked, head cocked to the right.

LeAnne rubbed the back of her gray-dusted black hair. "You're Dr. Owens."

He stretched out a long arm pointing at Nat. "The other Dr. Owens. She's overseeing our Flu Vaccine campaign this year."

With an embarrassed chuckle, LeAnne pivoted to face Nat. "Sorry, Nat! I forgot you were running it this year."

"It's okay, LeAnne," she assured, moving to the counter to take the clipboard.

"Nat, let me know if this is good, and I'll have Mrs. Owens put in the order."

Nat reviewed the list.

"LeAnne." Dad cleared his throat. "How come you call me Dr. Owens and call her Nat? We're both Dr. Owens."

Nat's head jerked at the firmness in Dad's voice. Not since she was seventeen and Dad caught her sneaking in thirty minutes after curfew had she heard that sternness in his tone. Dad's voice always dripped with soft-spoken sweetness.

"But she's always been Nat." LeAnne tilted her head, her face scrunched.

"True, but that was when she was our daughter. She's now our colleague. I'd like it if you'd call her Dr. Owens, or if you'd like to keep calling her Nat, then please call me Chris." Warmth radiated in his eyes.

"Of course…" LeAnne paused, looking between Nat and him. "…Chris." A hesitant smile bloomed. "I like calling her Nat, so I think I'd like to call you Chris. Makes me feel like we're all on equal footing."

"Thank you, LeAnne." He grinned, adjusting his yellow bow tie dotted with mini blue bow ties.

"Although, Chris…" She placed her hands on her ample hips. "…I have to say, Nat and you aren't equals." An emboldened sassiness seemed to have taken over her.

"Excuse me?" His lips pursed.

"She's a *way* better dresser than you." She pointed to Nat's shoes. "To quote my grandson, those shoes are on fleek, queen!"

Nat snorted and then curtsied.

Dad's brow wrinkled. "I like my bow ties, and so does Mrs. Owens. She says they're dapper."

"It's not the 1930s…you want to be on point or hot, not

dapper," LeAnne teased, waggling her eyebrows. "Speaking of Mrs. Owens, should I call her Heidi?"

He gnawed on the corner of his lip. "Probably best we all still call her Mrs. Owens. We all may be equal, but let us not forget who the boss is."

LeAnne playfully wagged her finger at him. "I bet you call her Mrs. Owens even at home, don't you?"

A soft blush kissed his cheeks. "Maybe."

"If my husband had called me Mrs. Samuels, I may not have divorced him," LeAnne sassed, turning to Nat. "Let me know about the list. I'm going to go restock the exam rooms before I leave."

As LeAnne disappeared through the red door, Nat slipped through the half door between the hall and the reception desk. She walked up to her dad, kissing his cheek. "Thank you."

Nat's heart had squeezed for the third time today at Dad's interaction with LeAnne. It was such a tiny thing, but the big things always were. She'd not asked him to do this. She'd not even complained to him about the staff calling her Nat and him Dr. Owens. It meant that he'd seen it too and fixed it in a very Dad way.

"I know I said it would take time and to be patient. I said that as your colleague. As your father, I lost my patience and did that." He draped his arm around her. "It's a bit of a tightrope we walk working together. I'll try to remember I am your colleague here, but it's hard when I am your father everywhere else."

She leaned into him. "I love you, Dad."

"I love you, Dr. Owens."

The happiness in her heart bloomed like a garden of sunflowers in the sunshine of his love and respect. They both may be Dr. Owens, but they were also father and daughter.

Perhaps, that was the most important role of all.

CHAPTER THIRTY-EIGHT

"…the love, respect, and confidence of my children was the sweetest reward I could receive for my efforts to be the woman I would have them copy." ~Louisa May Alcott, *Little Women*

Nat's heart raced. It actually fucking raced like a stallion rounding the bend at the Kentucky Derby. The last time her heart had beat like this as she sat at the dining room table of her parents' house was the morning after she'd lost her virginity. Convinced that somehow the recently-sexed pheromones were detectable, her heart pounded throughout their breakfast that day.

"I do love that I married a man who cooks," Mom crooned as Dad pushed open the door carrying in a glass bowl of taco-seasoned ground turkey.

Agreed. Nat's lips tugged up with devilish agreement. Not at her father's culinary skills, which were impressive, but by the many skills inside and outside of the kitchen held by her boyfriend. The novelty of Noah as her boyfriend had not worn off, nor had the queasiness about sharing their relationship with the family in two days' time, but she'd proceed. They were worth it, after all.

Fear had held her back far too long. *No more!* She would embrace the bravery that had been hidden within her all along.

"Well, I love that I married a woman who enjoys me feeding her." Dad bent to kiss Mom on the cheek.

I don't think I'll ever tire of feeding you. Noah's words danced in her thoughts as a far too big smile spread on her face. So, it appeared everything was going to make her think of Noah. Even her parents' unbridled affection for one another.

"Cut it out, you two, or I'll never give you grandchildren." Nat wagged a teasing finger.

"Well, at least I have Fitz and Lizzie." Mom shrugged, unfolding the blue cloth napkin and draping it on her lap.

"Oh, I have a feeling Natalie will give us human grandbabies someday." Dad winked at Nat as he took his seat.

Nat shot him an "I will kill you, old man!" look. He just unfolded his napkin and laughed silently at her. Thank the goddess, they'd be telling everyone Sunday because Dad was a week away from spilling the tea. In fact, Noah and she may want to walk through the door holding bedazzled signs proclaiming them as a couple, or else Dad would let it slip before the cheese board hit the coffee table.

After they'd served themselves some of Dad's delicious turkey tacos, black bean salad, and Spanish rice, they did the obligatory small talk chatting about Dad's latest detective novel, Mom's planned shopping trip with Maura on Saturday after the clinic closed, and the scrapbook Nat was making for Elle and Clayton to give them at the bridal shower in November.

"So, Natalie, you called this meeting to discuss some clinic business," Dad said with an encouraging smile.

Nat dabbed the napkin at her mouth and then placed it on her lap. "Yes. As you know over the years, we've discussed the expansion of the clinic to offer mental health services for our patients. With the shortage of licensed mental health providers and resources in the county, most people must drive to Rochester or Buffalo to access resources."

Mom sighed. "It is so frustrating. We've tried to attract a licensed psychologist or social worker to join us, but we haven't been successful. Even if they live in the area, they can get paid five to ten thousand dollars more a year in the cities."

Nat turned to Mom. "Yes, but I think if we focused on tele-health services, then we might have a better chance at attracting clinicians who would be open to making less money but having a job that provided them with the flexibility to see patients from home or, frankly, anywhere they can get an internet connection."

Dad and Mom's gazes met across the table, indulging in the kind of silent conversations that had annoyed Nat and her brothers. Those eye conversations were usually focused on something Clayton, Evan, or she had done wrong or shaded in a "bless their heart" hue as they passed parental judgment.

"I know Elle suggested Sloan-Whitney."

Mom's eyes narrowed. Dad fiddled with his bow tie.

"Which means affiliating with a third party. I agree with both of you that I don't want to give up control of the clinic. It's been run by our family for almost a hundred years. I think until there is no longer a Dr. Owens in Perry, it should remain as such. However, I do think there is merit in the idea of telehealth."

"I agree." Mom tapped her manicured red fingers on the smooth surface of the table. "We discussed that, but between the equipment, hiring a technician to run it, paying the thera-pist, the learning curve for patients, and marketing it was something we couldn't budget for this year. Maybe in a few."

Nat reached for her sleek, leather satchel, a gift from Elle when she started at the clinic to replace the canvas one she'd always used. Opening it, she pulled out the copies of the application packet she'd drafted. Pushing her plate to the side, she handed her parents each one.

"If you'd flip to the second page of the packet, it outlines the Clark Foundation and how we can utilize their grant program to pay for the startup costs for a telehealth program," Nat explained.

"Aren't they only for businesses? We're a medical clinic." Mom gnawed on her lower lip in thought.

"That's what I thought. But I spoke with them at length at…" Nat paused, looking at Dad's arched right brow. Of course, he knew when and where she'd spoken with the Clark Foundation's staff, and if she'd shared, so would Mom. Not wanting to raise Mom's suspicion, she lied. "…on the phone. They've never worked with a medical office, but they are very open to it. Their goal isn't just focused on businesses but cultivating thriving rural communities. A thriving rural community would include access to quality healthcare resources."

"This is very thorough and well-researched." Dad flipped through the packet. "I love the statistics about outcome measures related to mental health services and suicide rates in rural populations."

"What's this about a parent support group?" Mom asked, pointing to the third page of the documents.

Nat's giddiness couldn't be contained. Joy pulsed through her as if she was giving a talk during grand rounds in her Residency Program again. Goddess, she was such a school nerd. How she'd loved giving presentations in her academic career.

"I got the idea from Summer. It's a group for parents of kids with disabilities. Summer located other parents in the county who would be interested in the group. We reached out to a therapist who would be willing to host a virtual group for them. I'm proposing we get two sets of telehealth equipment to set up one in the third exam room we never use for individual appointments and one in our conference room to be used evenings and weekends for group therapy. We can start with the parent support group and then look at other groups, like for substance abuse or grief."

Nat's gaze flicked to her dad at the mention of a grief group. With a small smile, he nodded. Clayton, he, and she had met every Tuesday for the last few weeks while Mom was at her weekly Jazzercise class at the YMCA in Warsaw. The time together had been filled with many tears, hugs, and laughter about Evan. It also was filled with many conversations about how to best approach Mom. The mere mention of Evan seemed to grip her in debilitating grief where she couldn't speak or even seem to function.

An impressed grin sketched across Mom's face. "I think this is really good. Something we should explore. What do you think, Chris?"

"Agreed. Good work, Dr. Owens."

"Thanks." Nat did a wiggly happy dance in her seat. She didn't care that she was celebrating much like her five-year-old self when there was chocolate cake for dessert.

I bet Noah would make me chocolate cake to celebrate. She blushed at that. Yup, she was a goner. Summer was so right.

"I wish you'd brought me in sooner. I could have helped you with this," Mom said.

Nat blew out a breath. "I know. I wanted to show you that I can do both the clinical and the admin side of things. I wanted you to see that I can do it myself. That if Dad and you choose to retire, that I have this."

"Oh." A frown yanked down at Mom's lips as she placed the paperwork beside her plate.

Nat nibbled at her lower lip. Part of her wanted to just let it go, but the sadness almost screamed from Mom's downcast smile.

"What is it, Mom?"

"Nothing." Mom waved her hands in front of her face, almost seeming to flick off the idea that anything was wrong.

In the Owens family, if someone said they were "fine" or "nothing was wrong," then you just smiled and said, "Okay." It's how it had always been. Nat had done it so many times.

No more!

"There is something wrong." She shifted in her seat to face Mom straight on.

Mom's lips pursed. "Natalie, it's fine."

"No, it's not." She thumped her chest. "Talk to me."

"Natalie Joan, I told you everything is fine, so drop it." Mom's tone was as firm as her smile. "You did a nice job with this. I'll go over the application, and we can submit it by the deadline." She stood up, grabbing the stapled packet from the table.

Nat opened her mouth, but her reply was halted by Dad's hand resting on her shoulder. The squeeze of his hand was his silent command to stop. Dad knew Mom better than anyone. He'd advised patience, as Clayton and she discussed their concerns about Mom. As much as Nat wanted to yank her mom along with the rest of the family, she knew that everyone healed at their own pace. They waltzed a delicate dance.

"Heidi, please sit," Dad's request was gentle.

"This is silly. Everything is fine." Her face pinched.

"Damn it, Heidi." His demand, both pleading and firm, halted her steps.

Mouth slack, she swung back to him. "Excuse me?"

"I'm sorry," he said softly. "Please." His unwavering gaze turned steely.

While most of Nat's friends had fathers with stern "Dad" voices that made them cower when doing something wrong, Nat's dad lacked that particular verbal trick. A raised voice or shouts seldom breached his lips. She'd only ever had one stern-adjacent talking to from Dad. Even his cheers during their sporting events as kids were mild-mannered. A loud sigh or disappointed look was as rough as he'd ever been with them as kids. That had proven more effective than yelling with all three Owens siblings.

"Heidi, why did you frown?" he pushed, his gaze fixed on his wife.

"This is stupid." She tossed her hands up. "It was just a frown. I don't know why you're both making a federal case out of this."

"Because we've spent too long not talking about your frowns."

An instant protest choked Nat. Part of her wanted to dive over the table and tackle him to stop his words. They should wait as he'd counseled… Be patient. The other part of her sat in stunned awe.

"We've spent too long not speaking about things and that neglect has impacted our children."

"It has not," she snapped, her eyes narrowed. "Our children are fine."

"But we're not." Nat's confession came out as a whimper.

Mom's gray eyes, so similar to Nat's, glistened with disbelief or hurt. Nat wasn't sure, but she knew her words had struck as if she'd slapped her mother with her hand rather than the unwanted truth.

"Our children aren't okay. You're not okay. I'm not okay," Dad croaked. "The day we lost Evan, we started losing this family. We take the family photos with smiles. We have all the appropriate family dinners and events. We do all the things that make us look like a happy family, but we're not. We're broken."

Mom's hand shook as she gripped the papers. Her expression turned stormy, forecasting the coming tears.

"I don't want to lose my other two children because we don't talk about things." With a crack in his voice, tears rolled down his cheeks. "I don't want to lose you. I love you so much. You are my heart, and for the last ten years, my heart has been breaking every day. We will never be what we were before we lost Evan, but if we don't talk about it...if we don't grieve...we'll never be a family again."

Mom shook her head. "Chris, no. I can't. I can't. It hurts too much. I can't."

Nat reached out, taking Mom's free hand. "Mom, you can. I know you can because I did, and everyone says I'm like you. That means you're like me...You're brave."

The tears slipped down Mom's face as she looked at Nat.

"Dad, Clayton, and I have been talking about Evan. We want to help you...help us...move forward."

"Help me do what? Forget him? I can't forget him...there is a hole in my chest where he should be." She slammed her palm against her heart.

"Not forget. We'll never forget. But to forgive. To forgive yourself," Dad said, swallowing hard. "Just like I must forgive myself. The only reason he came home that weekend was to attend that father/son golf tournament with me the next day. He'd told us he was swamped with his residency program, but we pushed him to come home anyway. If we hadn't, he'd be alive."

"No." Nat shook her head in unwilling disbelief, vision shimmering with tears.

"I know," he said, his gaze meeting hers. "I know it's not our fault, just like it isn't yours, my dear girl."

Over the last two weeks, Nat had shared the knotted-up feelings of guilt, resentment, anger, and regret that had marred her grieving heart. Sharing the unspoken with Clayton and Dad was like rubbing alcohol on an emotional wound. It hurt like hell, but the ache started to dull with the sterilizing impact of talking.

Mom's gaze shifted to her. "What? What is your father saying?"

That painful lump attempted to choke the words away, but she pushed it down. "I was supposed to go on a run with Evan that night but didn't because we got in a fight. If I had gone running with him, we'd have been at the park. He wouldn't have been on that road…not meeting with that truck."

Mom shook her head. "It's not your fault…. it's not your fault."

"I know…well, I'm trying to know."

"Heidi, *our* children are hurting because we don't talk about things. For ten years, grief, pain, and guilt have imprisoned our daughter, our other son, and us." His glistening eyes warmed.

Mom swallowed thickly, no words coming. Her face was ashen.

"I've started seeing a counselor. It's helping. It hurts. I'm not going to pretend that there aren't lots of tears and times I don't want to do it. It's like any wound; it's going to hurt even while healing," Nat said, squeezing her mom's hand.

Rising, Dad walked to his wife's other side. Kneeling beside her, taking her other hand. "My love, even though we will heal, we will still have scars, but we'll learn to deal with them…Together. Our Evan wouldn't want this. That boy was joy in motion. Smiles and laughter followed him wherever he went. Let his leaving us to go to Heaven be the same. Even if we're not smiling, we need to talk about him. We need to do it as a family, and I think we need to see a therapist. It's time… it's time to talk."

Mom let out a shaky breath. "I don't know if I can. I don't know if I'm strong enough."

"Mom, we're strong enough for you. Let us support you. Let us hold your hand while you do hard things. Just like you held my hand until I was ready to walk on my own," she said, clasping her mom's delicate hands in her own, hoping each stroke coaxed her to say yes.

Gnawing on her lower lip, Mom looked between Nat and Dad.

"My love, we need you. You are our heart. We can't work without you," he said, brushing her satiny hair behind her ear.

"Alright." One breathless word laced with every emotion etched across Mom's face: sorrow, guilt, anger, longing, and the tiniest flicker of hope.

Rising, he pressed a tender kiss to her temple. "That's my warrior queen."

"I'm so proud of you, Mom." Amazed pride spread in Nat's chest. For both her parents.

Letting go of Nat's hand, Mom held up the packet of papers in her right hand. "And I'm so proud of you, my girl. You don't need me anymore. That's what the frown was about. My children don't need me anymore. I know it's silly. Clayton used to need me to watch Fitz, but that stopped when Elle came along. Now, you don't need me to run the business side of the clinic," she sniffled.

Nat's face lit with a silent chuckle. "Mom, we'll always need you, but more importantly, we want you. I don't want our relationship to be grounded in you taking care of me." She looked at her dad with a smile, and then back to Mom. "I know it's a tightrope to walk. You've been my mom longer than my colleague. You'll always be my mom, and I'll always want you, but maybe we can shift to friends. A relationship less about you taking care of me and more about just being with me."

"Can I still harass you about the shortness of your dresses?" Mom asked with a watery laugh.

"They are a little short." Dad chuckled.

CHAPTER THIRTY-NINE

"Well, I am happy, and I won't fret, but it does seem as if the more one gets the more one wants, doesn't it?" ~Louisa May Alcott, *Little Women*

The park brimmed with squealing children running across grass still damp from an early morning rainstorm. Sun poked through the gray sky, dissolving it into the soft blue of a sunny September day. Nat and Summer relaxed on the worn wooden bench overlooking the play area. Liam's happy shouts danced in the soft breeze as he climbed up the big slide at the other side of the playground. Smiling, Noah was two rungs below him. Reaching the top, Liam sat, and Noah scooted in behind him. Noah's hands were wrapped around Liam's middle, the little boy's arms waved in the air, and they both laughed as they slid down. Nat wasn't sure whose expression of delight was louder—Noah's or Liam's.

"He's so good with him." Summer nudged Nat's shoulder.

Nat's sigh dripped with happy contentment.

"I know it's early... but have you two discussed kids? You've always wanted kids. Does Noah?" Summer's eyes followed Liam as he and Noah ran to the metal jungle gym near the center of the park.

"He does." A goofy grin spread across her face.

Oh, my goddess, was she sitting at the park watching Noah play with Liam and daydreaming about the day he ran around the park with their kids? *Abso-fucking-lutely!*

"You are so ga-ga for that man." Summer's laughter came out like a bass drum.

Leaning her head against Summer's shoulder, she gushed with the fervor of a crush-sick teenager. "I am totally Lady Gaga for that man. I won't even pretend."

"Dork," she snorted. "So, are you two ready to tell your families tomorrow?"

"Yep."

"You've tackled a lot of big talks this week. This one will be a piece of cheesecake. I'm so proud of you and love calling you my best friend."

"Aw, you *love* me." Nat made kissy faces at Summer, who batted her away.

"You ruin all our moments," she laughed.

"Mom!" Liam's gleeful yell drew their attention.

They smiled and followed Liam's finger, which was aimed at Todd as he sauntered toward them, a huge grin on his face. A tail-wagging white huskie trotted beside him on a red leash. Nat and Summer rose and walked toward Liam and Noah, reaching the pair just as Todd did.

"Mom, look." Liam's voice reached a new octave of happiness. "She's so pretty."

"That she is," Todd said, his green eyes fixed on Summer.

Nat did not imagine the kiss of pink shading Summer's cheeks at that.

"What's her name?" Liam asked.

Todd turned to Liam. "This is Sheba."

"Why'd you name her that?"

"Because she's a queen." He scratched between the Huskie's ears.

Sheba placed her haunches on the ground. Her chest puffed out like the regal puppy she was.

"Do you want to pet her? She's very friendly."

Liam looked at his mom, who smiled. "Go ahead, baby."

He stroked his little hand along her chest. Both the boy and dog erupted in big smiles.

"I didn't know you had a dog," Summer said, stepping beside Liam and joining in the petting fest. "She's so soft."

"Todd rescued her two years ago. She was found abandoned at the side of the road with her two brothers and sister. She was the runt of the litter and had some health issues, so she hung out at the shelter for a bit until Todd came along," Noah explained.

"Is she okay now?" Liam asked, concern shaking his little voice.

"She's perfect. She can't hear, but I taught her different signs and touches for commands." Todd rubbed her ears.

Sheba looked up to her daddy, affection shining in her dark eyes. The same affection sparked in Summer's brown eyes as she stared at Todd. Nat fought the urge to high-five Todd for breaking through Summer's hard candy shell. Instead, she and Noah glanced at each other, big knowing expressions on their faces.

"Nat, want to meet her?" Liam tipped his head up to Nat.

"Of course." Nat crouched, running her hands over Sheba's silken coat. "Aren't you lovely?"

Sheba slapped her pink tongue against Nat's face in a wet doggy kiss. Squeaking, Nat fell back. Only she didn't fall far. Noah's legs braced her, keeping her in place.

Peering over her shoulder, she grinned. "Thank you."

"I've got you." An adoring gaze met her equally adoring gaze.

Yep. We both have it bad.

"Nat, is Noah your boyfriend?" Liam asked.

Both Nat and Noah's heads jerked to the little boy. His face scrunched as he stared at them. Todd snorted. Summer covered her mouth to stifle a laugh.

"Why do you ask?"

"Because you two look all goofy at each other like Grandma and Grandpa and Elle and Clayton."

"The kid is one smart cookie," Todd boasted, ruffling Liam's floppy chestnut hair.

"He sure is one perceptive kiddo." Nat looked to Noah and then back to Liam. "Yes, Noah is my boyfriend."

Pride filled her. Sure, it was just telling Liam that Noah and she were a couple, but it was the first step. Nat was owning her heart and sharing it with the world. Tomorrow she'd hold his hand and share with the rest of the world that this was her man, and she was his woman. They were each other's.

"Okay." Liam shrugged. "Todd, since Noah is Nat's boyfriend, do you want to be my mom's boyfriend? Then I can play with Sheba all the time."

Nat snorted and Noah stifled a laugh.

Summer sputtered and Todd grinned like the cat that got the canary. After Summer explained to Liam that it wasn't polite to ask people to be his mom's boyfriend, they headed home.

Nat and Noah left Todd to finish his walk with Sheba. They strolled toward Noah's house, leaving Nat's Jeep at the park. Over the last month, anytime she'd go to Noah's, she'd used the park as her alibi. Today would be the last day of that.

When they got back to Noah's, he made them lunch. It was her dad's turn to manage the Saturday clinic, allowing her the park playdate and now the afternoon to spend with Noah before he'd head to the Wine Down and then the brewery.

"Should we meddle with Summer and Todd, or just let it

happen?" Nat pondered, spooning up a bite of the vegetarian chili he'd had in the crockpot while they were at the park.

"Let's wait and see if they need a little push."

Nat leaned her chin on her hand. "Kind of like what you did for Clayton and Elle?"

Last summer, when Elle came back to town, Noah had a hand in encouraging the relationship. After Elle left to go back to her life in California, Noah worked his magic to get the cautious Clayton to get on a plane to surprise her and declare his love. Clayton had been so scared of losing Elle that he wouldn't push her to give them a real chance, and it had almost cost him the woman he loved.

"Did I ever tell you that you are adorable when you are modest?" she said in response to his mere shrug about the role he'd played in Elle and Clayton's romance.

"I think you're adorable all the time." He leaned across the table, capturing her lips in a slow, reverent kiss. "Especially when you're brave. Like yesterday with your mom and today with Liam."

Nat's lips quirked up. "I think Dad was the brave one. I can't believe he said anything."

"Now who's being modest?" He cocked an eyebrow.

Rather than copying his shrug, she bowed her head and made a magnanimous hand gesture.

A soft laugh escaped Noah's lips.

Taking a final bite, she reveled in that truth. She'd been brave. So had Dad. So had Mom. After more tears and talking, they'd called Clayton, who came by their parents' house after finishing up at the vet clinic for the day. The four of them opened a family album and flipped through each photograph from when they were the "Complete Owens' Family," talking, and crying. A long road still lay ahead of them, but as a family, they'd traverse it together.

"I've said it before; your dad never ceases to surprise me."

"I'm still nervous about telling Clayton about us, but I like knowing that Dad will be in our corner tomorrow. I think yesterday showed me that he's a fighter."

"He's scrappy like my girl." Noah nipped at her lips.

"Perhaps, we cease with the comparison of me to my dad when you are kissing me."

Noah's face scrunched in a grimace. "Good call."

"So, this is our last secret lunch." Her voice dropped, low and sultry, as she skated her hand up the sleeve of his blue Henley.

"It is."

"It's also our last time for super sexy secret sex," she purred, batting her long lashes.

Noah traced her lips with his index finger. "That it is," he said as he moved her bowl to the other side.

Heat prickled up her neck. Neediness radiated from her core as Noah stood up, coming to her side of the table. Pulling her into his arms, his mouth met hers. Opening to him, their tongues slowly danced. An insistent pulse thrummed between her legs as his hands traveled down her body to the hem of her T-shirt. Urging her arms upward, he yanked the soft fabric over her head. His hot mouth trailed kisses down her neck to her cleavage.

"Please." She moaned as his fingers unclasped her bra, freeing her aching breasts. The pink tips were taut and starving for his touch.

Her back arched as he licked down to capture a nipple in his mouth. Pleasure tingled as he rolled the hard peak with his tongue, followed by a long hard suck. Her breath grew ragged as he repeated the action on her other breast.

"My perfect girl." His husky voice rumbled straight to the growing slickness between her legs.

His praise. His touch. His kiss. No matter how many times she basked in his attention, she never got enough. Just the anticipation of knowing how his hands and mouth felt on her body and the way his words made her feel made her greedy for more. The only thing better than being touched by Noah was touching him.

She moved her hands down his torso, pulling at the hem of his shirt. Always her helper, he tugged it off himself. Their naked top halves met in a firm embrace as their kisses consumed one another. His strong hands gripped her ass, pulling her close to his growing arousal. Lifting her, Nat's legs wrapped around his middle. Spinning, he placed her on the table and rubbed against her as they kissed. The delicious friction of denim against denim pooled liquid heat at her core.

"Nothing between us," she panted.

It may have been gibberish, but he seemed to know what she meant. Stepping back, he unbuttoned, unzipped, and then pushed his jeans off. Smirking, he ripped off his socks.

He's perfect. Nat's entire body ached for this perfect, thoughtful, and fucking sexy man.

Removing his boxer briefs, he moved to her jeans. "Let's get these off you." It was almost a growl.

His hands worked quickly, removing her jeans, then her panties, and lastly her socks. Pushing her back, he spread her wide on the table. "Dessert," he purred, kneeling between her legs. His hot tongue slid down her center, finding her pulsing clit.

"Oh my..." Words were impossible as his mouth worked. The hard sucks and slow licks caused a tantalizing rigidity to seize every muscle in her body.

Eyes closed, she went between hands flat on the table and then gripping his head as he worked her. Her hips writhed against him, chasing the sweet release of climax. Slipping a finger inside her, he sent a jolt of pleasure cascading across her body.

"Fuck me...Noah!" she cried, allowing the orgasm to wash over her.

"As you wish," he said, his voice throaty.

Standing, he pulled her trembling body up. Flipping her,

he bent her over the table. Spreading her legs wide, she lifted her ass in the air. His hands caressed down her back to her backside, positioning himself at her entrance.

"Ready?" He rasped, both hunger and gentleness colored his tone.

"Yes." She moaned as he drove into her.

The delicious ache between her legs reached a fever pitch as he moved inside her. At first, his pumps were slow and soft, but soon he sped to deep, hard thrusts as she pushed her backside against him, coaxing him for more. Grasping her right leg, he bent it and lifted it onto the table, allowing himself to deepen his angle inside her.

"Fuck, Noah," she whimpered, slamming her hand against the smooth surface of the table. Goddess, it was so good. Every nerve in her body wound tight with promised release.

"I know, baby," he rasped, pulling out of her.

"What? Don't stop!" Her protest answered with him flipping her around and hoisting her up onto the table.

Settling between her legs, he thrust into her. "I want to see your face when you come for me." He pumped harder. "I want you to see what you do to me."

Nat dug her nails into his back, her legs tight around him. His cool ocean-blue eyes became a wildfire, their heat locked on her. Like a rising tide, the release started cresting. Their gazes remained woven. The unbroken eye contact intensified the pleasure coursing through her. She gave herself over to the ecstasy...over to him. A second orgasm ripped loose, rendering her limbs useless.

"Noah!"

"That's my girl," he grunted, his breath shallow, heralding his coming release. "Fuck!" The orgasm shuddered through them.

Their eyes remained tethered to each other. Something different crackled in the air. Not just the post-sex glow but something more. Something she'd not let herself think. Not let herself say.

Brushing her sweat-damp hair away from her face, his blazing eyes softened. "You're so beautiful," he murmured, pressing his lips against her temple. "Nat, I lo—"

"Shit! Sorry!" A deep voice shouted with embarrassment.

Noah's arms tightened around her back, trying to shield her naked body from the voice behind her. The voice she knew all too well.

"Fuck," Noah gasped, his eyes darting between Nat and the owner of that voice.

"Dude, I'm sorry. I should have knocked. I didn't know you—" The words stopped.

Turning her head, she faced that voice, Noah's arms still wrapped like armor around her.

"Clayton," she croaked.

Slack-jawed and holding a pizza box in his hands was her brother. His gray eyes widened with pained bewilderment. Noah pulled out of Nat, yanked her up, and shielded her with his body. His arms were protective and almost possessive.

Eyes closed and head shaking, Clayton turned abruptly, causing him to slam hard into the kitchen's entry archway. The momentum threw him to the ground, the pizza box skidding across the checkered tiled floor.

"Clayton!" Nat shrieked, running to her brother sprawled on the floor.

His hands covered his face. Blood poured from his nose when he removed his hands. His eyes squinted as if in pain.

"Are you okay?" she asked, reaching for him.

Clayton's eyes went wide as he pushed her away. "You're naked!"

Nat yelped, stepped back, and crossed her arms over her body. Noah handed her his Henley. He'd tugged on his boxer briefs. She slipped the Henley on. It hung on her like a loose dress, stopping mid-thigh.

"You're naked," Clayton repeated as if in a daze. He stood up facing them, blood raining down from his nose. "You… you were fu…fu…fu…fucking."

"Clayton." Noah's tone was quiet as he stepped beside Nat, placing his hand in hers. "We're—"

Clayton lifted his hands, stopping Noah's words. Then, his hands went to his face touching the blood. Pulling them back, he examined the red blots on his hand and then lifted his gaze to Nat. Disappointment swam in his eyes.

Nat's heart fell to the floor. As if she was a little girl again, caught by her big brother borrowing a toy she had been told not to play with.

Clayton shook his head and walked away.

CHAPTER FORTY

"…for love casts out fear, and gratitude can conquer pride."
~Louisa May Alcott, *Little Women*

Motionless and silent for several moments, Nat and Noah stared at Clayton as he retreated. The *thwack* of the front door slamming reverberated in the house. The disappointment that had shaded Clayton's gray eyes was the same emotion that swam in Evan's eyes when she'd argued with him. The night he'd died. The last image of Evan was of his disappointed eyes as she called him a jerk and walked away. Now, she'd done it to another brother.

I've disappointed him.

"Baby, no," Noah soothed, wrapping his arms around her.

Had she spoken her thoughts out loud? How did he know?

"It's not your fault." His hands caressed the length of her back.

Nat tipped her face up. "He shouldn't have found out like this. If I had listened to you and Summer, if we'd told everyone sooner, this wouldn't have happened."

Painful guilt clogged in her chest. The obsession with

waiting for the perfect time and perfect way to tell Clayton led to the most imperfect way for him to find out about them.

He kissed her forehead. "I don't like how Clayton found out about us, but we didn't do anything wrong. You didn't do anything wrong. Well, except I should have locked the front door."

She chuckled through her sniffles.

He cupped her face. "Let's get dressed. We'll go to Clayton's together. We'll talk to him together."

All the feelings curdled in her belly as they pulled into the farmhouse. The crunch of gravel beneath her sneakers with each step grated like bone-on-bone pain. Noah's outstretched hand beckoned her. Threading their fingers, they walked up the steps.

"Ready?" Noah asked, his gaze searched hers.

"Yes." She squeezed his hand, so strong and steady in her grip.

She held her breath as she knocked. The door swung open. Elle's face was drawn in a weary smile.

"May we come in?" Nat asked, scuffing the toe of her sneaker against the wooden porch.

"Of course," Elle said, her tone gentle. "He's in the kitchen."

Lizzie and Fitz barreled passed Elle to greet Nat and Noah. With quick pets, they followed her to the kitchen. Clayton sat at the dining room table, a frozen bag of peas over his right eye. Specks of dried blood stained his gray T-shirt.

"I can look at that if you want," Nat offered, pointing to Clayton's face. It probably wasn't the best opening line. Perhaps, "I am so sorry you walked in on your little sister post-mind-blowing sex on a kitchen table with your lifelong best friend still inside her" would be more appropriate.

Clayton plopped the bag of peas onto the table. "I'm fine."

Looking between one another, Nat and Noah's gazes debated who should speak first. Squeezing his hand, he nodded his understanding. It was her brother...she should start.

Heart pounding, she inhaled a deep calming breath. "I'm sorry you found out like this. We were—"

"Fucking on his kitchen table! On the same table where he and I played cards last week." Clayton interrupted with a slight sneer. "How many times? How long has this been hap...hap...happening? When did this start?"

Noah squeezed Nat's hand tighter. "We've been together for a little over a month," he said.

"My sister?" Clayton motioned to Nat. "You finally decide to end your almost monk-like existence, and you cho...cho... choose my little sister?"

"Clayton, I'm sorry—"

Clayton tossed up his hands. "Are you sorry I caught you? Or are you sorry you've been fucking my little sister?"

"Clayton," Elle cautioned. "Noah didn't react like this when he walked in on us."

Brow creased, he turned to her. "That's different. You're not Noah's sister. I wasn't taking advantage of you."

"Excuse me?" Nat hissed, angry fire burning in her belly. "What the fuck does that mean?" She'd never had an urge to slap her brother before. Good thing he already had a bloody nose and blooming black eye, or she'd have to give him one.

"You've had a crush on Noah since you were a little girl." He turned to Noah. "I thought you were a better man than this. To take advantage of Nat's feelings for you. I know I've been encouraging you to get back out there, but not with *my* little sister. Not like this."

Elle stepped beside him, placing a hand on his shoulder.

The clenched jaw softened at her touch. Clayton *never* lost his temper. His patience was as constant as the rising and setting of the sun. This was so unlike him, but it was what Nat had feared would happen. The urge to protect seemed to ripple Clayton's usually calm waters.

Eyes closed, he exhaled a heavy breath. "Why did you have to with my li…li…li…little sister?" he stuttered.

"She's not your sister to me. She's the woman I love," Noah declared, his gaze locked on Clayton. "This isn't what you're making it out to be. I am in love with Nat. I love her."

All the air in her lungs fled. Nat's chest rose and fell but the dizzy feeling didn't dissipate. *Noah loves me.* He was standing in front of her brother, clutching her hand, and telling him that he loved her. That he chose her.

Clayton just blinked. Noah's words took up all the space in the room, allowing no other words to be spoken. Shaking his head, Clayton turned and left the room. For a second time, he left a stunned silent Nat in a kitchen, wondering what the fuck had just happened.

Had the last twenty minutes really happened? Had Clayton caught her having sex with Noah? Had Noah said he loved her?

What the actual fuck? She blinked as if it was all a dream… both a nightmare and the sweetest of all dreams.

"He just needs time to process this," Elle breathed, her eyes darting to the now-empty entryway. "Noah…Nat, it's just a lot for him. He didn't mean what he said. You know that. He doesn't believe that about you, Noah. He's just shocked. He just needs time."

Noah nodded. In the span of Clayton and Noah's friendship, Nat cannot recall a single fight. There had been nothing but unwavering support for each other. As much as she knew Elle was correct that Clayton needed time to process this, she feared what the result would be at the end of that processing time.

"I'm going to go check on him." Elle sighed as she slipped out of the room.

Noah turned to Nat. "I meant what I said. I am in love with you, Nat. Right before your brother walked in, I was just about to say it. Hell, I almost said it half a dozen times over the last few weeks."

Nat's heart jumped into her throat, not allowing any words to come out.

Cradling her face, he said, "I love you, and it's okay if you're not ready to say it yet, but I want you to know that I love you and I still choose you. No matter what, I will remain yours."

Yet? How did he know? *Because he sees me, even when I am in the dark.*

"I love you, too," she croaked.

He swiped his thumb along her jawline before he pressed an almost reverent kiss. "Come home with me? We'll give him space to think. We can get your things from the Little Red Barn."

Nodding, she allowed Noah to guide her toward the door. Her steps were halted by a framed photo in the foyer, of Noah and Clayton in their blue high school graduation caps and gowns, a pint-size Nat between them flashing a peace sign. Evan leaned against Clayton, his hands flashing bunny ears behind his unsuspecting big brother. The image kept her in place. She'd lost one brother, but she wouldn't lose another one, nor would she lose Noah.

"Noah," she murmured.

He turned. "You're staying." It wasn't a question. He knew. He always knew.

"I think I need to. I should talk to Clayton." She clenched Noah's hand. "But I still choose you. I just won't accept that a choice needs to be made."

He dipped his head, pressing the tenderest of kisses against her lips. "My brave girl," he whispered, mere inches away from her lips, his hot breath offering comfort as he kissed her a second time. "Call me after. I'll come get you."

After Noah left, Nat walked to Elle's office. Tucked between two shelves stuffed with books sat an oversized leather chair that belonged to their grandfather. It was Clayton's favorite spot to think or sulk. She knew that's where he'd be. Walking through the ajar French doors, she found Clayton sitting in his chair, Fitz on his lap. Elle sat cross-legged on the window seat, Lizzie by her feet.

Elle looked up. "I'll give you two some privacy." She got up and walked to the door, where she paused to mouth to Nat *It will be okay*. Lizzie trotted behind her mommy.

Nat crossed her arms and stood in front of her brother. "You shouldn't have found out like that. Noah wanted us to tell people sooner, but I was apprehensive, and I should have listened to him. We were actually going to tell everyone tomorrow at dinner."

Clayton grunted.

"Although, I'm sure you would have had the same reaction if you found out tomorrow with everyone else. You're the reason I was hesitant to say anything."

"It didn't stop you from jumping into bed with Noah," he grumbled.

Nat smirked. "Well, at least you've moved on from the 'Noah took advantage of me' narrative you were peddling in the kitchen."

Clayton shifted in his seat, disturbing Fitz, who huffed his displeasure. "I shouldn't have said that. I just…"

"Being an ass," she scolded with a wry expression before sloshing a long breath. "Your overprotective mode was activated. This isn't about Noah, and you know it."

"He's my best friend!" Clayton pointed to himself.

"Yes, and he's the man I love." She pointed to herself.

"You love him?"

"Yes! I love him so much, and he loves me. Nobody has

ever seen me as fully and clearly as Noah. I can be completely myself. Messy. Goofy. Strong. Brave. Weak. I've never felt this way about anyone else. I know I've teased you over the last year about how hard you fell for Elle, but I get it. You may think this is just the residue of the crush I had on him, but the Noah I crushed on pales in comparison to the man I love." A steely resolve took control of her voice.

"I know I'm being a dick about this," he sighed. "It's just... You're my sister."

She pulled the chair from the desk over and sat beside him. "I know. You'd be a dick about any man you walked in on me having sex with."

He winced.

"Although, I think if it had been anyone but Noah you would have slugged them."

A quiet laugh softened his severe expression. "You're probably right."

"I'll always be your little sister, but I'm also an adult woman. I'm a doctor. I'm a sexually active—"

"Can we cease with the sex talk?" he groaned, pinching his nose and then wincing at the pain.

She grinned. "I don't mind that you want to look out for me. It's part of the big brother's job description. But I need you to respect my ability to know my own heart and make my own decisions. To respect those decisions...those choices. I choose Noah."

He nodded.

"If you pulled your head out of your ass, you'd realize he's the type of man you'd want for me. He's had your back your entire life. Don't you want a man like that with me?"

He stared out the window. Green trees with hints of fall gold danced in the breeze. The image of Nat jumping into the leaf pile that teenaged Clayton and Evan had raked in their backyard filled her vision. The slight exasperated pinch of

Clayton's face softened to laughter as he'd ultimately leaped into the pile with her and Evan.

"You're right," he murmured.

She smiled. *Just like the leaves.* Suddenly, the fear she'd harbored seemed silly. At the end of the day, Clayton always jumped in with her. He'd grumble. He'd narrow his eyes. He'd be a big brother about it, but when it was truly right and her happiness unquestionable, he'd join. That's what good big brothers did, and he was the best big brother. She knew the best, she'd had two.

He turned his gaze to her. "Having Noah as your boyfriend—" his forehead bunched "—would make it easier to look after you."

It was going to take him time, but he'd get there. She knew he would because he always did. She pinched him, though, because she was a little sister and that was her job.

"I'm sorry, Nat."

She leaned, wrapping her arms around him. "I love you, Clay Pot."

"I love you, Natster." He squeezed her tight.

Nat pulled away. "I think you owe Noah an apology."

"I think you two owe me a pi...pi...pizza." He paused. "You're right, though."

She rolled her eyes. "Why did you just walk in?"

"I knew he was working tonight, and he said he was just hang...hang...hanging out at home for the day, so I thought I'd surprise him with pizza. We've walked into each other's houses without knocking for years. I know he walked in on Elle and me, but I never thought I'd walk in on him with someone, especially my..." He paused with a firm smile. "... adult sister."

Amusement lifted her lips. "I think we should agree to always knock from now on."

He smirked.

"Why don't we grab Elle? We can order a replacement

pizza on the way and go to Noah's. You two can make up over pizza before he heads to work. I'll text him."

Elle poked her head in. "I've got the Daryl's app up. Do you want wings, too?"

Nat arched a brow. "Were you eavesdropping?"

"Well, I had to make sure you didn't kill my future husband. Even if he was being an ass, I love that ass." Elle grinned, batting her hazel eyes.

"My ass is one of your favorite parts," he said, winking at his fiancée.

"Ugh!" Nat gagged.

He *tsked.* "Those in glass houses…"

"Especially when they're naked on the kitchen table of said glasshouse getting nailed," Elle quipped.

"Too soon. WAY too soon."

After placing their order, the three hopped into Clayton's pickup. Bumping along the blacktop country road, Nat sank into the sensation that all was okay. She'd faced her fear and conquered it. Pulling her cell phone out of her sweatshirt pocket, she texted him.

Me: Clayton pulled his head out of his ass. *Smiley Face Emoji.* **All is well. We're on our way to your place with "Sorry for being a dick" pizza.** *Pizza Emoji.* **I love you, baby.**

A happy thrilled buzzed inside her at the freedom of those three little words living in the sunshine. She loved him, and he loved her.

No response came, so she slipped her phone back into the front pocket of her sweatshirt, knowing he'd respond soon. He always did.

"What the…" Clayton's words stopped, causing Nat to look forward.

A motorcycle lay on its side in the middle of the road. The rider sprawled on the hard pavement beside it, a cracked helmet a mere foot away, and blood dripping from his head. Clayton steered onto the narrow shoulder and parked. Nat's eyes scanned the scene and her breath caught at the sight of a familiar SUV wrapped around the telephone pole.

"Oh my…" she gasped.

"Noah!" Clayton croaked.

CHAPTER FORTY-ONE

"…feeling as if all the happiness and support of their lives was about to be taken from them." ~Louisa May Alcott, *Little Women*

Every nerve fired alive, sending fear quaking across Nat's body, her heart racing. For half a beat, they remained in the pickup. A never-ending horn blared, pulling Nat out of that gripping terror.

I am a doctor. I've been trained for this. She inhaled a steadying breath.

"Elle, call 911. Clayton, come with me," she commanded, jumping out of the car. Turning to the still open door, she ordered, "Elle, tell the operator you have a doctor on scene, put them on speaker, and bring it to me.".

Her training kicked in. *Triage patients.* She jogged first towards the motorcyclist The young man groaned, his eyes fluttering open. Pain creased his face as he sat up on the blacktop, a dazed look in his dark eyes. Scrapes, cuts, and blood ran down his bare arms. Flicking her eyes to Noah's vehicle, she saw no movement nor flicker of noise. No call for help. No moan of aching pain. No "Baby, I'm okay." All that filtered from his battered vehicle was the echoing horn.

Scarce resource protocol. Assess immediate versus nonimmediate care. From most likely to survive to... She wouldn't allow herself to finish that lesson learned from her medical training. She needed to focus on the patient in front of her. *You're my warrior.* Noah's voice whispered in her ears, reminding her to follow her training.

"Clayton, do you have a first aid kit in the truck?"

"Yes," he replied, his hoarse voice shaking.

"Grab it and bring it to me, then go check on Noah. Let me stabilize the motorcyclist," she ordered.

"On it," he said, running back to the truck.

"I'm Dr. Nat, I'm here to help. What's your name?" She knelt beside the man. Well, not a man. He seemed to hover between kid and manhood. Perhaps, seventeen...maybe eighteen.

"Doug," he said, his eyes blinking.

"Doug, can you tell me what hurts?"

"My head." He squinted, his hands pressing against his battered head.

"I see your helmet isn't on. Were you wearing it when you crashed?"

"Off...I to...to...took it off," he stuttered.

"Before or after you crashed?"

A furrow creased his bloody forehead. "After?" It came out more like a question than an answer.

Probable head injury or concussion, she thought, mentally flipping to head injury protocol from her ER rotation. It had been two years since she'd dealt with emergency medicine, but, like riding a bike, it was coming back to her.

"Here," Clayton rasped as he handed her the kit.

Nodding, she took it, listening to Clayton's swift feet sprint toward Noah. "I'm going to examine you. Is that okay?"

Nat opened the kit. *Thank the Goddess!* There were gloves, antiseptic cream, alcohol wipes, burn cream, bandages, ace bandages, ice pack, scissors, and tape. Dad had drilled this into all three of his children to have fully stocked first aid kids in their cars. Although, she wished she had hers from her Jeep, which had even more supplies.

Yanking on a pair of gloves, she started her examination. Groans escaped Doug as she touched him.

"I know it hurts, but I have to examine you to help you. Tell me what you feel as I touch," she assured.

Surveying Doug's body, she noted scrapes, cuts, and a bad case of road rash down his back. Nothing appeared to be broken, and his reflexes were intact. The teenager was sitting up, which helped her rule out a possible spinal injury, but Nat kept him seated until the ambulance could arrive, just to be on the safe side.

"Nat!" Clayton cried. "He won't wake up!"

Her heart screamed to run to Noah, but she knew she had to take care of the alert patient first. Move from less critical to most critical in situations like this. Nat's training steadied her shaking hands.

"Check his pulse!" Nat shouted in a steady voice.

A moment later, Clayton yelled. "It's there…It's steady."

Thank the goddess. She let out a heavy breath. "Keep talking to him. I'll be there as soon as I can." Her voice carried no hint of the fear rioting within her.

My brave girl. Noah's words bolstered her.

She focused on Doug, locating the cut in his hairline, and began cleaning it with an alcohol wipe. He winced.

"I know." She bit her lip as she cleaned the wound. He'd need stitches, but she couldn't do that now, even if she'd had the full kit she kept in her car. She grabbed the cotton balls to place over the wound to tape and slow the bleeding until the paramedics arrived.

"Doug, talk to me. Where were you headed today?" Nat knew she needed to keep him talking. The drooping eyes and dazed look indicated a possible concussion.

"To the bakery," he mumbled.

"What were you going to get there?" She pushed him to keep talking.

"Scones for my grandma."

Elle ran up, waving her cell phone. "Paramedics are on their way. They are on speaker."

Finally! "This is Dr. Nat Owens. We have two victims. One awake with a laceration along the hairline, cuts and scrapes along his arms and back, and possible concussion. The second victim is unconscious with a steady pulse."

Terror brightened Elle's eyes.

"The ambulance is on the way. ETA five to ten minutes, Dr. Owens," the operator said. "I'll remain on the line with you until they arrive."

Nat nodded as if the operator could see her. Looking at Elle, she ordered, "Grab a pair of gloves from the kit and put them on."

Elle placed the cell phone on the ground between them and complied.

Once Elle had the gloves on Nat said, "Keep Doug talking. If he passes out, scream for me. Also..." She grabbed Elle's hand, placing it over the head wound she'd bandaged. "...hold on to this tight. I'm going to check on Noah."

Elle nodded at Nat and then turned to Doug. "Hi, Doug, I'm Elle. Do you like books?"

Tugging off her gloves, she tossed them to the ground, put on a fresh pair, and then grabbed the cell phone. Jumping to her feet, and sucking in a deep breath, she ran to Noah's SUV.

Doctor first, girlfriend second. She willed panic down. Noah needed her to be his brave girl. To be his warrior.

Reaching the open driver's side door, she found Clayton. He stood there, hands on his head talking to Noah, who was slumped against the steering wheel, thin streams of blood ran down the side of his face.

"I didn't move him. I keep talking to him. He hasn't woken. He hasn't moved." His voice shook.

She handed the phone to him. "Hold this. The operator is on the line. Hold it up so I can hear and talk to them if needed."

Nodding, he took the phone. "Noah, Nat's here. She's going to fix you."

With a tentative reach, Nat touched Noah. "Baby, can you hear me? You've been in a car accident. You are on the side of the road in Perry." The last thing she wanted was for him to wake up thinking he was at that roadside in Iraq.

Heart still racing, she pressed shaking fingers to his neck, relieved to find a strong beat. "His pulse is good," she assured Clayton, who let out a thankful breath. He'd already checked Noah's pulse, but it appeared they both needed the confirmation.

Gently guiding Noah back against his seat, she turned to her brother. "Clayton, come hold his head up."

Clayton placed the phone on the ground and reached his long arms in to keep Noah's head up. Nat pulled up Noah's eyelids and shined her cell phone's flashlight into his eyes.

"Baby, can you hear me? It's Nat. I'm here, baby. I've got you." The forced steadiness in her began to break. She was losing the battle to remain Dr. Owens and not his Nat. "You need to wake up because Clayton needs to apologize for being an asshole."

"I do, and I want you to be awake when I do." His lips trembled. "I want you to be awake when I tell you how fu–fu–fu–fucking wrong I was. That I love you and I am ha...ha...happy you're with Nat. Although, if you hurt her, I'll ki...ki...kick your ass."

Nat flashed him a tight smile.

Sirens howled in the distance.

Noah remained unconscious. Nat's breath grew ragged,

and the tears pushed to the front of her eyes. *Fuck it!* She was no longer Dr. Owens; she was his Nat.

"Noah, you're not allowed to leave me. I won't allow it… Not when I'm finally yours, and you're mine. I love you. I love you. I love you," she wept, pressing her lips against his bruised and bloodied face.

Noah groaned, and his eyes fluttered open. "Nat?"

"I'm here, baby. I love you." She kissed his lips.

"I love you," Noah moaned, his eyes darting to the pair of hands holding his head up.

"It's Clayton. I'm here. We've got you. Nat and me," he said, relief softening his features.

CHAPTER FORTY-TWO

"Wouldn't it be fun if all the castles in the air we could make come true and we could live in them?" ~Louisa May Alcott, *Little Women*

Nat perched on the edge of Noah's hospital bed. She'd ridden in the ambulance with him using her girlfriend and doctor privileges. A girl must use all she's got to get what she wanted. And what she wanted at this moment was to not be apart from Noah. Elle and Clayton had gotten in touch of Noah's parents, theirs, and Todd, who would take care of the businesses for Noah. The families were in the waiting room for now, until Noah had been admitted, then they could visit him. He'd broken some ribs, and they wanted to keep him overnight for observation due to his concussion.

Doug, the motorcyclist, was still in the emergency room. Nat found out he would be released and not admitted. The police were still investigating, but it looked like Doug was speeding and ran the stop sign. When he weaved into Noah's path, out of instinct Noah swerved to miss him and slammed into the telephone pole. It could have been so much worse. Nat had overheard one of the police officers giving Doug quite a talking-to. Just overhearing the dressing down put the fear of the goddess in Nat, so she didn't have to stretch to imagine how the teenager felt.

"You love me." Noah smiled, looking up at her.

"Well, you said it first, so it was only fair," she teased.

Noah winced as he pushed himself up in his bed. "I do love your dedication to fairness."

"You love everything about me." She grinned as she leaned in.

"That I do." He pressed his smile against hers.

A loud clearing of a throat broke their kiss. Turning, she found Noah's parents, hers, and Elle and Clayton standing inside the room. Deep in their love bubble, neither had noticed their families slip in. Dad wore a big smile. Clayton tucked Elle into his chest, both grinning. Scott scratched his gray-speckled black beard. Mom and Maura high-fived.

Nat and Noah gaped at their mom's.

"I knew it!" Maura cheered.

"I was a little worried when Duncan came along, but you were right." Mom hip-checked Maura.

"Excuse me?" Nat's right brow lifted.

"Oh, Natalie Joan, don't look so shocked. I snuck around enough with your dad when we were teenagers to see all the signs of a secret romance," Mom said, winking at Dad.

Soft crimson colored Dad's cheeks, and he shrugged.

"I'm just happy this finally happened. We've been hoping for this for the last five years." Maura beamed.

"I guess I wasn't the only one who noticed the signs." Dad chuckled.

"A doctor? Nice going, son." Scott smirk covered face turned serious. "Jokes aside, thank god for Nat." He offered a thankful grin to Nat.

"Agreed. Thank you, Nat." With a concerned expression, Moira moved to her son's bedside. "How are you, honey?"

"I'm good. Thanks to Nat and Clayton." He looked between both.

Maura's blue eyes flicked between Nat and Clayton. "Thank you both. You've always had my son's back. He's lucky to have you two."

Clayton stepped up to the bed. "We're lucky to have him. I am lucky to have him not just as my friend but as my brother." He placed his hand on Noah's. "I love you, brother, and I'm sorry I was a dick."

"Why were you a dick to Noah?" Mom asked, hands on her hips.

"When I found out about Nat and Noah, I went all overprotective big brother."

"I did not raise my son to be a dick."

"I don't know if I like mom using the word 'dick' so much," Nat cringed.

"I'm really sorry, man. I shouldn't have reacted like that even…" He halted, his eyes bounced to his parents. "…if it was jarring to find out. You're a good man. The type of man I want for Nat. I'm sorry that I questioned that."

Noah squeezed Clayton's hand. "We're good. We're always good. I love you, brother."

Nat's heart erupted in happiness. Warmth spread through her limbs. It was as it should be. All of them, together.

CHAPTER FORTY-THREE

____

"Laurie, you're an angel! How shall I ever thank you?" ~Louisa
May Alcott, *Little Women*

The crisp autumn air pinked Nat's cheeks as she walked, hand clasped in Noah's through Fall Fest. It had been a week since the accident. He was still healing but was okay for a stroll through the festival. He had an apple dumpling to buy his girlfriend and some public kissing to do, after all.

Downtown Perry was closed to traffic. The windows of Main Street businesses were bedecked with red, orange, gold, and brown leaf wreaths. Clay pots with orange and red mums flanked each doorway. Rows of tables where vendors sold fall-themed food, goods, and products lined the closed streets. Children laughed as they weaved through clusters of wandering attendees. Country music hummed from the stage at the other end of the street.

"You did an amazing job with this!" Nat praised her friends as she and Noah approached the information booth being staffed by Carmen and Summer.

"It was all Summer," Carmen said, tipping the brim of her orange *Staff* hat to Summer.

"Thank you." Summer blushed.

Nat's lips tugged up for her friend. "This is a huge accomplishment. So much business flowing into downtown because of it."

"Yeah, Todd texted. They've been slammed at the brewery, bakery, and the wine bar. I feel like I should go over there." Noah rubbed his hand against the back of his head.

"Todd put us on strict orders to not let you go near any of your businesses until next week. You're still recovering." Summer wagged her finger, going full mama bear on him.

"*Oh,* we're following Todd's orders now, are we?" Nat waggled her eyebrows.

Summer's eyes narrowed. "Hush you, or I'll tell your mom about my friends and family discount on wedding planning services."

"Too late, my mom has sent me three Pinterest links this week." Noah laughed, pressing a kiss to Nat's temple.

Clearly their moms were team "Nat and Noah." Her heart soared. They could hold hands in public. They could kiss in public. Why on earth had she hesitated?

"I'll be good, though. Tell Todd I'll listen to him and my doctor. If not, my gorgeous girlfriend will kick my ass." His eyes shined with happiness as he looked at her.

The doctor had told Noah that he could go back to work next week but to take it easy. No heavy lifting, which had put a damper on their sexy activities. Although, Nat didn't mind. It was just nice to go to bed each night with Noah and wake up most mornings with him. There were still mornings when she woke up without him. It was okay because she'd come downstairs to his kitchen, where fresh coffee waited for her along with a smiling Noah and breakfast. It had only been a week, but the benefits of being out in the open were endless.

Leaving Summer and Carmen, they moved through the crowds and located Elle and Clayton in line for apple dumplings.

"There you are." Clayton hugged Nat and then turned to Noah. They did a fist bump and then the back-slapping, man-hug thing.

Nat noticed a slight wince flash across Noah's face as Clayton slapped just a little too hard. She'd like to pretend it was because he forgot his friend still had healing broken ribs, but she suspected it was because Nat had slept at Noah's since he had been released Sunday afternoon. Clayton was supportive of their relationship, but he was still a big brother. The four finally had that pizza Wednesday night when Elle and he had come over to Noah's. Nat's favorite kind of guests were the ones who brought pizza and the puppies.

"We'll get the dumplings and some water if you two want to grab us a table." Elle gestured across the street to the standing high-tops and folding round tables tucked beneath a large tent in the town hall parking lot. Hands clasped, they found an empty round table and claimed it. There may have been mild public kissing as they waited for Elle and Clayton.

"I need to see Dr. Owens!" A shrill voice yanked Nat out of her love bubble.

Looking up, she saw Mrs. Lewis amble toward their table. Her wrinkled face pinched in determination.

"Mrs. Lewis, my dad is at the clinic. He'll be here shortly," Nat offered, standing up to greet the woman.

"I said I wanted to see Dr. Owens." She placed her hands on her hips and eyed Nat. "The Dr. Owens who helped my grandson."

Nat's head ticked to the right. "Your grandson?"

"Douglas! Where are you?" she shouted.

Doug shuffled up to his grandma. His bruised face was scrunched in apology. "Mr. Wilson, I'm so sorry. I wasn't paying attention. Grand has warned me about my speed demon ways. I am so sorry you got hurt because of me."

Noah rose, reaching out a hand to Doug. "Thank you. I'm just glad we're both okay."

"And I'm sure we've learned a lesson." Mrs. Lewis tutted at her grandson.

"Yes, Grand," he said sheepishly.

Mrs. Lewis turned to Nat. "Thank you for helping him, Dr. Owens." She stepped close, wrapping her frail arms around Nat and squeezing tight. "You're a good girl...you're a good doctor."

"Thank you, Mrs. Lewis." Nat pulled back. "But Dr. Owens is my dad. You can call me Dr. Nat."

Doug ran his fingers through his black hair revealing the stitches at his hairline. "I told my Grand all about you. How you kept me calm and patched me up at the scene. How you helped Mr. Wilson."

"I am just so grateful to you, Dr. Nat." Mrs. Lewis teared up. "After Doug's parents died four years ago and my husband passed last year, he's all I have. Thank you for making sure I keep him."

Emotion fluttered in Nat's chest. If anyone understood the power that grief had on a heart, it was her. Had Mrs. Lewis' reluctance to see Nat rather than her father been more about holding on to what was familiar after losing so much already? Had it been less a proclamation on Nat but rather a desire to hold on to what she knew? Nat wasn't sure, but what she was sure of was second chances. About moving forward when mistakes had been made.

"Thank you, Dr. Owens." Mrs. Lewis hugged Nat tight before she took her grandson's arm and wandered away.

Noah looped his arms around Nat's middle, pulling her close to his chest. "That's my girl."

She tipped her head up. "I love being your girl."

"And I love being your everything." He pressed his smile to hers.

EPILOGUE

"Love covers a multitude of sins…" ~Louisa May Alcott, *Little Women*

Maybe the glitter eyeshadow was too much, but it was Halloween. Nat looked at herself in the full-length mirror hung on the back of the closet door. Hands on hips, she did her best Derrick Zoolander Blue Steele impression, admiring her short green dress and sparkly fairy wings. She was Tinkerbell, after all, so the glitter eyeshadow was on point. Blowing a kiss to herself in the mirror, she skipped out of Noah's bedroom and downstairs.

It had been just over a month since his accident and just over two months since they'd started dating. Most nights, Nat slept at Noah's, so it made sense that she'd commandeered the handing out of candy duties for Halloween. Noah was going to be at the brewery most of the night. Nat planned on handing out all the candy while eating the caramel popcorn she'd bought and watching *Hocus Pocus* until trick-or-treating wrapped up at eight. Then, she'd head to the brewery to meet Clayton and Elle for a drink while keeping Todd and Noah company until they closed at ten.

Then she'd let Noah peel off her little costume and do all sorts of depraved things to her and she'd return the favor as their Halloween treat to one another.

With the first ring of the doorbell, she fixed a big smile on her face. She danced to the door, and swung it open, holding a plastic witch caldron overflowing with candy.

"Happy Hall…" She stopped, eyes blinking. There weren't any adorably dressed up children at the door, but a basket with a tiny floppy-eared yellow lab puppy. "Who are you?" Nat crouched to examine the puppy, who took a tentative step out of the basket. Her uncoordinated puppy legs caused her to tumble out of the basket. Nat wasn't sure why she assumed the puppy was a girl, but she scooped her up to check.

"Yep, you're a girl," she cooed.

The puppy snuggled into Nat. Her silky fur was like the softest blanket against Nat's skin. Holding the puppy, Nat bent to retrieve a folded piece of paper from the basket.

"What's this?" she asked the puppy, who only snuggled deeper into Nat. Smiling, she unfolded the paper. "My name is Tink." Nat grinned at that and kept reading. "Will you live with me and my daddy?" Her heart sped. "What?"

"You're here every night, so it makes sense," Noah said, appearing from behind her.

Startled, Nat twisted to find him with an unabashed, hopeful smile on his face.

"I thought you were at the brewery," she said.

"I snuck away to introduce my girlfriend to the puppy I finally got after all her pestering me about getting a dog of my own."

Her face pinched in an indignant pout. "I didn't pester."

He stepped close, the heat from his body coiling around her. "I also came back to ask my amazing girlfriend to move in. I realize it may be a little too soon, but I don't want the appropriate things I should be doing to stop me from doing what I feel is right. Nat, I love you, and I want to make a home with you here…with me and Tink. Will you live with us?" he asked.

Nat looked down at the snoozing puppy and back to Noah. "Will you cook for me?"

Amusement pulled at the corners of his lips. "There's that savvy business mind of yours at work again. Yes, of course."

"Then I'll come home," she said, raising to her tiptoes, pressing a soft kiss against his lips.

"Come home?" His brow wrinkled.

"There's no making a home with you because with you, I'm already home." She nuzzled her nose against his.

"Welcome home." His smile met hers.

Please consider leaving a review for this book. Reviews are almost better than puppy kisses for an author.

Keep reading for a sneak peek of At First Smile.

AT FIRST SMILE

Disability advocate Pen Meadows is on a mission; grab a breakfast sandwich, find her gate, and listen to her smutty audiobook. Only, the sexy, tall man in front of her at Tim Hortons may prove a worthwhile distraction. His soft Irish lilt and mix of gruff sweetness make Rowan Iverson unlike any man she's ever met. After a brief meet/cute, and even briefer goodbye, the social media influencer ends up seated beside Rowan on a cross-country flight.

Rowan Iverson desperately wants to get back to Los Angeles without calling further attention to himself. A potentially career-ending incident at hockey's biggest game could transform the NHL's top defenseman into its most hated player. The last thing he wants is for his mess to trip up Pen. A mid-flight detour forces him to realize that his goal to resist her bright smile may be a game he's already lost.

Back in the reality of their jobs and lives in Los Angeles, Pen learns that the man she'd spent one incredible night with isn't who she thought. He's a player and Pen doesn't play games, especially when her heart is at stake. Can Rowan prove to Pen that he is who he wants to be…just hers?

SNEAK PEEK: AT FIRST SMILE

Chapter One
Cane Austen and Me
Pen

"Mommy, what's she doing?" The small chirp of a child's voice draws my attention.

I am not the aforementioned "mommy," but my head tilts toward the tiny human anyway. There's something in the shock and awe in their voice telling me there is a small finger pointing at me.

"It's her stick—"

It's a cane. I don't correct the wrong terminology. Instead, my smile tight and white cane ahead of me, I stroll down the not-yet-fully awake Buffalo-Niagara Airport terminal.

"It helps her see."

Ah, if only it were that magical. It's barely seven a.m. After spending a week with my mother, I lack the temperamental bandwidth to explain to this woman and her child the intricacies of being legally blind. It's a cane. It doesn't help me see, but rather it's a tool to allow me to use nonvisual cues to get from point A to point T. Right now, the point T I'm destined for is the Tim Hortons tucked into the airport's food court.

Aunt Bea always said I was a shining light illuminating the darkness in the world's understanding of what it means to be blind. It's why I've dedicated so much of the last ten years to educate people through my social media page, Cane Austen and Me. To my thirty-thousand followers, I'm the "It" blind girl, documenting my every day and big adventures with Cane Austen, my white cane, helping the non-visually impaired world's knowledge be just a little less obscured about vision loss.

The knowledge that I'm no longer Aunt Bea's little light aches deep in my heart. I can almost feel her soft arms folded around me as she cooed, "Pen, you'll help them understand." No matter how tired I was, she'd have expected me to stop. Explain how the cane works. Tell the child that not all blind people can't see. Set his mommy dearest straight on the blind people facts, helping their little human grow up without misinformation and ensuring that other little humans – ones like me with failing vision – don't repeat the storyline I'd faced as I grew up.

Clear their vision, Aunt Bea's sing-song words dance in my heart.

Sighing, I pivot on my strappy, wedge sandals and head toward the sound of the mother and child. A little boy sits, feet kicking, beside a woman, her long hair gathered into a messy bun, at a half-full gate.

"Hi. I'm Pen." My free hand gathers my long auburn hair, brushing it onto my right shoulder. The action soothes the pulse of anxiety. No matter how many times I do this, it's still awkward as fuck. *Good thing I love you, Aunt Bea.*

The little boy tips his head to his mom, whose forehead puckers in confusion.

Yep, I'm weirding them out. Frankly, I don't blame them. Most people don't have a lot of interactions with the legally blind. Let alone one who walks up to them and introduces themselves. Thanks to Aunt Bea, that is exactly who I am. Even if there are days – like today – where I wish I wasn't. Where I'd rather fade into the crowd, unseen and forgotten.

"I heard you ask about my cane," I lace just enough sweetness into my words to not send anyone into a sugar-rush. "This is Cane Austen. I'm legally blind, and she helps me stay safe. See how I sweep the cane? It's called constant contact and helps me trail things to guide my path or find things, so I don't trip and fall." With a tight upward curl of my mouth, I demonstrate how I use the cane.

"Are all canes girls?" The little boy's face twists into a pout.

A genuine smile kicks across my face. "Not all, but this one is."

"Why did you name it Cane Austen?" The woman's eyebrows knit.

"So she'll help me find my Mr. Darcy," I quip, making the woman snort with laughter.

It was the same reaction Aunt Bea had. This is my tenth Cane Austen. I've had a new one every year since I was sixteen. While everyone else was getting their first car, I was getting my first cane. The eye condition I have, retinitis pigmentosa, progressed to the point that a cane is necessary to keep me safe. I'd been diagnosed at age six, so I knew my vision was fading to black at a glacial pace…slow but unstoppable. The gradual progression of vision loss didn't lessen the painful realization that, while classmates were getting their licenses and cars, I was facing just another way in which I wasn't like them.

Not allowing me to wallow, Aunt Bea presented me with my first white cane. Blindfolding me – which she found hilarious – she dragged me into the driveway where she gifted me a white cane tied up with a giant red bow. She'd even put a Porsche sticker on it, winking as she affirmed that her niece would travel in style. "You gotta name this bad bitch," she'd crooned, explaining that the cane was my car, and everyone named their vehicles.

The little boy worries his lower lip, as if considering his words. "What does 'legally blind' mean?"

What, indeed? To the world blind means you can't see, but unsuspecting civilians didn't realize that blindness is served on a spectrum. The majority of legally blind people are like me, with some usable vision. There's a whole medical explanation that Trina, my ophthalmologist bestie, would bore people with at parties. I keep it simple, saying I have enough vision to get myself in trouble but not enough to always get myself out of it. Which is why I avoid trouble. As adventurous as Aunt Bea raised me to be, I don't take uncalculated risks.

After finishing my impromptu blindness in-service, I leave the smiling mother/son pair and redirect myself toward Tim Hortons. My flight to LAX doesn't board for another hour, so I have ample time to secure my sought after breakfast sandwich and make it to the gate to lose myself in my steamy romance audiobook. There's something delightful about listening to the swoony and sometimes illicit words of a favorite male narrator, with his hot guy voice, in public places. The idea of exposure makes the risk so much more rewarding. Whoever ends up sitting next to me on my flight home would, no doubt, turn a violent shade of red if they only knew what I was listening to.

Grinning, I stroll toward Tim Hortons. *Bless the airport gods!* I fight the urge to wiggle my hips, spotting only one other person in front of me. The sweet ecstasy of a multigrain breakfast sandwich and apple cinnamon tea is within my grasp. Besides seeing Trina, Tim Hortons was the only thing bringing me joy on this trip back to Buffalo. After moving to Seal Beach, California with Aunt Bea at seventeen, this Western New York staple was the only thing I missed. That includes my mother, who was already on husband number three at that time, and had *no* problem letting her teenaged daughter move cross country without her.

Whenever Aunt Bea and I went home, the first thing we'd do was hit Tim Hortons. Each Christmas, Mom sent us an assortment of teas, coffee, and hot chocolate from the retailer. Even this last Christmas. Though there's no longer a coffee drinker in the house.

I swallow the growing lump in my throat. Adjusting the large weekender bag on my shoulder, I force my focus to the back of the head in front of me. Only, in order for my gaze to actually land on the back of the man's head requires craning my neck. *How tall is he?* I'm five eight, but he's a giant.

"The card machine isn't working," the peppy cashier says to the tall man.

"Oh." His large hand slips to his pocket.

No doubt the action is to grab the wallet bulging from his back pocket and not to call attention to the way the faded jeans hug his firm backside. One that Trina would joke that she could bounce a quarter off. Although, I could think of far more pleasurable things to do with that ass.

Stop checking out his behind! Pushing my red-frame glasses atop my head, I twist my now extra foggy vision away from the tall man's cute butt. I mean, how would I feel if he was ogling me like I'm the last cupcake?

That might be a nice change. It's been a minute since someone looked at me with the same kind of covetous gaze that I'd used when looking at baked goods after that ill-begotten month I tried to give up carbs. Life's too short to not eat a cookie or ten.

"Shit!" he grumbles, closing his wallet. "Is there an ATM around?"

Second-hand embarrassment on his behalf flushes my cheeks. Few people carry cash on them. My always prepared motto means I'm not one of them. No matter what country I'm in, my wallet remains stocked.

The cashier taps the counter. "I think there's one down by gate twelve."

"Thanks. I'll run down and come back," he says, slipping his wallet into his back pocket.

Poor guy. My lips drag into a frown. Traveling is frustrating enough but to toss in an unnecessary trip across the airport terminal is obnoxious.

"No need, I got this," I offer, pulling my glasses back down. "I have cash."

"No, it's–" His words halt as he spins to face me. Beneath the brim of a blue cap, a smile curves at his lips. Its brightness is accentuated by his tidy dark beard.

A sudden swoop seizes my stomach, causing an explosion of butterflies. *That's new. Am I into men with beards?*

A navy Henley molds to his muscular frame. A fresh woodsy scent wafts from him, eliciting scenes of a pre-dawn walk through a dew-kissed forest. His entire aesthetic screams sexy lumberjack. Like someone who would press you against a tree, its rough bark biting into your bare ass, while even rougher hands held you in place.

Good lord, perhaps I need to cut down on my dirty audiobooks.

"That's kind of you, but I have cash. It's just in the bank." A gentle, barely noticeable Irish lilt mingles with his low gruff timbre.

I love the way unique voices tingle along my nerves. Perhaps my dulled vision heightens the way I hear the world, but I revel in the musicality of voices, picking out the unique notes that make each one distinct.

"Those pesky banks holding our cash hostage." My smile lifts, just a little bit more, with his soft chuckle. "It's really no big deal."

"Are you sure?"

"This will give me at least five karma points for the day." Stepping up, I join him at the counter.

"Are you in need of karma points?"

"Well, I did send my mother to voicemail this morning." *Twice.* But he doesn't need to know that.

This trip I lasted three of the five days I'd planned to stay at my mother's house, a new record, before I sought refuge. On day four, I retreated to Trina's, feigning that she had more reliable Wi-Fi for me to work from than the farmhouse my mother lives in with Charlie, her latest husband.

He grins. "I wouldn't want to get in the way of you reaching Nirvana."

"Thanks." I brush my long hair behind my ear, facing the cashier. "Can I get a large apple cinnamon tea and bacon, egg, and cheese breakfast sandwich on a multigrain bagel."

The cashier shakes their head, a big laugh bursting. "That's two apple cinnamon teas and bacon, egg, and cheese breakfast sandwiches on a multigrain bagel."

Twisted toward the man, my eyebrow arches. "Tea?"

He wags a finger. "That judgy eyebrow may cost you some of your karma points."

I gesture at him. "You just don't seem the *tea* type."

"What type do I seem?"

I frown and cock one hip. "Like 'drinks gasoline while eating a burger made out of the grizzly bear he just killed with his bare hands' type."

"That's preposterous," he scoffs. "Everyone knows moose make better burgers."

"I stand corrected." I laugh, pulling out my wallet.

After paying for our food, we slide down the counter. Drinks in hand, we stand waiting for our breakfast sandwiches. Other customers file up to the counter, while we remain in silence. Not uncomfortable or awkward silence, just companionable. Sipping my sweet, spicy tea, my eyes flick between the staff preparing our food and the sexy lumberjack beside me.

I play the game we all play when meeting someone: using the little external clues to put together a picture of who he is. His clothes are comfortable and well-worn, but clean. One hand grips the to-go cup, while the other brushes the back of his head as if he's nervous.

Do I make him nervous? *No, that can't be.* Men like him make people nervous, not the other way around.

Gnawing on my lower lip, I try to think of the last man I made nervous. Besides Cael, Trina's fiancé who was terrified that her oldest and closest friend wouldn't give him the stamp of approval, the last man with a wisp of nerves around me may have been Alex. *Ugh, Alex.*

"Pen," I blurt.

His head tips to the right. "Pencil?"

Laughter bubbles out of me. "My name is Pen. Well, it's actually Penelope Meadows, but my friends call me Pen."

He grins. "Rowan."

Of course, his name is Rowan. That name radiates big D hot guy energy. Not a Herman or Stanley vibe about him.

"Nice to meet you, Pen." His hand envelops mine, sending a jolt of something zipping along my nerves.

I try not to fixate on that little tingle but have to admit failure. When was the last time my body reacted to someone like this?

"So, are you coming or going?"

Seriously? Coming or going? Who am I? I school my features into a pleasant smile stamping out the blooming wince at my non-stellar verbal skills.

"Excuse me?"

"Are you coming into town or leaving?"

"Both."

"Overachiever," I tease, pivoting towards him, and my

arm brushes against his. My senses hum with the quick caress of his muscular body against mine.

He clears his throat. "I drove down from Hamilton, Ontario to catch my flight."

"So, where you heading to?"

"L.A."

"Me too!" I say with far too much pep.

What is wrong with me? I'm like an overexcited puppy. I should be cool and indifferent, not exclaim with the fevered devotion of two ten-year-olds exchanging friendship bracelets on the first day of camp.

"Well, *not* L.A. I live in Seal Beach, but LAX is a direct flight getting me the hell out of here sooner."

Why am I sputtering? *Awkward, party of one.*

"Not a fan of Buffalo?" He shifts, turning to face me.

"I have nothing against Buffalo as a city. People are nice. Love the wings. It's just…"

Stop talking, Pen! Do not emotionally vomit on this poor man. All he wanted was breakfast, not to have you overshare.

"…just prefer being home." I tighten my hold on Cane Austen's handle.

"Buffalo's not home?"

"Not anymore." I shake my head.

Rowan's hat brim shadows the upper half of his face, making it hard to read his expression. Reading facial expressions isn't my forte. Even with the limited vision I do have, it's often difficult to make out the tiny cues that can be found in someone's face. Aunt Bea always talked about the stories in the eyes. Those are stories I'm unable to read. If I'm close enough and the light is just right, I can make out some of the little eyebrow ticks, lip quirks, or forehead wrinkles.

My stories come from the voice and energy. Everyone has a kind of energy they exude. It may make me sound like the lady with a different crystal for each day of the week, but it's something I've learned to trust.

Right now, the energy coming off Rowan telegraphs annoyance, but I don't think it's directed at me. Despite my oversharing, his broad frame remains mere inches away. His obscured gaze fixed on me.

He nods. "I get it. I've only lived in L.A. for three years and it feels more like home than Hamilton where I grew up."

"Canadian boy, eh?"

He snorts at the terrible joke laced in my even worse Canadian accent.

Smirking, I raise my tea to my lips. "So, how did a nice Canadian lad end up in L.A.?"

His hand rubs his neck. "Work."

"What do you do for wo—"

"Christ," he groans, yanking out his cell from his back pocket. "Sorry, this is the fourth call in a row that I've ignored. I need to take this."

"Sure." I smile.

Holding the phone up, he grumbles, "This best be important." Pivoting, he strides away from the counter.

"Ma'am." The cashier holds up two bags with what I suspect are our breakfast sandwiches.

With a nodded "thank you," I take them. In literally five seconds, I've lost Rowan. Scanning the now bustling food court, he's disappeared into the crowd. Do I wait? Do I try to track him down? Do I just take his sandwich in hopes that I run into him again? What if he comes back and thinks I stole his sandwich? Although, I paid for it, so it's not stealing.

"Excuse me, do you see that man I was with?" I ask the cashier.

"He went over there." She points.

"Where? Can you verbally explain?" I hold up Cane Austen in a nonverbal reminder that pointing is not the best way to give direction to the visually impaired.

"Oh, sorry." The blush can be heard in her voice. "Far right corner... My right, not yours."

"Thanks."

Turning, I set off listening for his voice. Moving through the crowd, I make my way toward the far-right corner. Voice recognition is the best way for me to find people in large gatherings. Although, it's not ideal with someone I just met, there's something about Rowan's voice that has imprinted on me, both distinct yet familiar. Like nothing I've heard before but somehow something as well-known to me as my own.

"Damnit, I told you I don't want to do that," Rowan growls.

I halt. Not because I've found him, but due to the frustration underscoring his words. He's pissed.

"This is fucking bullshit."

Really pissed.

With his back to me, he carries on in an annoyed mutter with no idea I'm standing behind him, eavesdropping. It's not intentional, but I'm listening, nonetheless. Granted, my relationship with Rowan is five minutes old, but this anger reads wrong on him. Like an ill-fitting Halloween costume. Also, I'm not going to overthink my use of the word relationship.

Raking my teeth against my lower lip, I clutch the sandwich bag. I should turn, run away, and give the sandwich back to the cashier. Let them give it to the angry man. Not because I'm scared. There's no nip of fear telling me to stay away. Rather, it's more like witnessing someone do something they don't want to do.

"You're being a real motherfucker," he snarls, causing a few onlookers to clear their throats.

Ouch. I don't blame them. His tone is harsh.

Dropping his duffle by his feet, Rowan's rigid stance slumps. His free hand grips the back of his neck. The movement communicates regret.

"I'm sorry. That was uncalled for." Scuffing his sneakers along the floor, he lets out a beleaguered sigh. "I know. You're *my* motherfucker."

Aw. It's almost sweet the way it rolls off his tongue.

"We can discuss this when I get back. My flight gets in…" Pivoting, he comes face-to-face with me, mouth slack. "Pen." It comes out almost pained.

Crap! "I wasn't listening… Well, I was, but not intentionally. I—" I hoist up the Tim Hortons bag. "Breakfast!"

"Thanks," he says, drawing out the word and taking the offered bag.

"Sorry."

The muffled voice of whoever is on the other end of the call crackles between us.

"I should go." Frowning, I turn and hurry away.

So fricking embarrassing. Rowan is clearly having a day and I'm all like "Here I am holding your breakfast sandwich hostage while eavesdropping on your conversation with someone you fondly refer to as motherfucker."

Finding my gate, I fold myself into an uncomfortable plastic chair to devour my breakfast sandwich and fall into my latest audiobook. The sultry timbre of Wesley Williamson – my favorite narrator – helps me escape into the world of thousand-year-old hot vampires with Mr. Darcy vibes. The story being woven in my earbuds helps me leave the last week behind. Leave why I came back to Buffalo, the tension with my mother, and the awkward meet-cute with Rowan.

Rowan. My stomach flip-flops between a sigh and a flutter at the thought of him. I hope everything turns out okay with he and motherfucker. It seemed to have turned the corner before he'd caught me listening in. I scan the boarding area, wondering if he's here. He's not. At least, I don't see him which doesn't mean he's not here. He's bound for L.A. Are we on the same flight? The Buffalo-Niagara Airport is small, but not *that* small. There are several airlines flying direct to Los Angeles in this time window.

"Penelope Meadows, please see the agent at gate eleven's

counter." A voice booms over the sound system, interrupting the vampire/awkward girl meet-cute.

Hitting pause, I sling my bag over my shoulder and shuffle with Cane Austen to the counter. "I'm Penelope," I say, reaching the agent.

"Ms. Meadows." The agent beams. "Your seat has been upgraded. I have a new boarding pass for you."

"Upgraded?" I blink.

"You're still in a window seat, but you've been moved to first class. Seat one-A. We'll start pre-boarding in a few minutes for our passengers with disabilities. Would you like assistance going down the jetway?"

First class from Buffalo to Los Angeles? Perhaps I had earned some karma points after all. Thanking the agent and telling them I wouldn't need assistance, I head back to my seat.

Pulling my phone from my pocket, I check my messages. Despite the frown, guilt swirls in my stomach at the four unread messages from my mother. Sighing, I open them and respond.

Me: I'm at my gate.

Mom: Good! Did you click on the links I sent you to those clinical trials?

Eyes closed, I release a hard breath. If it isn't messages about my love life, it's ones about studies to cure my eye condition. *She means well,* Aunt Bea's cautious warning plays on repeat inside me. Opening my eyes, I reply.

Me: I'll look at them when I get home, so I can see them on the larger screen. I'll message when I'm home.

It's a lie, but my energy for this familiar conversation is nonexistent.

I swipe to my message with JoJo, my West Coast bestie. Trina is insistent that I'm allowed two best friends if I designate them by coasts. Trina Lyons, who is two years older than me, was my first bestie due to close proximity. She lived next door until I moved with Aunt Bea to California. I met JoJo Rivers a year later as freshmen in undergrad.

Me: Flight is on time. You still picking me up at the airport?

JoJo: Does a hobby horse have a hickory dick?

Me: A simple yes would do.

JoJo: Then I wouldn't be me. Tongue out emoji.

I snort just a bit. Even with the magnification program on my cell, I have the worst time with GIFs and emojis, so JoJo spells them out for me. It's both sweet and totally self-serving because I'm a hundred percent positive that a majority of the GIFs and emojis that she spells out do not exist.

JoJo: How are you doing, BTW?

God, that's a loaded question. My heart aches just thinking about the many, many responses rattling around in me. How does one respond when their entire world as they know it has been ripped away in a single moment?

Me: Okay.

JoJo: Acceptance smiley face when your friend is pretending they are okay when they're not emoji.

Me: Middle finger emoji.

JoJo: Gasp emoji.

Me: These aren't real emojis emoji.

JoJo: I love you emoji.

Me: I love you too emoji. We'll have all the LAX to Orange County traffic to dig into how I'm doing. I promise.

JoJo: Excited social worker friend emoji.

Hearing them announce pre-boarding, I text goodbye to JoJo and slip my phone into the pocket of my denim jacket. The late June weather is warm, allowing me to sport my favorite pale pink cotton sundress, but the jacket will keep me warm on the plane.

I won't pretend that excitement doesn't crisscross inside me at turning left while boarding the plane. The first-class lifestyle isn't something I've indulged in. Outside of that all-inclusive resort Aunt Bea took me to in celebration of my master's degree. As first-class as I typically get is getting to skip the wait at Bread, my favorite breakfast spot in downtown Seal Beach, because Aunt Bea and I've gone there every Saturday for the last nine years. *Almost every Saturday.*

Ignoring the twinge in my heart, I follow the flight attendant to my seat in the front row, which means more leg room. It also means all my things have to go up top. Pulling out the things I'll want quick access to – bottled water, bag of trail mix, phone, and earbuds – I toss my bag into the overhead bin and plop into my seat.

Head pressed against the window, I lose myself in my audiobook which drowns out the flight's boarding soundtrack – murmured apologies, cleared throats, and muttered, "I think that's my seat," and the repeated chastising of a passenger for blocking the aisle.

Someone takes the seat beside me. The furnace of their body laps against my skin. A fresh woodsy scent makes my eyelids flutter open. Straightening, I turn my face toward my seatmate.

"Pen," Rowan drawls.

Visit my Website www.melissawhitneywrites.com to find out where you can buy this book.

ACKNOWLEDGMENTS

It truly takes a village to write any book, especially a small town romance. I'd like to take a few moments to acknowledge everyone that helped *Coming Home* come to life.

My amazing husband, Mr. Whitney, gets top billing this time. Yes, he beat out the pugs. Baby, thank you for being my real life cinnamon roll/golden retriever MMC with grumpy tendencies. The inspiration for all my MMCs is wrapped up in how you love me.

Meghan Fisher, words will never express my deep gratitude for all you do. Thank you for cheering me on, telling me when I'm being silly, and allowing me to borrow some of your sparkle for Nat.

Thank you to my amazing editor, Gemma Brocato for your continued support and literary mama bear ways. You are truly a gardener of writers. Your guidance and support helps me blossom as an author.

A huge shout out to Dr. Amarpreet "Preety" Bath, who provided technical consultation for Nat. Not only did you offer your physician expertise, but your support as an amazing friend and human.

Thank you to the team from Happily Booked PR for your support with proofing and marketing.

Above all I want to thank you, my dear reader, for going on this journey with me. Whether this is your first or fourth Melissa Whitney book, I'd be NOWHERE without you. Thank you for your support. There are so many books in the world and the fact that you choose mine is humbling.

ABOUT THE AUTHOR

Melissa Whitney, who hails from the very real village of Perry, N.Y. depicted in this book, is a contemporary romance author. As a legally blind woman much of Melissa's work focuses on the exploration of disability, mental health, and trauma through a heartfelt, sexy, and comedic lens.

Melissa's debut novel *In the Hello and in the Goodbye* released in April 2024, and received a warm reception from readers for its thoughtful autism and mental health portrayal. Since then, she's released *Finding Home*, a Jane Austen-inspired small town romance, and *At First Smile*, an own voice hockey romance with blindness rep. Her work has been featured in several publications and on podcasts for its thoughtful, sensitive, and accurate representation of disability and mental health.

Ms. Whitney lives in Southern California with her husband and their rescue pug Milo. When not crafting her swoony stories, she's on the hunt for a pastry, brewing a cup of tea, and diving into her latest swoony romance.

To learn more about Melissa Whitney, you can visit www.melissawhitneywrites.com. Sign up for her newsletter to stay in the know on all things Melissa Whitney. Connect with her on social media (IG: @melissa_whitneyatuhor, Threads @melissa_whitneyauthor or TT: @melissasuewhitney).

ALSO BY MELISSA WHITNEY

Stand Alone Interconnected Series
The Hello Series (Two Books)
Book One: *In the Hello and in the Goodbye* (Now Available)
Book Two: *Our Now and Then* (Spring 2025)

The Home Series
Book One: Finding Home (Now Available)
Book Two: *Coming Home* (Now available)
Book Three: *Making Home* (Fall 2025)

Stand Alone Books
At First Smile (Now Available)
Happy Ever Afterlife (Summer 2025)

WHERE TO GET MELISSA'S BOOKS:

All books are available in e-book, paperback, and audio. You can get books at Amazon.com: Melissa Whitney: books, biography, latest update or be requesting at your local library or indie bookstore. Signed copies can be purchased through Heartbound Book Shop: Where Every Page is a Love Story.